Judi James was a highly successful fashion model before starting her own school of modelling in Chelsea and then becoming a management consultant. She now lectures to businesses on presentation skills. She has published two books for adults: *Carmine* and *The Ruby Palace*.

By the same author

Carmine
The Ruby Palace

JUDI JAMES

The Devil's Own Boy

Grafton
An Imprint of HarperCollins*Publishers*

Grafton
An Imprint of HarperCollins*Publishers*
75–85 Fulham Palace Road,
Hammersmith, London W6 8JB

Published by Grafton 1993
9 8 7 6 5 4 3 2 1

A catalogue record for this book is
available from the British Library

ISBN 0 586 21290 6

Set in Sabon

Printed in Great Britain by
Cox & Wyman Ltd, Reading, Berkshire

PROLOGUE

Ireland 1904

The day that his mother died was the day the boy had his first haircut. The cut had been long overdue but now he was shorn like a lamb. Cora watched his head over the tea-table and saw the soft downy dark hair that fitted the skull like a cap. She longed to raise a hand to cup the back of the skull into her palm and feel the hair and hard bone there, which she imagined would feel like that of a small bird, but she would never have dared and Niall would never have allowed her; he would have flinched away, she knew it.

His hair had no colour, just as his skin had no colour. His eyes were milk-white and the colour of dark puddles. His wire-rimmed glasses cut fierce furrows into the pale skin beside his ears.

All his curls were gone now and it tore at Cora's heart to see the bare-bone curves of the nape of his brittle neck.

'You'll have to start washing there now, you know,' she said, pointing towards his collar-line and smiling at his blushing. She was always one to embarrass him, despite her obvious affection. There were nearly ten years between them and she was often taken for his mother instead of his sister.

'What of this food then, Niall?' she asked as the first dish was set. 'Is there beauty enough on that plate for you, then? Does it please the old eye as well as the grumbling great belly?'

It was no way to speak to a child and he knew it. He glanced about at the other diners to see if they had heard.

Cora ate. The cloth before them was white and the china even whiter. A small silver fish lay on a bed of buttered black toast, its round eye pallid and filmy with death. He touched a fork with one finger to straighten it although he knew he should use it soon to mash the fish before eating it.

'Eat,' Cora ordered, and he picked up the fork reluctantly.

'Do you bone this, then?' he asked. He had a horror of fishbones.

Cora rose to lean over him, the very thing that he had hoped she would not do. He held his breath so as not to smell her as she took up his fish-knife and fork, slitting the fish in one cut from head to tail and lifting out the backbone in one piece. Cora smelt of church, despite the perfumes she wore.

'You can eat the rest,' she told him, sitting down again. 'They're quite soft, they won't choke you or stick in your throat.'

He pointed at the garnish. 'Did Missus Hickey lay that there egg, then?' he asked.

Cora snorted air through her nose. 'Don't be daft,' she told him. 'Did you think all the eggs in the world come from our bloomin' old hen? I should think not, Niall, no.' She took a last mouthful of fish and pushed her plate away, leaning back in her chair and patting her belly like a satisfied old man. 'Anyway,' she asked, 'who taught you to speak like that? "That-there-egg-then"? Who taught you like that? What are you, a wild boy or what? We'll be seeing you living in the bloomin' old gentlemen's houses when you're grown, at that rate. I shouldn't wonder at that, I really shouldn't wonder.'

She was enjoying herself greatly now and smoking as well, which was a huge disgrace. 'I wonder Papa lets you run wild like you do when you come home with language like that, you know.'

There was nothing wild in Cora's appearance, save a few wisps of hair that had worked loose from her bun. Cora's wildness manifested in her manner and her behaviour over tea, which had been outrageous. People were looking, but then people always did.

Cora looked nearer thirty than twenty and always had done for as long as Niall could remember. She sat askew in her chair and she wore colours that were wrong. There was a brown mole near her mouth that moved as she talked and her hair had the dull springiness of curled-up twine. There was life in her rust-coloured eyes but the white lashes robbed them of any distinction. Men would largely ignore Cora. They looked over her dull head in search of more elusive beauties. If pressed to recall Cora at all men would merely comment gravely that it was a terrible shame she'd none of her mother's looks.

'I want to go back,' Niall said before finishing his fish.

'Go?' Cora asked him, exhaling smoke from her nostrils. 'I shouldn't think so, Niall. Here we are in town at last in the finest tea-rooms in the whole of Clifden and we've yet to taste the pastries, which are the crowning glory of any tea-time, and you want to go? When I've been given a king's holy ransom at least to treat you to food the like of which you would not see on our old plates in a month of Sundays? Would you ever see fat old Maidie turning out a tea like this at our home, now? Rainbow sugar crystals and all the knives properly laid? Glacé fruits in a bowl? No. Not Maidie, no.' She licked a finger and dabbed sugar crystals up from the cloth around the cut-glass bowl. 'You should learn to appreciate fine foods, Niall,' she said, 'not that rare old holy stodge we get at home. It'll stand you in good stead some time, I shouldn't doubt. Women admire a man with a palate for good foods, you know.'

Niall rocked uncomfortably in his seat. 'I want to be with Mamma,' he said. His dark eyes gleamed wetly behind their gold frames. Any minute now he would begin to cry in earnest.

'And so you keep saying,' Cora said with a sigh, wetting a corner of her napkin with her tongue and dabbing it over her mouth. 'Jesus, but you're a mummy's boy! Did you ever pause to consider whether Mamma wants you with her right now? Don't you think she's enough to bother with without you going grizzling about her elbows? She's had seven of us already without the benefit of your old company, you know. I should think she would do better by herself now, so what do you say to that?'

But the tears came anyway.

'Oh, Holy Mother, but you're a pain!' Cora rolled her eyes to the ceiling, like the fish. She spat on her napkin and wiped it over his face, which he hated more than anything she had done that day.

'Stop it now, we'll go,' she said, but he had spoilt the whole excursion, he could tell. In a terrible huff, she tied her hat onto her head and threw the waitress a look when she enquired whether they had enjoyed their tea. They were halfway to home before she spoke to her brother again.

The house was in darkness on the lower two floors but Maidie had the door wrenched back before they had even knocked.

'Oh, Holy Mary, begging your pardon, Miss, but I'd thought you were the priest!' she said, covering her mouth with her fingers at the sound of her own blasphemy.

Cora threw down her hat and was off up the stairs like a dog. Maidie clapped her hands together over and again in despair, then followed Cora, though she was less agile and stumbled several times near the top.

Niall was alone then and the house seemed to die about him. There were voices above, but they were hushed and indistinct. He pulled off his cap and ran a hand over his furry scalp. His fingers still smelt of the fish that he had eaten. There seemed to be nothing that he could do. Usually when he entered the house he would search first thing for his mother, or she would be there, waiting. Now that seeing her was not allowed he did nothing instead. If he waited for her long enough she would be down again to care for him.

A door opened somewhere and a scream soared out like a trapped bird, banging around the walls until he pushed his fists against his ears to shut it out.

He was not allowed to run inside the house, not ever, but now he ran because there was no one there to stop him. He tore from room to room, his feet clattering on the bare, varnished boards. The house frightened him. A wind had blown up outside and the rain fell in a steady sigh. Soon he became breathless and his knees had started to ache.

Many rooms were locked to him so that, when one door did fall back, it seemed so strange that he paused on the threshold before entering. He had not expected any of the doors to open. The rooms were never opened now, not even for guests. Inside, the area was empty of furniture, save one wooden chair, which was placed in front of a stack of gilt-framed canvases, as though someone had recently been staring at them. The paintings were all covered in greying dust-sheets, apart from one, which had been pulled out and propped before the chair.

Niall stood, panting like a puppy, and then he moved in front of the chair to see which painting had been selected. His mother looked glorious in the moonlight. Tall and proud, she wore a black silk skirt and gloves so long they reached over her elbows. She smiled at Niall and Niall smiled back but, when he moved closer to see her, she vanished in a miasma of brushstrokes and only reappeared when he had returned to the chair. From there the pearls that she wore about her neck seemed real, but close to they had been nothing more than a few lazy cream curls, dotted with white. The likeness was not quite accurate but Niall liked it for the artist's attempt at a glassy-eyed perfection that was thrilling enough for a child.

Red was the colour that his papa most disliked yet it was the colour of his mother's chemise in the portrait. Perhaps that was why it was here instead of hanging in the hall as it once used to, according to Cora. In the background of the painting stood the house itself; an indistinct grey slab with a few licks of red to show its windows alight with the dying sun. How had the house been in the days when his mother had dared to dress in bright red? The artist, though, much to Niall's disappointment and no doubt distracted by his mamma's great beauty, had dealt with the house in so few strokes that, even from a distance, it was unclear.

'Sophia Henrietta Lloyd.' A voice spoke softly from the doorway and Niall looked up to see the young priest standing there. 'Such beauty that is terrible to behold,' the priest went on, then looked away from the portrait and smiled. 'Would you wish to speak with your mother now, Niall?' he asked softly.

Niall thought for a moment. No one had asked him such a question before; his mother was there to speak to when he wanted, that was all. The question itself filled him with a mild fear, so that he shook his head without speaking.

'Are you sure?' the priest persisted, bending to Niall's height and grasping him by the shoulders. 'It may be rather important that you speak with her right now.'

But Niall remembered what Cora had told him and knew that he was quite sure. He would speak to her later, when he had no need to be asked like this, when he would come home to the house and she would be there waiting for him, as usual. He should not go bothering her now, when she was busy giving birth.

'Your mother has given you a sister, Niall,' the priest said. 'She has named her already. She is called Constance. Will you look after her, Niall? Will you care for her as you should?'

Constance. The name sounded ugly.

'Would you care to help me bless the baby, then?' the priest asked, standing, and this time Niall nodded.

The baby was alone in the night nursery, which surprised the boy. A small fire had been lit in the grate but it had all but burnt out and threw long dark shadows that writhed across the ceiling above the cot. Niall had expected to find her the same small skinned-rabbity bundle that he had been told his other siblings were when they'd been washed and trussed up after their birth. The sight of this newest child, though, made him look back at the priest in shock.

Uncreased and unreddened by the effort of her birth, Constance was perfectly beautiful and at peace with the world. She made neither frown nor fist and for a moment Niall supposed her to be dead. The same glass-and-china look that his mother had in her portrait had been perfectly captured in the flesh of his sister's doll-like face. Her skin was powder-pale, touched only on the cheek and lips with the lightest, sea-shell pink. The ear that showed as she lay on her side was little more than a whitened curl surrounded by fine wisps of pale auburn hair.

Niall held out a finger to touch her, to see if she were real and alive and as their flesh touched he felt the warmth of her skin tingle up into his arm like a mild electric current. Then she opened her eyes to see who had woken her.

'Constance,' Niall whispered. Her eyes were silver-blue in the darkness, then they fell into shadow as the fire burned up and all that he could see were the milky-pale whites. She clasped at his finger in the way that babies do and he marvelled at her strength and thought that he would die before he ever pulled away.

He laughed aloud as she looked at him and, in his imagination, she returned the smile. Two shadows moved in the doorway behind him now, for beyond the priest stood Niall's father, rigid with rage and the pain of his recent loss.

'You two . . .' he began, 'with my . . . with my child?'

'William!' The priest's voice sounded calm enough; a voice of caution and reason in the face of terrible grief.

'Get him away from my child.'

The priest stepped forward as if to placate him but was literally pushed aside as the bigger man entered the room.

'Get . . . away!' he said, his voice rising almost to a shout as he looked at his son. 'Get away from her . . . go!'

'Mister Flavelle!' the priest implored, and William Charles Flavelle turned slowly on his heel to face him.

'It wasn't the boy's fault, you know,' the priest said. 'You can hardly blame him for this and all the others. He's a good little lad, just a small child himself. He's done no harm, William, let him be at peace now. You can't lay the blame at a small child for something that was in God's hands alone. Where's your sense of forgiveness, man? Do you think this is what your wife would have wanted? She loved the boy, too.'

'She's dead,' William Flavelle said. 'She's taken from me too now, and don't you dare go telling me that her death was the will of Our Lord!' His square dark beard shook with emotion as he spoke and he began to reel about the room as though drunk with the grief. 'This was the Devil's work, not the Lord's!' he shouted, and the priest quickly made the sign of the cross at his words.

'You!' William Flavelle pointed at his son and then slowly turned the same finger towards the priest. 'And you!' he screamed, so that the very room seemed to shake at his voice.

'Come, Niall,' the priest said, gathering the boy quickly and leading him out of the room.

'The baby,' Niall protested. He would have stayed to protect her but the priest acted firmly and slammed the door shut behind them.

Then the father was left alone with his child. He wiped a hand across his eyes and staggered like a blind man to the edge of the crib. The tiny face inside the blankets watched him silently and uncritically. William stared down at the clear blue eyes and something like a fist seemed to clench about his heart.

'Sophia,' he whispered, falling to his knees. 'Oh, dear God, Sophia, it's your face that she has. Oh God, Sophia, forgive me!' and his great body rocked back and forth with tears of uncontrollable grief.

BOOK I

CHAPTER ONE

Connemara 1896

A doughy morsel of McCullin's Best Fruited Tea-Cake had somehow lain stubbornly wedged between two of the old priest's remaining three teeth throughout the entire damp and unsettling afternoon. It was a small hard square of candied peel that was at fault. First the priest had sucked at it a while, enjoying the last of its spicy sweetness. Then its flavour had dulled, though, and it had become rapidly unpleasant to taste, so he had worked at it instead with the tip of his tongue, hoping in vain to dislodge it. Now he found himself losing both patience and manners as he set about it brutally, gaping his jaws wide and attacking the glutinous mass with the tip of an arthritic finger.

As he busily thrust and parried, the parish dog-cart suddenly slewed windward, leaving him abruptly and severely chastised for this furtive breach of etiquette by a stiff bolt of Connemara rain that cut him a quick keening blow to the face, knocking his index finger clear from his mouth and making him cry out from the suddenness of the attack.

Temporarily blinded, Father O'Malley wrestled impotently with the reins, tensing his body as his unpadded flanks prepared to do battle with the long and mercilessly pock-marked country road.

He was soaked like a sponge. The cold Atlantic wind bit deep into his atrophied old bones. His cassock was reduced to nothing more than a sodden black membrane that flapped to and fro about his scrawny legs. He was glad to be retiring, to be leaving these constant rounds of his behind, but he wished to God that he could retire with perhaps a little dignity intact. The arrival of the new priest

3

to his parish, though, had rendered that dignity entirely unobtainable.

Soon he would arrive at the house and at the great peat fire that burned constantly in its vestibule. His body yearned for the shelter and the heat that would dry him but he knew his relief and pleasure would be nullified by the knowledge that he would stand there dripping and steaming like some gawping old idiot; lips too frozen to speak and teeth chattering audibly, chafing his bloodless hands like bare bones before the fire, while the rain rolled in drops from the end of his long thin nose.

The priest looked up at his successor and was rewarded with a smile of pure concern from the younger man. Father Sebastian Devereux was, to all accounts, as personable a young man as had ever donned a priest's robe. Any moment now, the Father knew, he would be offering his waterproof for the fifth time that trip, and for the fifth time Father O'Malley knew he would hear himself refuse ungratefully. His misery and his discomfort had made him stubborn. He did not want the loan of the boy's waterproof and would have drowned in the blasted rain before he'd have accepted it.

If truth were told, there was something about the young priest that Father O'Malley, to his great shame, found deeply unpalatable. From the moment he had arrived in Connemara some two weeks previously the old man had found himself forced to search his own conscience for the root of these uncharitable thoughts. The boy was young; a mere twenty-four years, but that could hardly have been set against him since Father O'Malley himself had been just one year older when he had taken his first post away up the coast in Mulrany. He had been a great deal less confident than this young man, though, less at ease with his calling and the pressures it had hung about his narrow shoulders like a yoke. He had been haunted by the ghost of sin and plagued by the notion that he was somehow unequal to the task that he had been chosen to do. He had worn a perpetually haunted look that had begun to subside only in

4

middle age, for the sins that he heard in confession had seemed trivial compared to those that tormented his own young soul.

Father Devereux's soul, though, appeared in mint condition. If he did nightly battle with the Devil at all, then he seemed more than up to it, for he arose each day with an expression of such moral infallibility that the old priest found himself forced to wonder more than once whether he could possibly be possessed of all his wits. Surely such unquestioning faith could result only from gross ignorance? Yet Father Devereux had shown all the symptoms of intelligence and literacy.

If the young priest had a fault at all, then it was undoubtedly that of pride. Unlike most priests of his day he obviously came from a wealthy house, and that sense of worldly affluence was apparent in both his appearance and his manners. His manicured nails and his macassared hair had escaped no one's notice; nor had the fine worsted trousers or the best leather brogues, both of which would have been better suited to a dancehall in Killarney than the bogs of County Galway.

His cassock was unstained and seemed intent on remaining so, whatever the weather. Any creases would have vanished overnight and there were times on their tour of the parish when Father O'Malley had felt that he was escorting a bishop from Rome instead of a humble young priest.

One glance at the fine smart clothes and the sound of his fancy name and parlours had been opened to Father Devereux and the best china dusted down in his honour. Father O'Malley had found himself ushered into rooms that he had never known existed and he had watched as dour farmers from the heart of the moorland had stood scrubbed and tongue-tied before his new charge, rolling their caps in their great grimy hands as they tried to make sense of his cultivated voice.

Animals had been shooed from kitchens at Father Devereux's arrival, and the oldest of the Murphy lads, a roughish group of boys, had been heard to offer the loan of his father's old mare from the dairy, just for use on his rounds.

'She'll get you about all right, Father,' the boy had said, scratching his scalp and talking in accents so thick that Father O'Malley had been forced to serve as interpreter. 'Dada doesn't use her so much since his chariot broke and he got the new bike,' the boy had continued, his cheeks as red as hot coals. 'You won't want to be seen in that old thing of the Father's now, will you?' And, to Father O'Malley's great horror, the offer had been immediately accepted.

The mare had looked a sorry sight as she stood there in the rain, her ears flattened against her head and her great barrelled ribs heaving with the cold. With Father Devereux in the saddle, though, she had taken on a new lease of life, handling the pitted roads and hillsides with a grace that Father O'Malley, seated in his boneshaker, found unbearably depressing.

The young priest sat ramrod-straight, the reins held loose in one gloved hand, looking for all the world like a soldier of fortune off to do battle. If his sin was pride, then that had awakened something far worse in Father O'Malley. Watching his young companion sit dry and smart in the saddle, the old man felt the first uncomfortable flames of envy licking at his tinder-dry soul. It was knowing that this sin had been thrust upon him by the younger man that made him so uneasy and irritable.

Father Devereux had reined his horse about and was shouting something at Father O'Malley, though his words were lost in the wind. He pulled his mare closer to the cart, while the old man strained to listen.

' "Place me among the rocks that I love, Which sound to the ocean's wildest roar",' he quoted.

'What?' Father O'Malley bellowed, struggling with his own reins as his horse appeared to be trying to mount the roadside wall.

'Byron, Father!' the young priest called. 'I heard the ocean roar just then and the lines came to mind. Do you hear the sea, Father? I'm sure I can, even above this wind and the infernal rain.'

He bent to grab the reins of the old man's cart and steered it easily back on course, shushing and petting the horse as he did so. 'You're soaked, Father, soaked to the skin!' he said, looking back. 'Do we have much farther to travel before we reach the hallowed halls? I'm afraid you'll catch a chill if you stay out here much longer. Are you sure you won't take my coat?'

Byron! The old priest tutted to himself, but the weather prevented a stronger rebuke. 'We are onto Flavelle land once we pass through the gate piers ahead and to your left!' he shouted instead, then watched as Father Devereux dug his heels into the mare's ribs and rode on ahead to investigate.

The whitewashed gateposts rose like twin towers from the gloom. To either side ran ten-feet-thick stone walls that curved off until they disappeared in the vast demesne.

As Father O'Malley's cart rattled over metal gratings and onto a cinder track, the young priest returned with an expression of disappointment on his face.

'I thought we had left the old thatches of the clachan behind for a while, Father!' he said. 'I believe you promised me something grander once we reached your friends the Flavelles!'

Sheet lightning lit the parkland and Father O'Malley saw the young man's mistake. 'That's the farmhouse you've spotted,' he shouted, pleased to have the advantage for once. 'Look off to the east and you may find something a little more to your tastes.'

Father Devereux rose up in his stirrups and shielded his eyes from the rain. The estate stretched for miles but far away to his right he saw a large grey slab on the horizon. 'The dilapidated mansions of the landed gentry,' he whispered, for there was little to be described as splendid in the view that stood before him.

The house was large enough, though a sudden streak of

lightning showed its size to be the only frivolous thing about it. It was wonderfully ugly, almost humorously so, and totally devoid of any design or ornament that might have enhanced it. It was plain and leaden and Father Devereux felt his spirits drop.

'It is grand enough for you, then?' he heard the old priest ask.

'Very much so, Father,' was his reply, but he could not conceal the lie in his voice. 'How many live there?' he asked.

The old man shrugged. 'William Flavelle and Sophia, his wife,' he replied. 'Six surviving children and a handful of servants. As well as a few ghosts, I shouldn't wonder,' he added.

As if on cue they turned yet another corner of the long curling path and a low wall came into view, with a cluster of tombstones behind it. Through a ruined archway Father Devereux could see that the ancient stones were scattered without apparent pattern or design. He leant from his horse and, as the lightning flickered, could make out a handful of names on the largest of the stones.

'Liam Theodore O'Connell . . .' he read, 'and . . .' he added, peering, 'does that read . . .'

'Henrietta Maria Lloyd, beloved wife of the above,' Father O'Malley recited. 'May she who has created so much peace on this earth find eternal and everlasting peace in the arms of her maker.'

'Were these relations of Flavelle, Father?'

The old priest shook his head. 'Only by marriage. And if that sounds strange, then you will have to wait until you have met them and pieced together their story before you can know why I said it. Theo and Henrietta were Missus Flavelle's parents.'

'They died in the same year, then,' Father Devereux shouted back. 'And on the same day, too, in eighteen seventy-nine. Was this some great tragedy, Father?'

But Father O'Malley had had enough of a soaking and

whipped his horse in his impatience to get to the house. Father Devereux found himself forced to keep up, for fear of becoming lost in the vast grounds.

'So what of Missus Flavelle, then?' he asked, once their horses were level. 'Did she become mad at the tragedy or is she the grand old country matron of tradition; all flaming hair and ruddy red skin with a girth as large round as this horse and a brood of snivelling children hung about her full skirts? I've been warned about these wives of the landed gentry, Father, how they can be vipers when roused. Does she peck her husband into little pieces and then use him for the mincemeat, like I've been told?'

The old priest smiled beneath his hat as the rain ran from its brim down his collar. 'Missus Flavelle's hair could be described as red, yes,' he said. 'Though I think the word would do it an injustice. But then I am just a priest, not a poet too, Sebastian,' and that was all he would say in reply. Father O'Malley, known as a great gossip, for once found greater satisfaction in keeping his own counsel.

'Find out for yourself, my son,' he thought. 'Perhaps I shall see some of that self-righteousness of yours taking a bruising at last.'

'Is William Flavelle one of your better Catholics then, Father?' the young priest asked. 'You didn't point him out in church last Sunday, as far as I remember.'

'Oh, I shouldn't worry about our William's soul if I were you, Father Devereux,' Father O'Malley told him, 'despite the fact that he has not graced our pews with a visit in living memory, if I remember correctly. I do not believe either he or the Church would recognize himself as a Catholic, no.' He laughed quietly.

'Is he an atheist, then?' Father Devereux was clearly shocked and wondering now about the point of their tedious journey.

'An atheist? I should say not!' Father O'Malley said. 'No, no, not our Mister Flavelle, thank you very much, and I'd advise you not to say as much in his hearing. The only

9

reason you won't see William Flavelle in our church is because he's too busy praying to get there!' Clearly pleased at his joke, Father O'Malley reined in his horse and it was then that Father Devereux realized they had reached the tall oak doors of William Flavelle's mansion.

'He must be a wealthy man, though,' Father Devereux persisted, sliding from his wet saddle.

'The wealth was his wife's,' Father O'Malley told him and the young priest turned to hear more but the door opened and he found the moment was lost.

CHAPTER TWO

'The Church in itself is not a political creature and never will be. "Why?" you ask, and I will tell you why, Father. The Church is not a political animal because it cannot afford to be seen as one. That's the reason it has survived; it is its only method of survival; to see, yet not to get involved! Once it takes a side it risks the dishonour of defeat and that is something it could not afford at any price, am I right, Father?'

'The Father does not want to hear your political rantings.'

'Are you a political animal then, Father?'

'Were you a Maynooth man, Father? I believe our William here still teaches his children from the Maynooth Catechism. I'll swear he has a dog-eared copy of it lying somewhere about.'

'The Church is the Church and it does not give a fig for any human or political matter, as well you all should know. It exists merely to pursue its own interests as a Church. As a Church, d'you hear?'

'Perhaps you might tell us the Church's views on the emancipation of this country then, Father? Are you all for a call to arms like some of the boys or would a young man like yourself be content to sit back and watch his Church arse-lick the British backside once again? Eh?'

'The Church takes no stance because it has no stance to speak of! It is the referee at the boxing match who likes to be there in the thick of the action but without once taking his jacket off or getting his nose bloodied! It'll be there all right to raise the hand of the winner, though, you see if it won't! Now I'm as religious as the next man, Father, even Mister Flavelle here will testify to that, and you'll see me and mine there in the pew at the next mass, same as always,

11

but just what do you say to that comment of mine, eh? "Like a referee at a boxing match?" Eh? Now what do you have to say to something like that?'

'Sit him down, he's drunk, the bastard!'

'Shut up now, and let a man speak!'

'You should understand that Mister Mulkerrin here was an O'Connell man, Father.'

'The proudest ever to wear the name! I was there in 'forty-three, Father, marching beside him with the Young Irelanders. He arrived in a Bianconi coach, I'll never forget it. "The Liberator" we called him then and a handsome figure he was as well.'

'Then eight years later the whole of Clifden was up for sale and you'd got poor old Hyacinth sat up in her castle, waiting to be dispossessed.'

'He was a good man. He was a saint. I'll not hear bad about him.'

'Quick, pass him a handkerchief, someone, he's getting damp about the eyes. He'll be singing too, in a minute, and then you'll all be sorry, for we'll be here the entire night!'

There was laughter at that, and Dan Mulkerrin leant over to spit into the grate.

'You're a damn fool, O'Neill; all of you, damn fools. We're owned by the British now, thanks to idiots like yourselves who could do nothing but laugh!'

'Come on then, Father, let's hear your voice? What do you say of it all? And let us know first if it's the Church we'll hear talking or your own voice!'

Father Devereux cleared his throat, but Father O'Malley spoke for him.

'I believe you'll find your new priest here is more a poet than a politician, Brendan,' he said, his rheumy eyes glittering in the light from the candles.

'Even a poet may dabble in politics, Father, if you don't mind the correction. Edward Martyn is chairman of The Society and I hear that Yeats himself is always hanging about at meetings.'

12

'I want to hear the new Father now on my notion of the Church and the boxing match. I say it would never get its nose bloodied in the political arena, now what would your thoughts be?'

Father Devereux looked about the table and a dozen pairs of eyes looked back. A stout man to his right filled his pipe-bowl carefully with Gallaher's and tamped it down thoughtfully with his thumb.

The meal had been half-finished by the time they had reached William Flavelle's table and the other men had been sitting back in their seats, allowing their bellies to settle around the large oak table.

'They will be on to their pipes and their politics by now,' their host had warned them as he had pulled the double doors back and he had not been mistaken in his forecast, so the two priests had sat to their supper beneath a suffocating fug of both.

As his meal was delivered, Father Devereux pulled his napkin from its silver ring and went to smooth it onto his lap but a discreet cough from Father O'Malley's end of the table alerted him to the fact that the others still wore theirs tucked beneath their chins and so he quickly fixed his into his collar instead.

'I have to confess,' he began, feeling a fool to be addressing the table with this bib beneath his chin, 'I was something of a pugilist in my college days. It is this fact that accounts for the slight flattening of the cartilage of the nose that I'm sure those of you seated closest to me will not have failed to notice.' He pointed out the spot with his dinner fork and several of the men leant closer to look and nod verification to the rest of the table.

'Far from being a mere bystander at the ringside then, I can honestly reassure you all that I was there in the very thick of the action every time. My nose was broken and of course it bled, old man, it bled like the very devil!'

The room fell silent and several of the men sat back in their chairs, confused. Then William Flavelle began to laugh and tap the side of his spoon against the rim of his glass. The others followed suit and Father Devereux found himself patted on the back and called a 'good fellow' for being so sharp.

'Well done, Father, you parried that one well, if you'll excuse my continuing the metaphor!' William said, raising his glass.

O'Neill's confusion deepened further still. Had his question been answered, or what? He half-rose from his chair but the drink had made him unsteady and he fell back again, which made the other men roar.

A plate of steaming food was placed in front of Father Devereux. 'Minced beef-cake, boiled greens and potatoes!' William Flavelle announced, gesturing grandly. 'We eat plain food in this house, Father, just as the Lord did in His day. It's a point I'm sure you'll appreciate, being a man of the cloth. Plain food, combined with fasting and abstinence; it's the self-denial that frees the soul, don't you think? If we are able to deny ourselves in things lawful, we shall be better able to deny ourselves in things unlawful. Eh, Father?'

Father Devereux nodded and smiled vaguely, though his spirits had sunk at the sight of the food before him.

'Plain food and prayer provide the spiritual backbone of this household,' William told him.

The plate the food sat on was finest glazed bone china; Worcester, the young priest thought, though he had no desire to pick it up for closer inspection. The food that lay heaped upon it was, as his host had seen fit to boast, basic in the extreme. The steaming mounds of boiled greens, blanched potatoes and watery mince had long since become indistinguishable from one another, while the slab of bread on his gold-rimmed side-plate had become hardened with age.

'Wine, Father?' the maid whispered but, spotting the plain water in his host's glass and guessing the man to be teetotal, Father Devereux declined.

'Pity, Sebastian,' Father O'Malley called from the

opposite end of the table. 'Mister Flavelle here keeps one of the finest cellars in Galway. I'll help myself to a little more of your exquisite Burgundy if I may, William?' He raised his brimming glass in a silent toast to his host. The room seemed to relax at his words and conversations were resumed.

'You're a young man,' Father Devereux was informed. 'Are you French at all, then?'

The young priest shook his head. 'You're referring to my surname, of course?' he asked, dabbing with his napkin at some water that the maid had spilled on his sleeve. 'Though I believe my ancestors were Huguenots who fled to Britain.'

He noticed the raised eyebrows around him. Mulkerrin had been lighting his pipe for the fifth time that night and had stopped instead with his match in his hand, waiting until it burned his fingers until he threw it down with a quiet curse.

'That was in the seventeenth century, of course,' Father Devereux added. 'I believe that has left us with a full two hundred years to realize the error of our ways!'

William Flavelle slapped the palm of his hand full against the varnished wood of the table at this, causing the Sheffield plate cutlery to jump and the candles in the flint-glass lustres to flicker. He was an alarming man, even in a good humour. Not tall, but square-set enough to be called big, he was easily able to dominate a room without once being called upon to speak. He had insisted Father Devereux take his own seat at the head of the table, but he held control well enough from the side with his strange dark eyes that flicked about the room, following every word that was spoken. Bearded like Moses and with the wild stare of a prophet, William Flavelle, in his long black frock-coat and high starched collar, looked for all the world like a fierce lay-preacher of the hellfire-and-brimstone variety.

'Did you hear about the Clifden riots, Father?' Father Devereux heard himself asked, but he found that he could not answer. Like an unseen ghost, a figure had moved

15

around the table and into his line of sight, drifting silently between the pools of golden candlelight and in and out of the shadowy gloom.

O'Toole to his right was quoting Grattan and Griffith in a voice so full of reverence that it finally broke with the emotion. He saw tantalizing glimpses of russet-coloured hair and translucent-pale skin but all other detail was denied him by the darkness of the echoing room.

'It was a bloody fine fight, that; begging your pardon, Missus Flavelle,' O'Neill said, and it was only by that comment that Father Devereux realized that the others saw his vision as well. Flavelle's wife. Yet they all seemed fairly oblivious of her. Mulkerrin half-rose from his seat but she extended a slim pale hand to show she expected no such niceties. The whole room seemed full of her perfume and, as she found her chair to the left of the priest, he set his eyes upon her face at last.

CHAPTER THREE

Sophia Flavelle sat, head leant in one hand in the languid pose of the day, smiling in tolerant amusement at the debate that raged so furiously about her.

'How was your food, Father?' she asked.

'Good,' Father Devereux told her. 'Very good.'

'Really?' she raised one eyebrow high. 'I thought it rather insipid.'

She was laughing at him, at his obvious lie. He dabbed his lips with the napkin and returned the smile, fighting back the blush that threatened to spread across his entire face.

She laid her fingers across her lips and her pale hazel eyes held him fast in their myopic stare. Her beauty was dramatic but also frustratingly unspecific; when placed under closer inspection it vanished altogether and there was no one feature to be singled out to inspire the young priest's poetry. And yet the beauty was there, and in overwhelming abundance.

'Did you ever see such a gathering of old goats?' she asked, and Father Devereux laughed out loud, for none of the other men heard her.

Her nose was too long and too straight and her lips rather thin with a pale ochre tint that matched the freckles that speckled her high brow.

'Should I peel this, do you think, or would anyone notice if I popped it in whole?' She held up a single purple grape for Father Devereux's inspection.

Father Devereux looked about the room. 'I should believe you'd escape notice this once, Missus Flavelle,' he said.

As he spoke, another of the gentlemen spat loudly into the fire, sending a loud hiss from the hot ashes.

17

'And you'll forgive the brief lapse of etiquette at such a high-mannered gathering?' Sophia asked, and the grape disappeared between her lips.

'Of course,' Father Devereux told her. 'Just this once, at least.'

When she laughed she tipped her head back and he could see her white teeth and the pulse that throbbed on her thin pale neck.

It was only Father O'Malley who watched them now and he wore a smile that bordered dangerously on the smug. He raised his wineglass in a silent toast, enjoying himself at last.

'So here's to your "grand old country matron",' he thought. 'All flaming red hair and a waist as great as your mare!' His eyes flicked to Sophia Flavelle. 'Gaze upon her, boy!' he thought. 'Drink every drop of that wondrous beauty and then tell me what all your posturing poets would have to say; then tell me how wrong you can be, with your pompous pride and your terrible, ghastly arrogance of youth.'

Sophia Flavelle rose from her seat and the candle flames guttered slightly in her wake. She walked from the room and Father Devereux felt an idiotic sense of having been somehow deserted. He caught the last of her; a final sweeping of some pale, faded rose stuff that was the fabric of her skirts and then there remained only the old men's conversation to fill the breach that she had left.

Then he heard the first notes from the piano.

She began with Brahms, but the men still talked and so she switched to some Irish ballads instead and, one by one, they fell silent to listen. The style in which she played became unashamedly sentimental and increasingly so, until Father Devereux was forced to cover his mouth with his napkin, to hide his smile of delight at her mocking of them.

She finished with 'A Londonderry Air' and the mood became unbearable until the men about the table sat back into their seats, their thumbs tucked into their waistcoats, to gaze at the ceiling and dream. By the last verse several

18

were dabbing at their eyes and Mulkerrin was openly blubbing. The decanter of port stayed untouched and the only movement came when a large and very raw green baked apple covered with thick custard sauce was placed before Father Devereux.

O'Toole was the first to his feet. 'To the good Lord and to Ireland!' he said in a voice shrill with emotion, and the men raised their glasses to join him in his patriotic toast.

It was well after midnight by the time they had reached the hall and were struggling into their coats. The cold air there sobered them a little and they fell quiet. Mulkerrin took a hat-brush down from a shelf in the dark oak closet and set about brushing his high-crowned bowler with angry, vigorous strokes.

'Christina, my dear!' Father O'Malley exclaimed as he took his hat from the solemn-faced girl who stood by the door. 'What keeps you up at this hour?'

He stamped his old feet on the flagstones as though already feeling the frost that would greet them outside.

'Mama said I might stay up to see to the guests,' the girl told him, blinking furiously with some nervous affliction. A small pair of wire-framed spectacles hung from a chain around her neck but either vanity or forgetfulness had prevented her wearing them.

'You were wet when you arrived, Father,' she said. 'I stuffed your hat with paper and held it by the fire to keep its shape.'

'You looked such a sight, Father!' came another child's voice from behind them. 'I saw you from the stairs! You looked such a sight, honest to God! You looked like a wet bat from the belfry!'

There was another girl by the foot of the stairs, smaller and less plain than the first, though still a long way from being anything near pretty.

'Does God not supply you with an umbrella then, Father?' she asked. 'If He could send Noah a bloomin' great ark you'd think He'd at least have run to an old waterproof for

19

one of His priests, now, wouldn't you? Doesn't He know you could catch your death on a night like this?'

Before Father O'Malley could reply to her cheek the older girl had crossed the hall and, with a cry of 'Blasphemer!', had dealt the young girl such a hard blow about the face that both priests winced in sympathy.

Cora said nothing and she barely flinched.

'Cora?' Father O'Malley opened an arm out to her but she let out a little laugh and skipped away from him.

'You looked like a bloomin' great bat you know, Father!' she shouted, and this time she was off up the stairs before her sister could reach her.

'You could have hung by your heels to dry off by the fire!' she shouted from the landing and then there was just the sound of her feet, running off to another part of the house.

'Not so hasty, Father!' They turned to see William Flavelle walk into the hall, his arms outstretched. 'I've barely had time to meet the new priest! I had hoped to get down to some real discussion of current theology now that those drunken sops are left; perhaps over some glasses of antique brandy, Father? There's a fire lit ready in the study, if you've a mind.'

Father Devereux looked to Father O'Malley with an expression of deepest anxiety on his face. The old priest sighed and closed his eyes in silent prayer.

'It's terribly late, Father,' Father Devereux said, but his words were wasted. They were led into a study and shown to two large leather chairs. William Flavelle stood before them, warming his arse over the insubstantial peat fire.

'I saw you had noticed my wife, Father,' William began, turning to the young priest.

Father Devereux felt himself begin to redden. He thought that he should say something; felt it was expected of him but he found himself at a loss for the appropriate words.

'Your wife is a beautiful woman, William,' Father O'Malley said, yawning. 'And I'm sure all men must stare

20

at her. But I thought it was theology we were here to discuss.'
He settled deeper into his chair and, to the young priest's
horror, his eyes slowly closed and his head nodded forward
onto his chest.

The room fell silent and Father Devereux heard his
shoe-leather squeak as he changed position in the chair.

There was a soft knocking at the door and William called,
'Enter' so loudly that Father O'Malley's head started back
against the antimacassar.

'Will you hear the boys' confessions, Father?' William
asked the old priest as his two sons entered the room.

'Francis? Thomas?' Father O'Malley asked, looking confused. 'But surely you would rather come to the church . . .'

'It's not good to sleep on a conscience that is tormented
by guilt, Father,' William Flavelle said. 'I told them they
could come to you once the others were gone.'

'But it's past midnight!' Father O'Malley said, pulling
himself up in his chair.

'Will you hear them, Father?' William cut in. 'Or are you
too tired?'

He motioned the eldest boy, an awkward, stringy-looking
lad, to kneel in front of the priest.

Father O'Malley shrugged and the boy began a whispered
list of all his petty misdemeanours. When he had finished,
the second boy, a stockier, ruddy-faced lad took his place
and began his own whispered litany. Father Devereux could
catch only a few of their words but he found the sins being
squeezed from their lips so turgid and unimportant that he
had no desire to hear more. He was cold and getting colder
by the minute and his body ached for its bed.

'They are wicked, filthy sinners, Father,' he heard William
Flavelle say. 'And we should now pray for their impure
souls.' Their host knelt between his sons and placed a hand
onto each of their heads. He started a prayer that lasted an
hour and twenty-two minutes; Father Devereux timed every
second on the mantel clock behind them. When it was over
it took them another quarter-hour of coaxing before Father

O'Malley's bones would unknit enough for him to be walked to his carriage and the frost was as thick as cake-icing by the time they finally took their leave.

Father O'Malley was asleep at once and even the jolting of his cart as it ran over the rocks was not sufficient to wake him. The wind caught his thin white hair, blowing it around his bare skull like a lady's fan and Father Devereux stretched over to pull on the old man's hat to keep his head warm on the return journey.

CHAPTER FOUR

Father O'Malley scooped the yellow skin from the top of his warm milk and threw it to the floor, where it was eaten by the cat. The fire crackled comfortably and its flames lit the old man's eyes like twin candles.

'Theo O'Connell was poor Sophia's father,' he began, pausing to inhale the sickly smell from his mug. Father Devereux realized with a sigh that he would be needing the proverbial patience of a saint just to see the story through. Patience was a luxury only the old could afford. Father Devereux found himself looking out of the window as his foot tapped against the floor.

'Theo was a great man, Sebastian; a delight to know,' the old priest went on. 'He left Ireland many years ago for America where he felt, like many others before him, that he could make his fortune; the difference between Theo and most men being that he did just that and, once it was made, he returned to Ireland to find himself some peace.'

Father Devereux smiled and shook his head. His pink reptile tongue flicked over the milk moustache that had formed across his top lip.

'Alas,' he laughed, 'peace was the last thing that poor Theo was to find around here, for he had not reckoned on the tenacity of Irish motherhood in full feckless flight! Theo was still a bachelor, you see; a little elderly, perhaps, and a little prone to using the kind of language that might have made a sailor blush, but he was a bachelor nevertheless and these problems were nothing that could not be overlooked once the rumours had spread concerning the size of his fortune. Wealth like that might make even the most blasphemous curses suddenly and wonderfully acceptable.'

The old priest chuckled and Father Devereux waited. First

William Flavelle in his study and now this. He wondered if it had begun to get light outside. When they had left for the great house that evening he had never supposed that he would not be seeing his bed again. The old priest's cat coiled itself about his legs, looking expectantly up at his lap. Father Devereux thought of its tabby fur over his clean black cassock and leant forward quickly, resting his elbows onto his knees to curtail its leap from the floor. Father O'Malley took this gesture as a sign of increased interest in his tale and stirred himself in his chair to continue with renewed vigour.

'Theo remembered the great house from his youth, when he and other local poor lads from the clachan had been called up to stand shivering in the hall and be presented with an orange each from the owner. By then the house was empty though, and in a sad, dilapidated state, but Theo bought it anyway in the vain hope that its remote location would mean he could seek sanctuary within its walls, perhaps until he died.

'He had his servants put it about that he was in poor health, though nothing could have been further from the truth, in fact, for a more robust man I've yet to see.' He rubbed his hands together with delight.

'The local mothers would have none of it, though!' he chuckled. 'They smelt out their prey and they filled poor Theo's drive with their carriages; all stuffed to their brims with a rare old assortment of women and girls of supposedly marriageable age. Theo took one look at the descending hordes and fled to the safety of his study; the very room that we sat talking in tonight, but the women had travelled a long way for the most part and were not to be thwarted that easily. They left their cards and, when no reply was forthcoming, they returned to leave printed invitations to this do and that, all arranged on the trot, and entirely for poor Theo's benefit. When he could stand the siege no more and was forced to venture out from his seclusion they even contrived to waylay him in the streets.

'I believe they would have driven him back to the relative peace of New York had he not finally come up with a plan to thwart the lot of them for good; he married Henrietta Lloyd, and in doing so rid himself of the troublesome women in one fell swoop!

'Oh yes, there were more noses put out of joint when that match was announced than I've seen around here for many a day!' The old priest laughed.

'And what,' Father Devereux asked, picking cat hairs from the hem of his robe, 'made Henrietta such a paragon of her sex? Why did Theo pick her out from all the others on offer? Was she as beautiful as her daughter? Was that what made her so different?'

Father O'Malley started a laugh that finished as a fierce hacking cough. 'Oh, Henrietta was different, right enough,' he said, wiping his eyes on his sleeve. 'In fact she was the local disgrace; a woman to be ignored by all but the most charitably-minded. She had it all against her, Sebastian, and what I believe Theo saw in Henrietta was the ultimate protection against all the scavengers.

'Henrietta was English, you see, Sebastian; she was a Protestant; she was well past her prime as far as marriage was concerned and, worst of all, I believe, she had a son, who had been born well out of any notions of wedlock. The poor child had died soon after its birth but the village had never forgotten. And it was she, Sebastian, this terrible, sinful scarlet woman; a woman who had been the recipient of the charity basket each harvest for five years running, on account of her having fallen so low, it was this woman, Sebastian, that Theo saw fit to choose above all the local beauties!

'Oh!' he exclaimed, slapping his hands onto his thighs. 'It was like a keg of powder placed beneath the local community and Theo had dared to light the fuse! It was terrible to hear the baying for blood that followed, Sebastian, I promise you!'

Father Devereux stopped picking at his robes and cupped

25

his chin in his hands, his interest genuinely evoked at last.

'Did you visit them after their marriage?' he asked.

'I did,' the old priest replied, defiantly. 'And I was proud to go, though there were those around here that would have written to Rome to get him excommunicated, if they could. You see I liked Theo, I had a soft spot for the old rogue, in fact, and I must confess I'd always had an affection for Henrietta, too, believe it or not. She had sinned, yes of course, but she was an intelligent and lively woman and good company, as well.'

'But to marry a woman like that just to get the rest of them off his back!' Father Devereux said.

Father O'Malley laughed at that and leant across to tap him on the knee. 'But now there's another shock in store for you!' he said. 'And not nearly half as much of a shock as it was to old Theo at the time, I believe. You see he fell in love with Henrietta after their marriage! Now that should gladden that poetic soul of yours, Sebastian! He married the woman out of barest necessity and then he found himself in love with her into the bargain!'

'And did she feel the same?' Father Devereux asked.

'Why, of course, or my story would not have been as perfect!' the old priest told him. 'Or did you never hanker after a happy ending, Sebastian?

'Theo became a changed man. He was happy; deliriously so, bubbling over with his luck like some dried-up old river that finds itself suddenly flowing with fresh springwater. It was a joy to behold, Sebastian, I can tell you. He placed the whole house in Henrietta's name as a belated wedding gift and she repaid that favour by filling the place with life for him.

'Henrietta was no great beauty, Sebastian; nothing like her daughter, you understand. She was a big woman, strong and rather heavy-boned for most tastes, but she had the capacity to create beauty and that can be one of the greatest of God's gifts, I believe. The house became glorious; she had it painted base to roof and then she filled it with the most wonderful furnishings and wild flowers and dogs and the sound of her laughter; when I first visited Theo after his marriage I believed him the luckiest man alive, can you believe that? A man of God smitten with envy over another man's marriage to a woman his Church would have shunned?

'They opened the house up and threw party after party, so keen were they to let all share in their joint good fortune. I attended the first ball myself and there were more servants there than guests. Henrietta sat alone on her brocade chair in the middle of the empty ballroom while Theo stood in the hall, waiting to welcome the arrivals. When the guests did not show, Theo merely led his wife out onto the floor and they danced there alone until the sun came up. I believe it made little difference to them whether guests were there to see or not.

'The village would not come, you see, as I said; they'd their noses so out of joint they might never have breathed fresh air again. I had expected tears from Henrietta but I had not reckoned on her resolve, or the strength of the love that she had for Theo. She merely sat there happily enough in between dances. "They'll come," she told me. "Not this time and maybe not the next either, but they'll come here eventually, Father, you see if they don't. They'll be burning with curiosity and even their pride won't be enough to keep them away."

'And she was right. They came in time; first a trickle and then a flood, as word got about how grand the place was and all, and when they came they found that they received such hospitality that they'd never before seen in their lives.'

'And all this met with your approval, Father?' the young priest asked.

'Not approval exactly, no,' Father O'Malley told him. 'Though it would have been difficult enough to have stood about, clucking away like some disapproving old hen in the face of all the guileless charm that those two were capable

of exuding. Their joy was infectious, Sebastian and, besides,'
he tapped the side of his nose, 'our Theo was a generous
man; as generous to the Church as he was to all his
neighbours. The place would be without a roof today if it
had not been for Theo's kind patronage, you know!'

Father O'Malley leant back in his chair and yawned,
clasping his hands across his chest and studying his bare
toes thoughtfully. 'You know one can get chilblains by
toasting one's feet near to the fire in such a way, Sebastian?'
he asked, yawning again, slowly. Then his old eyes spotted
the impatience in Father Devereux's face.

'It was eight years or so before our Sophia came along,'
he said, quickly resuming his tale, 'and you may just imagine
the shock for all involved! There was Theo, by now the
respected local statesman; all grizzled grey hair and mutton-
chop whiskers and there was his wife giving birth to a child,
for all the world like some eager young bride!

'You'd have thought it the only baby on God's earth too,
for all the fuss that was made of it. Theo was so puffed up
with pride that I feared he might burst! As I remember it
they would both sit around that cot making faces and stupid
noises at that poor child, so that it's a wonder the lass slept
at all in her first years, for they were all there to hug her
and play with her, whether she wanted it or not.

'They employed a nanny too, but only because it was the
thing to do, for I'll swear the girl got not so much as one
touch of her charge for all the time she was there!

'Sophia was spoilt then, you see; there is no doubt of that,
though the spoiling never actually spoilt her, if you understand my meaning. She grew up as used to all the fussing
and the luxury and the love as you and I would to, say,
prayer and breathing. She and her father were inseparable
until the day that he went away to America to take a look
at how his business was going on, and the day that Theo
left I thought Sophia's heart would break for sure. It was
the only time I have ever seen Sophia Flavelle cry, for, as I
told you, she was not a spoilt child as such, though she was

used to having her heart's desire and this was the first occasion that she could not get it, I believe.

'At the age of fifteen she had got herself engaged to be married to some suave young Englishman who shared her passion for horses and it was the following year, on her sixteenth birthday, in fact, that the tragedy that we spoke of earlier was finally to strike.'

Father O'Malley's voice grew quieter as though the next part of the tale were still painful for him to relate. Father Devereux pulled his chair closer to avoid missing any of his words.

'As expected,' the old priest began, 'there was a grand ball planned for Sophia's birthday and they threw the house open to over a hundred guests. The weather was mild that night and the veranda doors had been opened so that the dancing could spill over onto the lawns. There were candles and flares burning throughout the gardens and the place could have been compared to a faerie palace; if you'd a mind to be so fanciful, that is.

'The house as it was then in no way resembled the place that you visited this evening, Sebastian, you have to understand that. I expect you found it a little bare, did you not?'

Father Devereux nodded. 'The only room I saw fully furnished was William's study, where we finished the evening,' he agreed. 'The rest of the place made me think that the family had hit upon hard times and been forced to sell all their furniture, stick by stick.

'What they did have left was good, mind you. I believe that was Chippendale that we sat upon at dinner and there was an exquisite satinwood cabinet that I glimpsed in the dark of the hall. There were a few American pieces there too, I believe. Theo must have had them sent over when he came to live here.'

Now it was Father O'Malley's turn to nod. 'What you see today is a tenth of what there was,' he said. 'William considered the display of wealth indecent and most of the finer pieces lay covered in dust-sheets in the cellars.' He sighed. 'But I am losing my drift,' he said, settling back in his chair.

'Arthur Denham, Sophia's fiancé, had invited some young friends from England and as the evening progressed there was a certain amount of high-spirited horseplay, as is inevitable when young people and alcohol are mixed in liberal quantities.

'It was past midnight when one of the locals happened to mention to young Arthur the tradition known as "about the house". Now that concerned the record, held by Theo himself, I might add, for driving a carriage and pair out of the drive and through the gates, then around the demesne and back up to the house again. No sooner had young Arthur heard this tale than he had taken it as a challenge, and he and a friend from London took it upon themselves to break Theo's record, for the honour of their country. He did it to impress Sophia too, of course, for the challenge had been made in her hearing and she was much for seeing her beau as the local hero. At first she was all for going with them, though she was somehow persuaded to change her mind and watch instead, thank the Lord, and the pair went off alone while all the others stood watching.

'By all accounts Arthur and his companion ripped through those gateposts like demons out of hell; Arthur steering, his greatcoat flying, a whip held high in his hand, and his friend clinging to the sides of the carriage for dear life. The whole party came out to cheer them on and you could hear their shouts echoing for miles back in the clachan. Once they'd ridden out of sight the guests all stood there counting the seconds off aloud, but the counting subsided when, one after another, they caught sight of the other carriage in the distant drive.

'Henrietta had promised young Sophia an extra surprise after midnight on her birthday and it was their carriage the guests saw, bringing them slowly up towards the drive. She had slipped away unseen, you see, to collect Theo from the town, as he'd made the long trip back from America to

30

Ireland just to be at Sophia's birthday and there he was, leaning from the carriage window, waving for all he was worth.

'Sophia spotted him first and let out a scream of delight, though that scream of pleasure turned to one of terror when she saw Arthur's carriage tearing towards them from the opposite direction. Her screams soon found company. People shouted, hollered, waved their arms and stamped up and down, imploring Arthur to rein in before it was too late, but he was too far away to hear and so the guests were given no alternative but to watch in growing horror.'

The old priest paused a while and Father Devereux watched in silence as he dabbed a tear away from his eye and licked his tongue across his dry lips. He placed a hand to his brow to hide his face as he spoke the next words.

'Arthur's carriage hit Theo's coach broadside-on and Sophia watched her beloved mother and father crushed to death as they sat in their seats.'

Father O'Malley's voice broke at this point and it was a few minutes before he could resume.

'Sixteen years old,' he said, 'rich, spoilt and beautiful and in a moment it was all taken from her. Now there's your tragedy, Sebastian. Can you wonder why it still hurts me to talk about it, even after all these years? Can you see the look on the poor girl's face as the people she loves most in life are stolen from her in an instant?'

Father O'Malley's mouth puckered. He moved a little closer to the fire and in a moment it was scorching his cassock; they could smell the smouldering cloth.

Father Devereux placed his index fingers across his lips and gazed thoughtfully into the fire. 'What happened?' he asked at last. 'Who did she turn to? Her fiancé? The Church?'

'No, Sebastian,' Father O'Malley said quietly, 'she rejected us both, I'm afraid. The thing had been an accident and Arthur was never openly blamed for the deaths but Sophia let it be known that he was no longer welcome at

31

the house. She could not bear to look at him, you see, knowing that he had been responsible for the deaths of her beloved parents.

'I made frequent visits to the house in the weeks after the tragedy but I was received by her only once and then it could have been a stranger that I was talking to, for she had changed so much I would barely have known her. The life had gone from her, Sebastian; her spirit had died. I know that was to be expected under the circumstances, but the changes had been so great that they were pitiful to see in one that I had known from birth.

'She refused all offers to stay with her mother's relatives in England and she locked herself up in that old house with only the servants for company.

'She invited no one to the funerals, Sebastian, and when I saw that child standing alone at the gravesides, her cold white face peeking out from under the black bonnet, why, I thought my heart might break for her. It is at times like that that the Church should provide comfort, I know, but it was difficult to explain to her that God might be exempt from blame in the whole affair and I believe that she shunned Him for the same reasons that she had shunned her fiancé.

'I had bought her a fine gold rosary that day, Sebastian, possibly as a means of reparation, I don't know, and I handed it to her at the graveside, after the service. She took it from me with a polite word of thanks, though I thought for one minute she intended to drop it into the grave. Then I watched her walk back from that desolate spot to the house and that was the last that I saw of her for many months.

'It was the vicious cold winter of 'seventy-nine, Sebastian, I don't know if you'll remember. There were sheep frozen in the fields and for weeks there were houses cut off from the rest of the clachan, so things got put aside in the bitter battle to see the year through.

'It was late spring before I was to see Sophia again and a pale, funny-looking creature she had turned into in the meantime, though I suppose you would still have found her beautiful, for she fitted what I would take to be the poet's ideal. She came to me, Sebastian, she walked right into the Church and, once I was over the shock of her poor pinched face and her dulled-looking hair she shocked me again by asking me right out if I would take the service at her wedding.

'At first I thought she'd come back to us, Sebastian, and my heart took a leap, I can tell you. I thought she'd forgiven poor Arthur and was again set to marry him, but I was wrong, as you will know.

'William Flavelle was the man at the local end of managing Theo's affairs and his estate. The main bulk of the work was done off in Dublin but William had been chosen as agent to see to things this end. It turned out that he had been the only person outside the estate that Sophia had had contact with through the winter, and that through necessity alone; or at least it had been.

'William was well known in the clachan as a self-made man with aspirations. He had come from the poorest of families but a relative in America had paid for his education and he had seen the chance when offered him and seized it with both hands. He had gone on to study law and then had offered his services to Theo, knowing himself to be the only man for miles with such qualification and that therefore the man would have little choice but to use him. William was a respected young chap, but I could not say that he was well liked, for all that. He had a commanding presence even then, and I believe it would be fair to say that those who met him would find themselves rather in awe of the man. You've met him yourself now, Sebastian, and I'm sure you'd agree that the same is true enough today. He is not an easy man to know. He has standards higher than most and can be difficult to talk to. I believe that he strives for perfection in all things, and none more so than in his religion. He takes his theology a little too seriously for most tastes, Sebastian; mine included, I might add!

'I believe that when he met Sophia he saw her as some

divine mission in his life. There was this poor girl that he knew to have once been so spoilt and so worldly and he had found her lifestyle sinful in the extreme. I believe he thought that God had exacted the ultimate penalty from her in taking her family at a stroke, and that it had been given to him to lead her back onto the path of righteousness once again. He must have felt that what had happened to Sophia had exonerated all his strong-held ethics of hard work and abstinence, Sebastian; I heard him say as much at the time and I've heard it repeated many times since, even within Sophia's hearing, if you can believe that!'

The old priest sighed again and Father Devereux saw the outline of his narrow ribcage as it rose and fell beneath his robes.

'Sophia must have seen the strength in William,' he continued, 'and she clung to that strength like a drowning man to a rock. Under William's tutelage I saw her begin to be slowly consumed by her own guilt and I saw she truly believed that only William could save her from herself. He taught her the error of her ways and showed her how the life she had led before was sinful in the eyes of the Lord. It was to blame for the tragedy; *she* was to blame for the tragedy! She had been given too much in life and of course it had been taken away. She leant on William, Sebastian, and she married him, and that was over sixteen years and six offspring ago.

'You have met Christina and Cora, then there is a third daughter, little Edith, born just a few months ago. Francis and Thomas are the eldest two boys; Francis is a big lad of fifteen and Thomas a few years younger. The other boy, James, is still in the nursery with Edith.

'The last child nearly killed Sophia, I believe. I was called in three times to administer the last rites but she pulled through by the grace of God and the determination of Doctor O'Sullivan, though the doctor asked me to warn William not to make major demands on his wife again if he wants her to live. It is a difficult thing to discuss with

34

any man, as you may imagine, but William took the news quite well, I believe. It is possible that a further abstinence will appeal to him, I don't know.'

He looked to the young priest for comment but Father Devereux did not move his gaze from the fire.

'And what became of all her wealth?' he asked the old priest. 'The house looks so barren; what became of her father's business in America?'

The old man shrugged. 'The money went to William after their marriage and was his to do with as he saw fit, I suppose. I don't know what happened to Theo's business, perhaps it was sold. He owned paper mills, I believe. The whole house is William's now and I'm sure you might hear Theo turn stiffly in his grave at the Spartan way that the place is run. Perhaps William gave his riches away to some deserving cause or other, who knows? He did not discuss it with me. I'm sure it has been put to more worthy use than in Theo's day, though I know many around here who mourned the going of the balls and all the finery.'

'Yet he sees fit to decorate his own rooms with enough show!' Father Devereux said angrily. William's study had contained all the fine pieces and decorations that the rest of the house had lacked. There had been rich Chinese rugs on the floor and heavy purple velvet hung at the windows. William's desk had been heavy mahogany but the room had been dominated by an elaborately-carved dresser that Father Devereux supposed to have been rescued from the dining-room at some time. The piece was fascinating and he had found his gaze wandering to it as William had continued his diatribe. The thing was enormous; divided at the front into six panels and each representing the temptations of Christ in imaginative and rather luridly-carved detail.

There had been an even more elaborate Italian gilt mahogany chaise-longue by the fireside and beside it a mahogany reading-stand with a candle-stand attached and a gold-leafed book lying open upon it. An enormous Bible had been placed on a delicate japanned pedestal desk that seemed barely equal to taking such weight, and above it hung an exquisite oil-lamp chandelier.

The whole room had seemed full of a richness and opulence that was sorely lacking in the rest of the house, as though William had plundered the place for the benefit of his own quarters.

By contrast, Father Devereux remembered the bleak hallway with its one solitary closet that could not hold all the guests' coats, so that they had to be heaped upon a nearby chair, and the bare oak table that had been the only other furniture; with its lone silver salver that had long been empty of visiting cards.

The panelled walls had been impressive, though the panelling had been badly in need of a polish, as had the imposing stone staircase with its plain mahogany banisters. There had been black bog-oak shutters on the windows and most had been closed against the storm, giving the place a most gloomy and melancholy aspect.

'Was there nothing that you could have done, Father?' the young priest asked.

Father O'Malley shook his head sadly. 'What was there to do?' he asked. 'Tell a religious, God-fearing man to stop giving his money away to the needy and spend it on his poor wife instead? Ask him to refuse to marry her and leave her alone in a house full of memories? Should I have demanded he buy curtains for rooms they no longer use and spend less time on prayer and fasting and more time feasting on quail's eggs and caviar? It was Theo I needed to speak to, Sebastian, not William. It was Theo who had defied the Church with his rash marriage and his reckless lifestyle. William is a frugal man, and he follows most of the laws of the Church to the letter. We should praise him for that, I believe. As a friend of poor Theo's there was a lot that I could have said but, as a priest, I found my lips were, of necessity, sealed. Officially I can only commend William's actions, my boy.'

There was silence in the room before the old priest rose unsteadily to his feet.

'You are tired,' he told Father Devereux. 'When you get to my age sleep is no longer so important. Take my bed, my son; it is too late to go saddling your horse. I will stay here a little longer by the fire, watching the flames die down.

'The story has brought back memories and I am too melancholy for sleep. I shall probably doze off here, in fact; it has been my habit of late.' He waved an arm at Father Devereux. 'Sleep well, my son. Do not let my story disturb you. There have been many more tears shed by many others between that time and now, so do not concern yourself too much with the plight of Sophia Flavelle and her brood. They have eaten tonight and they are warm in their beds, which is more than you can say for many of the parish.'

Father Devereux took the candle he was offered, spending some time lighting it in the draughts from the door and the ill-fitting windows. Once it was finally lit he stared down at the old priest and found him already asleep. His cadaverous face looked like the skull of a sheep in the firelight. One hand was laid feebly across his chest and a thin line of spittle had leaked from his mouth onto his chin. For a moment Father Devereux took him for dead but then a soft rattling snore reassured him that he was not.

'Sleep well yourself, Father,' the young priest whispered. 'For I'm sure your sleep will be sounder than any in the great house tonight.'

CHAPTER FIVE

'Sophia?' Naked and anointed with oil, William Flavelle had entered his wife's bedroom. His huge erect penis stood out proudly before him, like an eager sword in the hand of Christ. He had come to do good works. He had come to show to Sophia the way of the Lord.

The bedroom smelt of Eau de Bois which was the perfume she wore when alone, for she knew that he did not approve. It would cling to her clothes, though, and he would show his displeasure, not in words, but in his actions towards her.

'Sophia?'

Silence answered him. So she was already asleep. He knelt beside her bed and he prayed, his hands clasped before him on her satin quilt. He could hear her breathing and smell her sweet breath upon his face. His erection quivered and he clasped his hands firmer and screwed his eyes tighter shut so that she should not distract him from his conversation with God.

He would not bow to temptation, of that much he was sure. She was the whore come to tempt him and yet he could overcome his lusts, and by doing so find the path to spiritual salvation.

He looked again at her face as it lay, silvered in the moonlight and pressed hard into her pillow. Her lips were partly opened, so that he could see her teeth. One arm lay across her hair; wrist-side up, as though warding off a blow. How vulnerable that wrist looked, like the belly of a reptile. He thought of Adam and Eve in the garden. If he cut that wrist she would die in an instant and yet she turned it towards him, as though in defence.

How opposite to him she was! That she could have sinned

so much and yet could lay, asleep and blameless like a child in her bed, while he was destined to kneel in an agony of doubt and self-loathing! The blood poured in a torrent through his veins now; deafening him to his prayers and blinding him to all but his wife's pale flesh.

His prayers became louder but his voice was less sure, for the Devil's poison flowed along with the blood, weakening all parts of his body save one. The throb of his groin burned upward, consuming his other senses, so that even his prayers tasted carnal in his mouth. He tried to wrestle the Devil with his prayers but his body was no longer his own and the words that he searched for would not come.

Father O'Malley's thin golden rosary hung from her bedpost before him, swaying to and fro like the pendulum of a clock in the breeze from the window, clicking occasionally as it hit the wall, and William gazed at it, mesmerized.

'Blessed Father,' he began, for the words had come to him at last, 'grant me the strength to fight this temptation.'

He watched his shaking hand reach across the bedclothes, pulling them gently back as he eased his great body down beside her.

'Look down upon me, thine servant, O Lord!' he whispered. He ran his hand over his oiled chest and onto his rounded belly. 'Holy Father, look down upon me now!'

She moved in her sleep then, her hand fell from her face, and he fancied he heard her murmur his name. Her lips moved; he watched as her tongue reached to moisten them, like an animal that smells its prey, and in that one small movement she had unwittingly severed the single thread of her husband's self-control.

He fell upon her. She awoke with a start but then was not alarmed, for it had been like this before. He pushed her nightgown upward to her waist and she closed her eyes tight as he entered her.

She could not bear to see his face. His eyes had bulged in their sockets from the strain and his teeth had become clenched as he began the final throes of battle with the Devil. He cursed aloud and called her a whore, all the time his body pumped up and down and the bed shook until it rattled against the wall.

He pushed forward with a cry and the bedsprings screamed in rusty indignation. Three more violent thrusts, three more strangled cries and then his spine wrenched back in a spasm that seemed to last an eternity. Then he threw himself from her and fell back onto the pillows, fighting for breath.

'William?' Her voice was like a soothing balm. She stretched out an arm and her cool hand felt for him, smoothing his hair that was plastered to his brow as she would do to calm a sick child. But William shrank from her, pulling away from her touch. He rose from the bed; a dark and silent figure in the moonlight, walking across the bare boards of the floor and pulling the door back to vanish into the shadows of the house.

Sophia raised herself on her pillows, pulling her knees up and hugging them into her body after first covering them again with her nightgown.

There was a small cup of water on her nightstand, covered with a cap of beaded muslin to keep any dust from settling onto the surface. She removed the cover slowly, dipping her handkerchief into the water and pressing it to her temples. She felt the persistent throbbing there that she knew would soon turn into a headache.

Allowing her head to fall back onto the pillows, she opened her eyes to see the rosary, hanging directly above her head. Reaching up to pull it down, she pressed the cold metal cross against her lips and, closing her eyes again with a sigh, settled back into the sleep from which her husband had woken her.

William Flavelle, meanwhile, had reached the sanctuary of his bedroom and, locking the door behind him, crossed to his own nightstand, where he surveyed his image in the speckled glass of the ancient mirror. Sweat filmed his face and clung like dew to his black woolly beard. He had pulled on his nightshirt and it was already soaked; sticking to his flesh like wet plaster, so that he could no longer bear its touch. In a sudden rage he ripped it over his head and threw it in a ball onto the floor. Now he stood naked again before God, naked and defenceless in the face of his sin. He watched his barrel chest heaving in the mirror, its thick black hair matted and wet.

The sweat began to evaporate in the breeze from the half-open window and the heaving subsided as he felt his self-control return. He cleared his throat and joined his hands. Now came the time for penance and for punishment. His God was a forgiving God, but his sin that night had been great.

Now he heard God's voice above the roar of his blood, and the instructions that He gave him were clear. 'Like the beasts of the fields,' he heard the voice admonish, and knew the voice was right. His eyes filled with quick tears of shame at his actions, though the tears as he wiped them were opaque and heavy; more like mucus than real tears.

'Bless me, Father, for I have sinned,' he began, falling to his knees in prayer and clutching his Bible before him. He had no need of priests and their churches, not when he could hear God's own voice direct in his head. He stayed there on the hard floor for hours, praying for God's forgiveness until his body was frozen and his bones cried out with the pain. He prayed until the dull burden of guilt began to ease from his mind and then at last he rose to complete the penance.

He was ready for his punishment now, though he knew it was to be harsh. There was an enamel bowl on the washstand in front of him and he filled it with the cold water that stood in a matching jug. Immersing his hands and forearms to the elbow he set about washing; first with soda and then with carbolic until his flesh stung with the scrubbing he gave it. He liked the smell of the carbolic, it made him feel cleaner and purer. It blocked the evil stench of his wife's perfumes from his nostrils and he inhaled the aroma greedily, until his lungs were full of it.

When the first ablutions were over he dried his hands quickly and set about the harder work. Picking up a bristle floor brush from beside the bowl, he worked it into a cake of yellow soap and scrubbed at his nails until the flesh around them was raw and starting to bleed. In time all the skin from his fingers to his elbows was reddened and scratched and only then did he pause to dry his arms and throw the scum-covered water in the basin away.

Dusting the raw skin with violet-scented powder, William Flavelle turned his face again to the mirror and was pleased to see a man who looked calmer and more composed.

There was only one more duty that the voice had asked of him and then he could allow himself some sleep. With a sigh that filled his broad chest, he lifted the jug once more and filled the bowl with clean fresh water.

'Holy Father,' he said, over and over again, like a chant. 'Forgive me for I have sinned.'

There was more to be cleaned; there was the core of his flesh and the very weapon of his sin. His cheeks burning with righteousness, William Flavelle poured out more soda and picked up the scrubbing brush to set about his final task with grim enthusiasm.

CHAPTER SIX

There was some sun in Connemara that winter; it glistened on the frost for a full three days and Sophia Flavelle took the chance to take a long walk alone, to blow some of the dust from her soul and to breathe the fresh sea air into her lungs once again.

And so there she was, wandering in the demesne, her coat buttoned to her neck and her face made pink by the wind. She reached the brow of a hill and then suddenly she stopped. 'Oh, my dear Lord!' she whispered, and her bare hands flew to clutch at her neck.

Not far below her but across the glassy field lay stretched out an enormous undulating sack of brilliant emerald green silk. The great sheet of fabric turned into the sun, shimmering so bright in its rays that it all but blinded her for the second. She placed her hand over her eyes to shield them. There was something attached to the by now half-risen sack – a round basket – and there was a figure hanging from the basket. She saw its shoes glimmer as they too caught the light.

Sophia picked up her skirts and ran without hesitation, her feet pattering small steps onto the frozen grass as she attempted to keep her balance on the descent of the hill.

'Father Devereux!' She had stopped by the basket, as the balloon now rose above it in its fully-inflated splendour. The priest was busy with the controls. His head was bare as he leant back to look upwards. Sophia thought he looked strange in the brown tweeds he had chosen to wear for his trip.

'A priest in a hot-air balloon!' Sophia laughed aloud. 'Now there's a sight worth running for!'

He saw her then and she noticed the blush that spread

over his features in an instant, as though she had caught him at something obscene.

'Missus Flavelle!' he cried, and the basket tipped a little as he leant over to greet her.

'I would never have guessed, Father!' she laughed, clutching her hat.

'It's a sport I enjoyed in my college years!' the priest shouted. 'I was delighted to find a club so close to Connemara. Have you ever been in a balloon, Missus Flavelle?' he asked, suddenly.

Sophia took a step backwards. 'No, no, I have not!' she said.

The fresh air had gone to the young priest's head. He felt alive and impulsive. 'Would you care to ride with me, now?' he asked. 'It's perfectly safe and we don't need to go far.' He extended a hand towards her.

'I hardly think I can ...' Sophia began.

'Look, there are steps,' Father Devereux told her. He enjoyed the look that had burnt up in her eyes. 'There is a blanket, too, that you can throw about your shoulders in case you get cold,' he added.

She was like a nervous animal that is tempted by food. A sudden laugh emerged from her mouth and she looked shocked at the sound.

'It's hardly fitting, you know!' she said, but she had taken his hand by then and he was helping her to climb in. She was amazingly agile, he found. His other hand had barely touched about her waist before she had made a little leap and steadied herself immediately, clutching the sides of the basket and panting clouds of warm steam from her mouth.

She ran a hand to push her hair back into the sides of her hat and then she laughed. 'I had never thought that I would find myself being shocked by a priest!' she said.

Father Devereux smiled. He pulled at a brass chain and flames belched out above them and the ground fell away under their feet. Her eyes were bright, like a child's.

'I don't believe this is too shocking,' the priest said.

'Anything is shocking in Connemara.' Sophia laughed. 'You'll discover that for yourself once you've been here a while.'

'I suppose the place must have its compensations,' he remarked.

He watched her lean over the edge of the basket to gaze at the circling earth below and as he looked at her cold bare hands he thought of the story that Father O'Malley had told him, of how she had lost all that she had in that terrible tragedy.

'Then I would just like to hear you name one!' She laughed, turning to him and tapping her hand against his arm.

A pheasant took off from the ground to their left and they watched its brown wings flap wildly in an attempt to keep its bulbous body aloft in the grey skies.

Sophia clapped it on in its exertions and Father Devereux blew into his hands and stuffed them into his pockets. He was a handsome, rather vain man and he wished now that he had not met her when his cheeks were blue and his eyes full of water from the wind.

'Do you think the rocks and the bogs look prettier from up here, Father?' she asked him.

He could never have answered her truthfully. Not only was the view of the wild Atlantic coast sufficient, at times, to make him cry with its beauty, but there was also the spiritual succour that he felt as he dangled up there, halfway between heaven and the earth. It made him feel infinitely closer to his maker than other mortals and he, proud man that he was, felt this led to an almost unique kinship with God.

'There's the Twelve Bens down there, look, do you see?' he asked, pointing.

She watched his face, smiling at him as though she indulged a child; he saw her watching and blushed again. The sky above them turned turquoise and the clouds were salmon-pink. The huge envelope of green silk rippled in the winds like the sail of a proud galleon. Compared to all that celestial beauty the bleak grey lands below brought goose-bumps to his skin.

'You remind me of Icarus,' Sophia said quietly, still smiling, and he felt once again that she was mocking him.

The sea broke onto the black cliffs below them and a miserable cloud of seagulls cackled and cursed above it. He saw the untidy cluster of whitewashed cottages that would one day be his parish, and the hills beyond them that were an intense grape-blue against the fine pale green of the misty sky. He could almost smell the rotted seaweed that lay in great heaps along the shoreline and in his imagination he heard it popping as it dried out in the sun.

Sophia shivered and he bent quickly to pick up the tartan blanket and lay it carefully about her shoulders.

'It is not the cold,' she whispered once his face was close. 'I have seen my house. We have just passed above it.'

Father Sebastian found that his arm was still about her shoulders. He allowed it to slide away naturally, not wanting to appear to be refusing her comfort.

Light-headed with recent fasting, William Flavelle watched the balloon from the window of his bedroom. At first it had been a blurred speck in the distance but as it glided nearer the shape had taken form until he had known it for what it was. Then he had recognized the occupants of the basket that hung below it and, barely aware whether what he saw was a vision or reality, he had thrown himself down onto his knees in ferocious prayer.

He had seen his wife laughing, though he had not heard her laughter through the glass, and he had seen the new priest with his arm about her shoulders. His entire body began to tremble as the meaning of the vision slowly became clear to him.

'Fornicator!' he mumbled into clasped hands that were pressed against his mouth. 'Adulterer!'

He had seen the glances that had passed between them in

his own home the other night. He had prayed for guidance then but had felt himself reprimanded for daring to distrust a priest. Now he had been shown that he was right. His wife and the young handsome priest. His God had shown him. William knew that he was being punished in the most terrible way. William Flavelle remained on his knees, praying for forgiveness and deliverance until he heard his God tell him to go to his Bible and that he would be shown what action to take.

Walking slowly, painfully across the floor he reached his book-stand and began slowly to turn the pages.

As the balloon passed above Christina Flavelle, as she stood in the garden, she believed that she, too, had seen a holy vision but, unlike her father, it seemed to her like those received by Saint Bernadette, and she found herself throwing up prayers of thanksgiving, rather than forgiveness.

She had prayed for such a vision since she had first read of the lives of the saints and today seemed like the perfect day for her to have received such a reward for her prayers, when the sky was a brilliant green and the clouds were being blasted on their way by the most celestial of winds.

She had found herself subdued to silence and inactivity at the sight and had been standing, staring at the house, when she had felt the dark shadow as it passed over her and had looked up in time to spot the miracle apparition as it passed. She had not had her glasses with her but it did not matter, for God had appeared to her as a vast green undulating orb and beneath that holy orb she had been surprised to make out two of his angels, waving clearly at her to show that the vision was for her eyes alone.

Christina did not wave back. She had been unable to move and she was to regret this lack of response for the rest of her life. What if she had been able to wave? Would her life have been transformed? Would the angels have alighted and taken her back to heaven with them? Instead she had fallen on her face in the dirt and sent up a stream of childish prayer. She had been beaten later by her papa for the state of her frock but she had not minded the beating for she had known by then that she was chosen by God.

' "His palette gleamed with burnished green, Bright as a dragon-fly's skin",' Father Devereux said, looking up at the balloon as the wind whipped them onward and they floated high above the prostrate child in the garden.

'I don't believe she saw us.' Sophia smiled, turning back to him. 'She seems to have fallen over as I waved. Wordsworth?' she asked, almost absent-mindedly.

Father Devereux looked quickly at her face, delighted by her knowledge. He had not known that she would have an ear for poetry. 'Thornbury,' he corrected her. 'A new favourite of mine.'

They laughed at that, for no reason they could have named, and their laughter echoed like a peal of bells in the ears of the praying child, down below.

CHAPTER SEVEN

Winter left Connemara late that year and its going was barely noticed during the miserable summer that followed. It was autumn again before the lands were given a chance to dry out from the rains and there was barely a day that passed without Father Devereux needing the protection of his waterproof and his scarves as he made his way about the clachan.

It had been five long years since Willian Flavelle last made an appearance in Doctor O'Sullivan's surgery and now the doctor noted with a sigh of irritation that he had chosen the very day that he had hoped to close his business early for a much longed-for dinner of boiled mutton and gravy.

It was not that the doctor was unwilling to hear an inventory of the man's half-imagined complaints but, knowing William as he did, he guessed the list to be endless. His stomach growled hungrily in thwarted anticipation and his hopes dropped still further as he made out the earnest and troubled expression on the man's face as he entered the small room.

In a moment of panic the doctor found himself bending quickly to enjoy the aroma of some flowers that Bridie O'Reilly had insisted on placing in a vase upon his desk as a gesture of thanks for his treatment of her goitre. Bridie also cleaned the local church, though, and it was from there that the doctor suspected the flowers had come.

Doctor O'Sullivan was not yet an elderly man but his empathy with his patients stemmed from the fact that he tended to share their suffering himself. A muscle in his back sent a searing pain throughout his spine at the sudden movement as he stooped. The pain, he found, was squandered; William was not deterred by the fact that his office appeared to be empty, and the flowers smelt of nothing more than cat's pee and wax polish. Or perhaps it was his own catarrh that he smelt, and which had plagued him now since the onset of the previous winter.

'Doctor,' was all that William said in curt greeting, pulling the hat from his head and throwing himself down onto the small bentwood chair in front of the doctor's desk without waiting for the seat to be offered.

'William!' the doctor replied with feigned surprise. He attempted to straighten to greet him properly but his spine had locked fast, sending out distress flares of pain with every movement.

'I'd like a few words with you, Doctor, if you don't mind,' William Flavelle said, oblivious to the other man's predicament.

Doctor O'Sullivan crooked an arm and placed a shaking hand into the small of his back.

'A few words, William?' he asked, his voice wavering with pain and indecision as he saw the plate of boiled mutton that awaited him fade slowly from his view.

'Yes, Doctor,' William said, turning his hat in his hands. There was something in his tone that cut short any excuses the doctor was in the throes of dreaming up, and even his spine seemed to unknit for a second, so that he was able to straighten enough to steady himself against the brass rail around his desk.

'There are things that have been troubling me; things to do with my wife,' William went on.

The two men regarded each other for a while and then Doctor O'Sullivan nodded.

'Very well, William,' he said. 'Of course I shall hear your problems.'

He pushed his chair back and noted with irritation the duster and the polish that his housekeeper had left standing upon it. By the time he had moved them to the floor, an operation that took some few minutes, on account of his back, William was staring at the ceiling and clicking his tongue quietly with impatience. Doctor O'Sullivan took his seat and crossed his arms over his belly.

There was silence.

The doctor cleared his throat, wishing with sudden anxiety that he had blown his nose before they had started. It was patently too late now to be thinking of such a thing. The catarrh pricked the back of his eyeballs, forcing tears to well up and spill down onto his withered cheeks.

He used the silence to search his pockets in vain for a handkerchief and panic rose with the tears when he was unable to find one. William Flavelle was sure to start speaking soon, and he could hardly ask him to wait once he had started.

For a moment the doctor considered the use of his sleeve; the Lord knew that it was filthy enough already with the mud and dirt that accumulated each morning on his rounds, but then he spotted the duster lying by his feet on the floor and he let out a sigh of quiet relief.

While blowing his nose he heard William begin and he worried that he might have taken his sigh as one of irritation for the time that he was taking.

'As I said, Doctor, it is my wife that I have come about . . .' William began.

Doctor O'Sullivan gazed into the yellow duster. Was that blood he saw, mingled with the mucus? Alarmed, he held the rag up to the thin light to see the dark spots there more clearly.

As William Flavelle commenced his list of problems, Doctor O'Sullivan found his attention wandering, so worried was he that he may have discovered symptoms of the onset of tuberculosis.

'And then . . . and then there is the child,' he heard William saying at last, and he pulled his attention back, as the man's voice had dropped and it needed all his concentration to hear him.

So that was why William had come today; there was some

to-do over one of the children. In the long silence that followed, the doctor found himself wondering which one had caused the trouble this time and why William Flavelle had come to his surgery instead of calling him to the great house, as usual. His money would have been on Cora for a bout of the influenza, of course, though Thomas was a spirited boy and he had not seen him for a while.

'It's the child that my wife is carrying, Doctor,' William said as though he had read the doctor's thoughts.

'Ah, the new baby!' Doctor O'Sullivan said, shifting comfortably in his chair. He pushed his sandy hair back off his face and treated William Flavelle to one of his most patronizing smiles. This child at least could not be causing trouble as it had yet to see the light of day, poor thing. 'It is not nearing its time yet, William,' he continued affably. 'Don't tell me it is worrying you already.'

He watched William's hand as it rose to his face.

'As you know, there is another month to go yet, Doctor,' he said, and his head dropped. 'I am afraid that it will kill her,' he whispered. 'I am afraid that she will not survive it!' His voice broke and Doctor O'Sullivan closed his eyes slowly to the sound of his sobs. He was unable to hide his irritation.

'I warned you, William,' he said. 'Father O'Malley warned you and I warned you what you would be doing if you approached your wife again. We told you after the last child that you should exercise restraint. Still,' he sighed, 'I suppose it is what the priest would call God's will and you must leave your wife's fate to God's tender mercy. I will tend to them both as best I can.'

He had heard the same story every day for years: 'Doctor, we cannot afford this new child!'; 'Doctor, my wife will die if she has another!' Always the men sought him out and always only once it was too late.

'Why do they come to me at all?' he wondered. 'It is their problem entirely, they have brought it on themselves, why can they not employ a measure of restraint? They are insatiable in their lusts and their desires, how do they think I can help them now?'

'It was not my fault, Doctor!' William Flavelle exclaimed, and the doctor sighed again at the cliché, the cry of a million husbands before him. Yet officially their Church would take their side. Doctor O'Sullivan's back was aching, though, and he did not care to hear official Church talk. He was a medical man, not a religious one, and he hoped William Flavelle had not come to pin him down with one of his endless theological discussions.

'You cannot blame your wife, you know,' he said, angrily. 'The women cannot be held responsible. Men are stronger and the control lies in their hands. Women are told often enough that it is their wifely duty to comply when their husbands approach them. I believe they think they are failing in their Christian duty if they dare to refuse.'

There was a long pause after this outburst and then William Flavelle finally spoke.

'The child is not mine, Doctor!' he said, so quietly that Doctor O'Sullivan thought at first that he had misheard.

'Not yours?' he asked, shocked. The professional tone of calm objectivity had left his voice altogether now. 'Can you be sure of what you are saying?'

'Yes, Doctor,' William told him gravely. 'I am sure.'

Doctor O'Sullivan rocked to and fro in his seat, his hands clasped between his knees, his previous pains forgotten. It was not strictly speaking his problem and he found himself acutely embarrassed to be hearing it.

'You should be telling this to Father O'Malley . . .' he began, but then he saw the desperation in William's eyes. He had thought the man on the brink of clinical insanity for quite a while. Now he suspected that he may have fallen over the precipice at last. 'Has your wife . . . has she admitted this adultery?' he asked. He saw William's head shaking in the darkness of the gathering shadows.

'No.'

'Then how can you be so sure?' He almost laughed with

the relief. William had fallen prey to wicked gossip, then, that was all. 'Your wife is a good woman, William, I have known her from birth. I am sure she is innocent of any accusations . . . you should not listen to idle gossip, trust in your wife and in the fact that the child is your own. You should try not to dwell on such morbid doubts again, do you hear me?'

'I *am* sure, Doctor,' William Flavelle repeated, stubbornly.

The doctor paused, his mind racing over all the possibilities that this statement induced. If William were not insane it could mean only one thing. He wiped his long fingers across his mouth, sorely in need now of a swallow of brandy.

'Do you mean you . . .' he began. Had the man seen the actual adultery? His mouth dried at the thought. How else, though, could he be so sure? He searched for the right words. He hated to be specific about such things that should, by rights, have been private between husband and wife. It was an aversion from which he had always suffered and which he nevertheless tried his best to keep hidden. These were problems that, as a bachelor, he always felt desperately unqualified to deal with and he had never come to terms with his queasiness over such things.

It was then that a new thought struck him. 'Are you saying, William, that you had not been intimate . . .' he cleared his throat and began again. The longer the pause, he knew, the harder it would be to continue. 'Do you mean you had no . . . no knowledge of your wife at the time that the child was conceived?' His face had reddened and he was glad the room had become darkened.

William did not answer immediately and the doctor wondered whether he, too, was suffering a seizure of embarrassment.

'No,' came the answer at last. 'I did have relations with my wife around that time . . .'

'Then the child will be yours!' Doctor O'Sullivan exclaimed, taking William for a damned fool now.

'No, Doctor,' William insisted. 'I sinned with my wife,

yes. I should not have touched her and I prayed to God to give me the strength not to do so, but I do not believe that the child came from that union.

'I prayed, Doctor,' he went on, 'I prayed to God that no child would come from our couplings and the Lord told me of my penance and I suffered it duly. God would not deceive me, Doctor, I am sure of that. The child did not come from our union; if I am to believe that it did then I am to lose faith in all that my God has to tell me. He would not have refused me that night, Doctor, I know he would not.'

'You cannot blame God for your sins!' Doctor O'Sullivan was no longer able to hide his irritation. 'Nor should you put the blame upon your poor wife! This is a medical matter you are talking of; this is science and nature! Any man in his right mind knows that if he couples with his wife a child may result from the union! You cannot believe that mere prayer alone will alter the course of such a natural process! And then to accuse your wife of adultery as a result!

'Good heavens, man, go off and tell your priest what you have told me and I am sure his response will be much the same as mine! Speak to Father Devereux, William. He appears to have a sensible head on his body, for all I have heard.'

He laid his long hands upon the desk to show that he wished to hear no more, but William would not be cut short.

'I believe it is the Devil's child!' he shouted, and the words rattled through the doctor's nervous system and down into his very soul.

He scratched at his scalp and sighed.

'Tell me, Doctor,' William asked, pushing his face closer across the table. 'What would you call the child of a priest?'

Doctor O'Sullivan felt a sudden nausea in the pit of his empty stomach, followed by an urgent desire to laugh aloud.

'Father Devereux,' William said. 'I believe the child to be Father Devereux's!'

The doctor felt a strange sense of relief at the statement,

as though it confirmed his diagnosis of William Flavelle's insanity. Then the thought that such an idea should have appeared in his head at all occurred to him and again he found himself suppressing a desire to laugh. And then Father Devereux's name filtered into his consciousness and an aching began somewhere behind his temples, making him rub at the throbbing veins with his fingertips.

'Do you know what it is you are saying, man?' he asked, feeling suddenly very tired and very old. He did not feel equal to dealing with the man, suddenly. William Flavelle could be a terrifying man at times and never as much as he was at that moment.

William's head nodded. 'Yes.'

The doctor sighed. His chair had suddenly become very hard and he felt cold, so cold that his hands had turned blue.

'You are accusing a priest of God of committing adultery; of breaking one of the Ten Commandments of Moses, with your wife?' He swallowed carefully, trying to get a tone of gravity and of terrible rebuke in his voice. 'Do you know the day of the week, William?' Then, more gently, 'Can you tell me all the names of your children?' He had to be professional, he realized. He had to check the state of the man's mind.

William Flavelle was on his feet in an instant. 'You believe I am insane!'

Doctor O'Sullivan shook his head quickly. 'Do you have any actual evidence of this dreadful sin, supposing that it ever took place at all?'

William stared long at his hands. 'I saw them together in the demesne . . .' he began.

'You saw them?' the doctor asked, suddenly very alert. 'You actually saw them together? Is that what you mean? You saw them committing this sin together?'

There was a pause that lasted all eternity and Doctor O'Sullivan was disturbed to find himself wishing William would answer in the affirmative. It would at least reassure him of the man's sanity and he would not then have to try to test his reasoning again. It was as he sat questioning his conscience over his own maliciousness at this that he heard the word 'No' uttered from William's mouth.

'You did not see them?' He sounded irritated now.

'I saw them together . . . God led me to the window and I saw them there. She was laughing. He had his arm about her shoulders.'

'And that was all?'

'Yes.'

The doctor exhaled held breath in a slow and steady wheeze. 'Then you are deluded, William,' he said, the anger building again. 'You should be ashamed of your own thoughts! To accuse a man of God and your wife of such things without evidence is wicked. You believe they may have walked together once; is that proof of these terrible accusations? He had his arm about her; perhaps he was offering her comfort! Perhaps she is as frightened of her pregnancy as you! Did that not occur to you?'

There was no sound now from the man who stood before him.

'Did you not think?' he asked.

There was a noise from William that he took to be assent.

'Go and speak to Father O'Malley,' the doctor began. 'Tell him what you have told me. See if he doesn't echo my sentiments entirely . . .' but William Flavelle was gone from the room before he could finish his words.

The doctor sat pondering in the empty room for many minutes after the man had left. Should he tell Father Devereux? He itched to tell the young man, both to warn him and to worry him, for if William Flavelle were in fact in the grip of a bout of temporary insanity then who could know what the outcome might be? He thought long and hard and in the end decided against disclosure. There was, after all, little to be gained by putting the young priest on his guard, when perhaps it might merely be worry over the baby's birth that had caused William's mind to erupt as it had. There was more to be gained by silent vigil, Doctor O'Sullivan decided. He would watch and he would wait and, if all went well, he would not be called upon to discuss the matter again.

Niall Eugene Randall Flavelle took his first breaths of life during the last watery hours of a fragile autumn day. Sophia had survived the birth well but it was her son that Doctor O'Sullivan did not expect to live.

When the old priest had picked the child up to anoint his small red screwed face with holy water he had thought for a terrible moment that its head would roll off, for it lolled back over his arm in an alarming, lifeless way while its gummy mouth had fallen open without so much as a whimper.

There had been trouble in persuading Sophia to part with the boy at all; despite the exertions of giving birth, she had proved to have quite a strong grip and had wept so many tears above the poor baby's head that they had thought it would die of drowning before it could fade from more natural causes.

The four eldest children had been allowed in to kiss the child's brow before it died and Father O'Malley noticed more than one of them pull back with distaste once they saw the livid red bundle he cradled in his arms.

It was the sight of Cora's face, wrinkled with repugnance, that had caused the child's first keening cries and with those cries came the first warning signs that he might, after all, live. Cora, of course, was delighted and claimed to have saved the poor thing's life, and perhaps it was that incident that was to make them so close.

To William Flavelle, though, the screams were a voice from hell. Kneeling alone in his study he ceased his prayers at the sound, clapping his hands over his ears and crying out aloud at the new intrusion into his household.

It was Father O'Malley who found him, still kneeling in the darkness by his desk, and he watched William's great broad back for a while, not wishing to eavesdrop on his prayers.

The study had changed since Theo's day, he noticed, when it had been full of books and rarely used, for Theo had had no use for solitude once he had married Sophia's mother. There had been so many books there that they had spilled off the shelves and formed stacks upon the floor. Now those same shelves sat empty, save for one or two heavy religious tomes.

The family Bible lay open before William on the desk. It was a large, elaborate affair, bound in purple chamois leather and with its pages edged in gold leaf. It had been gaudily illustrated by hand, and ordered direct from Rome by William on the day of his marriage; the only incidence of extravagance that Father O'Malley could remember the man being guilty of. That Bible was William Flavelle's proudest possession. He read from it each day and carried it at night to the dinner-table.

Rising on his toes to see what passage William had turned to for comfort, Father O'Malley was instantly aware of the joints of his feet cracking like pistol-shots in the silent room.

He waited for William to turn at the noise but the quietly whispering voice did not falter as he prayed to God Almighty to spare the life of his wife. There was something on the Bible's page, the priest could see, something that he recognized. It was a miniature of Sophia, done in oils; a painting that Theo had commissioned shortly before he had died.

It had been a rather daring portrait for its time, with Sophia's neck bare to the shoulders and her long hair loose about her face. She was laughing in a way that the priest had not seen since the day her parents had died.

The priest was surprised to find the painting in William's possession at all, let alone lying atop his cherished Bible. He cleared his throat loudly to announce his presence in the room and this time William heard him, for his hand shot out to grab the portrait and bury it quickly in his inside pocket.

William Flavelle's face, when he turned, was terrible to see in the half-light. It was the face of a man suffering the deepest of torment. His eyes were mad with fear and his features were bloated and wet from all his tears.

'He looks like a man who has drowned,' Father O'Malley thought, averting his gaze to avoid embarrassing the man further.

'How is she?' William asked.

'She is well, I believe,' the old priest told him.

'She will live?' William asked, as quick as a shot.

'Oh, yes, the doctor seems to have no reason to think that she will not survive this time,' Father O'Malley said. 'In fact he seems quite surprised by her resilience; so much so that he has had to reward himself with a glass or two of your best malt to wet the baby's head. The child is well too, by the way.'

William sank back onto his knees and his head fell to his hands.

'It was the child that gave more cause for concern at first; it is a boy, by the way,' the priest continued, 'but now the poor scrap seems to have enough breath in his lungs and I believe the good doctor is merely waiting for Francis to saddle his horse again before he takes his leave for the night.'

There was a vast array of rubbish displayed upon William's desk, he noted, which seemed doubly surprising for a man so obsessed with cleanliness and order. There were scraps of faded paper with odd scribblings and drawings upon them; a small ribbon of hand-made lace that someone had obviously abandoned unfinished; some gaudily painted stones and a misshapen piece of whittled wood. Father O'Malley had supposed them to be rubbish but then the thought occurred to him that they may in fact be mementoes of the children, and he looked again at the man who crouched before him.

William Flavelle's shoes were polished like glass, he noticed, even the soles, and his black hair had been greased with pomade to shine like patent leather. He did not appear to be as vain as Father Devereux and yet he was by nature an immaculate man and a perfectionist in all things. He was obsessed with cleanliness and there was a basin by his desk in which he would wash his hands a hundred times a day, and always before touching his beloved Bible.

'God has spared her,' William said.

'Yes, yes,' the old priest agreed, 'she is perfectly safe, and the boy too, as I said. You have another son, William, did you hear me tell you just now?'

William said nothing, just rose silently to his feet.

'He's a small, weak little thing, William, as I mentioned, and not much to look at at the moment but he has a good pair of lungs, as no doubt you'll have heard. Did you select a name for him yet? Or were you sifting through your Bible to make your choice?'

It was William Flavelle's silence that caused the old man to jabber on as he did.

'Would you like me to fetch the child?' he asked at last.

'No,' William cut him short and a frown of concern crossed the old man's face.

'But you will see your wife?' he asked.

William nodded.

'I thought . . .' the priest began.

'Yes?' William asked, turning to him.

'I thought a man would be eager to see his new son,' Father O'Malley said, confused by William's attitude.

William walked across to his Bible, spreading his hands upon its open pages. 'Do not expect to see me in your church, Father, giving thanks for the child's safe delivery,' he said quietly. 'I would rather it had died, and that is the truth. It would have been better dead, Father; do not ask me to explain why.'

Father O'Malley felt a chill at the man's words. He waited a while, pondering his reaction, but William ignored him, studying his precious Bible and so, after a while, the old priest retired quietly from the dark room.

CHAPTER EIGHT

They were pushing Father O'Malley around in a chair for six months before he died, and a sorry sight he made too, with his shakes and the appearance of his poor face. It had somehow taken on the aspect of intense and unspeakable sorrow after the stroke and huge tears would roll constantly from his great bulging cod-fish eyes, while his gaping jaw would jabber on just as though he'd glimpsed the approach of the apocalypse and was set on warning all who saw him of the terrible impending doom.

He frightened the parishioners as he was taken about. They were superstitious folk and, understanding him to be near to death, therefore took his demeanour to be a dire portent from one who has glimpsed the afterlife and not been overly taken with what he might have seen.

The old priest had lost the power of speech completely yet he still seemed frantic to communicate. He would grab at the nearest hands and sleeves instead; clutching them in a surprisingly vice-like grip and subjecting their owners to such a wild array of grimaces and utterances that even the bravest would become nervous at the sight and more than one poor soul had been known to faint clean away.

It fell, of course, to Father Devereux to push this harbinger of doom about the parish and even he found his local popularity waning as a result. Their visits to the great house, though, had become more frequent, mainly because the young priest thought he detected an unexplained but nevertheless noticeable improvement in the old man's condition when he was there.

His expression would seem less anxious during those visits and his tenacious grip would relax completely, especially when the children were present. The children, fortunately, paid him no heed, and Christina seemed to positively relish his visits. She would sit by his chair, reading to him from the Bible and one time when the young priest found them, the old man's hand was resting lightly upon the girl's bowed head, as she read.

The children of William Flavelle were a strange brood, Father Devereux discovered; mostly plain in appearance and quaintly old-fashioned by nature. At first he had thought them all as dull as ditchwater but, as time went by, he found himself increasingly fascinated by their strange but often charmless characters.

It was the harsh religious regime imposed by their father that the young priest most blamed for their idiosyncrasies. William had them pray seven times a day, strict on the Canonical hours, and there was mass each day, although William himself did not attend. Meal times were an occasion for further prayer and restraint, when the children would sit in silence with their communion medals safety-pinned to their jackets, waiting to be called upon to quote a list of venial or mortal or cardinal sins, or to recite their responses from the catechism.

Their affection for their mother was manifest, though some had more trouble in expressing it than others. Sophia might not have been the easiest woman for a child to love, either, he found. She spent much time with them, he saw, and was always visually accessible, but she appeared distant to them mentally, having a somewhat distracted air about her for most of the time.

She would play with her youngest children and cover them with kisses and embraces but the priest found her rather languid in her affection, perceiving such a sadness behind her smiles that he could not help but feel that the children must yearn for more robustly maternal arms.

Francis, the eldest boy, though more man than boy by now, looked and acted the sullen farmhand rather than son and heir to a wealthy estate.

He was a tall runt of a lad who was rarely seen inside the house, except at meal times, and who would speak only in reply to direct questioning, and even then with a distinct lack of enthusiasm. There was a smallholding on the estate, which encompassed the cottage that Father Devereux had seen by the gates, and it was there that Francis appeared to prefer to mooch about, in the shadow of his grandfather's tombstone.

It was Thomas, his younger brother, who resembled his father, being stocky but not quite as dark. He was intelligent and engaging and, despite his homely features, was known to be more popular among the local girls than Francis, who was popular only among the owners of the local drinking-houses who profited considerably from his patronage.

Christina had not grown out of her plainness and the poor eyesight that dogged the entire brood seemed to have afflicted her the most. Rather than improving, her nervous blinking had grown worse with age, and she had to suffer the added indignity of Thomas's thoughtless teasing.

Christina was her father's most loyal disciple in the house, despite the fact that it accorded her no special favour from him, and she made it her job to police his meticulous strictures of her siblings whenever he was absent.

Cora caused her the greatest anguish for, although the two girls were inseparable, they were completely opposite in nature, and each was a constant thorn in the other's side. While Christina appeared solemn and earnest but with a vindictive streak, Cora was reckless and unmanageable; her only softness being in her fondness for both Niall, whom she mothered, and Thomas, whom she worshipped.

For all her wild displays of temperament Cora was mostly ignored by her father, the priest noted, though whether his habit of turning a blind eye to her wilfulness was due to indulgent parental affection or actual indifference, he could never be sure.

It was the blight of Christina's life, though, to watch as her sister's outrageous behaviour remained unadmonished

64

by their father. She would squirm at the unfairness of it all and, when the squirming became unbearable, would be forced to draw the latest misdemeanour to her father's attention.

His response always frustrated her, though, for he would tell her merely that her sister would get her reward in heaven, whereas Christina would have preferred to watch Cora being dealt her overdue punishment long before she was dead.

Father Devereux barely saw the three youngest children, for they were kept ensconced in the nursery for most of the time. It seemed that William would not tolerate their noise and mindless chatter about the house. They would all arrive at meal times, though, to be made to repeat their catechism, with the exception of Niall, who was still too young to manage more than a half-dozen words.

Niall was the strangest child, Father Devereux thought. He seemed isolated from the others and not merely on account of his age. He found himself watching the boy with growing interest, and discovered Father O'Malley showing as much close attention himself.

At first Father Devereux was inclined to put this isolation down to shyness on the boy's part, but then he discovered that the problem stemmed from the father's behaviour, not the son's. Niall was treated differently from the others by William; of that fact the priest soon became sure. It was not so much that William ignored him, for he ignored all his offspring in one way or another; no, the thing was, Father Devereux decided, that he acted as though the boy did not exist, which was another matter entirely. It was the strangest thing. While the others were either ignored or bullied under their father's strict regime, Niall escaped all notice or mention, at least while William was around. He was petted enough by his mother and all but spoilt by Cora, but this barely compensated for the peculiar mental torture inflicted upon him when the whole family was present.

The child was not neglected; Sophia more than tended to

his needs. He was paler than the others and a little thinner but he had been a sickly baby and that was only to have been expected. No, Niall moved about his father's house like a little ghost and, on the rare occasion when William had no alternative but to look upon the boy, the priest saw an expression in the man's eyes that he could only identify as one of fear.

Father O'Malley regarded the boy with a look of fear, too, but it was a fear born of pity, if Father Devereux read it right.

'Is there something wrong with the boy?' he had asked the old priest one day, when Father O'Malley was still capable of speech.

They had returned from a late supper at the great house and were quietly digesting it in front of the fire. It was the first time that Father Devereux had noticed anything abnormal in William Flavelle's attitude towards his son, but the old priest had merely shaken his head and sat sucking at his gums.

'It's just that I noticed Mister Flavelle treats the boy queerly, that's all,' Father Devereux went on. 'I don't mean that he is cruel in any physical sense, it's just that . . . well, he seems unaware that he has a fourth son at all! I felt such pity for the boy today that I even picked him up myself, poor little thing!'

The priest's head snapped up at that news and there was a look of concern on his face. 'Did William see you handle the boy?' he asked.

Father Devereux laughed. 'Well, yes, I should imagine he did,' he said. 'And why not? If he will pay no attention to the boy himself then he cannot expect his visitors to ignore him as well. He's a fine little lad, Father; a trifle pale in complexion, perhaps, but then so are all the others, and I must say he's finer featured than the rest of the brood put together. He's inherited some of William's better looks, thank God, don't you think? I'll admit he has the appearance of a little fish at the moment; all white-skinned and bug-eyed as he sits gazing about the room, but he may grow into something more special, I believe.

'You can't help but pity him, poor lad, and yet he fought like crazy to get away when I gave him a hug. Do you think he's a little simple, Father? Could that be why his own father rejects him as he does?'

The old priest formed his words slowly. 'Sophia loves the boy and so does God, Sebastian,' he began. 'And I believe young Cora would kill for him, given half the opportunity. He is loved enough.'

He paused to let out a sigh and run a shaking hand over his bare scalp.

Sophia Flavelle puzzled Father Devereux, too. They had not been alone together since the winter's day that they had taken their trip in the balloon and, when he had finally come across her again a few days ago, he had found himself hurrying away from her before she saw him.

It was the first walk that he had taken alone in their grounds for many months, and he had been wondering why he had stayed away for so long, for the skylarks wheeled overhead in the sun and he could smell the sea on the winds that buffeted about his face, and taste its salt upon his lips.

It had been a glorious day; by far the best since he had first arrived in Connemara. He had been reading of local legends and so his head had been filled with tales of Shees and Banshees and changeling children and, as he had set about climbing the hill, he had turned halfway up to see the purple fields and dark grey bogs below him and, for once, could almost believe the tales to be true.

He had gazed down at the limewashed cabins of the clachan, with their thin lines of peat-smoke that rose up from the small thatched roofs, and he watched a farmer, stripped to the waist in the sunshine, cut trenches of turf from the bog, throwing each sod to the surface with a quick twist of his muscular arm.

The Twelve Bens had stood, shrouded and magnificent in the distance and the sight of them had caused him to shiver, despite the warm day. Then he had looked upward to the brow of his hill and he had seen the small kite that flew there, circling and diving like a small bird.

He had supposed it to be the children and had rushed further up the slope to catch them at their game, but there had been no children on the hill, only Sophia Flavelle, laughing aloud as the wind caught her kite, and running with the string that held it, her russet hair flying wildly behind her.

He had considered joining her, but had thought better of it, finding himself all at once embarrassed and wondering at her strange behaviour, which he had found curiously unsettling.

She had not seen him and for that much he had been grateful, and had retreated quickly down the hill before she had been given a chance to do so. The sighting had puzzled Father Devereux ever since, though for the life of him he could not have said why.

On the day that Father O'Malley finally died the wind had howled about the houses of Connemara as though God had grown impatient in His heaven and was loudly berating the old man for his stubborn refusal to quit the mortal coil.

The vast Atlantic breakers had turned thunder-grey at the sound and their buffeting blows to the rocks around the coastline had sent out ground-tremors that could be felt in all the homes nearby.

Yet still the old man took his time about dying. At six in the morning his weak rattling breaths had had the doctor in his silk hat paying fourpence to the housekeeper's boy to cycle to the midwife to fetch her for the laying-out.

The boy had been blown clean off his bike on the first bend he took and Father Devereux had watched him from the house, worrying that the doctor's skills might be needed afresh, but the poor lad had scrambled back to his feet and, after pausing to dust himself down, had disappeared from sight in the murky, gusting drizzle.

By noon, though, the old priest had rallied and was sitting up in his bed supping a cup of hot gravy. He had called for water and, when his mouth was moist enough and his belly charged with food, had managed one word of request in Father Devereux's ear: 'Caution.'

Father Devereux had looked puzzled.

'William Flavelle,' the old man went on. 'Caution, my son.'

'Father?'

But he was too late.

The old priest had died.

CHAPTER NINE

William Flavelle received Father Devereux in the sitting-room of the great house. It was a ladies' room, he found; fussy and over-furnished, entirely incongruous in that great empty mausoleum of a place.

The room was stuffy and dusty and yet there was a fire lit in the hearth and a yawning dog laid out in front of it. The heavy satin curtains were pulled closed and candles had been lit, though there were still several hours of light before sunset. A baby grand stood before the largest of the windows and Father Devereux realized that it was the one that Sophia had played on his first visit to the house, when she had made the men cry over their dinners.

William Flavelle stood with his back to the fire and motioned the priest onto a small scroll-backed settee. The settee was low to the ground and Father Devereux felt decidedly uncomfortable sitting on it. There was a rosewood cabinet beside him, full of cranberry glass and he busied himself studying these rather gaudy ornaments while his host stood clearing his throat, pacing to and fro and otherwise generally asserting himself upon the room.

Huge shadows reared up the walls as the fire responded to the draught that roared down the chimney. With each gust the room was filled with white ash and peat-smoke and William's dark suit was soon speckled like an egg.

When his host was done clearing his larynx, Father Devereux informed him of the old priest's demise. William turned to the fire at once, leaning his hands against the black marble mantel, his head bent as though in prayer.

'He was a good man,' he said at last. 'One of God's own. Our Father will receive him now and he will be safe enough in the blessed arms of the great Lord Almighty. I will pray for him tonight, just as he prayed in his lifetime for me and for mine. May the Lord receive him and the Lord watch over him in his eternal rest.'

There was a pause and Father Devereux joined in with an 'Amen' for want of a more suitable response. The word seemed to startle his host who looked round with an expression of surprise as though having forgotten he was there at all.

Father Devereux had been offered dinner and so, once his audience with William was over, he was to follow his host into the dining-room where the rest of the family were waiting. He rose to his feet with difficulty, nearly over-turning an inlaid mahogany card-table in the process. Two pieces of Limoges rocked side by side with a porcelain tinkle that presaged further disaster but they steadied themselves and Father Devereux breathed a quiet sigh of relief.

The children were present at supper; a line of solemn faces in front of him, all set to sit and stare as they spooned their food into their open mouths. Their eyes were uncannily alike, Father Devereux noticed; washed of all discernible colour and with the unfocused stare of the short-sighted. He attempted a smile but not one of them smiled back.

The silence at table was oppressive, magnifying all other sounds until it was excruciating to either move or eat. Father Devereux said the grace but his heart was not in the job and he found himself watching instead the heads that were now bowed before him in prayer.

Francis made the strangest sight. Fresh-washed from the fields, his coarse dark hair had been wetted in an attempt to make it lie flat. As the water dried in the warm room, though, large tufts had begun to spring upright so that he looked like a scarecrow.

Then the prayers were over and the priest felt their eyes fix upon him again and heard their breathing as they waited for permission to eat.

'Did you light a candle for the Father in church today?' he asked Christina as the bowls were passed around. The girl's eyes widened and she watched him, still in silence.

'There is no conversation allowed from the children at table, Father,' William Flavelle told him.

'I'm sorry,' Father Devereux began, 'I thought . . .' He had thought that the rule must apply to the smaller children only. He looked at the two eldest boys and Thomas raised his brows, shrugging a little to show the rule applied to them as well.

'Saving the pleases and thank-yous of common courtesy, that is,' William went on. 'Will you bring some more cold pressed tongue for the Father, please?' he asked his wife.

Sophia made no motion to rise from her chair and Father Devereux held his hand across his plate to show that he had enough.

The eating commenced but William's plate sat empty.

'A fast day,' Sophia murmured. 'My husband sets great store in the power of fasting. Often the children join him, too. It gives the nurse the devil of a job at bedtime though for she cannot get them down when their stomachs are rumbling like thunder. I discovered a small tin of biscuits beneath the girl's bed the other night and, do you know, I believe she has been feeding them to the children just to see them get off! Now whose sin is that do you think, Father? The nurse's for feeding them on a fast day or the poor hungry little creatures for eating them? I know who my husband would blame if he found them with the crumbs about their mouths!'

Father Devereux studied his own food, a sodden mound of glistening cold meat and hot vegetables, and then looked to William's plate, which sat, gleaming white, before him. 'Why the plate then?' he wondered. 'If he is not to eat at all?'

'If you are so keen to speak, Christina,' William said, so suddenly that even the priest's head snapped up to listen, 'perhaps you would like to read to us instead, while we eat.' He pushed his chair back, grasping the arms with both hands. 'I have the transcript of a sermon from the Jesuits in

Dublin, sent just this day in the post. I'm sure the Father would be interested in hearing it too now, wouldn't you, Father?' He did not wait for a reply.

'Take it, take it, Christina!' he shouted. 'It's folded there in the Bible! Now none of your mumbling, mind! God will be waiting to listen as well as the Father. Clear your throat and read to us in your best voice.'

Christina rose shyly from her chair, pausing once to look about her audience before reaching into a small velvet bag that hung about her waist and pulling out her spectacles. She hooked the wire frames around her ears and then wiped her fingers one by one on her skirt as though frightened of soiling the pages of her father's Bible.

She had eaten nothing and her food sat untouched. Father Devereux went to protest, to insist that she started after she had eaten, but once again he thought better of it and so sat with his head bowed in silent contemplation above his hands as he awaited the first of the young girl's words.

Christina watched them solemnly. Her facial twitches increased and she tried to clear her throat with a short, high-pitched cough.

A small foot kicked Father Devereux neatly across the shinbone of his right leg and he looked across the table to catch Cora's wink.

There was the sound of wafer-thin pages being turned before the sermon was finally discovered between the first two pages of Corinthians. Father Devereux watched as Christina unfolded the paper and his heart sank a little as he saw at least six full sides of foolscap, all printed in the same minute and meticulous type.

Christina began to read, her voice high and piping with a peculiar soporific drone in that warm and airless room. Her nervousness took most of the pitch and inflection from her tone so that the words became meaningless without the most strenuous attempt at concentration on the part of her audience.

Much of it sounded to Father Devereux like the heaviest and most leaden type of rhetoric, as dull and as sodden as the food that lay before him on his plate. His ears yearned for some poetry to aid his digestion. Dessert was served and soon Christina's voice became no more than a backdrop to the scraping of spoons against china. Sophia smiled at him. Was his pudding good? 'Yes,' he mouthed back, 'very good indeed.' He noticed she had left hers largely untouched.

The children ate little but this, the priest noticed, came more from their having to chew each mouthful many times before swallowing than through lack of appetite. Only the two eldest seemed exempt from this chore and they both ate quickly, spooning second helpings onto their plates while the youngest watched with envy in their faces.

Francis had his eyes upon the table for the entire meal but Thomas sat back easily in his chair once he was finished eating, yawning and stretching, looking every inch the young country squire in his lightweight tweed jacket and his fancy silk cravat. At one point he rested his hand lightly upon his mother's bare arm and she leant quickly across to kiss him fondly on the cheek.

The youngest children became restive once their pudding was eaten. Cora wound ringlets in the serviette with her fingers and the babies sat, bug-eyed from the effort of sitting still and silent for so long.

Christina's voice droned on, meanwhile, as she began a discussion of the seven deadly sins. Aware that she had lost the attention of at least two-thirds of the room, her voice had grown a little with the confidence of those who know they are ignored, and had taken on a passable imitation of the tone of the sermon's author.

She had reached the sin of adultery and was making much of it; as had the Jesuits who had written the tract. In a vast cathedral the rafters would have been made to quake at such words as Christina read aloud now, though in that some-what more modest dining-room their only immediate effect was in making Father Devereux look to his host, aware as he had become that the text was surely inappropriate for a young girl to be reading.

He was surprised and shocked that she was allowed to continue. It appeared that the Jesuits, though, were only just warming to their theme. Christina's shrill piping voice told of the evils of adultery and of the terrible punishments that its perpetrators might expect to receive in the afterlife. Her voice rose to a shriek as she spelled out the hellfire and damnation that awaited them and, as she turned to the last page of the tract, the priest was concerned to see the fear on the face of William's youngest son as he listened with rapt attention.

Niall's face twisted and the tears squeezed from his eyes. Probably he had not understood his sister's words, yet her tone was enough to have alarmed him badly. He held his arms out to his mother for comfort and Sophia would have risen from her seat to lift him, had her husband not stopped her. He said nothing, merely pointed to the full plate that sat before the boy. Sophia looked from her husband to her small son in obvious anguish and slowly took her seat again.

'Nobody will move until the food is eaten,' William said.

Sophia smiled. 'Why, none of the babies has been able to finish today,' she said quickly, patting crumbs from her lap as she spoke. 'The suet was too heavy and I believe the portions were rather large. I'll ask cook to put less fat in it next time or it will sit in all our poor stomachs like lead.'

William looked at his wife and then stared across at the priest, his face seeming to contort like his son's, so that Father Devereux almost expected to see tears forming in his eyes.

'Tell him to finish,' he said, quietly, 'or we will sit here waiting the rest of the night.'

Father Devereux could see the anger in his face now. He watched Sophia rise from her chair and, throwing her napkin onto the table in a tight ball, move quickly from the room. His own chair scraped across the floor as he tried to stand in an attempt at gallantry, but she had left long before he could find his feet.

William watched her go without expression, even when the door slammed behind her and the china jumped on the sideboard.

'Shall we retire to the study, Father?' he asked once she was gone. The frown had fled from his face and the affable host had returned. 'I'd like your views on the tract we heard just now. It was something to send the blood coursing through a man's veins, don't you think? Eh?'

He patted the priest on the shoulder as he led him towards the door. Father Devereux looked back just the once at the children and their pale eyes stared back, expressionless.

'Eat your bloody food, Niall, you great baby!' Cora said once the priest and their father were gone. 'Or I swear he'll have us here the rest of the week if you don't! Is that what you want, eh? To see us sitting here growing old around you while that food there becomes green with the mould and you'll still have to eat it anyway?'

'Why don't you eat it yourself?' Thomas asked, yawning. 'Papa will never know.'

'Oh, but he will!' Cora told him. 'Because Christina here will tell him, won't you, Christina? You know she will, Thomas, you know Christina tells everything.'

Christina had moved back to her seat and sat, red-faced and silent, staring down at her hands.

Francis stood up impatiently and walked over to the fireplace where he pulled a wad of tobacco from his trouser pocket and set about rolling himself a cigarette.

'Eat your food,' he ordered Niall, licking the edge of the paper and spitting tobacco from his tongue. Niall shook his head uncertainly, his watery eyes full of fear at his own daring.

'I shall tip it over your head if you don't,' Francis warned. 'I've work to do outside still and I'm damned if I'll waste what is left of the light just because you won't stuff a few mouthfuls of suet down your throat!'

Alarmed by her brother's tone, Cora picked the spoon out of Niall's bowl and held it to his closed mouth. 'Eat it, darling,' she coaxed, trying to push the food between his lips. 'See?' she asked, pretending to taste it herself. 'It's quite good! The others have eaten theirs! It's only you, Niall, yet we all have to wait. Eat some for me? Won't you be a good boy?'

The boy's lips parted reluctantly but Thomas leant across the table as he was about to take the first mouthful.

'It's slimy and it's mouldy, Niall, and they make it from snails from the garden,' he said, and pushed his chair back, laughing, as the small boy's mouth shut like a trap.

Francis swore at his brother but Thomas just laughed all the more and Niall, who adored him, forgot to cry and joined in the laughter. Thomas whistled loudly through his teeth then, and a large yellow dog padded into the room, its long pink tongue hanging expectantly from its open mouth. Thomas took his brother's bowl and placed it on the floor before the dog. They all watched enthralled as the dog noisily ate the suet, slurping the syrup from its chops, and Niall laughed so loud at the sounds the dog made that Cora had to shush him, in case their father heard.

'And you can even tell if you like, Tina,' Thomas told his sister, 'for, to be honest, I couldn't give a halfpenny sod!'

Christina stared down at her fingers. 'I don't have to tell,' she said, quietly. 'God knows already.'

'God sees everything then, does He?' Cora asked, leaning from her chair.

Christina nodded. 'You know He does.'

'Then I hope He saw what a bloody idiot you made of yourself over that flamin' sermon just now!' Cora said. 'Just who do you think you were? Wailing and carrying on like some flamin' old priest. You were only asked to read it, you didn't have to go putting in such an embarrassing performance! Was it supposed to be for the Father's benefit, or what? Did you know she's a passion for the Father, Thomas? Him with all his good looks and Christina with her ugly old face? Did you know she carries a flower she saw him sniffing once, pressed between the pages of her prayer-book? And I'll bet she wears it pressed to the bodice of her nightgown when she's in her bed at night, too! You embarrassed the Father with your rantings, Christina, did you see his face as he walked from the room? You embarrassed him speechless, going on as you did, there's no doubt about it, poor man, no doubt at all!'

Thomas grinned at Cora but he shook his head to tell her she should stop.

Christina picked at her nails under the table until they bled, but she would not cry. She turned her mind instead to the Bible and the prayers that she had memorized to say in her bed that night.

When Father Devereux had finally gone, William Flavelle knelt alone in his study and sent his own prayers up to God.

'He is one of your priests, oh Lord,' he whispered, 'and I cannot argue with your choosing. I know also that I must receive him into my house and watch him sitting at my table, eating of my food, for he is still chosen by you to do your work in Connemara and I know that I must welcome him, no matter how hard that might be.

'I have forgiven my wife for I believe her to be an innocent in all of this and I believe she was only led astray by the Devil as a punishment to me. She is weak, Lord, and the Devil knew how to use her against me. I cannot forgive him, though, and I feel I never shall.

'I shall have your handsome young priest in my house, then, and watch as he talks to my wife; knowing what I know and knowing how hard this cross is for me to bear. I also shall feed the boy that I know is not my son, but the son of the Devil.

'Tell me, Lord, that I am right; send me a sign to reassure me. I am too weak to fight this alone, Lord, I must know that you hear me, and then no cross will be too great for me to bear.'

His leather shoes creaked as he changed his position on the floor.

'Am I right, Lord?' he asked, begging a reply. 'Or is the doctor right when he tells me I am deluded? I need your guidance, Lord, I need a sign. Am I wrong? Tell me!'

Sophia bent over Niall's cot to tuck the blanket around his small body and to kiss him goodnight. As her lips touched gently onto his brow she pulled away suddenly and leant back to study his sleeping face.

'His forehead is burning,' she said to the maid, who was immediately dispatched for some water to bathe him. Then the child's nursemaid was called from her bed.

'He is a little feverish,' she agreed, and she smiled in an attempt to calm the boy's mother.

'He was wilful today, over his food,' Sophia whispered. 'His papa was angry. Perhaps the excitement has upset him, do you think?'

The girl nodded. 'That's very likely it,' she said, though she had little if any idea, if the truth were told.

She dipped a handkerchief into the water and pressed it across the child's brow. 'He is a sensitive little boy,' she said, 'and it could easily have upset him. Perhaps he will be better after a sleep.'

Sophia smiled at her words and straightened from the bed with a yawn. She looked down at her son, who appeared not to have woken. She knew she was overprotective and that the nursemaid was probably right.

'I'll be in first thing in the morning,' she whispered, and tiptoed softly from the room.

'A sign, Lord!' William repeated, pleading, in his room. 'Is the boy mine or the son of the Devil? I have to know if I am ever to have any peace. I cannot live without knowing for sure. Send me a sign, that my soul shall not forever be in torment!'

79

CHAPTER TEN

A veil of fine drizzling rain shrouded the countryside around Connemara and lay like beaded cobwebs in the young priest's thick hair as he stood up to his thighs in the water of the icy river. He had gone there to fish but, as with most anglers, the truth was that he wanted to be alone.

He had never sought solitude before as his vanity normally demanded an audience but now, with Father O'Malley dead and his responsibilities about to increase twofold, he found himself suddenly able to appreciate the indulgence of his own company. Alone at last he found himself to be a young man and a poet rather than the responsible bearer of God's word upon the earth.

On this particular morning, though, as the young man and the poet were just reeling in a rather undernourished pike, Father Devereux found his solitary musings over Byron and Tennyson interrupted by the rattling wheels of a box-cart, apparently taking the pitted track at a greater speed than caution would ordinarily allow. Curious and somewhat annoyed at the intrusion, Father Devereux waded towards the bank, trying to see the carriage in the distance, but the mists were too thick, and he was not afforded a good view until the thing was nearly upon him.

It slewed around the corner, the horse's hooves sliding in the mud, and for one terrible moment the cart rocked on its side and the priest thought the whole contraption might turn over. The horse let out a whinny of fright and its eyes rolled in their sockets as Father Devereux fancied he felt the startled beast's hot breath upon his face.

It steadied at the last moment though, but by then the priest had thrown himself backwards to avoid the lethal collision that he feared must be imminent, and was lying in the thickest of the mud as the rig pulled to a halt some few yards further along the road.

'Father! Are you all right? I cannot see for this damn mist!'

It was the doctor calling him, he recognized his voice despite all the mud that had collected about his ears. He slithered to find a foothold on the bank then ran towards the box-cart in as gainly a fashion as his dripping rubber waders would allow. His rod trailed brokenly behind him, its hook and fly catching in the grass and the weeds.

'Father!' the doctor called again, this time with relief as he saw the priest appear before him relatively unharmed. Doctor O'Sullivan was not known as an immaculate man but now his face was ashen and his smart silk top hat had tilted to the side.

'Your housekeeper told me you may be up here, Father!' he said, extending a hand as the priest approached. 'God knows but I thought that I'd killed you when I came upon you like that on the bend! I hate to disturb you like this; even God must have His day off sometimes, but the case is urgent and I know how you Catholics are if you die without your prayers being said!'

Father Devereux attempted to dust himself down but the mud was still wet. 'Who is it who's dying, Doctor?' he asked.

'It's up at the great house,' Doctor O'Sullivan told him. 'I'm afraid you'll be needed, Father. I've been up there all night and am just returning this morning. Come, get into the cart and I'll tell you the details as we travel.'

Father Devereux clambered into the box-cart and sat to pull off his waders. 'Who is it, then?' he asked once the difficult chore was completed.

'The youngest, I'm afraid, young Niall Flavelle. I am sorry to say that it is the diphtheria. If I'm right, and I believe I am, then he may not live to see the day out, poor thing.' He paused to concentrate on the reins as the cart juddered over a particularly ferocious sequence of pot-holes.

'There's been an epidemic, as you well know, Father,' he said once the cart had straightened. 'Six children lost in the next village in as many days, you know. This is the first case here, though. I thought that we might have been spared when we missed the first wave.'

'Is there nothing you can do for him?' the priest asked. He found a handkerchief in his trouser pocket that had somehow remained free of mud and used it to wipe his face. Some dirt had got onto his teeth and tasted bitter in his mouth. He spat into the handkerchief and rubbed his gums with a finger.

The doctor shrugged. 'I've done as much as experience and the books tell me to. Now I believe it must all be down to your prayers.'

Father Devereux laughed. 'Do you see the Church as a last resort then, Doctor?' he asked.

'There's some around here who believe the lame can walk if they get their prayers right,' the doctor told him. 'I just know that if you don't say the last rites over the poor little thing then it is to be imagined his young soul will be floating for all eternity in some ghastly netherworld.'

Father Devereux studied the doctor's face more closely. 'You're a Protestant, then?'

The doctor let out a brief, barking laugh. 'Don't tell me you didn't know!' he exclaimed. He sat in silence for a while. 'There's a lot of us around if you look closely, you know,' he said, affably enough. 'Does it bother you, Father? A Protestant doctor tending your Catholic flock?'

'I'm surprised one or two of your patients don't mind,' Father Devereux remarked, grinning. 'They're not noted for their tolerance around here, though you seem to have ingratiated yourself into the local community all right.'

'And that was more down to necessity than tolerance, Father,' the doctor said, laughing, 'at least in the first place. They were slow enough to call me in to start with but when they saw it was a clean choice between life and death, well, they managed to come around somehow.

'They have their own way of dealing with religious perverts around here, you know, Father, as I expect you've realized. In my case they simply decided to ignore my heresies as if they were some mild form of eccentricity. You'll have noticed the type of behaviour in the house we're about to visit.'

'William Flavelle, you mean?' the priest asked.

'William, yes,' the doctor answered. 'Do you see the man much in church?'

Father Devereux laughed. 'Never,' he said. 'He's hardly what you might call a proper Catholic.'

'And what about Missus Flavelle? What about Sophia?' He was watching the young priest now, from the corner of his eye.

Father Devereux looked surprised. 'She is there for most services, as far as I know. Father O'Malley never said that she missed. William never, though, I'm afraid.'

'William Flavelle,' the doctor mused. 'Now there's a man to be reckoned with. A strange child of the Catholic faith, if ever I saw one. I should suspect he even outstrips your own knowledge of the Great Book, eh, Father? What they call an obsessive personality, I believe. Did you know that I dabble in psychology too, Father?' He was smiling and the priest smiled back.

'Yet I believe William takes less interest in my treatment of his son than he would if he had called the veterinary to one of his animals.'

Father Devereux watched the doctor drive the cart and noticed that his starched collar was grey with age and his fingernails rimmed with black dirt. His florid complexion showed him to be a drinker, like many of the men around those parts, though the priest knew him to be partial to brandy and fine wines, unlike the poorer men of the clachan, with their poteen and their ale.

'So you have seen a certain amount of indifference on William's behalf?' Father Devereux asked.

'Always,' the doctor replied, 'though you'd barely notice

with all the weeping and wailing the boy's mother is doing. She'll be the next to go down, I don't doubt. Perhaps you should have a word with her, Father; tell her of all the rewards her suffering will gain for her in heaven, or something. Give her some comfort. Though I believe she still has more faith in her old religion, for all her husband has done to persuade her otherwise.'

'Her old religion?' Father Devereux asked.

'She was raised more Protestant than Catholic. That was her mother's religion, as I'm sure you will have been told. A fine woman, Henrietta, what a terrible tragedy that was, to be sure . . .'

He stopped his chatter to concentrate as the cart circled the pitted drive and Maidie came running up to take his hat and bag as he made the descent to terra firma.

As she moved to let them pass the doctor paused to feel the sides of her neck with his fingers. 'You should be away from here a while, Maidie,' he said. 'I told you as much last night and I'm surprised to find you still here this morning. Do you not have some family you can stay with until the sickness has passed? I don't want you going down with the blasted thing too, you know!'

'I'm to stay with my auntie tonight,' the girl said.

'Good, good, now mind that you do.' The doctor patted her head and she turned to lead them to the nursery.

'The missus said I was to ask if you'd like some tea, Father?' she said as they approached the darkened room. A warm smell of sickness filled the priest's nostrils as the door was opened, making him feel vaguely queasy.

'No tea, thank you, Maidie,' he said, trying to smile. 'Just some fresh water, if you've the time to spare.'

The girl smiled at the priest's handsome face and threw a quick curtsy before closing the door behind them.

It was a while before his eyes adjusted to the gloom, but he could hear the child's laboured breathing long before his pupils had dilated. The blinds had been pulled and the only light in the room was the dull reddish glow of a night-light that had been left on a small table at the head of the child's cot.

As his vision adjusted he saw the figure that lay prostrate on the bed beside the sick child. It was Sophia Flavelle, still dressed in her nightclothes, her arms thrown about the child as though protecting him from a blow and her head pressed beside him on the pillow.

She awoke as the doctor unclipped his bag and the priest saw her look from one to another, confused, until reality dawned and the anguish appeared in her face. She looked at the priest and realized at once why he had come.

'No!' she cried. 'You shall not have him!'

It was the doctor who took her by the arm and led her to a chair by the fire, though she was unsteady on her feet and twice had to be prevented from falling.

'Courage, Missus Flavelle,' he told her, sitting her down and patting her hand. 'I've just come to check on the boy. I'm sure you'd rather the priest were here than not. We can all pray that he'll not be needed.'

He crossed to the bed, taking a wooden spatula from his breast pocket and bending to examine his patient. The laboured breathing turned to a rattling gasp as he did so and Sophia made to rise from her chair in alarm at the sound. She waited in silence and then the doctor straightened, rubbing at his spine as though in pain himself, and nodded for Father Devereux to take over tending to the young boy's soul.

It was the thing that Sophia had dreaded. As Father Devereux began his prayers his voice was drowned by her despairing screams and she had to be led forcibly from the room before he was able to continue.

'No!' He heard a different cry from the passage outside. 'You cannot let him die! He did mean to eat his dinner, I know that he did! It was Thomas who fed his food to the dog, I saw him! Oh, don't allow God to punish him in this way, Father, he is only a small child! Please, Father, please!' It was Cora's voice this time and she fell into hysterical sobbing that grew quieter as she too was led further away from the sick-room.

Father Devereux laid down his prayer-book and walked out into the passage to see to the girl. The nurse had her by the arm but, when she saw the priest, she pulled away at once and went running towards him, her face red with the effort.

'He's so little, Father!' she cried. 'And usually so good! Couldn't God turn a blind eye and forgive him just this once? We all egged him on, Father, it wasn't Niall's fault!'

Father Devereux took the child by the arms and bent until their faces were even. 'This illness of your brother's is not a punishment from God,' he said, gravely. 'Now where did such an idea come from, eh?'

Cora looked at him and wiped her nose with her fingers. 'Papa told us,' she coughed. 'We wanted to pray for Niall but Papa told us we were not to, for it was God's punishment for his sins and only God would decide whether he lived or he died. But Niall is so quiet, Father!' she went on. 'The quietest of us all! He was only naughty over the pudding because it was suet and he does not care for suet, it makes him sick and Thomas told him it was slime, too! You speak to God, Father, tell Him it was not Niall's fault! Please, Father! Papa says he will most likely die!' She choked on her words then and fell into sobbing so that the nurse was able to come and lead her away at last.

The doctor stopped her, whispering to her above the child's head. 'I told Mister Flavelle these children should be gone from the house!' he said. 'Why are they still here?'

The nurse shook her head slowly. 'He will not have it,' she said.

'My husband has no fear for the other children, Doctor.' A voice came from behind them and they turned to see Sophia Flavelle standing, more composed now, in the doorway of the sick-room.

'But he must know that the illness can be caught by any of them if they remain here!'

Sophia shook her head. 'No. He is quite firm on this matter. God has selected Niall alone for this punishment. The other children are safe.'

The doctor let out a curse and did not apologize to either woman for having done so.

'Where is he?' he demanded. 'Let me speak to him! He must be made to understand the dangers of what he is doing! You should be gone yourself, Missus Flavelle! The whole house will be down with it before the end of the week if you don't.'

'I can't go,' Sophia said, wearily. 'I only wish my children could. We had the carriage waiting at the door but he would not allow them to enter it. He says that it is God's will, Doctor, and he will not hear any argument. Try again if you will, but I know he will not be shifted in this matter.'

'I should speak to him,' Father Devereux said, and the doctor nodded as Sophia began to cry once again.

The priest entered William Flavelle's study without knocking, so intense was his anger at the man's stubbornness.

'Father!' William hid his irritation at the intrusion and rose from his chair, throwing the papers that he had been working on into an open desk drawer. He motioned the priest towards a chair but Father Devereux shook his head, declining the offer.

'I have given the last rites,' he said, his voice measured.

'Good, good,' William answered, turning his hands on the desk and studying them as though fascinated by his own flesh.

There was a period of angry silence as the priest chose the right words.

'Would you join me in prayers for the boy?' he asked at last.

William looked up in apparent surprise and Father Devereux was astonished to see tears upon his face.

'I can't pray for him, Father,' he said, quietly. 'The words will not come while I know that what has happened is God's divine will.'

'The boy may die, Mister Flavelle. Surely you cannot want . . .'

'What I want is irrelevant,' William cut in. 'The boy's life is in God's hands now, not mine.'

'And the others?'

'The others?' William looked confused.

'The other children,' the priest explained. 'Are their lives not still in your hands? You have been told they must leave here or they all might die. That is not God's will, Mister Flavelle, that is yours!'

William smiled. 'I have no fears for the others, Father,' he said. 'They will be safe, I am sure of it.'

'How can you possibly be so sure?' the priest asked.

William Flavelle walked around his desk, staring at the priest. 'I asked God for a sign, Father, and he has given me one. I expect nothing further. The other children are innocent.'

'But you cannot see this illness as some divine punishment!' Father Devereux said. 'Why, Cora told me you have the other children thinking their brother may die because he did not eat his dinner! You cannot allow them to think that, Mister Flavelle! Innocent children, afraid to leave the food on their plates in case God will see and strike them dead! This illness is an epidemic, the doctor has just told me! You cannot put it down to divine retribution!'

'Cora is confused,' William began. 'I said nothing about punishment for not eating food, and I should remind you that all are guilty in the eyes of God, Father, even new-born babies.'

'You must pray for your son, Mister Flavelle,' Father Devereux said, 'and, by God's mercy, he may be spared. Kneel with me now; you cannot refuse to try.'

As he stared at William a door opened behind them and the doctor entered the room.

'Your prayers are too tardy, gentlemen,' he said. 'I believe the boy is over his crisis. While you bluster over your theology I believe the physician's art may have saved his life after all. I should apologize to you for stealing some of your thunder. What price your Catholicism now, eh, Father?' He smiled at the priest as though they shared a joke. 'I'm afraid it was left skulking in the wings on this occasion, Mister Flavelle!' He laughed, placing his bill upon William's desk and taking his leave of them before either man could speak.

Barely three weeks had passed before Father Devereux was called again to the house. This time it was the maid who came for him, the ribbons of her bonnet loose and blowing about her round face with the wind as she ran through the streets to fetch him.

'Father! Father!' she called, shouting right inside the church where he was praying. 'The doctor says you're to come again; it's the other youngest who are stricken this time and both are bad, so it seems! I cannot go with you for my auntie won't allow it but the boy has a cart waiting and they say you're to come at once or it may be too late!'

Father Devereux rose to his feet with a sigh. It was a beautiful day, full of promise and good hopes, and he had fancied he could smell the summer in every breath he took. Each gust of wind that blew into his church had seemed to him scented with poignant nostalgia for the summers of his childhood and he had watched as each puff swept up to the nave, sending small clouds of winter dust into the air to hang immobile in the shards of coloured sun from the stained-glass windows.

Nature's chest had to be swollen with pride to produce a day like that, he had thought, and now this. Death was a dark stain that had tarnished the day and he had his invitation to enter the world of sickness and mourning and unbearable grief.

To have to smell the sick and to watch over the dying. He breathed his last breath of sweet summer air but already it was tainted by his imagination. It would be up to him to explain over and again how God could allow such suffering of innocents. Would the Flavelle children receive their rewards in heaven, he wondered. Would they be fed at some divine dinner-table where no prayers were to be read and where suet was permanently off the menu?

There would be no more catechism when visitors were present and the dog would always be there under the table to eat the leavings from their plates. Perhaps they would lose their glassy-eyed pallor and learn to laugh like other children at last.

A stray breeze hit the organ-pipes and they emitted a ghastly moan that brought the young priest back from his musings. The girl still stood before him, red-faced and panting, holding her bosom down with both hands as though her run had disturbed its equilibrium.

She expected urgent action from him and he suddenly and depressingly felt unequal to the task. Sighing again then, he lifted his hat to his head and reached for his overcoat and scarf, for his heavy heart and his dulled soul had chilled his flesh, despite the mildness of the day.

The two young Flavelle children clung feebly onto life for a further three days and then they both suddenly died, within hours of one another and the house was plunged into mourning.

Sophia merely vanished with her grief. Entombed in one of the vast dark rooms of the house that the priest was never invited to enter, she was made inaccessible to visitors offering either spiritual or mental comfort. The five surviving children suffered in turn from bouts of either anger or deepest distress.

Francis and Thomas made some effort at discretion in their displays of emotion but Cora was openly distraught. It evolved that much of this was brought on by the fact that, during Niall's illness, she had made a pact with God to the effect that He could take anything from her if only He would let the boy live. Was that why the others had died, she wanted to know; had God taken the other young children in return for Niall's life?

William had his own questions, but they were aimed more at the doctor than the priest. How was it that the illness had come into his household? If it were not retribution from God then how had it occurred, and why? Why had they been chosen when no others in the clachan had been touched? Why was it that Niall had survived when the other two youngest had died?

They sat in William's study for hours locked in such debates and the doctor found the conversations bearable only on account of the fine antique brandy that was dispensed with comforting regularity into his glass.

In time, though, the doctor came to enjoy these discussions. They gave him the opportunity to expound his latest medical theories and in William he found a captive and attentive audience. His dissertations on the transmission of diseases by germs were wordy and complex but he discovered William's fascination for the subject to be as endless as his own.

William would listen to the doctor's theories for a day or so at a time, as though finding comfort in the vagaries of medical science. He obviously did his own research too, for some mornings he would present fresh arguments that were exceptionally well-informed. The problem with William's theorizing, the doctor found, was that it was of course too much centred around his religion and, as the doctor had discovered many times to his disadvantage, medicine and religion just did not mix. The two were incompatible. He prided himself on the clean and clinical study of medicine as a pure science and became increasingly irritated at William's insistence on a spiritual dimension to all ailments and their accompanying remedies.

'I am not some winged messenger of the Gods, you know!' he would shout at William when their discussions became heated. 'I am a scientist, pure and simple. If someone is sick I provide a scientific cure! There is no room for your God in our laboratories! I am not some medieval medicine man providing spiritual mumbo-jumbo. We know why treatments work these days, William, we no longer put it down to the miraculous vagaries of nature in her full glory! I work with my own hands and not the hand of God!'

'But who is it provides the essence for your cures?' William would ask. 'And who guides your hand to find them? Who decided where your germs will strike next and whether or not that strike will be lethal?'

And then, slowly, the doctor could see that William Flavelle had tired of their discussions, so that they became less frequent until they ended all together. He had heard the evidence, the doctor realized, and had come to a decision. His interest in medical matters in general began to wane and he appeared to have found the answers to questions that had been troubling him since his children's deaths.

Doctor O'Sullivan could guess what those questions might have been, but he had no idea of the answers William Flavelle had discovered, nor why those answers should have given him such spiritual relief. In the doctor's eyes it was William who was to blame for the deaths of those children, by refusing to send them away. The only insight he was to have into William's apportioning of the blame came during one of their last suppers together.

'You believe that it was the germs that brought the diphtheria to my house, then?' William asked.

The table was bare, save for their two places, which had been set, as was the custom during this series of discussions, facing across the width at the end furthest from the door and any potential interruption. Food was brought in but not served, so that the men could continue unabated, serving themselves when a natural lull occurred.

'That is my theory, William, yes,' the doctor said with his mouth full of Stilton. It was a theory he had expounded many times at great length and yet his host still had to hear it repeated. 'I believe there are others, well-respected in my profession I must add, who would be called to deny my ideas, but I feel the evidence gathered must needs point in that inevitable direction, yes.'

The doctor, of course, was no research specialist himself but he liked to give the impression of being no mere humble practitioner in a tiny village on the west coast, where his everyday duties extended to little more than the diagnosis of rheumatics or attending difficult births. His main sources of research were to be found in the pages of elderly medical journals, which provided many of the expert opinions that he had become so fond of expounding.

William leant back in his chair with a sigh, clasping his hands across his belly and fixing the doctor with an intense, questioning look.

'And would you say it was God who planted these so-called germs of yours in such a fashion?' he asked.

The doctor placed his knife carefully by his plate and took up his napkin to wipe butter and crumbs from his fingers. He thought for a while, chewing the last of his cheese, then finally swallowed and began to clear his throat.

'Religious theory is not my field, William,' he began cautiously, 'as I have told you many, many times before. You would do better to speak to young Father Devereux than myself. I cannot help and you know it; it really isn't my subject.'

William leant forward across the table. 'But you would say that there is no evidence in all your medical research to prove that God did not pass these germs on?' he asked.

The doctor pushed his plate away with a sigh of resignation. He pulled a snuffbox from his pocket and tipped some of the powder onto the back of his hand, inhaling it deeply with his eyes closed.

'No, William,' he said, eventually, 'I do not believe that there is.'

William Flavelle nodded, obviously satisfied with his answer.

'But that is not to say that there never will be,' the doctor added, hastily. 'I do not necessarily believe science to be an enemy of religion, William, but I do know we are chasing its tail! Why, look at some of those miracles described in the Bible! Many can now be explained away as mere natural phenomena, thought by an unprogressive civilization to be evidence of some greater hand at work!'

William waved the doctor's words away angrily. 'Atheist rubbish!' he said. 'It is my own situation that interests me, Doctor. I believe that the youngest child may be responsible for the deaths of the other two.'

The doctor looked up, horrified. 'You cannot blame that innocent child for contracting diphtheria, William!' he said. 'No more than you can blame him for surviving while the other poor children died!'

William looked at the doctor from the side of his eyes. 'It was he who first had the germs,' he said. 'And it was he who passed them to the other two. You told me as much yourself.'

'Yes!' the doctor exclaimed, appalled. 'But when I said that I did not think . . . You cannot believe . . . William, you are deluded by your grief, man! Surely you cannot think that, during all our discussions, I was laying the blame at your poor son's doorstep!'

'But I did not suffer the illness,' William replied, 'nor did the servants, or my wife, for that matter.'

'Pure luck!' the doctor cried. 'It could have afflicted anyone; it may still afflict you, though I pray that it will not.'

William smiled at the use of the doctor's word 'pray' and the doctor reddened, feeling he had somehow been tricked.

'You may call it luck, Doctor,' William said in a voice so low it was almost a whisper, 'but then I would accuse you of paganism. I would call it God's hand, Doctor; God's hand or the Devil's.'

The doctor struggled to rise from his chair, realizing as he stood that his intake of William's brandy had been considerable that night. 'I cannot stay to hear more of this, William!' he said as the ceiling spun about his head. 'I believe you to be unbalanced by your own grief and I hope to hear later that you have come to your senses and realized the terrible implications of these immoral claims! I may not be your doctor, William, but I would suggest you allow me to prescribe you a powder to help you come to terms with what has occurred in this house.' He waited unsteadily for an answer but William Flavelle sat deep in thought, staring ahead at the table.

When the doctor had gone he sat there an hour longer, stroking his beard as he discovered the truth from a tangled situation.

'I asked for a sign,' he said, clasping his hands in prayer, 'and you have given me one, though not in the manner that I would have liked. The boy has been sent by the Devil and his presence here is a curse upon my family.

'If he had not been the son of the Devil he would not have survived his illness but instead he lived to pass it on to my innocent children and it was they who died instead of him. I can forgive my wife, God, and I must try to forgive your priest, but I must above all protect my family from this evil that resides in its midst. I cannot allow it to grow to destroy us all. Let me act now, Lord, or we are all to be doomed!'

CHAPTER ELEVEN

Two years had passed since the deaths of the babies. Their small bodies lay buried in the grounds of the great house and William, in his grief, had paid for a grand marble monument to be erected above them. A craftsman had been brought in from Dublin for the task and the statue he had fashioned had been visited and marvelled at by all those able to make the journey.

The edifice took the form of a huge carved angel seated on an ivy-covered rock. The angel had one cloaked arm held up across its face in mourning and those bold enough to clamber over the crumbling wall for a better look said that the angel, behind its sleeve, had an expression sad enough to bring tears in an instant to the strongest man's eyes. They also said that it had the face of Sophia Flavelle, though that may have been just fancy.

Sophia had the loss of three of her children to suffer, for Niall had been sent away from the house; first to convalesce his illness and then to a school that William claimed to have had recommended to him, despite the fact that the other children had all been educated at home in their earlier years.

Niall had taken these separations with apparent lack of emotion although he became more withdrawn than usual, speaking, so it seemed, only to his sister Cora. She and her mother were distraught enough to fight William over the decision to send him away, though they knew in their hearts they had no chance of winning.

William fought them with science. The boy carried germs, he told them; Doctor O'Sullivan had said as much. So little was still known about germs and diseases that it would be better if Niall were away from the house, he said, so that there was no risk of further contamination. There was no knowing how long these germs could be carried and he did not want to risk any more of his children dying.

'Then I shall go with him!' Sophia had cried, but then Cora had started the hysterics at the thought that they should lose both their brother and their mother. It was more than she could possibly bear.

'You have four other children here, Sophia,' William told her.

'They are all nearly grown!' Sophia pleaded. 'Niall is just a baby, William, he needs me, I know he does!'

But William was, of course, adamant. 'Niall is nearly five. He was strong enough to survive diphtheria and the doctor has assured me it has done no lasting damage. He will be strong enough for a temporary separation. He will be well looked after by the Jesuits, Sophia; there is not a better upbringing to be had, as I well know. It was only through a Jesuit education that I was able to better myself and they will stand the boy in good stead, too. They have given me every assurance that they can care for his spiritual and physical well-being in a way that I fear neither you nor I are capable.'

Sophia began to sob then and was unable to argue further which frustrated poor Cora and made her angry. It was the first time in her life that she knew her papa to be wrong. If Niall was as full of lethal germs as her father had said, why were the Jesuits so keen to take him?

'Please, Mama,' she begged, 'tell Papa he is not being fair! Niall will be so lonely without us, I cannot see him living with strangers at all! The school will not suit him, either, I know it won't! I've heard such dreadful tales of the Jesuits! Nurse tells us they torture small boys who do not know their catechism! Please, Mama, please speak to him again!'

But her father had gone and her mother just sighed and raised her hands palm-upward in a gesture of resignation.

'There is nothing more I can do,' she said. 'I will visit him as often as I can.'

'He can't sleep in the dark, Mama!' Cora pleaded. 'They may not allow him a night-light, just imagine!'

'It is a good school, Cora,' Sophia told her patiently, 'you should not describe it in such a terrible way. I'm sure they will allow Niall a night-light and whatever else it is that he needs. You mustn't worry, Cora!'

'But you are worried, Mama!' Cora said. 'I can tell by your face! Look, you are crying again.'

Sophia had turned her face away then so that Cora should not see her tears. She was worried, of course she was, but she had delegated all her authority and her finances to her husband many years ago. He controlled her life; there was nothing more she could do.

Cora and Niall went along to mass that week. It was the first Friday in the month and she told him that it would be proper. He said nothing on the way to the church, just walked clutching her hand, stopping only once to stare without comment at some sheep that were being herded onto a sparse patch of land by a boy not much older than himself.

It was a grand, well-attended service and they had sat in the front pew, Cora singing out the hymns as though her very life were dependent upon it. The church glowed yellow with candle-flame, and when Niall looked up his sister saw the flames reflected in the round lenses of his glasses, so that he had small fires for eyes.

With the rain outside, the place smelt of wild flowers and wet tweed. Niall watched the altar-boys go solemnly about their business and wondered if Father Devereux would select him for the job when he was old enough. One of the boys had mud on the lace of his cassock and Niall saw him pass a boiled sweet from his pocket when he thought no one saw. Niall smiled at this but the boy just pressed the sweet into the side of his mouth and did not smile back.

He watched Cora shuffle in a queue to the altar-rail and saw her pale face when she returned.

'Jesus, I hate those wafers!' she told him. 'They always

stick to the roof of your mouth. You're not to bite them so they end up choking you instead!' She licked her lips and pulled a face.

The men in church prayed with heads bowed, Niall noticed, their elbows resting on the pew in front and their hands up to cover their eyes. Cora sat bolt-straight, though, her lips pressed against her fingers as though frightened the words of her prayer might escape from her mouth.

There was a dog in the church, smelling the place out with its wet ragged coat. Niall went to pet it when they walked from their pew but Cora pulled him away and said he shouldn't touch, it could have the mange.

The departing congregation formed a jam around the exit. When they had reached the marble basin that stood in the centre of the aisle, Cora lifted Niall and he dipped his fingers into the holy water, touching it to his forehead, sternum, left shoulder and then right, as he had been taught. Some water dripped onto his jacket and he wondered if God would be angry at the waste.

When they had left the crowd Cora pulled him around to a small side-altar where a painted statue of Our Lady of Eternal Succour stood, her eyes rolled heavenward, in such a conflagration of candle-flame that Niall thought she might melt, as though made of wax.

Before the altar stood a large wooden box with a slit in the top for their letters.

'What's it for?' Niall asked, looking down the hole.

Cora pulled him back by the collar of his jacket. 'It's a petition box,' she told him. 'And you're a right idiot not to know. You light a candle for all the poor souls in purgatory and then you post a note in there for God and then God will read your petition.'

She knelt before the statue and crossed herself quickly.

'And then what?'

'Then He grants your request, I suppose,' Cora said.

'Any request?' Niall asked, staring at the Lady's face.

Cora sighed. 'It's not Saint Nicholas, you know. You're

not just to ask for sweets or toys. The requests must be special and important enough for God to hear. You can't go wasting His time with nonsense.'

'Are the other babies in purgatory?'

Cora shook her head. 'I shouldn't think so. The Father was with them at the end.'

'Can I have a candle for them anyway?'

Cora rose to her feet, banging dust off her skirt with her hands. 'I don't have the money on me,' she said. 'And, besides, I told you they won't be there anyway. It would be a waste of the beeswax.'

'May I write a note then?' Niall pointed to the small pile of old paper and the blunt-ended pencil that lay tethered to the box.

'It's not a bloody mailbox!' Cora looked about to see if anyone was watching. 'You don't just post a note in there and expect the dead to get it! Besides,' she added, 'how is God to read it when you can barely write your own name?'

'If I write it God will understand it,' Niall insisted.

'Don't be such a bloody fool!' Cora laughed.

She watched her brother walk forward and winced as he licked the stub of the pencil before he began to write his little note. It was mainly scribble, she saw, but he took the task so seriously one would have thought it was his best script.

He folded the paper enough times to make her tut aloud and then pushed it through the hole in the box, pressing his eye to the slit as it fell to make sure it had dropped all the way in.

Cora placed an arm about his shoulders. 'Who was your note for?' she asked.

'It wasn't a note,' he said, seriously. 'It was a petition, like you said.'

'So what was it you wished for?'

He pulled away from her then and scratched his shoulder uncomfortably. 'I shouldn't tell,' he whispered. 'Or it won't happen.'

'Jesus, it's not some child's game this, you know, Niall!' Cora was exasperated. 'It's not like crossing your fingers or holding your breath when a tinker passes you on the road! You've written to God now, Niall, and He will read it whether you tell or not!'

'I wished for something bad,' Niall admitted slowly, biting at the side of his mouth. His face turned red but, when he looked up at her, she saw that his eyes were clear. 'I asked God for Papa to die,' he said.

Cora stared at her brother a while. 'That was very wicked of you,' she said at last, but there was no conviction in her voice as she spoke.

CHAPTER TWELVE

There had been many times since the death of her children that Sophia Flavelle had prayed to be allowed to die as well but her prayers had not been answered; she was alive still, though anyone seeing her would have wondered how much alive she really was.

Every time she had bent to kiss her small wide-eyed son on the cheek as she left him each term at the school she would be greeted by such a wave of silent misery that she could barely find the words to bid him goodbye. She would promise that he would be able to come home again soon, but she knew she lied, for his father would not have it and there was nothing she could do to change his mind.

The grief that she suffered had taken its toll upon her health. She had tried lately to regain her strength for the sake of the other children but she had fallen prey to various ailments and was often confined to her bed.

William no longer came to her room at night and for that much she felt she should have been grateful, though she missed his touch, no matter how grudging it may have been.

It was late in the spring of 1903, then, before Sophia felt well enough to walk as far as the church to pray for her dead children and it was here that Father Devereux found her, kneeling straight-backed in the empty pews, her gloved hands clasped before her as she whispered her entreaties for a release from the life that she led.

Thinking that his church was empty, he had hoped for the opportunity to peruse a new Bible that he had received that day in the post. The binding of the small book was exceptionally fine and he carried a letter-knife in one hand, with which to slit open the gold-leafed pages.

He had first opened the book at the poems and the one

that he read was a particular favourite. It was during the second stanza, as his glance left the page for a moment to allow his mind to digest the richly-beautiful prose, that he had spotted Sophia in front of him for the very first time. She had not heard him approach and his initial impulse was to tiptoe away unseen. Sophia's misery and her grief were all too obvious, despite the tautness of her spine, and the young priest felt he had no more words to offer by way of consolation than those that had already been said. Then, for no reason that he could name, he suddenly changed his mind. Sliding his paper-knife between the pages to keep his place, Father Devereux snapped his Bible shut and walked silently down the aisle to join the praying woman.

She looked up, startled, as he sat beside her in the pew and for an awkward moment he thought she might faint clean away. Then some colour returned to her pallid cheeks and he found himself smiling to reassure her all was well.

She started to cry then and he was mortified to think that he could have been the instigator of those tears. He sat in embarrassed silence as she wept and was unable either to move or speak until her sobbing was over.

She stopped suddenly, with one huge sigh that seemed to shake her entire body. Father Devereux was astonished at the suddenness with which the tears ceased, as though they were dried up at source, like a river. Until that moment he had feared they would never stop, for there had been no indication that they would.

The sky outside darkened with a storm and then suddenly cleared again, sending shards of bright ruby light through the window of Saint Augustine. Sophia looked at the priest and he knew then what it was people had seen in the face of the marble angel, to describe it as possessing the power to drive grown men to tears.

'Father,' she said at last, her hazel eyes pools of tears, 'am I to be sad for the rest of my life? For I do not think I can bear it if I am, and would rather be dead right now.' And then her head sank back onto her hands.

Father Devereux thought hard before speaking. He had no personal experience of grief and mourning, though he had seen more of both during his first years as a priest than most men see in a lifetime. He was unable, therefore, to supply Sophia with the honest answer that she so obviously needed. Looking about for some other diversion to cheer her with, his eyes alighted on the new Bible; the knife still resting between the pages he had been reading.

On impulse he took the knife up and used its sharp tip to slice the page cleanly from its spine, then handed Sophia the thin paper in the hope that the poem would lift her heart as it had done his own. He had forgotten its nature entirely and thought only of the words themselves. They had been beautiful and must, therefore, offer some comfort.

Sophia took the paper from him and read in silence, save the odd gulp or two.

'The joints of thy thighs are like jewels,' she read. 'Thy navel is like a round goblet, which wanteth not liquor; thy belly is like an heap of wheat . . .' She turned once to stare at the priest and then went back to the prose.

'Thy two breasts are like two young roes . . .'

She paused for a moment, closing her eyes, then read on.

'This thy stature is like to a palm tree and thy breasts are clusters of grapes . . . I will take hold of the boughs thereof; now also thy breasts shall be as clusters of the vine, and the smell of thy nose like apples . . .'

There was more, but Sophia had felt that her heart had ceased to beat within her chest. The blood drained entirely from her face. She looked at the priest again and only one word escaped her pale lips: 'Oh!'

It was more a murmur than a word yet it was a complete embodiment of all her passions and desires. It was the sound that her soul made as it found wings once more and soared towards freedom, causing Father Devereux to look up from his book with an expression of anxious dismay.

The paper fluttered like a moth in Sophia's hands and the young priest caught it as it fell in a spiral to the floor. He turned again to Sophia's face and found the expression to be the same. It was not the look he had expected. He had thought to see pleasure or even shared delight at the poetry, but her countenance was rapturous and that seemed, even to an avid poet like himself, a little extravagant to say the least.

Then his glance fell upon the page, the words written there, and he became immediately overcome with the most ghastly embarrassment.

'I must apologize, Missus Flavelle . . .' he began. 'I did not intend . . . you cannot possibly suppose . . .' but he looked again at Sophia and realized at once that she had supposed. She had taken his poem not only as a declaration of his love for her, but a deep and very real passion as well. The verse was fairly steeped in sexual innuendo.

'Missus Flavelle . . .' he began again, 'I should never have . . .'

Her eyes had dried now and were like fine precious stones that have emerged from the bottom of a lake. There was such hope and longing and desire expressed in those eyes that the priest felt himself lost within their power and incapable of any attempts at contradiction.

It was there, in the church then, that Father Devereux realized another truth: in his heart at least, he had no desire to refuse her. He was aware in an instant that he loved Sophia; might always have loved her from the first moment of seeing her, though it was only now that he knew it. It was as though his skull had been cracked in two and the truth had escaped at last, blinding him to all but the power of his own passion.

Their faces hung together in the dusty, sun-riddled air, then he bent and touched his lips against her mouth. He had never kissed a woman before, had only pecked the dry old cheeks of elderly ladies. He had expected the same powdery feel but there was life in Sophia's lips and the press of them, moist and warm against his own, startled him.

He dared not get closer, dared not touch her body, for

fear he might die. Instead he clung to the wooden back of the pew as to life itself and their heads fell apart, though he could still taste her in his mouth.

They stared at the altar.

'Missus Flavelle,' he said again.

'Sophia,' she corrected. 'You must call me Sophia.'

The priest sighed at the authority in her tone. So he was to have no choice, then. 'You *must* call me Sophia,' she had said. It was an order, and he felt his will receding at her words. It was amazing how her strength had grown and his willpower had diminished after one very small kiss. Her hands seemed so thin around her purse, they were as fine as the claws of a bird.

'May I kiss you again?' he heard himself ask.

'Yes,' Sophia replied, 'but not in the church.' She laughed at that and he knew he was lost.

CHAPTER THIRTEEN

Sophia Flavelle stood on the high and very windy hilltop where the white clouds blew so low that she felt she might almost touch them with her hand.

She flew her small kite, something she had not done for an age; not since the young priest had watched her, and that had been some three years previously.

The kite had become faded and tattered with age and she had had to mend its holes with a lattice-work of tape. Its tail, though, had been lengthened by as many as ten twists of paper and it was the sight of these bobbing sheets that brought a smile to her face and even made her think about laughing again.

The wind gusted harder and the spool of string spun in her hands as the kite rose still higher. It swooped and dived with its long tail following after and each twist of paper was so dear to Sophia that she thrilled to see them hanging there where none but she could reach them.

There was a fresh sheet in her hand. Securing the string about her waist to free her hands, she settled down onto the grass to read it before consigning it to the same fate as the others. It was a letter, a love-letter, its prose so lurid that it brought a blush to her cheeks. It was both passionate and romantic, she decided, running her fingers along each line as she read before closing her eyes and kissing the fingertips that had touched such dizzying and enchanting words.

'My darling,' it read, 'I wish to have you lie your dear head upon my chest; to feel your sweet breath upon my face; to smell the perfumes of your body; to taste your flesh; to feel myself around you like the air and inside you like the spirit of love itself. My body aches in wanting as I write

107

and it can only be your presence once again in my arms that will help to ease this terrible pain.'

Sophia gasped at this and clutched the note to her bosom. 'My darling,' she said, reciting the next words by heart, for she had them all entrusted to memory. 'My flesh dies without you, yet needs only your dear touch to give it life again. How cruel is fate to deny me such a humble favour!'

It was all too much. The words had plucked a note deep inside Sophia's soul and the chord reverberated until her entire body quivered with longing. Once the seizure had passed she smoothed her hair to her head and, feeling calm once again, quickly wound in the kite and tied the note to its tail.

She released it immediately for she felt it pull away from her hands, so keen did it seem to become airborne. The tail flicked behind the kite like that of an irate cat and the spool spun hard between Sophia's pale and slender fingers.

There was a pleasant choking in her throat that she had not felt for years. She was loved again; adored, in fact. The words of her letters confirmed as much. She watched the kite fly free above her and knew she was happy again at last, that this was the only true happiness she had experienced since the day her parents had died.

She started to run and found that she could not stop on the slope. Her bronze hair blew like flames around her face. Strands fell into her eyes and mouth as she laughed, and she shook her head to free them. When she stopped her cheeks were bright apple-red and she bent over double, fighting for breath. Ten letters! So her love was ten weeks old then; so young, in fact, yet it felt as though it had burnt within her forever. A letter a week, and each left for her behind a stone of her dear papa's grave.

CHAPTER FOURTEEN

There should have been guilt and recriminations, but somehow there were none. A young and handsome priest, so bravely in love with a married parishioner; by right his nights should have been filled with anguish and deliberations, his waking days a nightmare of torment and indecision. Sophia, too, should have suffered equally in her choice between wifely duties and forbidden love and yet both priest and wife appeared to flourish in the glow of their mutual adoration.

Their time spent apart was bitter enough, but then she had his letters and he had the pleasure of composing them. Under the approving gaze of his new muse, Father Devereux became the skilled poet that he had always longed to be. Passion had smitten him just as surely as his faith. He was an intellectual man, but surprisingly simple in his beliefs. He had never questioned his religion and he did not question his passion for Sophia. To him they were both natural occurrences and he would have thought no more of questioning their existence than he would have thought to question the fact that the sun rose each day in the sky.

If his passion for his Church was right, then so must his passion for Sophia be, for they felt the same to him; there was nothing to choose between then. Both then, according to his logic, must have come from the same source. He had seen Sophia's face in the face of the marble angel and such expressions could surely belong only to heaven.

He had told her this once and she had laughed at him. 'If our sins were etched on our faces we'd all be an ugly lot!' she had said, but he had not joined in her laughter.

How were they to know that they consummated an affair that William had created in his mind years before? All of his suspicions had been right but they had been of the wrong time. How could they have known that a young boy already suffered through William's obsession with their affair? Or that they were about to commit a sin for which Sophia's husband had already forgiven her?

Ten long weeks passed, then, and now the priest craved Sophia Flavelle as he craved nothing else in his life. He longed to take her and for her to take him and in his mind that longed-for union would be in the open where they could lie naked before his God. There would be no robes then, to remind him of his duty as a priest and he could become a young man once again, paying homage at the altar of Sophia's beauty.

They met at dawn, when the family in the great house still slept, and the mists were so heavy on the ground that they could imagine themselves invisible to all.

He took her to the hill and she carried her kite, though she knew it would not fly that day. They stood on the wet grass that was shrouded in a fine veil of threads beaded with pearls of dew and they watched the mists roll from the rivers down into the sea.

Sophia's hand shivered as he took it. Only then did Father Devereux realize exactly what it had cost her to come to him. His journey had been simple; he had merely saddled his horse and made his way leisurely across the demesne. Sophia had had to make her escape from her home, aware that her husband could have discovered her at any moment. The priest became filled with admiration at her bravery.

'Were you scared as you left?' he asked.

She shook her head defiantly but did not speak. She had felt as though she were leaving her home forever. She had crept like a ghost along endless darkened corridors but silence had been impossible on the bare and ageing boards. Each crack of the wood underfoot had sent a shock through her heart, stilling it once until she thought it would never beat again.

They reached the brow of the hill and turned to gaze at

one another, each finding the other beautiful. He knew he had only to touch her cheek with his fingers for her eyes to close and her lips to part in a sigh. She knew that one kiss from her would have him shaking with desire. He held his palm to her face and she pressed her mouth against it.

How should he undress her? he wondered. He longed to see her naked! They kissed once more, and this time their lips met in earnest. It was Sophia who pulled away from the embrace to whisper against his ear.

'I have never before been kissed like that,' she murmured, her hand clutched to her chest. 'My husband would never kiss me.'

Father Devereux was immediately both thrilled and saddened; thrilled to be the first man to have kissed her in such a way and sad to think that her beauty had been left neglected for so many years.

He had not supposed Sophia to be in any way an innocent and his own virginity had hung like a yoke about his shoulders. He had never known passion with a woman; merely some childish fumblings with other boys at his college. Their bodies had been reassuringly familiar to his own, though, while what lay beneath Sophia's layers of skirts and corsets was a mystery he found himself hesitant to discover.

He watched as her hands reached to her neck and her fingers danced over a line of small pearl buttons there. As if by magic they fell back at her touch. The buttons reminded him of children's teeth; so milk-white and perfect, they opened into a grin. She barely moved and yet her dress was swept away onto the ground and, to his amazement, she stood before him naked, just as he had longed for and dreamed of!

She was so slim beneath her clothes that her body was not unlike those of the slender boys he had known back at the college. This was a relief to him, for he had feared her strangeness.

She shivered in the morning air, yet she stood so proud

111

and grand before him. There was almost no flesh on her and yet her breasts were heavy and her hips seemed wide. She had no modesty, either, which surprised him; that she could stand there naked yet not cover her body with her hands. It suited him that she did not, for he wished to devour every inch of her with his eyes. Her pubic hair was russet and coarse, as bright as a flame against the paleness of her skin. The skin was fine enough but became almost transparent where it stretched taut across the bones of her hips and he could see the mauve veins across her soft stomach and inner arms.

There were creases in the flesh of her belly, which he supposed to be the scars of childbirth. She turned beneath his gaze, as proud as any statue, and he found himself profoundly affected by the run of her spine and the way it curved into the small of her back, then arched out again into the softness of her buttocks.

His hands caught at his own clothes. He became suddenly clumsy, faltering over actions that he performed so smoothly every day. He would have ripped at them, had they not been such good quality.

At last he was as naked as she. He stood behind her and pressed his flesh against her, taking her breasts into his palms. They felt cold to the touch. He heard her sigh and then he kissed the back of her neck, where the spine ran in a line like glass marbles.

'My darling Sophia,' he whispered into her hair and she let out a sound that was like a sob as they fell to the ground together to consummate their lusts and their mutual desires.

They felt to him like the last words that he would ever speak.

CHAPTER FIFTEEN

Their love should have lasted an eternity; in fact it survived barely to the end of the summer. They met one day on their hill, when the first cruel winds of autumn blew Sophia's hair into a mane of wild fronds. Father Devereux watched as they licked against the pale pink softness of the afternoon sky while the ocean's roar in the background presaged the first stirrings of storms to come.

Sophia pulled a scarf from her coat and tied it about her hair. He thought how cold and pinched she looked and found it sad that she should hide one of her finest assets beneath a length of raw Donegal tweed. He smiled as she looked up at him, for her nose was red and her eyes as bright as jewels.

She talked a lot as they walked, which was unusual, for she liked to listen while he recited his poetry. He had no verse in his pocket that day, though, and so was relieved at her mood.

She told him of Cora and Christina and of Niall, whom she had visited again that day. He had been quiet and she had prayed that he would enjoy school more this term. He had not clung to her at all, she said, which was promising, and he looked quite grown up in his navy wool. Besides, she added, apparently talking to herself now, he would be home soon enough for the holidays, as long as William allowed it. And then she had stopped quite suddenly and turned to look at the priest.

'Oh, my darling boy!' she said, excited. 'You will never guess!' She clutched her hands together before her like a child with a secret to share.

He had never seen her in this playful mood before and it

unsettled him for it did not align with his poetic melancholy. He forced a smile that he did not feel.

'Guess what?' he asked. 'A secret?' She nodded. This childishness, he thought, did not suit her one bit.

'From me?' he asked, attempting to share her mood. 'You know you cannot keep a secret from me, Sophia!' He clutched at her waist, feeling faintly ridiculous. She turned away from him and ran to the nearest tree.

'Let me think,' he said, frowning. 'Christina has seen her second vision? Cora has an admirer and is all set to wed?'

Sophia laughed aloud and shook her head.

'You have written me a poem?' he went on. 'Your cook has finally mastered the art of a light suet?'

Sophia placed her hands together over her face and he thought at first that she was laughing again but when she looked up he saw her eyes were sad.

'Oh, my darling,' she told him, watching his face all the while, 'my darling boy, my love; I have news for you; I am carrying your child!'

He pulled away from her spasmodically, though it seemed a decade later before her words finally reached his brain. He felt a sudden need to sit down upon the ground and yet would not have done so, for the grass was wet and his clothes newly-pressed.

'A child?' he had echoed, mindlessly.

He saw her face and the hope that was suddenly extinguished in her eyes, like a snuffed candle.

She pulled at his sleeve. 'Did you never think of it?' she asked. 'Did you never imagine it could happen?'

'Never!' he said in horror, and he spoke the truth, for it had never once occurred to him that their couplings could have resulted in anything more than mutual bliss. Of course he knew all about nature, but their affair had seemed to defy all such laws. It had been illusory and magical; reality should never have intruded.

'Did you not understand the mysteries of nature, then?' Sophia asked, smiling at him.

'Of course!' he told her, embarrassed. 'But I never thought . . . I thought somehow . . .'

'You thought it did not apply to us, is that right? You thought we were in some divine state of grace that would make us exempt from all worldly matters, is that it?'

That was exactly it. That was precisely how the priest had felt. He walked away from her, feeling the need to keep moving. He did not care whether she followed him or not.

'What are we to do, then?' Sophia asked. She appeared so calm that it frightened him.

'Do?' he asked, and in that one word, by the tone of his voice and by the expression on his face, he killed their love forever.

'We must do nothing,' he told her. 'There is nothing to be done.'

Her hand flew to her face and she stepped back from him. She had had her happiness and now she saw that it was at an end.

'But my husband . . .' she said, though her voice had grown weak.

'He will believe it to be his!' the priest said. 'It is essential that he should believe that!' He looked at Sophia's face and saw the disbelief there.

'Did you think we would have any option?' he asked. 'Did you think I could possibly claim the child as my own? I am a priest, Sophia! My career would be finished! Your family, too!' he added, desperate to convince her. 'You would lose everything you have; all that is dearest to you!'

She was shaking now, he saw, and her eyes had filled with tears. 'You are all that is dearest to me, Sebastian!' she said, clutching his arm. 'There is nothing else that I cherish, nothing!'

He was horrified at her words; that she could have so little concern for her husband and her children.

'You couldn't bear to lose your children, Sophia,' he said in his priest's voice. 'I know that you couldn't.'

115

'Niall is the only one who needs me now!' she said. 'And he has been taken from me!'

He took her by the shoulders, almost shaking her to persuade her he was right. 'How did you think we could do it? Where did you think we could go?'

She stopped breathing as she stared at him. Her eyes became wild and she spoke in a whisper. 'We could have left here . . .' she said. 'We could have gone in your balloon . . . flown away somewhere where no one could find us . . .'

His hands dropped to his sides. He felt himself capable of killing her. What she said made no sense and a dreadful fear crept into the pit of his stomach.

'Niall is only at school,' he said, ignoring her words, 'and you will have the new child to care for.'

It was as though he had hit her. He would never forget the expression in her eyes as, finally, she tied her scarf more firmly beneath her chin, turned her collar to the cold and walked away down the hill.

'Sophia!' he called. He felt only a great fear. There was more that he needed to say and yet he wanted her gone with every ounce of his being. He felt the cold creep into his bones and he, too, pulled his collar against the wind. He watched her back as it grew smaller and then vanished and he wished that she could be gone that easily from his life.

CHAPTER SIXTEEN

And so poor Sophia received yet another cruel blow, and this time it was to prove fatal for there ceased to be meaning to her existence; her last chance of happiness had passed. Sebastian Devereux had been her one hope and without his love she was lost.

As his child grew inside her so she slowly lost her reason and the words of the priest's poetry tumbled in her head like the endless spurting of a fountain. She sought sometimes to recite them, to make meaning of the ceaseless jumble, but they slipped from her grasp as she caught for them; refusing to congeal into line or verse.

She took to standing on their hill, wide-eyed and dishevelled, her coat unbuttoned to the wicked chill winds and her poor mind seeking sense when there was none to be found. She fancied the child inside her to be deformed; to be mutating as it grew. The doctor was called to reassure her but she would not be calmed.

The swell of her belly appalled her. It was her punishment, she said, and no one could understand what she meant.

'She becomes irrational,' William told the doctor. 'I even fear that she may attempt to take her own life.'

The doctor smiled. 'I have seen many pregnant women behave in this way,' he told him. 'But they do not come to any harm as a rule. It is merely a form of hysterics, brought on, I believe, by the child pressing on a nerve that in turn starves the brain of some of its oxygen.'

William paced the room before him. 'This child is special to me, Doctor,' he said.

'Special, William?' Doctor O'Sullivan asked. 'Surely all of your children are special to you.'

William stopped to look out of the window, with his back turned to the doctor.

'I told you the circumstances of the last child's conception,' he said, quietly.

'You told me a lot of strange nonsense, William, yes . . .' the doctor began.

'God decided that I had been punished enough,' William continued. 'He has sent me this child by way of reparation for all the suffering. It is my gift, Doctor. I know it to be my gift from God just as Joseph knew the Lord Jesus to be God's gift to the earth. The circumstances were the same.'

The doctor looked confused. 'Are you saying your wife conceived this child without your help, William?' He pushed a hand through his hair, suppressing the desire to laugh.

'It is God's child.' William nodded. 'My child. The Lord's gift to me.'

He turned to face the doctor, his eyes wide and shining with conviction.

'The baby will turn soon, William,' the doctor told him, unable to pursue the subject any longer, 'and then there will be peace in this house once again, I assure you. In the meantime,' he added, washing his hands at the basin in William's room, 'I suggest you hire a private nurse to sit with your wife, and then you can put your staff onto other duties. Insanity, however temporary, can be an alarming thing to witness. I believe your wife would be less distressed once the problem is over if she were to know that there were the least number of witnesses to her suffering.'

He paused in his washing and looked about in vain for a towel.

'Your wife is a fine lady, William,' he said, patting his hands dry on the legs of his trousers. 'Very fine and very proud. She'll suffer when she discovers the fuss she has caused at this time. A nurse can leave as soon as she's over it. What do you say, William, shall I book one or not?'

William stood silently by the washstand, apparently

absorbed by a cake of soap that he kept turning over in his hand.

'Very well,' he said, finally, and the doctor smiled with relief.

'Good man,' he said, patting William on the back. 'Good man.'

The nurse arrived the following week and for a while all appeared to go as the doctor had predicted. In the sixth month of her pregnancy Sophia was discovered in the kitchens, dressed in her favourite linen morning-dress with the white organdie collar; her hair neatly coiled in a russet garland about her head. She was planning the coming week's menus as though she had never been ill or confused.

The cook, knowing of her problems, eyed her warily at first. Sophia, she noticed, was still so slender that the child barely showed and she was alarmed at the twin circles of mauve beneath her eyes. She was strong enough to stand, though, refusing all offers of a chair, and she read through the menus in a most rational way, even remembering the doctor's planned visit for the following Friday and how he could not tolerate steamed fish so would be offered baked trout instead.

It was as Sophia was leaving the kitchen that the cook, still worried by her mistress's undernourished appearance, pulled a tray of fresh-baked cakes from the oven and, wrapping one in greaseproof to avoid burning her fingers, pressed it into Sophia's palm. The delight on Sophia's face told her at once how the gesture was appreciated.

'Madeleines!' she said. 'Is Papa due home, then?'

The cook looked confused.

'You know they are his favourites!' Sophia said, smiling as she bit into the sponge. 'Oh, it must mean that he is due back tonight, in time for my party! I wondered what the surprise was!' She looked at the cook and laughed, pressing a finger to her lips. 'Don't worry,' she said, patting the woman's plump arm. 'You're not allowed to tell, I know.

119

I shan't tell Papa that I've guessed.' Her hand was icy-cold, despite the warmth of the kitchen.

The cook felt the hairs stand up on her neck as she realized that Sophia had completely lost her reason.

That was to be the last phase of Sophia's illness then, and for six more weeks she was to be found wandering in the house, apparently blissfully happy, humming quietly as she planned for a birthday party at which her dead father was to be guest of honour. No one told her that the party had been over a quarter of a century ago for no one wished to see the pain return to her eyes.

Constance, who had been conceived on the hill in the demesne, in the dew of mid-summer, chose a cold winter's day for her birth. While the barber's shears clipped around Niall's neck, at the fine wisps of hair that hung about his pink ears, so his tiny new sister was filling her lungs with her first few breaths of pure Irish air. As she was placed for the first and last time at her mother's breast she let out her first small mew of contentment at finding herself born so perfect. Niall, meanwhile, had gazed at his sardine tea, wondering at Cora's nerve, to be smoking cigarettes in a public place.

It was the ultimate irony of Sophia's life that it should have been Father Devereux's place to sit at her bedside offering spiritual succour as he read the last rites softly into her ear. The litany sounded like the words of love he had whispered to her and for a moment she had become confused, thinking they were back on their hill and about to make love.

The pain of childbirth had subsided at last but her eyes were unfocused and she found herself too weak and confused to move. She became only vaguely aware at last that what she heard was prayer, not passion, and then she knew that she was dying and her heart lifted with relief at the thought.

'For thou hast delivered my soul from death,' Father Devereux read softly beside her, 'mine eyes from tears, and my feet from falling. I will walk before the Lord in the land of the living . . .'

Sophia turned her head towards the speaker of these words and her eyes focused at last. The priest's voice faltered, but in fear, not in sadness. It was her confession he feared; that it might be overheard by others. He had hoped she would slip into death without regaining consciousness but now he saw her eyes clear the hand of fear gripped his heart like a vice.

He looked across at the nurse, but she appeared to be asleep. Sophia's lips moved and he wanted to smother her: she could destroy him with her last breath, he knew.

Sophia saw the priest's face in the candlelight and thought for the last time how handsome he looked. His brows were drawn with concentration, for the light was poor and the print of the Bible small and faint with age. Had he come to her at last? She tried to raise a hand to him, to smooth the frown from his brow. She would tell him how she loved him still, yet she found that she could not move and when her lips formed around the words, she saw the fear that sprang up in his eyes and the words never came.

'Care for our child,' she whispered instead and watched as his face became as pale as her own.

'I will take the cup of salvation,' he read loudly, drowning her words.

Had he wept for her? His eyes looked clear as they fixed upon the pages of his Bible.

'Did you love me, Sebastian?' she asked. 'Did you love me truly? With all your heart and your body and your soul?'

'Open to me the gates of righteousness,' he read. 'I will go into them and I will praise the Lord.'

'Tell me that you loved me,' Sophia whispered, her voice growing fainter. 'Give me your hand,' she begged. 'Let me feel the warmth of your body one last time.'

Panic filled the priest's eyes. He turned the pages of the Bible quickly, pulling at a plait of silk that he had placed between the pages. The silk had been plaited by her, he suddenly remembered, and his fingers fell from it as though repelled by its touch.

'When thou liest down,' he read, his voice unsteady, 'thou shalt not be afraid.'

The hired nurse stirred in her chair.

'Thou shalt lie down,' he continued, 'and thy sleep shall be sweet.'

'I cannot die without knowing, Sebastian!' Sophia pleaded. 'Did you love me? I cannot tell now, I cannot remember . . . it seems so long ago . . .' She suddenly grew restless. 'My child!' she said. 'My baby!'

Father Devereux forced himself to place a restraining hand upon her arm. Her skin felt already dead. She had not lost her beauty but her skin had lost its life and warmth.

'Your baby is well,' he assured her. 'You have a beautiful daughter.' He spoke the words in dread, fearing her response.

'Name her Constance,' she said. 'And take her away from here, Sebastian, please, I beg of you! If you love me, if you ever loved me, take her away from this house. If he guesses the truth I will fear for her life. I will not be here to care for her, Sebastian. In God's name, promise me you will take her away!'

Father Devereux backed away from the bed. He looked across at the nurse but the shadows were too deep in the room to see her face or its expression.

'For pity's sake!' Sophia cried and then fell back onto her pillows, her face quite grey and her mouth half-open with the effort of drawing air into her lungs. The priest knew he should call the doctor and that perhaps she might be saved, but he could not risk it for he did not know to whom she might make her confession.

'The box,' she gasped at last. 'Take the box from beneath my pillow. Do not forget me, Sebastian. Our child, take our child . . .'

Sophia's last breath came as a rattle from the back of her throat. He seemed to feel the sound in his own gullet. He could not breathe; an emotion he could not name choked him so that he thought he should die with her. He had an urge to shake her, to bring her back to life, yet relief overwhelmed him that her lips were silenced at last.

'Don't leave me, Sophia!' he heard a voice say, but it was the whisper of a young man that had loved her while he stood there in his capacity as a priest. He closed Sophia's eyes with his fingers and pulled the wooden box from beneath her pillow. Her head lolled to the side as he did so.

'Nurse!' he called, and it was the priest's voice that spoke now, not the voice of the lover and poet who had seen all that he loved pass away before him.

The nurse stirred slowly in her chair and he almost wept with relief as he realized she had been in a deep sleep all the time. They finished their duties then, the nurse and the priest, and when William arrived to find his wife dead he let out such a roar of grief that the old nurse almost passed out with the shock as Father Devereux led her from the room.

CHAPTER SEVENTEEN

That evening, alone and unable to mourn, Father Devereux opened the box that Sophia had given him. It contained every one of his letters, each still tied with the string of the kite, and he sat wondering why they were bound in such a fashion, for he had never seen them flying in the air.

Beneath the letters lay a folder of red velvet and coiled inside the pouch was a lock of Sophia's russet hair; the type of keepsake any young woman might give to her lover. He cupped the hair in his hand – it still held her precious scent and it was as though she were in the room with him. The memories it stirred kept him pacing the house for the rest of the night whilst the young man within him wept noisily and openly for his dead love.

He wept for her body, which lay cold between two candles. He yearned for the warm touch of her flesh and for the sight of her again. Her perfume aroused a picture in his mind. He saw her standing on the hill where they had first made love. He watched as her thin dress slipped off her naked body and she stood, white and ghost-like, before him. He saw her face, golden in the candle-flame as she had sat beside him at the dinner when they had first met ... Choking, he threw the wooden box away from him in anger and fear of the memories that its contents evoked.

He realized in a wild burst of grief that she was the only woman he would ever know, for he could never risk such a liaison again. He had not thought his actions would lead him to this. Poems and words of love spilled into his head, only now he knew their impotence, now there was no one to write them for.

Celibacy had never bothered him while he had been a romantic and an idealist but he had tasted the pleasures of the flesh and his physical desires would haunt him for the rest of his life.

He fell to the floor and crawled in his self-pity. His narrow, empty bed seemed to mock him. He thought of leaving the parish, as though his memories might fade with the distance, but he was an ambitious man and knew his leaving would be viewed with suspicion. Rumours would start and the thought that his affair might come to light filled him with terror.

Playing the role of priest came naturally to Sebastian Devereux, though, and he soon took control of his emotions as he went about his ecclesiastical business. The carved wooden box was placed away on a high shelf in his house, which is where he also consigned his grief for Sophia. He did not have to see the box and, therefore, he did not have to think about her. He wished he could burn it, to have it exorcized forever, but a superstitious fear that surprised even him overruled the idea.

As a priest he had duties to perform and he fell into his work with renewed enthusiasm. With time he found he could admonish his sinning parishioners without any twinge of reciprocal guilt and the whole episode became to his mind a test of his powers of recuperation and resilience. He was soon astride his mare once more, his back as straight as it always had been and his eye fixed firmly upon the spiritual education of his flock.

Only one dark thought haunted his quieter moments and disturbed his sleep and that was of his child and how she would grow. What if she were to resemble him? The likeness between himself and his own siblings was remarkable; anyone who looked at them knew them immediately for brothers and sisters. What if the same similarity should be re-created in his daughter?

He came to fear the sight of the child as he feared nothing else in his life. Was her face growing into a mirror image of his own even as he slept in his bed at night? Was her wispy hair darkening as babies' hair often did and had she lost her mother's pallor with the first taste of the sun? But Constance was William's child, he told himself, and the lie almost became the truth for he recited it so often to himself, hiding all other possibilities away as he had hidden Sophia's wooden box.

Sophia's funeral was the bleakest affair, made more so by the fact that it was the worst day for rain that anyone, even in that rain-sodden county, could remember. It threw a veil of deepest mourning about the house, obscuring all but the nearest trees and pathways. Hanging as heavy as dense fog, it stung the faces of the mourners if they looked up from the grave and ran down their necks if they did not. The mud was treacherous enough underfoot for only the youngest and nimblest to show, while the rest stayed at home, for fear of breaking their necks.

It fell to Father Devereux to lead the service and he found himself intrigued and not a little concerned by the sight of William Flavelle in the front pew. As the rain thundered down on the roof, William stood, erect and proud; cradling his small child in his great arms. When the first hymn was sung Constance awoke and, hearing the singing, began to wail. Her cries continued throughout the service but William's face remained impassive and he made no move to silence her.

Father Devereux was puzzled but more than a little relieved that her noise drowned out his words, hypocritical as they were. 'Devoted mother and devoted wife . . .' he heard himself say and any moment a shard of white light should have torn through the rafters to burn his tongue out.

White-faced and dull-eyed with grief, Sophia's other five children waited huddled beside her grave like a clutch of helpless birds. Thomas stood between his sisters and managed to mouth a few lines of the responses while Cora aimlessly turned the pages of Niall's prayer-book for want of some distraction from her grief.

Niall was still banished to the end of the family line, an exile from the heart of the small group. It pained Father

Devereux to see the small boy stand so isolated and to watch the look of longing that he threw to his small sister when she cried.

As he recited the words above Sophia's coffin, Father Devereux chanced to glance up and found himself staring into the face of the carved marble angel that kept watch over the children's graves. For a second, in the rain, he thought that it was Sophia's face he had seen and her words flashed through his mind: 'Our child, my love, take our child!'

He stammered his words and then stopped completely. Some twenty or so faces stared at him from the graveside as he paused. Had they all heard her voice? They stood like wet seals, waiting for him to start again, their coats black and shiny with the rain. In a seizure of panic Father Devereux looked down into the open grave and across at his daughter, a tiny bundle in William's arms. He stepped back from the narrow gaping hole as though fearful of its contents and, in doing so, almost lost his footing in the mud.

The baby had stopped crying and he fancied it had stopped for him, awaiting his decision on its mother's request.

'Heavenly Father . . .' he began, for he was a priest first and foremost and he had a duty to perform. A sheet of bright lightning rent the sky overhead and Constance let out another anguished yell. Father Devereux felt a hand on his sleeve and turned, white-faced, to find the doctor beside him.

'Do you not think you should make a speedy service of it, Father?' the doctor asked in a whisper that was barely audible above the rain. 'Or we'll be drowned as we stand here; either that or we'll be fried in our boots by the lightning!' As he spoke another bolt speared the grey skies.

'My surgery will be full enough with coughs and wheezes tomorrow as it is!' the doctor added.

Father Devereux nodded.

'Good man!' the doctor said, and retired to the back of the crowd.

'Ashes to ashes . . .' the priest intoned. The words came

easily to him now. He finished the service and all but William turned gratefully from the graveside. The nurse prised the baby from his arms and, when the priest looked back, he saw William standing alone, a dark bowed figure against the pitch of the sky. The mourners were running now, trying to get to the shelter of the house before they contracted pneumonia. Father Devereux stopped, though, for he thought he saw someone waiting behind William, half-concealed by a tree.

'Francis?' he asked himself, trying to make the figure out in the gloom, why would Francis be waiting there? The boy was over twenty years of age now, and yet so in awe still of his father that the priest could not see him waiting alone to offer his condolences.

'Come along, man!' the doctor said, suddenly appearing at his side and waving him towards the house.

The priest laughed. 'Do you never stop tending to the welfare of your patients?' he asked.

The doctor grinned. 'Do you ever stop tending the morals of your flock?'

Father Devereux looked back once to the two men below him before joining the other mourners in the mad dash to the house.

CHAPTER EIGHTEEN

'Father?'

William Flavelle turned round in surprise and annoyance at the sound of his eldest son's voice. He had thought himself alone at last with his wife and wished to say more prayers above her coffin. Francis stood before him, tall and awkward as usual, his head bowed and his hair plastered to his face.

'Get back to the house, Francis!' William shouted to the boy. 'I want to say my prayers in solitude. I need some peaceful time together with your mother.'

He waited for his son to move but Francis merely raised his head to look his father in the eye.

'She had no peace,' he said quietly. 'And there will be no peace for any of us now, will there, Father?'

'What?' William shouted. 'What in God's name are you trying to say?' He strode nearer his son, pulling his coat up about his ears for shelter.

Francis backed away as he approached. 'I'm going away, Father,' he said. 'I've decided. I'm leaving here. I can't stay now that she's dead.'

William laughed humourlessly. 'Since when were you such a mother's boy, Francis?' he asked. His son stood still before him, staring miserably at his shoes. He had said all that he needed to say and thought it would be enough. He had not wanted a conversation or a discussion with his father, and now just wished to go back to the house and make arrangements for his departure.

He turned to go, but William caught him by the arm.

'So where are you off to, then?' he asked. His face was close to his son's and Francis felt the first stabbing pang of fear in his stomach as he saw the expression in his father's eyes.

'I mean to make my own way . . .' he began, less sure of himself now, 'and some of the boys have told me there's work to be had in the towns. If I can see my way to Clifden or even Dublin or somesuch . . .'

'The boys!' William said, releasing his son with a smile on his face. 'So it's the boys now, is it? The ones you spend so much time drinking with of an evening, they're the ones you would turn to for advice now, are they? Since when do scoundrels like that give advice worth its weight, I'd like to know? Eh?' He shook his head like a wet dog and water sprayed out from his beard.

'You're my son, Francis,' he said. 'My son and my heir and God help me you will not leave this house until I am dead and unable to prevent you! Do you hear what I say?'

Francis's legs were gripped with the shakes but he held his ground. 'I'm a grown man, Father,' he said. 'You can do nothing to stop me. My mind is made up.'

They stared at each other as the rain beat down onto their faces. William's eyes had a mad, staring look and for a moment Francis thought he might try to strike him but then the madness went and his body seemed to relax.

'Very well,' he said, moving aside to let his son pass.

Francis looked shocked. He was unable to believe his father's words but then his heart lifted and he turned to run back to the house.

'Where are you going, Francis?' William had him again by the arm.

Francis turned. 'To the house,' he said.

William stared solemnly at his son. 'I thought you said you were leaving,' he said.

Francis's mouth dropped. 'In a few weeks . . .' he began. 'I did not mean now . . . I have to get the farm in order and save some money for the fare . . . I have to get a suit and some luggage . . .'

'If you leave you leave now!' William told him. 'You do not go inside that house again.'

'But we have Mama's funeral to see out!' Francis said. 'I

130

have no things with me and I'm soaked through!' He pointed at the water oozing from his best shoes. 'I don't have so much as a penny on me; you can't expect . . . !'

'Let your friends get you the money!' William shouted. 'They are so free with their advice they should be pleased to help you out with the cash! Take your sad stories to them, Francis! I don't want to hear them and I don't care to see your face again.'

He turned from his son and strode towards the house, leaving Francis standing forlornly in his wake.

Francis watched the dark shape of his father's back until it dissolved into the rain and mists of the demesne. He watched until there was nothing more to see and then he heard his father's voice, roaring so loud that it echoed about the grounds. 'God will punish you!' he shouted. 'You will be back, Francis; one day you will return. You can none of you leave this house without my blessing. You will come back here, Francis, and God help you when you do, for I shall not!'

Francis waited a while, but no more words came. He stared towards the house but the rain did not clear enough to afford him a last view. Soaked already, he turned up his collar and shoved his hands deep into his pockets before setting off across the bogs.

CHAPTER NINETEEN

The great empty room struck warm after the chilling wetness of the afternoon. Two peat fires had been lighted, one at either end, and it was around them that the funeral guests congregated like two warring factions, stamping the rain off their shoes and standing so close to the flames that a smell of scorched tweed permeated the entire house within minutes.

Tea and sherry were served, the tea mainly preferred for there was whisky to come later. Once that arrived the men appeared to relax, closing their eyes as they sipped and smacking their lips together with pleasure while the women watched, tutting at the sight.

Death was the favoured topic of the day and understandably so for there had been three deaths so far in Connemara that week. It was a subject the villagers held close to their hearts and it was one on which they could all have pronounced themselves to be experts. As they discussed the matter with some pride at their expertise the doctor found himself called upon to cross the long room many times as his professional opinions were required to settle this or that dispute. As the afternoon wore on and the whisky bottles emptied, so the doctor's navigation of the space between the two fireplaces became erratic and laboured, for he was being poured drinks at each end.

By five o'clock the rain was forgotten and it was condensation instead that ran in thin ribbons down the windows and the mood of the two groups was such that no one noticed William enter the room to stand by the largest window with Constance held in his arms. He had changed into dry clothes but his beard was still wild and his dark hair dishevelled as he gazed from the window as though expecting the return of his wife.

He was offered a sherry by the timid maid but made no move to accept it. It was Father Devereux who first noticed him and who first felt obliged to murmur the usual words of condolence that the occasion required.

As he approached, the maid crept gratefully away to fetch more water for the tea. It occurred to the priest as he saw William's wild staring face that he would have given a large fortune not to have to talk to him.

'The child has a fine pair of lungs!' he said, showing a great deal more humour than he felt. 'She drowned my poor service out more effectively than the rain!'

In the silence that followed Father Devereux broke off a piece of the sponge cake he was carrying on a small bone china plate and popped it into his mouth, for want of anything better to do.

'Such a terrible day,' he continued once he had forced the cake the entire length of his parched throat. 'The mud was quite treacherous underfoot.'

William turned to look at him but he did not answer. His face was devoid of all emotion or thought. The bundle in his arms moved slightly and Father Devereux was suddenly filled with dread at the sight.

He cleared his throat finally with a cough, placing one hand politely to his mouth as he did so. 'Mourning is a queer thing, Mister Flavelle,' he intoned. 'It can make a man very insular, very alone. It is a difficult thing to share, I know, very difficult.'

He was offered tea and accepted it gratefully, pausing to sip it and burning his tongue in the process.

'You must try not to isolate yourself in your grief, though,' he said. 'You should allow the children to share the mourning with you. They will be a comfort to you, Mister Flavelle, and you to them. It is important you are close at a time like this, do not lock yourself away.'

He had been particularly troubled by the sight of poor

Niall who had made a pathetic vision all day, standing alone as he did from all the others. Only Cora seemed to have noticed him and then just the once, to give him some tea and a sandwich after which, with a look to her father, she had retreated to the end of the room.

'Your children feel the loss of your wife just as keenly as you, Mister Flavelle,' the priest went on, 'especially the younger ones. They can help you with your burden if you will allow them, I have seen it happen many times before, I can assure you. Look at your youngest boy, look at poor Niall! He is still just a child yet and he cannot have grasped the enormity of his loss. It will hit him hard when he does, I'm sure.'

William Flavelle looked across in the boy's direction but his expression did not change.

'He was taken to see her in her coffin,' he said dully. 'He knows well enough that she has gone; they all do.'

Father Devereux shook his head. 'It affects some in different ways,' he said, rubbing the back of his neck. 'You should see your way to keeping him close just now. He will need equilibrium in his life after such a loss.'

William looked back at the priest and his eyes seemed focused for the first time that afternoon.

'Is that God's opinion, Father?' he asked. 'Or merely your own?'

Father Devereux looked startled. 'I should have thought it's just Christian charity, Mister Flavelle. I should think . . .'

'Are you speaking as God's messenger on earth, Father?' William persisted. 'Is this God's will you're ordering me to obey or are you just giving me the benefit of your own opinion? Is it the priest telling me I should keep the boy close or just the man inside the robes? Eh?'

Father Devereux looked confused. 'I should have thought any caring person would have told you the same, Mister Flavelle,' he said. 'I don't believe you need to see it as a command from God, merely an opinion that anyone could have offered with the best of intentions . . .'

'The boy is to board full-time with the Jesuits from next month,' William interrupted. 'They will be there to provide all the equilibrium he will need, Father.'

'The Jesuits?' Father Devereux raised his eyebrows. 'But ought you to send him away at such a time? With his mother just dead I should have thought . . .'

'Why such an interest in the boy, Father?' William suddenly shouted. 'There are four more children here today that are missing a mother and one older boy out there in the demesne right now that I would have thought more than deserving of your spiritual salvation!' He looked to the window as he spoke, to the path Francis had taken. 'Why Niall, Father?' he shouted. 'Why that one?'

As his voice rose Constance stirred in his arms and her small fists became visible above the shawl in which she was wrapped.

'The Jesuits can deal with the boy's soul, Father,' William continued, turning again to face the priest. 'They will see to him far more ably than I ever could. They will see the evil there in him and rid him of it in ways that I am not capable of.'

'Evil?' Father Devereux asked, but his host was moving away.

He looked at the small boy once again, with his shorn head and his wire-rimmed spectacles. 'Won't you reconsider?' he asked William, moved to speak by a sudden rush of compassion. He even dared to catch his host by the sleeve. 'I feel you are being unnecessarily cruel to the boy.'

William turned suddenly at his touch and the expression on his face made the priest step back quickly away from him.

'IS THAT GOD'S VOICE SPEAKING THROUGH YOU AGAIN, FATHER?' William shouted, so that the whole room turned around to listen. 'OR DOES THIS ADVICE COME FROM THE MAN AGAIN, RATHER THAN THE PRIEST?'

Father Devereux's hand fell away to his side and he stood there foolishly, glancing about at the faces that watched them with grave interest and wondering what would be said next.

'WOULD YOU TAKE HIM THEN, FATHER?' William bellowed even more loudly, and the child in his arms began to cry. 'ARE YOU TO CLAIM YOUR OWN AT LAST?'

There were gasps from some of the women and the priest looked down at the baby in William's arms, his face burning.

Hearing the rumpus, the child's nurse, in a moment of uncharacteristic daring, rushed across to take Constance from William, but he pushed her roughly away.

'TAKE HIM, FATHER! IF THAT IS GOD'S WILL, THEN TAKE HIM!' William pointed across at Niall and the boy seemed to shrink away at the sudden attention.

Father Devereux was confused. 'The boy?' he asked in a whisper. 'Why should I take the boy?'

William's great shoulders started to heave then and the shaking soon gripped his entire frame so that when the nurse moved forward a second time she was easily able to take Constance from his arms. Huge tears poured from William's eyes and rolled down onto his cheeks. He made an attempt to speak but no words came and instead he ran from the room, cutting a wide pathway through the bunches of silent guests.

The room was quiet for what seemed an eternity and then O'Reilly, the local magistrate, lifted his glass in a toast and shouted drunkenly, 'Cheers!', which only he found amusing. But the ice was broken, for some of the younger men began sniggering at the man's lack of tact and the women fell to tutting again, registering their disapproval. When general conversation resumed, though, most were of the opinion that it had been well worth braving the rain after all to witness such a scandalous scene.

The doctor staggered forward to clap Father Devereux across the shoulder-blades as only a drunken Protestant would have dared. 'Take absolutely no notice, my boy!' he said cheerfully. 'The poor man is out of his wits with the grief. He should blame himself, though. I told him another would kill her.'

'He does not know what he is saying, then?' Father Devereux asked, still confused at William's outburst and shaken by so nearly being accused in public.

'It is my professional opinion that he does not, no!' the doctor said, shaking his head and almost losing his balance into the bargain.

Father Devereux looked hastily about the room. The guests had stopped staring and the incident did, indeed, seem to have been passed off. He breathed a deep and audible sigh of relief. His secret had been spared, then. William was merely confused and did not know what he was saying. The tray of drinks passed by and he took up a glass of whisky and threw it down his throat in one swallow.

'Well now, Father!' the doctor said, delighted. 'That drink found a welcome home for itself and no mistake!' He held his own half-full glass to the light and inspected the amber-coloured contents with a smile of satisfaction. 'You know, for all the jallop that I deal out during the day to those that are suffering, there's none so efficient at raising a smile and a twinkle of life to the eye as this pure Irish brew I have held here in my hand!' he announced.

Several men nearby laughed at this and Father Devereux grinned. The whisky felt good in his stomach. Surely if God had wanted him to give up the cloth He would have had him unmasked there and then, but He had not. That He had not was a sure sign to Father Devereux's mind that his calling was safe after all. Peace and warmth slipped through him like rich fire. He had stood near the brink, on the very precipice of discovery, and God had pulled him back and told him he was forgiven. His future secure then, Father Devereux turned to the doctor to listen with amusement and contentment to the tales with which he regaled his audience, righteousness suffusing his soul while the spirit of the whisky filled his veins.

CHAPTER TWENTY

'So how's this fine school of yours, then?' Cora asked when Niall returned home after his first term. 'Jesus, I can see they're giving you growing lessons there if nothing else!' She took him to the wall in the yard to see how he measured against the chalk marks. 'I'm sure you'll have grown half a yard since I last did you. Your blazer's looking a fit already and I thought it'd be a year or two before we could say that. What are they feeding you on, Niall? Elephant steaks and holy water, I should imagine!'

She pushed his cap off and placed the flat of her hand along the top of his head. 'Look!' she said. 'No, don't turn or you'll have chalk all over your bloomin' jacket, now. Stay still, that's the boy! See! You're to be the giant of the family all right. You're twice the height of Thomas at the same age! I thought you'd be the tadpole, Niall, but it seems I was wrong. Did you think about growing outwards too, though?' she asked, pulling at his belt. 'You're as skinny as a weed!'

Niall smiled and she caught him by the shoulders. 'Is the school all right then, Niall? I've had the devil of a time worrying about you, you know. Are you making your mark? Do you have a grand time with the other boys? Did you bite one of the old Jesuits for me yet? Do you get up to all sorts once the priests' backs are turned?'

Niall shrugged and kicked at the ground with the toe of his shoe.

'Aw come on and tell me!' Cora insisted. 'I'm not like Christina, I won't go blabbing to Papa, you know. Tell me all your stories, Niall, I've been dying back here to hear them!'

Niall took his cap from her hands and placed it carefully

back onto his head. 'They beat you,' he said, quietly.

'Beat you?' Cora laughed. 'Well they have to beat the bad boys, don't they? Or they'd end up with the Devil in them like Thomas! And look how bad I turned out because Papa never raised a hand to me! Don't you think I would have done better for the odd beating or two? Now tell me the rest, Niall, I want to hear it all.'

Niall shook his head, his eyes fixed on the ground. 'They have a paddle,' he said. 'Or the strap, which is worse. It's wood between leather and it can make you scream if you're out to appear a baby.'

'But that's if you're bad!' Cora insisted. She bent to face her brother. 'Were you ever bad, Niall?' she asked. 'Did they use the paddle on you?'

The child nodded and she whistled between her teeth.

'Holy Mother of God!' she said. 'So old Maidie's tales of the Jesuits were true. All that putting the fear of God into us when we were younger and I thought she was having us on all the time! All those nights when she said the Jesuits would creep out from under our beds and steal us away in the night if we didn't sleep! For God's sake behave yourself there, Niall! I don't want you coming home with your bones in plaster every term!'

Niall looked about the garden, anxious to change the subject.

'It smells funny here now,' he said.

Cora sighed. 'It's the apples. Papa left them to rot in the apple house after Francis left. It was the same with the stables, too. He sold half the horses for the devil of a low price and the rest would've starved if Maidie's young brother hadn't come in for nothing to care for them. They looked pitiful until then, Niall, it would've broke your heart to see them. When Francis comes back it will break his too, I don't doubt.'

'Did Francis not come back yet?'

'Not yet,' Cora told him as they set off to the cliffs. 'Papa says he will be back any day now, though you're not to mention it yourself for it makes him mad, I can tell you!'

'Everything makes Papa angry,' Niall said quietly and Cora bent to pull up a handful of long grass to throw at him. The dirt stuck to his face and she rushed over, suddenly concerned. She pulled a hankie from her pocket and spat into it to wash his face.

'We'll have a walk,' she said, 'but you're to stay smart. Papa has asked to see you in his study after the tea.'

Niall looked anxious again.

'Did you learn all you have to say at table?' she asked him.

He nodded. 'Take the food from our mouths blessed Father . . .' he began but Cora stopped him.

'I don't want to hear that old rubbish now,' she said. 'You can save his old prayers to bore us with over our tea. They're too stuffy for the garden, don't you think? Now you behave yourself tonight, Niall, and maybe Papa will let you off any more of that terrible old school of yours.'

She had promised him a walk and she started off but turned before they had gone a few paces. 'I wouldn't say anything to Papa about the beatings at the school, if I were you,' she said before flouncing off again.

They passed the machinery that Francis had talked his father into installing in the yard to crush oilcake for the cattle. It had been their brother's pride and joy though its constant whining hum had been an irritation to the cook, who had said she heard it from the kitchens and that it stopped her from thinking straight. It stood silent and rusted now and Cora pulled Niall away as he stood on tiptoe to stare at it.

'You'll get filth all over your clothes,' was all the comment she made.

They took the path to the sea. The walk took an age and Niall thought he would be an old man before they finally reached their destination. Cora stopped at every small stream to unbutton her boots and wade barefoot. On the opposite bank she made her brother wait again while she

dried her feet on her hankie and pulled her boots back on.
When he saw the sea again, though, he knew all the waiting
had been worth it. He stood at the top of the cliff, a slight
figure like a heron on skinny white legs, and felt the wind
blow across his face and scalp, tasting the salt on his teeth.
He dug his hands into his pockets although Cora shouted
to him to take care.

When he looked back she was laid out on the tufted grass
like a pile of fat brown rags, so he stole as close to the edge
as he dared and when he looked down to the sea he saw he
was higher than the gulls and the sight of the heaving water
excited him as it cracked across the black rocks below.

The wind was terrific. He held his thin arms out to his
sides and his jacket became a sail so that he felt himself
swayed on his feet and wondered if it could be strong
enough to blow him clean away. The tide was pulling out,
leaving thick heaps of shiny seaweed in its wake, and he
watched the gulls swoop onto it with cries like the scream
of a child.

He had never been down to the beach for he had been
told the climb was too steep. There were sandy indents in
the rock face to his right and he put his shoe upon the first
step then looked back to see if Cora watched him.

'You'll break your bloody neck, you idiot,' she said
lazily – she was propped on her elbows now, not missing a
trick.

'Can we go down a little?' Niall asked. A fresh gust of
wind caught him and he clutched at the long grasses with
his hands.

'You'll dirty yourself,' Cora said, but she was already on
her feet, sizing up the drop.

'I won't,' Niall promised. 'I can leave my blazer at the
top here.'

He folded his jacket into a neat square then set it on the
ground, Cora watching him as he carefully selected a large
stone to weight it down.

She put a hand to her eyes to shield them from the sun.

'Come on, then,' she said, and Niall felt joyous as he stretched to take her hand.

They reached a thin sand-rooted sward that overlooked the beach. Cora would go no further for she said she saw two men on the shoreline collecting seaweed for their potato-patches, and if the men saw them they'd be there all day listening to their talk. Instead she pulled Niall down to sit and as she did so he saw she crossed herself, which he thought strange. Then he noticed the small circle of stones to their left and the bunches of dead flowers dotted about them and Cora told him in a whisper that they were sitting beside a killeen where the unbaptized babies were buried.

Niall stared at the small sad graves and at the wind-whipped grasses that grew around them. 'Why aren't they buried beside other people?' he asked.

Cora pulled up a long blade of grass and chewed it between her teeth. 'Because they are unbaptized, you idiot,' she said. 'The dead would turn in their graves to have them next to them. They have to put them here. It's a shame the priest did not get to them all in time, then they could have been buried properly like our babies were.'

Niall stood up, eager now to leave. He shivered as though a cloud had passed across the sun, feeling black and depressed at the thought of all the lonely dead babies that lay beneath the dry sand.

'Can we get back?' he asked.

'First you couldn't wait to climb down here and now you're here you want to be off,' Cora tutted, brushing the sand off her skirt.

The two men had got nearer and Niall saw they pulled a small donkey between them. They wore tweed trousers and Tam o' Shanters and Niall stopped to wave at them. One of the men waved back.

'Can I see the baby when we get home?' Niall asked as they made their way to the house. Cora walked ahead, annoyed with him for wanting to leave so soon.

His one thought on returning home had been to see his

little sister and to marvel once again at her beauty. She seemed to him an enchanted thing like a faerie; the sort nurse had told them danced on the top of the stone gate piers at night.

He had been away from home for so many months that he feared she may have become ugly like the rest of them and he wanted badly to know that she still lay in her cot, as sweet as a little doll, her small head pressed into her pillow and her pink fingers clutching her quilt.

'Is she still pretty?' he asked Cora.

'More so, if anything. Too pretty for her own good, I suspect. You know the pretty ones get taken by the Shee and the weak little changelings are left in their place? One time we'll find an ugly skinny little thing like you were lying quiet in her cot to die instead. I know nurse watches all night by her bedside just in case, though exactly what she'd do if the Shee turned up, God alone knows. She's a fit of the vapours at the mention of the name!'

She stopped walking and turned to face him. 'I doubt if you'll see Constance, Niall,' she told her brother. 'Papa keeps her to him like a prize pet. I think perhaps he knows the sight of our ugly faces about her cot would be more than the poor thing could stand, being so exquisite herself.'

Niall grinned. 'She's too little,' he said. 'She can't tell who's ugly or not!'

'Shows how much you know, mister clever-sticks!' Cora placed her hands on her hips. 'Our Constance is a proper little lady I'll have you know and when she grows she'll be a *great* lady too, like our mama was once. Even now she would spot if you'd not combed your hair or had dirt under your nails as you do at this moment.' She pulled his hands out of his pockets and slapped his fingers when she saw them.

'Little as she is,' she went on, 'I'd swear she would know, Niall, so you'd better wash yourself and take your spectacles off if you see her or you'll frighten her to death.'

She pulled a watch from her pocket and raised her

eyebrows at the time. 'We'd best be back for tea. I don't want you late for Papa. You know how he'll be if he has to wait for you.'

William Flavelle did not appear at tea and the first time Niall saw him was when he arrived in his study that evening. Cora walked him to the door of the room and motioned to him to knock. She knew she was not to follow him inside and so dared to lean her head against the frame to listen instead. She soon became bored, though, for the wood was too thick and she could hear none of their words once Niall was inside.

The musty smell of the books that had once lined the room had lived on much longer than the tomes themselves and it mingled with ghosts of other comfortable smells like tobacco and wood polish and the smoke from the peat in the hearth. The illusion of comfort was confined to the one sense, though, for, as he stood before his father's desk, Niall felt more uncomfortable in every other respect than at any time before in his life.

It was the first time that he could remember his father ever paying him attention and he felt apprehension and dread mixed with a tremendous desire to please.

He looked up at the chair that stood behind the vast desk and realized with a new jolt of fear that it was empty.

'Are you prepared to repent your sins, Niall?' A voice came from behind him and fear almost made him lose control of his bladder. He did not dare turn to look his father in the eye and his bare knees shook so hard his grey knitted socks slipped a few inches further down his legs.

He could not begin to speak. He did not know what answer he should give and, if he had, his voice would have failed him. His father walked slowly into his line of sight, carrying the great heavy Bible open in his hands. There was a cloth-covered reading-table behind the desk and he placed the book carefully upon this, smoothing the open pages with the flat of his hand before turning his terrible gaze upon his son.

'Did you make your confession at school?' he asked. His nostrils were like great dark caverns to the small boy, and his beard and his eyes looked blacker than hell.

'Yes, Papa.' Niall's voice was little more than a whisper.

'Regularly?' William asked, and his son nodded once again, staring at the small cap held between his hands.

William clasped his hands before him. 'And were the Jesuits pleased with your confessions, Niall? Did you confess to every sin? Did you miss none of them? None at all?'

Niall searched desperately for the correct answer that would please his father. Had the Jesuits suspected him of more sins than he admitted and contacted his father to complain? He had told everything, he was sure, but perhaps they still suspected more. Niall's head felt hot, as though he had a fever.

'Read from this,' William said when he did not answer, and moved from the table to take his seat behind his desk.

Niall walked to the Bible and looked across its pages at the back of his father's dark head. He was nearly too small to reach the book and almost wept with fear at not being able to do his father's bidding. Then, with relief, he saw the sheets of hand-written paper that William had placed across the pages and stood on tiptoe to read from them.

The room was dark and the handwriting unclear but he saw his father was waiting and so started as best he could.

'I looked into the sinner's eyes,' he began, 'and I saw the Devil hiding there. For what is a man but the receptacle of his soul, and what is that soul if it be given over to evil?'

There was more, much more, and Niall was left to struggle over every long, unpronounceable word. Twice during the reading he broke down in tears for the text was too difficult for him and he thought that he would never finish. His father sat in silence as he cried, though, and did not move at all to help him.

By the time he was finished his forehead was beaded with sweat and his hands so damp they were stuck to the Bible's leather binding.

He waited, shaking, as his father slowly turned to face him.

'Did you understand those words, Niall?' William asked his son.

'Yes, Papa,' Niall lied.

'Every one?'

'Yes, Papa.'

'They are good words, Niall,' William told him, standing to indicate their meeting was at an end.

'Good words and honest words,' he said, opening the door. 'You will learn them by heart before you return to your school.'

CHAPTER TWENTY-ONE

1911

Dark mosses grew over Sophia's headstone and visits to her grave grew fewer, though fresh lilac was placed there every week in summer and evergreen branches when the weather turned chill. She lay between her parents and her children and did not return to haunt her lover, the priest, even though he never once visited her grave to lay flowers by her stone. He made a point of taking the longer route to the house to avoid passing the graves altogether.

William became Sophia's only constant mourner, arriving each morning as the sun's weak rays cut their first pale swathes through the trees, speaking to her in death as he had been unable to speak to her in life.

It was at Sophia's graveside that William professed his love for his wife at last, now that her ears were closed by death and no longer able to hear his words. Now her flesh was rotted he told her of her magnificent beauty and, her eyes forever closed, he begged her to see him and to forgive him.

He read the lies carved into her tombstone and soon those lies became a sacred and sacrosanct truth. 'Adored wife ... devoted, beloved mother.' The mosses had laid claim to the rest of the stone and tentacles of ivy fingered each remaining word. William had clawed it away with his bare hands to read the rest, leaving the stone stained green. 'Loyal and dutiful ...' it went on, 'virtuous and devout ...' The weeds had not been allowed to spin their web of shame about such deceit.

'I forgive you, Sophia,' he would cry as he stood there alone. 'You were as pure in your innocence as a child. It was not your fault that you were so tempted by the Devil.

147

You were weak and I should have been there to save you as I had been so many times before. Rest in peace, Sophia, for God forgives you, too.'

He forgave his dead wife her imagined sins and was forced to welcome the priest to his house, for who was he to revile a man of God? It was the boy that William could not forgive for he was the living embodiment of their guilt. Without him the sin could perhaps have been forgotten or ignored, but instead this wicked fruit of their union lived on as a constant reminder.

It was Constance who was to become William's salvation in life as in her he saw still the proof that God was all-seeing and all-forgiving. She was a miracle and a gift to him for all that he had had to suffer in the past. She was as beautiful as she was perfect and he thanked God daily for blessing his life with such a prize.

Two nurses had been dismissed in quick succession for daring to correct her; one for speaking sharply when she refused to eat her food and the other for taking her pram around the demesne when it was obvious to William that Constance had no desire to make such a journey when the sky was full of snow.

A girl from the clachan was finally found who was patient and indulgent, so over-awed by her tiny charge as to pander to her every whim. Even so it was fortunate that Constance had a good enough disposition for William was apt to blame the girl every time he heard the baby cry.

By day her cradle would be placed in William's study, near the fire, so that he could watch her as he worked. Never before had he paid so much attention to a child and never before had he lavished so much affection on another being.

When she became old enough to walk a few steps he had a small pen built so that she could totter about in complete safety. Her first word was 'Papa' and her first gift a tiny white kid-bound Bible. When she cried in his study William would quiet her by reading to her from Psalms.

'Thou art fairer than the children of men,' he would read.

148

'Grace is poured into thy lips; therefore God hath blessed thee forever.' And Constance would become quiet again as he read, which gave William unmeasurable pleasure.

The other children rarely saw their younger sister although Niall was the only one to be truly troubled by that fact. Thomas and Cora were pleased that their father paid them less attention as it gave them more freedom than they had had before in their lives. Thomas took up smoking cigars wherever he chose and his wardrobe became more dapper than usual.

Cora maintained that he courted three girls at once: one girl she considered common lived in the clachan and wore the red skirts and plaid wool shawl typical of peasant women; the other two were more refined, sisters on a visit from the college in Clifden. Thomas kept his silence about all three girls though, despite Cora's constant teasing.

Cora herself had no beaux to boast about and she and Christina were early consigned to old-maid status. Their standing in the community deterred any local lads from making their acquaintance, whilst their plain features and eccentric manner put paid to any young men from further afield.

Cora had a dream that her forays into town to take Niall to tea when he returned from school would lead to her meeting a handsome and well-mannered gentleman who would have an instant passion for her. Her eyes would therefore scour every shop and tea-room and tramcar that they entered, in the hope that just such a man would be present. Her plan was to appeal to this eligible man to rescue her from her dreary fate but no such knight appeared to take up the challenge and she became increasingly bitter.

What was denied her in life became known to her in print. She took to reading with a voracious appetite once her father no longer took an interest in what she read. Novels of unrequited love and passion were devoured nightly in her room until her eyes became too weak to read by candlelight

149

and then, if Niall were home, she would call upon him to read aloud to her instead.

Christina was more private in her passion. Her childhood vision had been the greatest turning point in her life and she had built a grotto in the demesne to mark that conversion. What had begun as a small rockery of stones had become something much grander. She would spend most of her days clambering over the rocks to polish and whitewash them and to paint and repaint the plaster statues of the saints that she had collected together.

They stood in a crazily-tilted half-circle, looking for all the world like a group of gaudy farm-folk stopped to pass the time of day upon the slope. On closer inspection the placidly-fixed expressions became visible, together with the biblical tracts that were painstakingly painted onto the stones about their feet. Christina spent much of her day at those rocks, searching the skies and waiting for a second sight of the angels that had so inspired her.

Her heart had long ago been secretly pledged to her handsome young priest, Father Devereux, and she bore her silent sufferings of this unrequited love with all the brave discretion of the holy saints and martyrs. She made it her duty to see to his well-being in life and duly spent many hours on her knees at her grotto, praying for his safety and salvation.

Visitors to the house were rare, and the two women were forced to seek companionship in one another's company. They were forever fighting and arguing but knew they had little choice but to spend their time together.

Francis was never spoken of; his room was kept as it had been left and his jobs on the small farm were done only at the whim of Maidie's younger brother. William behaved as though he were expected home at any time, having his place laid at supper every evening and even sending Thomas from the room when he dared to sit in his seat.

Niall's holidays from school would always follow the same routine; on his first evening home he would be taken to his father's study where he would be questioned about his school work and made to read passages from the Bible.

He was forbidden to see Constance, for fear, William said, of contamination, and allowed to visit his mother's grave only when either Christina or Thomas were available to accompany him. On two occasions Cora took him into the gardens when Constance was playing there and she let him watch her but only when William was away from the house.

He became quieter and more introverted with every term at the school although it seemed to be only Cora who either noticed or cared. Sometimes he would mention the name of a boy from his class but Cora had the impression that he was as lonely and isolated at his school as he was at his home.

'If you grow big enough you'll be able to show those old Jesuits what for!' she would tell him, and it was as though he took notice of her for he continued to grow at an alarming rate, but showed little sign of filling out his frame. His shoulders became wider and his hair darker, more like his father's in its thickness and colour. His shyness made him stoop though, so that Cora would nag at him to hold his height well and to walk like a gentleman.

'Look at our Thomas now!' she would tell him. 'He's a spine as straight as a stick! It makes him look an honest, open man and that makes other men admire him. Curled up like you are you look a proper wet and a coward, so no wonder you get all the beatings!' And so Niall tried, for his sister's sake at least, to walk in a straight and proud way or, he was told, Constance would be ashamed of him when she became such a great lady.

They were sitting in the dining-room the following year, Thomas teaching Niall to smoke cigars like a man while Niall choked on the sickening, thick smoke he had inhaled, when their father arrived and announced he would be hosting a party.

151

His four eldest children sat silent in their chairs at this news, immobilized with the shock. Thomas had barely time to fan smoke away from the table but the news stopped him in an instant and he sat staring, as startled as his siblings.

'A party!' Cora whispered, instantly transported to the world of her imagination where dashing young men queued for hours to fill her dance card.

Christina opened her mouth to speak but a fierce volley of blinks and twitches distorted her features before she could get the words out.

William appeared unwilling to say more on the matter and they had to sit and watch him eat his meal before wiping his mouth with his napkin to continue.

'It is Constance's eighth birthday this year,' he told them. 'I believe her mother had her first taste of society at that age and I intend the same for her.'

Christina and Cora looked stunned. There had been no parties for them, not even to announce a coming-out. Now their sister was to come out at the tender age of eight. The idea was preposterous but neither sister dared voice an opinion. Instead it was Thomas who spoke.

'And will there be some young gentlemen invited to keep our sister company?' he asked. 'There must be some we could ask to ensure she has sufficient partners for the dancefloor!' He laughed at his own joke but the others watched him in silence.

William was out of his seat and around the table in an instant and had struck his son a heavy blow about the face before the smile was gone from his lips.

Thomas rocked in his chair from the shock but recovered quickly enough to jump from his seat and square up to his father. The two men were nearly the same height, though William was the more solid, with fists the size of bread-plates. There was a terrible moment as the two men glared and the sisters clutched one another, screaming in fear.

'Silence!' William roared, turning his back on his son.

When they were able to sit quietly he turned to face Thomas once again.

'If I hear you utter one more filthy word like that about your sister I will throw you out of this house as empty-handed as I did your brother!' he shouted, his head shaking with rage.

'It was a joke, Father,' Thomas said, as calmly as he could manage. 'I didn't mean anything by it.' The mark of his father's blow was still clearly printed upon his cheek.

'Then your jokes are in bad taste!' William straightened his jacket and smoothed his hair with his hand. He stared at his son and Thomas raised his arms in a gesture of submission.

'I apologize,' he said. 'I did not intend to be insulting. I just thought that our sister might be a bit young to appreciate an adult party, that's all. I meant no harm. You saw things in my words that were never there.'

Christina and Cora looked pleadingly at their father for the thought had occurred to them that he might be sufficiently angered to cancel the party altogether. If there was one thing worse than that their younger sister should be treated to a party when they had not, it was the idea that the party should not take place at all. The thought was unbearable to them. They could not speak, they could only clutch one another and use their eyes to plead silently. Cries of fear at the fight turned to sobs of despair in their throats. They even looked at Thomas with hatred in their eyes. How dare he upset their papa at such a treasured moment in their lives? How could he have jeopardized their only chance of happiness? They no longer cared about the reason for the party, nor how unjust that reason might be. They only cared that the party be held at all. And it was this sense of desperation that drove Christina to tell the first lie of her life.

'Constance will have her heart set on the party by now,' she told her brother. 'And, besides, there is nothing strange in the idea. I have read that in London children as young

153

as five are allowed their own society parties as long as they are capable of presenting themselves in an adult manner, which Constance surely is. She dances like an angel and plays the piano almost as well as did dear Mama. It would be a crying shame to keep her back a few more years because of the dictates of convention. And she's such a beauty, too,' she added as no one had contradicted her. 'If Mama was allowed parties I don't see why she can't.'

Thomas took his seat again and Cora gazed at her sister in disbelief at her cunning. It was the only time in her life that she was to feel respect for Christina and she found herself nodding quickly to show her approval at her words.

William stood stroking his beard. He did not want the party now. His son's words had filled him with horror at the thought that it might be a forerunner of the day when Constance first stepped into the world to choose a husband of her own. The thought had not occurred to him before and now it filled him with dread.

It was Constance who had wanted the party, though, and he had been fool enough to indulge her. He could imagine the scenes if he attempted to tell her it had been cancelled, after all. It had been her first request when he had asked her what she would like for her birthday and he knew he could not deny her, not now that the promise had been made.

He looked about the table. Thomas's head was sunk into his shoulders but Cora and Christina sat as eager-eyed as puppies. Niall sat quietly in his seat, for once not the main protagonist, his eyes, though, fixed firmly on his brother's smarting face.

'I see only lies and deception about this table today!' William shouted. 'Cora!' His daughter jumped from her seat. 'Fetch me the Bible!'

Cora ran across the room and fetched the heavy book from the sideboard. It was difficult for her to lift and as she struggled with it its pages fell open sending a handful of markers fluttering to the floor. Thomas leapt to help her but

William grabbed his son by the arm and pulled him back into his chair.

William took the Bible from his daughter and then slammed it down on the table in front of Niall.

'Saint Luke: Eleven,' he said and there was a quiet rustling as Niall searched for the page. When it was found William ran a hand across the page and pressed the tip of his index finger onto the passage that was to be read.

'The light of thine body is the eye,' Niall read in a whisper.

'Louder!' William ordered.

Niall lifted his head to look his father direct in the eye and held his gaze for the rest of the passage for he had it to memory and did not need to refer again to the page.

'Therefore when thine eye is single, thy whole body also is full of light,' he recited, 'but when thine eye is evil thy body also is full of darkness.' He continued to stare at his father and it was William who first looked away.

'Shameless, corrupt and malevolent!' William said quietly with fear in his eyes. 'The Jesuits have done nothing for your soul, boy, I can tell that now.'

He looked down at Niall's hand on his Bible and pulled the book from him, slamming its pages shut so quickly that dust flew into the air and his fingers were almost trapped.

Niall's eyes still did not leave his father's face. William raised a hand as if to strike him as he had struck his other son.

'Niall!' Cora cried in panic, but the boy refused to avert his gaze.

'Take heed therefore that the light which is in thee be not darkness,' he said, continuing the quote quietly.

William rose from his seat so quickly that his chair tumbled to the floor behind him. 'Blasphemer!' he cried, lifting the Bible above his head in rage.

Cora's hand flew to her mouth but Niall did not move. Maidie appeared in the doorway to clear the plates and, seeing the scene before her, let out a little cry and backed quickly out of the room, her tray banging the door and chipping a few flakes of paint onto the floor as she reversed.

The noise seemed to jolt William into sense and he slowly let the Bible drop, then followed the maid from the room. Once he had gone it was Thomas who jumped from his seat to congratulate his brother.

'Well done, Niall!' he said, clapping the boy across the shoulders. He took the brandy decanter from the sideboard and poured some of the liquid into a glass. 'Here,' he said, offering it to his brother, 'hold your nose and slug this back. It'll do you good; no, don't sip it, throw it down your throat. It'll choke you at first but you'll feel better after, I promise.'

Niall gulped the drink and then started to cough, his eyes watering more than they had after the cigar.

Christina tutted. 'Do you want the boy to end up like Francis?' she asked.

'Are you saying you know how Francis has ended up, Christina?' Thomas asked.

'Of course I don't!' she retorted.

'Do you think he's drunk his way to Dublin by now?' Cora asked.

'More like slumped in some barn or other if he's found a farmer who'll take pity on him,' Christina remarked.

Thomas leant across the table, angry again. 'Now who's to say he's not made his fortune by now and has his pockets stuffed with cash? He's more guts than the rest of us, that much I know at least! I don't know how you have the nerve to mock him, Christina. At least he's away from this house, which takes more courage than you or I have. We should all be away from here but we don't have Francis's nerve, that's all, so we'll live here till we rot, I suppose. Niall was the only one with the guts to stand up to the old man and he nearly got a pasting like me for his troubles!'

'We'll leave when we marry!' Cora said.

Thomas turned to look at her with an expression of pity on his face. 'And when might that be, darling?' he asked. 'When the pigs learn to fly or when hell freezes over? I'm sorry, Cora, but you must see the truth for what it is, not imagine the sort of romantic rubbish those old books of yours are full of.

'How old are you two now? Twenty-five and twenty-eight? There's girls in the village that have a marriage and nine children by the time they're your age. And you two have not had as much as one suitor between you.

'Did you think Papa would allow you to marry once Mama was gone? He wants you here; he wants us all here, Cora, with the exception of young Niall there and God alone knows what it was he did to offend him so much!'

'You could bring some of your men friends home to meet us!' Cora cried. 'It's Papa's fault that we haven't married, he never allows us parties and balls. This one for Constance will be the first we have had here and I dare say he won't pay for new clothes for the evening so we'll end up in our old stuff. Did you know other women in our position change their outfits as much as ten times a day? I don't have that many dresses in a week, that's my trouble!'

Thomas looked across the table at his two sisters and he saw two plain-faced women with few, if any, of the qualities that might commend them to a potential husband. Christina was an ugly thing with her pinched little face ruddied from standing at her grotto in all weathers. Her features danced continually, her hair was severe and her clothes out-of-date. She tried hard to be as devout as her father but even a young William Flavelle would have found her a daunting prospect as a wife.

Cora had more life to her but she still had the look of an old maid.

'A lot of girls marry their brother's friends,' she said. 'It's an acceptable form of introduction and I'm sure Papa would not object.'

Thomas studied the tablecloth carefully, feeling suddenly rather depressed. He wished he had not brought up the subject of marriage at all.

'Oh, you'd find my friends really rather rough, Cora,' he said. 'They're not at all the sort a man would bring home for his sister. I'm sure you could both do far better for yourselves. Perhaps you'll meet someone at Constance's party.'

Cora opened her mouth to disagree but Thomas was quick to stop her.

'Besides,' he said, 'there's been no party of that sort in this area for years. The men will be falling over themselves for an invite. You'll probably have your pick, you know. You'd do much better than with my lot.'

'Can you imagine who Papa will be inviting?' Cora said quietly. 'Especially after what you said to him just now. He'll have no one under eighty, you can be assured of that!'

Thomas laughed. 'There'll be Christina's handsome young priest!' he said. 'You won't find many men better looking than Father Devereux. I know he won't do for a husband but I'm sure he'll take a turn about the floor and you can always close your eyes and pretend while he has you in his arms, Christina.'

Christina's face reddened, which prompted her sister to join in the teasing.

'Priests can't dance!' she said. 'Why there'd be a right holy commotion if Father Devereux was caught jigging about on the floor with Christina held in his arms! You could just see him with his black skirts flying!' She laughed, rising from her seat and spinning about the room so quickly that her own skirt flew out and pins fell from her hair.

'You should not mock the Father!' Christina shouted so loudly that Cora stopped at once, red-faced and panting. Christina stood beside her chair, staring at the others and trembling with anger. Her eyes blinked wildly behind their gold-wire frames. 'Besides,' she said when her temper had calmed, 'I dare say Papa will cancel the whole event now that Thomas has opened his mouth.'

'No,' Niall said suddenly and they turned to him in surprise – he had been so quiet since their father had left the room. The brandy had made him lightheaded and his cheeks were red, his eyes bright as buttons. 'Could you see him

158

telling Constance it is cancelled?' he asked. 'Could you see him disappointing her?'

He sat so solemnly in his chair that he suddenly looked older than his fourteen years and Cora leant across to pat him on the arm.

'Do you know, I believe the drunken young rascal's right!' she said. 'Papa would not risk upsetting our sister and I believe by his face just now that he had promised her the party already.'

'You see?' Thomas said, smiling. 'There's no harm done, Christina, whatever I said. And thank you, Niall,' he bowed to his brother, 'for introducing a note of manly sense into this hysterical scene.'

He raised his brandy glass in a toast and clapped his free hand to his chest. 'To the party!' he cried and downed his drink in one.

CHAPTER TWENTY-TWO

The chill night air was full of the scent of wild heather as the carts and carriages pulled between the great white-painted gate piers and into the demesne onto the overgrown road that would take them to the house.

Father Devereux stepped into the glowing hall and found the perfume inside the house was man-made rather than natural; women's colognes, camphor, cachous and hair-oil all lay in the air mingling with the more normal aromas of warm flesh perspiring in the heat of the fire and dripping candle-wax.

There was much commotion and noise in the hall behind him as the local folk arrived all at once, for the invites had said six and they had no notion of etiquette, which would decree that a late arrival is the grandest of entrances. They had come in a racing of carriages for fear of being last and missing some of the fun, much preferring to stand wedged in the hall than to miss any of the food laid out upon the tables.

Once their coats and hats were shed the men stood about rubbing their hands to show they were ready for their drink. It was left to the women to signal their lack of manners with a tap on the arm with a fan or a series of sharp looks that led to much good-natured grumbling.

Cora had been right in her assessment of the guests' ages. As the priest looked around he noted that most of them were, if not over eighty, then at least beyond forty, and a strange lot they looked as well; all herded together like cows for the milking, showing yards of bleached and yellowing flesh that had not seen the light of day for many years past, with their creased old dresses just out of brown tissue and their ill-fitting suits that retained the impressions of their coat-hangers.

Everywhere were smiling, lined faces and worn starched-stiff collars. Fingers bent with arthritis fussed nervously over clasps and buttons to check that all were secure. Feathers, their spines cracked with age, moulted until the floor underfoot took on the look of the bottom of a cage of exotic dying birds.

Christina had affixed herself to the priest's elbow from the moment he arrived and she would not be budged, no matter how he tried to shake her off. It was not that he wished to offend the girl, who was looking more plain than normal in an unflattering gown of sugar-pink brocade, but he was embarrassed by the way that she would peer up at him with such devotion in her eyes that he was sure all the other guests must notice.

It was in the midst of this gathering of ancients that Constance arrived to greet her guests shyly, stepping carefully down each stair of the wide stone staircase, holding her long skirt to one side and the banister with her free hand. Her skin was as pale as marble and her expression solemn, to suit the grand occasion, and her long auburn hair had been curled and pinned about her small head.

'Mama's dress!' Christina exclaimed when she saw her. 'He has had Mama's dress made for her!'

Father Devereux looked up and felt his heart stop. It was the dress from the portrait that she wore; perfectly reproduced but in a child's size. The deep red velvet chemise fitted perfectly about Constance's small waist and the long skirt billowed around her, giving her all the solemn poise of a twenty-year-old woman.

'Are you all right, Father?' the priest heard Christina ask. 'Would you like me to fetch you a glass of water, or some champagne?'

'No,' he was able to mutter. 'No . . . thank you.'

There was so much about Constance to remind him of her mother, and in that one moment he missed Sophia in a way that he would never have thought possible. His face went from pallid to bright red. He could not stop staring at the girl, though he was aware how he must look.

'Does she know?' he heard himself ask Christina. 'Has she seen her mother's portrait?'

Christina shrugged. 'Of course not,' she told him. 'Do you think I should tell her, though, Father? Everyone else must know.'

Father Devereux grabbed the girl quickly by the arm. 'Don't say anything,' he said quietly. 'It might upset her. It may spoil her big day.'

As Constance reached the bottom step she smiled charmingly about her. All the guests smiled back, and some clapped their hands; she looked so lovely that a few actually cried.

It was astounding, they said later, how she had learnt each guest's name. Not only their names, for William had forced into her head all their business as well and had taught her to enquire politely about the health of their offspring or their livestock with genuine concern. Yet all the time her bright eyes scoured the room for a sight of her brother Niall, who she had been praying would be allowed to be there. She had rarely seen him and so she was fascinated by him. In her mind he had become a heroic figure, turned away from his home and only able to visit at her Papa's discretion.

Every guest who entered the house that night would pause to marvel at William's apparent and uncommon extravagance. Chandeliers had been lit and curtains replaced in every room. Furniture that had been in store for years had been brought out and polished up to look like new and french windows had been flung back to provide access to the sloping gardens that stood below. All the lawns had been lit with tapers to give an eerie yellow glow and there were garlands of sweet-smelling elderflower strung about the entire house.

Constance's gown had been ordered from Dublin and so taken had she been with it that she had begged her papa to

162

order dresses for her sisters as well. She would refuse, she said, to be attired in the finest stuff if they were to wear only their old things. And so Cora and Christina were turned out in palest pink trimmed with tiny white daisies and stiffened organdie. She had wished to transform them in the way that she had seen herself transformed when she had first tried on her gown and looked at herself in the mirror, but instead she had consigned her sisters to the most ghastly of fates for, though they looked splendidly pretty in Constance's eyes, their sweet dresses made them appear sallow and ugly.

'She is so like Sophia!' William heard all his guests whisper and his lungs nearly burst from being so puffed with pride. He watched her in the hallway and he would have caught her up into his arms had she not looked so much the lady.

She *was* like her mother; their beauty was the same although their features differed. She had her mother's freckles; a fine dusting of palest gold across her nose and her back and her slender young arms. Unlike her mother, though, Constance's beauty was no mere illusion, her features were perfect and could brave the closest scrutiny. Her eyes were large and palest blue, her lashes long, like a doll's. Her nose was slim but not as long as her mother's had been; her lips were pinker and more clearly defined.

She had inherited none of her mother's languor, either, and danced about with the excitement of the occasion whenever her dress permitted. She was quiet enough to be thoughtful but she managed to appear vivacious as well, looking about with delight at all the sights and sounds of the newly-decorated house.

'Won't you go into the ballroom?' Thomas asked each visitor once Maidie had seen them out of their coats and they had a full glass in their hands. He knew full well there was no such room in the house, for the ballroom had long since been converted into a dining- and smoking-room, but they had a large room put aside for the dancing and some

163

boys from Galway had been paid well to provide the music. They were waiting in the room now, in their ill-fitting dress suits that had been hired for the occasion, putting down glasses of beer and trying to make the most of Sophia's untuned piano before the guests arrived and they were called upon to play.

In the old smoking-room a table had been laid with Henrietta's finest linen and then covered every inch with food that had taken two days to prepare. At the centre lay two trout, so huge that their tails overhung the great plate they were laid upon, their dull dead eyes surveying the dark ringed stains above the gas-lamps on the ceiling. Cucumber slices lay curling around them in the heat and beside them stood the magnificent shining domed peaks of jellies and rice-moulds, their gleaming towers quivering with pride as each guest strode across to admire them.

The guests congregated hungrily about the banquet but their host seemed reluctant to give the order to eat. The men tugged at the ends of their waxed moustaches as their eyes took in the sight of the boiled hams and the accompanying bowls of cold pickles. Conversation ebbed as the aroma of warm cheese pastry and freshly-baked rolls filled the air but the command was not given and the guests became anxious.

'We are not all present yet,' William announced and everyone looked about, wondering who it was that kept them from their food. A quick check revealed that all the decent folk from the county were present. Iced punch was served and the guests took their cups gratefully, draining them quickly and then chewing on the fruit inside to silence their groaning stomachs.

'I believe we may await the arrival of the Holy Ghost himself!' the doctor was heard to whisper and guests nearby laughed more loudly than they should have for the spirit in the punch had settled badly on their empty stomachs.

'Do you have any idea who this mystery guest is, Father?' he asked, moving across to the priest. 'It's a quarter past eight now and I fear we'll all be laid out on the floor if he does not serve some food to mop up all the alcohol and gastric juices that our stomachs are drowning in.'

Father Devereux looked to Doctor O'Sullivan like a man aroused from a dream. 'I've no idea who it can be,' he said quietly, and with apparent disinterest.

'I quizzed Christina but she seems as ignorant as the rest of us,' the doctor told him. 'It's a wonder you get any word out of that poor girl yourself, Father,' he added, watching Christina from a distance as she fussed her way quietly about the room, smoothing tablecloths and straightening rugs with the toe of her shoe. 'You do know she's a thing about you, don't you?' he added slyly, looking from the corner of his eye.

'Don't talk nonsense, man!' Father Devereux said, taking notice at last.

'Oh, it's true, poor thing!' the doctor told him. 'You only need eyes to see what's plain in front of your face, Father. But don't tell me you're surprised. A good-looking man like yourself must have had hundreds of poor women making cow-eyes at you. It must come with the job, surely! We all want what we can't have, Father, and that job of yours must put you in a class of your own with the women. You must have a hell of a job keeping them at bay! It's only to be expected with some of them, though,' he added, nodding towards Christina, 'when the only men that girl's likely to see from one day's end to the next are her father and her brothers.

'Did I tell you the figures I read on incest just this last week, Father?' he continued. 'Do you know the estimated percentage of incidents in a small backwater like this one?'

Father Devereux raised a hand quickly to stop him. 'I hardly think . . .' he began, hoping desperately to stop the man's flow as William Flavelle had returned to the room and was walking in their direction.

'Oh it's more common than you'd imagine!' the doctor went on, warming to his theme. 'Or perhaps you are aware after all, Father, for you must hear tales to make your hair curl in that confession box of yours, eh? Would a man be possessed enough to confess a crime as grave as that to his priest though, I wonder?'

William Flavelle was at his elbow now and a deep frown had cut into his forehead.

'Could you ever imagine telling such a thing to any living soul?' the doctor asked. 'And then to expect your God to let you off with a few Hail Marys! Now that's the joke of it, Father, you have to admit! What a wonderful vanishing act after all! A few magic words and your sins disappear and you are as blameless and innocent as the day you were born! It's like wiping chalk from a blackboard, don't you think? Free to return to the bosom of your family and sin again as you like.

'What poor poor creatures those wives and daughters must be, Father Devereux, to be sinned against until all eternity and no one to turn to with your finger of guilt. What a wonderful religion, to be sure!'

Father Devereux attempted a stern expression to impress his host but William's presence inhibited him and he found himself deliberating before attacking the doctor over his words.

'Well then, Father!' the doctor said, drunkenly. 'I'll take your silence as an admission of defeat! You've no argument against me at last and, if you're half the man I think you are, you'll admit it!'

The doctor laughed but he laughed alone. Father Devereux turned to study his host's face. William looked troubled. How much had he heard of the doctor's monologue? He waited for the man's temper to rise but a commotion in the hall provided a timely diversion.

'Perhaps you would like to discuss the vagaries of our religion with the bishop, Doctor, if you feel Father Devereux is not up to the confrontation?' William said. There was a smile on his lips as he spoke.

'The bishop?' the doctor cried. 'So there's your esteemed

guest at last, William. Praise to God that he's here and now we can eat!'

William took the doctor's arm to lead him to the new guest but the doctor moved smartly out of arm's reach. 'Oh no!' he said. 'I could never meet a bishop on an empty stomach! I know when I'm outclassed all right; leave me to chew the fat with our priest here, for he takes my drunken hectoring in good part. He's still too young and too polite to call me an old fool, I believe. You can keep your bishops for the time being, William, but lead me to the cold cuts before I die of hunger!'

William was still smiling as he left them to welcome his guest. The elderly bishop was led about the room by his host, smiling at some of the guests and stopping to be introduced to others. If he appeared less grand than expected then the party he arrived with more than made up the deficit.

Behind him and around him, slowly removing their gloves as they surveyed the rest of the room with expressions bordering on distaste, stood an elegant middle-aged couple, a younger, haughty-faced woman, three younger girls all dressed in identical fashions and a young and very bored-looking man.

The sudden appearance of such a group in a room filled with so many creaking, over-stuffed bodices and mouldstained suits had an instant and devastating effect. All conversation ceased abruptly, much to William's embarrassment, and the music died with the sounds of speech, for the musicians were as inquisitive as the next man and had laid down their instruments to take a better look. The only sound in the large and echoing hall was the ticking of the clock on the mantel and the only movement the relentless swing of its heavy brass pendulum.

William Flavelle seemed seized with an agony of indecision. Should he continue to escort the bishop and, in doing so, turn his back on the grand-looking group? His eyes cast about for little Constance but she had abandoned her post for the moment to pet an old lady's dog and to fetch it water as its mistress claimed it suffered dehydration in the warmth of the room.

In the moment of silence the bishop cast his eye about the room and spotted Father Devereux standing with his flock.

'Father!' the old man cried and motioned for the young priest to join him. The two men shook hands warmly and William was forgotten for a moment and free to tend to his other guests.

'We'll talk later, Father!' the bishop said to the priest. 'But first I must introduce you to some new friends of mine; more than friends, Father,' he added, smiling warmly, 'veritable samaritans, in fact!' He led the priest across towards the party that had arrived with him.

'These good people here took it upon themselves to share their carriage with me when my own, alas, had failed me.' He shook his head at the couple beside him and they smiled graciously to show they shared his joke.

'Father Devereux . . .' the bishop said, waving a hand, 'may I introduce Mister Robert Westerham and his wife . . .' The pair extended cool hands and Father Devereux offered his own with a warm smile of welcome.

'And Miss Catherine Lloyd, Missus Westerham's sister,' he continued and the younger woman stepped forward.

'Lloyd?' Father Devereux asked.

The young woman smiled. 'I see you recognize the name,' she said with an English accent.

'We are cousins of Sophia Flavelle,' her sister told him. 'Lloyd was her mother's maiden name. Her mother Henrietta was our father's youngest sister. This is our son, Alexander,' she said, 'and these are our three girls.'

The young man came forward reluctantly to take Father Devereux's hand and the three girls threw brief bobbing curtsies but remained in the background.

'I was named after the Greek emperor,' the young man told him. 'My namesake conquered half the world. I expect Mama assumes the same fate for me. I told her it is a ponderous burden for any young man to live with.' He smiled at that and his face became charming, losing all of its sulkiness.

'Alexander is in Ireland to complete his education, Father,' Missus Westerham told him. 'We were here to pay him a visit and then we received William's invitation . . . '

'You have never been to Ireland before, then?' Father Devereux asked.

'Once,' the woman told him. 'Many years before when Catherine and I were small children. We came to this house, Father Devereux, on the occasion of our poor cousin's birthday, but that was the only time. Our father moved back to London as a young man and lived there the rest of his life. I was pleased for Alexander to visit, though, to see where our cousin was born.'

Father Devereux smiled. 'And what do you think of us, then, Mister Westerham?' he asked her son.

Alexander rolled his eyes. 'If I could see you through the rain I might tell you!' he said. 'I believe my only sight of Dublin has been from beneath the brim of my ancient sou'wester. This must be the driest part of the country; or do you stop the rain for birthdays and bank holidays, Father?'

The Westerham clan burst out laughing at that and none laughed louder than young Alexander himself. Once the laughing had stopped his mother sought out William and took him by the arm. 'I am hoping Alexander will be welcome to spend a few weeks here, William,' she said. 'He has inherited a weak chest from his father's side of the family and the doctors in London say the sea air will do him good. Could you bear to put up with him, William?' she asked charmingly, watching her son with doting eyes. 'I am sure he will have the colour back into his cheeks within weeks.'

William looked shocked but the bishop cut in before he could speak.

'The air here is the best in all the world, Missus Westerham!' he said, inhaling deeply as though to make his point felt. 'Is that not so, William?'

'Then that's settled then!' Missus Westerham said. 'And Alexander will provide some company for your own children, William,' she added, looking about the room with a disapproving eye. 'They must be rather isolated here I should think. Very little company of their own age? Alexander is nineteen. You have boys I believe, don't you?'

'William has two strapping sons, so I hear!' the bishop said. 'And three lovely daughters; where is the little angel whose birthday we are here to celebrate?' he asked, looking about.

William called Constance's name and she appeared at his side at once, smiling shyly as she was introduced to the waiting party.

'What a delightful child!' the bishop exclaimed. 'Come, my dear,' he said, leading her to a nearby chair, 'won't you stand by me and then you can introduce me to all the other pretty people here.'

'She has inherited her mother's beauty,' Missus Westerham told William. 'If your two other daughters have done the same I shall have to think twice about leaving poor Alexander with you. So much beauty will go to his head!'

But all was well for Christina and Cora chose that moment to arrive in the room and, once she had seen them, Alexander's mother no longer had fears for his virtue. When they were introduced to their new guest and discovered he would be staying at the house for a while, their faces pinked with excitement and they began to fuss about him shyly, fetching him drinks and small plates of food.

Alexander was like a creature from another world; dazzling, elegant, quick-witted and bright, talking in an accent that they could barely understand at first, but which they thought the greatest thing, nevertheless.

He had none of the clean-cut handsomeness of Father Devereux but the priest looked like a moth beside a butterfly when he stood near Alexander, who was dark-haired and slim and had the face of a sullen angel. Cora knew nothing of style or fashion, yet found his velvet-collared suit and his gold-embroidered waistcoat with its pattern of entwined peacocks fascinating.

He appeared unimpressed with absolutely everything and this, in turn, impressed the sisters enormously. That he should come to the grandest ball Connemara had known for years and stand there yawning was, they felt, most wonderfully outrageous. He studied his nails when the bishop spoke to him as though he conversed with such men every day of his life and he all but ignored their sister Constance as though her beauty was a matter of no consequence at all. He merely glanced once in her direction and then looked away as though thoroughly bored.

Alexander brightened only once that evening, in fact, and that was when he was taken to meet the old ladies of Connemara, who had requisitioned a vast area of the room for their own purposes. They sat near to the fireplace and the silver tea-urn, away from any draughts, and it was there that the most comfortable chairs had been arranged in such a way as to emphasize the strict pecking order that existed among them.

The ladies gossiped and stared, they discussed all those that were present and those that were not and one had brought knitting for she said her knuckles would fuse if her hands were idle. Their flirting and cooing had until that moment been exclusively reserved for Father Devereux or for the small dog that one of the ladies had enthroned on her lap. They tried to tempt both with choice titbits from the table but their simpering found a new quarry when Alexander approached.

He was a beautiful boy, they said, and well-mannered too, unlike William's sons who kept their distance from the group. Alexander seemed surprisingly content to join in their gossip even though he knew none of the victims of their wagging tongues. Cora and Christina fetched him glasses of punch and iced lemonade and it was there that he sat for

171

the rest of the evening, being perfectly spoilt and cosseted, despite Cora's entreaties to get up and dance.

As the music started the floor cleared before them and it was William who led his small daughter out for the first dance of the evening. As she stood on tiptoe to take her father's hand there was an 'Ah!' from the watching guests and, as she began to spin prettily around, there was even a patter of spontaneous applause.

William was surprisingly light on his feet for such a big man and as they made their solemn way about the floor so more dancers joined them until the space was filled with slow-swirling couples. As the music grew faster, though, the older guests began to sit out.

'No more,' William panted, halfway through a fast waltz, and Constance laughed when she looked at him for his brow was wet with the exertion.

'Just one more dance, Papa!' she begged, but he shook his head and led her to the side. 'There is your present yet to come,' he told her. 'When would you like it, Constance?'

She smiled. 'Now, Papa!' she said, her eyes alight with excitement. 'I would like it now, if I may!'

He led her across the room and out through the french windows. She stepped into the darkness and the sound of a hundred crickets came from the gardens that lay before her. The flares at the end of the lawn sent strange shadows across the grass and their flickering light made the whole scene before her look flat and unreal.

Her father stood still at her side and she hardly dared move in case she missed one exciting second of what was to come. A shape appeared from out of the shadows at the end of the lawn. It was Sean, Maidie's brother, and Constance wondered what he could possibly be doing there. Then she saw her present and she let out a scream of delight.

The boy led a small grey pony behind him; she heard its gentle snorting and saw its soft head bobbing as it followed obediently along.

'Papa!' Constance cried, rushing to see her new present. When William finally joined her her eyes were bright with pleasure and she rose at once to hug him, calling out a thousand words of thanks as she did so.

William felt the small arms about his waist but was unable to reciprocate her affection. He remembered how Sophia had embraced the children so openly and a small tear of self-pity fell down his cheek at the thought of his own inability. Instead he pulled her arms from him and turned away in anguish.

'May I name him, Papa?' Constance asked, stroking the horse's mane and his soft velvet ears.

'Of course,' William told her and his voice sounded strange. 'He is your pony, Constance, you must do whatever you want with him.'

'May I take him into the party then, Papa? To show to all the guests?' she asked at once.

He went to stop her but found he could deny her nothing and so instead he watched in silence as she mounted the pony and rode it bare-back across the lawns. They disappeared through the french windows and William laughed quietly to himself as he heard the beast's hooves on the wooden dancefloor and the old ladies' screams as it clattered about, dispersing all the dancers.

Once the pony was tethered safe outside again Constance saw her youngest brother standing alone by the door and rushed across to join him.

'I wasn't sure that you were coming,' she said. 'Papa told me you were kept at school.'

Niall looked awkward, staring at the floor.

'Did you see my pony?' she asked and he nodded.

'Did you all get ponies for your eighth birthdays?'

Niall laughed. 'No, Constance,' he said. 'We did not.'

'Well, you must have been away at school, then,' she said, smiling. 'I expect that was the reason. You are never home, Niall,' she added. 'Why are you always away?'

Her brother looked anxiously about to see if their father

was watching. 'I believe Papa prefers it like that,' he said. 'I believe he wishes us to be kept apart.'

Constance laughed at him. 'Oh, why should he want that?' she asked. 'I can't believe you, Niall! I think you must have been very bad and that Papa sent you away for being naughty. He must have forgiven you now, though, or he would never have let you come to my party. Would you like to ride my pony? You can if you want.'

She placed her hand in his and it was the first time he had touched her since she had lain in her crib. He smiled lovingly at her yet felt clumsy and ugly beside her.

The music started again and she looked about excitedly. 'Will you dance with me, then?' she pleaded.

'I can't dance,' he said, knowing that he should not.

'Then you should learn as I had to,' she told him, pulling his arm. 'Or you will never find yourself a bride, Niall.'

Niall laughed. 'Who told you that old rubbish? Cora?'

'No, nurse,' she corrected him. 'She said that gentlemen meet their brides on the dancefloor and that is why Cora and Christina have been moping about that boy all evening, hoping he will ask them for a dance and then propose, did you notice? You'll never marry if you aren't light on your feet!'

'Then I will stay unmarried the rest of my life,' Niall told her.

'Don't you want a bride?'

'Not yet,' he said. 'Not ever. I'd rather stay here and look after you.'

'Oh I don't need looking after!' She laughed.

'Not yet you don't,' he said, 'but I'll be there when you do.'

She stared at him and then smiled again, thinking he was joking.

'Come on,' she said, tugging again at his hand. 'I can teach you a few steps.'

'Papa would not like it, Constance,' he told her.

'Papa has said I can do as I like tonight,' she insisted.

'And it is quite the done thing for a young girl to dance with her brother. Thomas would not dance with me, though, and that only leaves Papa and he is too old and keeps getting out of breath. If you don't take me, Niall, then I shall ask the bishop and then everyone will be shocked, you see!'

So Niall allowed himself to be led reluctantly onto the dancefloor where they stood face-to-face while Constance showed him the first steps.

She placed her small hand in his and attempted to put her other onto his shoulder but found she could not reach and so took hold of his forearm instead. 'Now, you place your hand about my waist like . . . so . . . And then I will count the beat and you move your feet in time with mine.'

He looked down at her tiny feet in their satin slippers and his heart sank at the thought that he might tread upon them.

'Move my feet where?' he asked. That made her laugh and he found himself joining in.

'Oh, anywhere that my feet go!' she told him. 'You'll see!'

She began to move and Niall stumbled in an effort to keep up with her, which made her laugh some more.

The old bishop smiled as they passed him and Constance raised her hand to wave, which made Niall trip again.

'Who is that young boy with Constance?' the bishop asked Father Devereux as he watched them.

'That's Niall, her youngest brother,' the priest said and the bishop turned with a frown on his face.

'I thought she had just the two older brothers,' he said. 'I'm sure William told me that he has only two sons.'

'Perhaps you were mistaken,' Father Devereux replied, but the bishop shook his head, puzzled.

'They make a pretty couple,' he said. 'It's good to see a boy so fond of his younger sister.'

'We should stop,' Niall told Constance, for she was dancing faster now that he had picked up the steps and no longer stumbled.

He was lightheaded with joy to be dancing with her but

he felt terrified at the same time. He wished the whole world to see him dancing with his beautiful sister but he was afraid his father might see, too. She looked so happy, though, and eventually her happiness overcame his fears.

The fiddler rose from his seat and broke into a jig; a favourite number that had all the guests clapping their hands. Niall went to return to his post by the door but Constance kept hold of his arm, shaking her head so that her auburn curls bounced. She threw herself into the dance and Niall could not help but follow. Besides, the music was livelier than before and he found the steps easier to follow.

Constance laughed aloud with excitement as her long skirts flew, and Niall heard himself laughing too for he had not known so much fun before in his life. She twirled in front of him and all the guests clapped in time for they were enjoying the sight immensely. He saw the watching people in a blur about him and then one face in particular, white with fury. He recognized his father and stopped dancing in an instant.

'Constance!' he heard William shout. The music stopped and all the guests turned to listen. Only Constance had not heard. She spun about, smiling, and then Niall saw the expression on her face change as she heard her father's voice at last. Her feet stopped but her long skirts did not. She twisted in the fabric and found her legs trapped. Niall saw her start to fall and he ran to catch her but she slipped from his grasp and landed on the floor with a small scream of pain.

William was upon them in an instant, pushing his son roughly out of the way and lifting Constance up in his arms. For a terrible moment her head lolled back lifelessly and, looking at her ashen face, Niall supposed her to be dead. Then he heard her voice and relief flooded through every inch of his body.

'No, Papa, I am quite all right,' she said faintly. 'Let me dance, please, let me down.'

William studied her small pale face and then looked across at his son. 'This is your fault, Niall! Your fault again! I have lost two children and a wife to you but you shall not have this one as well, I swear it! I swear it on my life!'

With Constance still held in his arms he strode towards the door, the guests parting quickly to allow him to pass. They looked shocked for they had all heard what he said. They turned to Niall and he saw their staring faces as he stood alone on the dancefloor, at the spot where his sister had fallen.

Constance was precious to him, he would not have hurt her for the world. He would have died for his beautiful sister, who looked so much like their mother, and now he was accused by his father of harming her.

He remembered the brother and sister who had died. How had that been his fault? And his mother, too? Had she caught his illness as well? The blood drained from his face and the room seemed to move before his eyes. He saw the doctor step out of the crowd and walk towards him.

'Come on, lad,' he said. 'You should take no notice of your father for he's just upset and does not know what he says.'

'Go and help Constance!' Niall cried, pushing him away. 'She could die! You have to help her!'

'Very well, very well,' the doctor said. 'Though I think the only thing that young lady has injured is her pride! Don't worry about her, Niall, she will be all right, she was just startled by the fall, that's all. You must not get so upset.'

Cora pushed in beside him as he spoke. 'You great idiot!' she told Niall. 'What did you go thinking of, dancing with Constance like that? Did you not know she is kept wrapped in tissue all the year like a piece of prize glassware? Whatever possessed you to go galumphing around like a crazy fool with her for? You should have known Papa would throw a fit like he did! It took me a month to get him to allow you here in the first place and now you go and get all the blame when madam goes and twists her fine little ankle! Whatever were you thinking?'

'She's not going to die, then?' Niall asked, confused, and Cora and the doctor both laughed at him.

'Did you not hear her squealing and complaining as Papa carried her up the stairs and away from her precious party?' Cora asked. 'She was the noisiest corpse that I've ever seen if she was! No, she's still with us, Niall, thank God. I couldn't see that one being taken before her time. He'd have His hands full if He did, I can tell you!'

She handed her brother a glass of iced water and he sipped it gratefully.

'Cora,' he asked, 'did I kill the two babies that died? And Mama? Papa said it was my fault.'

Cora shook her head. 'Of course you didn't kill them, not unless your name is God you didn't, anyway. Ask Father Devereux. It's God who decides who is to live and who's to die, not some stupid great schoolboy who can't dance without tripping! And, as the doctor told you, Papa was too upset to know what he was saying.'

Niall sucked at some ice as he looked about the room. 'I believe Papa thinks that I did,' he said. 'I think he knew what he said.'

But Cora snorted, declaring that she would hear no more of it and went off to search out Father Devereux, to see if he would have a dance after all.

CHAPTER TWENTY-THREE

'It's terribly decent of your papa to leave us alone so much,' Alexander said, lifting the lid of the teapot to see if there was enough liquid inside for a fourth cup. He placed the silver strainer over his cup and poured from the pot, nearly upending it in the effort to drain it. The two sisters watched quietly as he sipped at his drink, pulled a face, then replaced the cup onto its saucer and pushed the two aside with an expression of distaste.

'Oh, don't worry on that score,' Cora laughed. 'He's employed the local priest to act as chaperon. Father Devereux is just a little late, that's all. It's why Christina's eyes have not moved from the face of the clock this past hour, though I doubt she can see the hands at all, without her glasses.'

Alexander pulled a silver fob-watch from his waistcoat pocket and it was as he flipped back the engraved lid with his thumb that Father Devereux made his entrance.

'Father!' Christina was up from her chair in an instant.

'Did you meet our cousin, Father?' Cora asked, wiping the rim of a clean cup onto her skirt.

'You were at Constance's party,' Father Devereux said, extending his hand. Alexander's hand felt soft and cold but his gaze was direct enough.

'Ah yes!' Alexander said, waving his teaspoon in the air. 'The wondrous brat! So tell me, Cora, how is the poor angel's leg this morning? Will she live to dance the pas de deux again? Should Covent Garden be informed of the talent it has been denied?' Cora laughed and Christina's shoulders shook slightly.

'Constance is quite well now,' she said. 'Though Papa will not believe so.'

'Perhaps we should order a crystal bathchair like a faerie coach for the poor creature!' Alexander said and this time both sisters laughed.

'Could you work a miracle on her, d'you think, Father?'

Father Devereux raised his palms upward. 'Not quite in my capacity, I'm afraid,' he said, shaking his head.

The sisters obviously found Alexander droll and witty, he thought, to judge by their expressions. Starved of all companionship save their own, Cora and Christina felt that the introduction of such a young man into their lives had brought some sorely-needed excitement.

'So now your dear papa has fled to Dublin on business, having seen your sister to rights and banished your younger brother from the house, am I right?' Alexander asked. 'Do you know I thought I might be bored here but instead I find myself in the middle of some amazing melodrama!

'I thought your papa admitted to only two sons, by the way,' he added. 'When now I discover that he has no less than three! What a mysterious man! To forget your own son! I must say, though,' he told them, 'I wish my father would forget me now and again. To hear him informing some bishop that he has just the three daughters and that is all would have my heart in palpitations of delight! Except when the allowances are being paid out, of course.

'How does one achieve the honour of being forgotten by one's father? Do you commit some terrible crime? Yet Niall looked like such a quiet young man! Tell all, Cora, darling, I do so love a scandal!'

Cora dropped the cake she held when she heard herself referred to as 'darling' and she looked across at Christina in time to see her eyes narrow with envy. 'Another cake?' she asked Alexander, holding the plate out before him.

Alexander patted his stomach, leaving crumbs on the deep pile of his velvet waistcoat. 'A little heavy for me, thanks,' he said, eyeing the fat buns with trepidation. 'I prefer the frothy light confections that one buys from the French patisseries in London.'

Cora returned the plate to its place on the table.

'Niall is not Papa's favourite son,' she said, quietly. 'We do not know why, but I suppose such things must occur in other families. He is always well-behaved, though.'

Alexander pulled a face. 'How boring!' he said. 'I was never well-behaved as a child if I could help it. I was unpardonably cruel to my sisters and yet my papa never as much as raised his voice to me once. All I saw your poor brother do was to dance with the little sprite; not very well, I have to admit, but then surely bad dancing cannot merit such harsh treatment? Where has he been banished to, by the way?'

'Back to school. They said they would take him out of term time. He is being educated by the Jesuits.'

'So that's why he talks differently from the rest of you!' Alexander said. 'You know I had only been in this country three weeks before I had an ear for its dialects! You girls speak pure country, of course, but at least I can understand it. That young boy was nearly incoherent. I thought he was speaking Gaelic when I first heard him.'

'We don't speak country Irish!' Cora looked affronted.

'Yes, you do, darling,' Alexander insisted, dusting his lap down and patting his mouth with his napkin. 'You say "tree" instead of "three" and other things like that. "Der are tree tings on dis table . . ." that's you, Cora, have you never heard yourself?' He laughed but Cora blushed with shame and sat chewing at her lip.

'I told you I could be cruel,' Alexander said, patting her hand. 'I hope you are not about to sulk or anything like that. I hate girls who sulk, it makes them look so ugly. My sisters can sulk for hours on end and I tell them it puts wrinkles on their faces.'

He turned to smile at Christina. 'Tell me of your other brother, the one who has left altogether,' he said. 'Was he banished, too?'

'No,' Christina said. 'Francis ran away.'

'And have you never seen him since?'

'No.'

'Is there no news from Francis, Christina?' Father Devereux asked. He was becoming irritated by the boy's tone and was keen to show more serious concern. 'Has he never written?'

'Not once,' Cora replied.

Alexander swung back in his chair. 'Lord!' he said. 'How romantic!'

'Poor Francis was hardly the romantic,' Father Devereux said quickly. It was difficult now to keep the irritation from his voice.

'No,' Christina whispered, 'he was very down-to-earth.'

She looked across to her sister for agreement and it was then that she first noticed something strange about Cora's appearance. Fishing in the small purse she wore around her waist, she pulled out her glasses and hooked them about her ears, watching as her sister's face slid into clearer focus.

She was right; Cora was wearing powder on her face and, if Christina was not mistaken, a smudge of rouge on either cheek, too! Christina's mouth fell open with the shock. She looked across at Father Devereux, to see if he had noticed, but he was attacking his cake with a fork and so she looked instead at Alexander and caught him winking at her sister. She rose unsteadily from the table, dropping her napkin as she did so and sending her cake-fork flying onto the floor.

She would tell Papa. She would tell him right away. But then she remembered he was off in Dublin and realized that she would have to bite her tongue until he returned.

'Would you call Maidie to clear the things?' she asked instead, to explain her sudden behaviour.

'I'll tell you what,' Alexander said, stretching, 'shall we take a small trip out to town tomorrow? I'm bored with the bogs and bleakness and am feeling the need of a few tall buildings and a little traffic on the roads. We could see a play, perhaps, or a music-hall. It would be fun, don't you think? You could come, too, if you like, Father,' he added. 'Even priests must have a day off now and then, don't they?'

182

Cora was instantly in agreement but Father Devereux found himself shaking his head with a few muttered excuses, while Christina, still not recovered from her shock, was slower to register her approval of the plan.

'You're wearing powder!' she remarked to her sister as they helped carry trays to the kitchen.

'Am I?' Cora asked. 'Now there's a thing.' She was careful to pronounce the 'th' now, after Alexander's teasing of her accent.

'And rouge!' Christina whispered angrily. 'And in front of the Father, too! How could you, Cora? You're a complete disgrace! What do you think you look like?'

But Cora merely smiled, aggravating Christina further.

'Alexander said all the women in London wear it now,' she said, pushing the kitchen door open with her foot. 'So it's no disgrace that I know of.'

'You look common,' Christina told her, flinching as the door hit her tray and the plates on it slewed towards the edge. 'And Papa will be furious, you know he will.'

Cora rounded on her. 'Papa will only know if you tell him,' she said. 'And if you do tell him I will inform him of the sketch of Father Devereux you keep pressed between the pages of your prayer-book!'

Christina's face turned bright crimson. 'You will see your reward in hell, Cora!' she stuttered, her eyes blinking furiously, and she pushed past her sister to unload her tray before there were more sharp words and the plates were broken.

When the others were gone Maidie took Father Devereux to see the sick child. He expected to follow her to the nursery but, to his shock, she halted outside the door of Sophia's room instead. 'Miss Constance sleeps in here now,' she whispered before opening the door. 'Her Papa insisted upon it, though secretly the child's terrified with the thoughts of ghosts, and all.'

It was not just the child that was terrified by the ghosts. Father Devereux found himself standing in the doorway, reluctant to enter the room; fearing it would smell still of Sophia's perfume or that the mere essence of her presence would overwhelm him once he was inside.

Constance lay in the bed, a small shape propped up on a large mound of pillows.

'Come in, Father,' Maidie said, taking his reluctance for manners.

Looking down at the child that he knew to be his daughter, Father Devereux felt himself torn in many directions, by his heart and his mind and his calling. She was William's daughter, she was his daughter, she was a child of his parish. She was beautiful, he noticed, with her small pale face pressed against the white pillows and her hair fanned out about her shoulders. He searched each of her features for any trace of his own but found that he could not tell for he could not be impartial.

'She is tired out, Father,' Maidie said beside him. 'She would not sleep last night for complaining. All she wants to do is get up and visit that blasted horse.'

'How are you, Constance?' Father Devereux asked, his tone professional and priestly.

'Quite well, thank you, Father,' she said quietly. 'Though Papa will not let me out of bed.'

'And what does the doctor say?' the priest asked.

Constance giggled. 'He says I must practise my dance steps a little more carefully.'

Father Devereux looked across at the maid and she raised her eyes to the ceiling.

'The doctor says she is well enough,' she mouthed at the priest, 'it's her father who believes she is an invalid.'

Father Devereux looked back at the child. There was a frozen bleakness growing inside him, a mixture of fear and guilt that he fought hard to suppress. 'Do you say your prayers to God?' he said softly. The child nodded.

'Good, good,' he whispered. There seemed little more to be said.

* * *

William Flavelle sat in the bishop's office in Dublin, his body sunk deep into the folds of an ancient horse-hair armchair and a copy of the Bible in his hand.

'You say you want a transcript of one of my sermons?' the bishop asked, sorting through a pile of dust-covered papers and waving the dust away with one hand as he spoke. 'Can you be a little more precise with the date, do you think? I believe they are filed under content and subject matter, though there may be some chronological order to them.'

The room they sat in was barely used and William supposed the bishop must have grander offices at the front of the house.

'The nuns are excellent housekeepers, of course,' the bishop apologized, 'but they refuse to come in here for they say they would not know where to start with it!'

Piles of books and religious tracts obscured the walls of the room from view and each tall pile was shrouded in its own grey mantle of thick dust.

'I rarely use this room,' the bishop explained. 'The grounds of the school stretch beyond the windows there and the noise of the children disturbs any concentration . . . children are not as they were in my day . . . nor yours, I suspect . . . no discipline to speak of now . . . no discipline at all . . .' He stopped talking to tug at a wodge of papers at the bottom of a tall pile. 'Balls bouncing against the walls and windows . . .' he continued, 'one nearly cracked a pane of glass just the other day . . .'

William looked across at the diamond-shaped panes. It appeared that most of them were cracked but it was hard to tell with all the dirt on the outside.

'The subject of the sermon was sin,' William informed the old man. 'Cardinal sin; sin of the gravest kind.' He had the bishop's full attention now.

'What kind of sin, my son?' the old man asked.

'It was . . . ah . . . quite specific, according to those who heard it,' William said, feeling suddenly uncomfortable in that hot, airless room. 'Incest,' he said at last. 'You made reference to incest.'

The bishop looked surprised, his thick white brows rising above the plain frames of his glasses.

'Incest?' He placed a fat finger across his pink lips. 'Ah, yes, I remember the occasion clearly. I had attended a seminar given by some luminary or other; I don't remember his name, but he was alarmingly convincing about his claims of the incidence of incest in the rural areas of our country. I remember thinking that I should make mention of it in my next sermon; not that there would be anything to worry about in a place like this, you know, but one cannot ignore these things, it is the Church's place to speak out, don't you think? Shocking to contemplate though, isn't it? Quite shocking!'

William bowed his head in agreement.

'It seems the danger is higher in the more remote areas,' he went on, shuffling through the paper. 'In some countries it is quite the norm, can you imagine? I believe the lecturer must have been referring to those countries where the entire concept of sin is a hazy one.'

William leant forward in his chair. 'How does the sin take place?' he asked. 'What are the greatest dangers?'

The bishop sighed. 'Oh, brothers and sisters mainly, I suppose,' he said. 'Too young or too ignorant to know any better than to sin their entire lives. Then there are the fathers too, you know. I heard of one man . . .' But he had found the papers he had been looking for at last, pulling them out from the pile with a flourish that raised a large cloud of dust.

'Here we are then!' he said. 'I told you I had a record of every one of them!' He held the notes close to his nose and frowned. '. . . none shall commit grievous sin . . .' he read. Gradually, his reading became more sure, his voice and pace gained momentum until he was suddenly in the pulpit, gazing down upon his congregation, and William found himself treated to a full and animated reading of the entire lengthy sermon.

186

There was sweat on the bishop's brow by the time he had finished and William had missed his last train to the west coast. The old man lowered himself slowly onto his leather armchair, removing his glasses as he focused on the solitary member of his audience. 'Is that the sermon you wanted?' he asked, puffing.

William nodded. 'Very succinct,' he said. 'Very forceful.'

'Ah yes, it made its point, as I remember. But may I ask why you wanted that particular one?'

William stroked his beard thoughtfully. 'As you say, you never know where it might be needed. Ours is a tight-knit community and I heard the doctor bring the subject up just the other day. The idea of it worried me, as it has done yourself. It's a disturbing notion all right. I thought I might show this to our Father Devereux,' he said, taking the sheets that the bishop offered him, 'he may like to include some mention of it in one of his sermons, you never know. One has to be vigilant. They are simple people in our part of the country, as you saw for yourself the other evening. I felt afraid. Complacency is a sin itself in my book.'

The bishop smiled as he shook him by the hand. 'The flock are in safe hands with young Father Devereux,' he said. 'He has a wise head upon his shoulders and has more than filled Father O'Malley's shoes. Speak to him if you are worried, though, William,' he added. 'I'm sure he will give some words of reassurance.'

William rolled the papers into a tube in his hands. 'Thank you, I will,' he said.

'And you will send my fondest regards to that little angel of yours?' The bishop nodded. 'Is she up and about yet?'

'Almost,' William told him. 'There was no lasting damage, thank God.' He crossed himself as he spoke.

'You are a lucky man. Five wonderful children. They must be a credit to you, my son.' He watched William's face carefully, waiting to be corrected. How could a man make a mistake about the number of his sons?

The sunlight blinded them as the nun opened the front door for William to leave.

'Five children, yes,' William said, not smiling. 'A lucky man, to be sure.'

CHAPTER TWENTY-FOUR

Alexander and the girls made a queer trio as they walked about the town. The boy had dressed in his best for the occasion and Alexander's best was a whole world of difference from anything any of the other young men they passed had to offer in the way of fashionable clothing.

His suit was pale beige linen and he had a large paisley handkerchief emerging from its breast pocket like a burst of bright flowers. Beneath the suit he wore a dazzling waistcoat, embroidered with oriental dragons and buttoned with a line of ornate golden studs. On his head a bowler that he claimed to have bought in Dublin perched at quite an angle, more to poke fun, he said, than to take the thing seriously.

He would raise his hat to all the ladies that they passed, wishing them a good-day as though he were a local boy and proud of it. With his thumbs tucked into his waistcoat and a sister on each arm he seemed in the best of spirits and the two girls could not help but find his mood contagious.

They looked dour there beside him, hanging to his elbows like two ugly bats, their plain sallow faces peering out from two of the dullest hats that Alexander had seen in a long time. Their heavy brown plaid skirts dragged about their legs as they fought to keep up with their cousin's longer stride.

Alexander was interested in everything. He insisted they rode the tram and rowed on the river so that they could throw bread rolls to the ducks and swans. He tossed coins to the hurdy-gurdy man and laughed with delight when the monkey caught his pennies in a small metal cup. They took tea in Cora's favourite tea-rooms and made such a commotion there that the other diners turned to stare.

'It's so dull in here, as dull as death, don't you think?' Alexander asked the waitress as she brought the hot water to their table.

'I thought you were having a grand time!' Cora said, turning to him in surprise.

'Oh, I generally manage to amuse myself wherever I am. But it is truly, breathtakingly dull in this place, I promise you.'

'Is London so much better then?' Christina asked.

'Better?' Alexander laughed so loud that he almost choked on his scone. 'It's London you have to live in if you're looking for any fun. We'll go there some day and I'll show you about, then you see if you don't love it like I do.'

Christina and Cora stared at their cousin but he did not look up from his plate, so they were left with no idea which one of them had just received the invitation. Both women would have loved to have visited London with him but now neither of them could accept.

'What does London have to offer that Dublin does not?' Cora asked, fingering her napkin.

Alexander looked surprised. 'Well, just about anything, I should say! Anything you might care to name! There's nothing you can't find in London, I promise you.'

Christina poured him a second tea and Cora leant across to grab the tongs and drop two small cubes of sugar into his cup.

'Do you think that boy could play "The Londonderry Air"?' Alexander asked, referring to the young man who sat in the corner of the room, serenading the diners on a small harp. 'I'd so love to see all these old girls here weeping into their tea-cups. You know there's no song like it in England? It's the stirring stuff that gets the British blood boiling. Do you think it's the rain that makes the people here so sentimental? It only takes one old man in a pub to fill himself with ale and then rise to his feet to sing a few bars and the whole room is blubbering, I've seen it myself. It's wonderful stuff; I'm sure the British could do with a bit of it themselves.

We're all terrible stuffed shirts over there, did you know?'

'Perhaps the Irish have more to cry about,' Cora said quietly.

'Maybe so,' Alexander told her, 'but we are still brought up to think that it's unmanly. Papa would beat me for a week if he caught me blubbing; it's supposedly one of the worst things a chap can do.'

'I thought you said your father didn't chastise you?' Cora asked.

'Not about the big things, no! But to catch a chap crying, well!' Alexander pulled a face that made both girls laugh. Their laughter encouraged him to worse excesses and he went back to balancing his tea-cup on his forearm, much to the disapproval of all the ladies nearby.

Niall sat in the confession box of the school chapel, turning his hat nervously in his hands. He was a tall, angular, awkward-looking boy with a glowering, sullen expression which caused his teachers much irritation.

The air in the box choked him. He hated the smell of that chapel for it had none of the comforting odours of the old church at home. The mustiness of the prayer-books reminded him of his father's study and that thought, in turn, formed a hard wedge of fear in the pit of his stomach.

He had wanted only to please his father; to please him and be loved by him as Constance was. When he had seen the affection and pride in his father's eyes as he looked towards his sister, though, he knew that this gift would be denied him, whatever he did and however hard he tried.

There was an impatient rustling in the cubicle beside him. He cleared his throat, licking his lips nervously.

'Bless me, Father, for I have sinned,' he began. He wished the priest that sat beside him was Father Devereux for he had always found the younger man easier to talk to.

'What are your sins, my son?' The priest sounded bored and irritated. A dozen boys waited outside in a queue.

Niall longed to offer him a clean slate; to shock him with

his goodness. But to say that he had not sinned would have been called a lie and he would have been beaten. He sighed. His sins did not feel so great to him and sometimes he made a few up. It was just that his father and his masters seemed to find him so wicked.

He paused a while, thinking.

There was a long sigh from the box beside him. 'You were sent back early from your holidays,' the priest prompted. 'What sin did you commit to merit such a punishment?'

Niall studied the roof of the box. Sinning at home was easy though he could not always explain what it was he was blamed for.

'I fought with my brother,' he said.

'Fought with him?' the priest asked. 'In anger?'

'No,' Niall said quickly, 'but we annoyed the cook and upset some of her things . . .'

'What else? Is there nothing else you wish to tell me? Nothing greater you wish to confess?'

Niall sat in silence.

'You are a young man, now,' the voice said. 'Is there nothing more? Nothing that you can think of? Nothing you have wished for that you should not? No desires that God would judge unnatural?'

Still Niall was silent.

'You have a sister, do you not?' the priest asked, sounding exasperated now. 'A younger sister?'

'Yes,' Niall whispered. What did Constance have to do with his confession?

'Your father is concerned about you . . .' the voice said. 'He is concerned for your relationship.'

Niall felt his entire body break out in sweat. 'I hardly see her,' he said. 'I meant her no harm. She just wanted us to dance.'

'What happened?'

'She fell. I didn't drop her, she just fell.'

'What else?'

'Nothing else,' Niall said. 'She wasn't hurt.'

'I'm not asking about the fall,' the voice persisted. 'I want to know what else happened.'

Niall sat in silence.

'What are your feelings for your sister?'

'I love her.' Niall wiped his hands on his trousers. Surely that was the right answer. A brother should love his sister. He loved Constance; he even loved Cora and he supposed he might love Christina too, though she was more difficult.

The priest coughed. His voice still sounded bored. 'Do you love her in a pure way, Niall?'

Niall felt the sick rise in the back of his throat. What could be wrong? What had he done now? His mind raced, trying to make sense of it all.

'I . . . I don't understand, Father,' he said. He felt like a child, with tears stinging the backs of his eyes.

'Do you have impure thoughts?' the voice asked.

'Yes, but not . . .' Not of my sister he wanted to say, but he could not believe that was what the priest could mean. He thought of the party and of the dancing, his mind racing back and forth, but still he found no clues.

There was a deeper sigh from beside him and Niall realized that once again he had done wrong. Yet what should he have confesssed?

'Say twelve Hail Marys and report to my office after mass,' the priest whispered to him.

When he walked into the Father's office he realized at once that he was in for a beating, for the man stood behind his desk, the paddle in his hand.

'You are a liar!' he said, as he delivered the first blow. The paddle hit the soft flesh of Niall's hands and the pain stung his entire body a moment or two later. The second struck his fingers and he tried not to wince, but his hands curled reflexively and he was ordered to open them again. And so the beating went on, until his palms were blue and red, his arms shaking.

Then the priest came to a halt, his face sweating and his

eyes bulging. 'Your father sent you to us for good reason,' he said. 'You must repent your sins to be saved!' He lowered the paddle and wiped it carefully on his robes. 'We need your co-operation if you are to be helped. So what do you say to that? Will you be saved or will you be damned?'

Niall looked at the priest's face. 'I will co-operate,' he said, unable to argue.

'And how will you help us, now?' The priest was almost smiling. Perhaps the punishment was over, after all.

'I will help in any way that I can,' Niall said. What was he to say? He would even have lied to keep the priest happy at that moment.

'Then will you confess your true thoughts to me, Niall Flavelle?'

Niall's head dropped, exhausted, onto his chest. 'I have told you everything,' he said quietly.

'And that is what I am to tell your father?' the priest asked.

Niall was silent.

'Very well,' he was told, 'you can go.'

When he reached the corridor Niall paused for air, leaning his back to the wall and letting his head rest on the cool stone behind him. All his life he had been blamed, but for what he did not know. He read his Bible regularly and could recite huge passages from it. He prayed when he had to and generally behaved himself. He had loved his father and his family and had longed to be loved in return. Now he felt himself beginning to hate them all instead; his father, the priests, the dull dreary sermons he was forced to memorize. He even hated his mother, for leaving him alone when she died. He recalled her gentle beauty and he pressed his sore hands against the wall to stop himself from crying.

What would his mother have thought of his beatings? But she was no longer there to be shocked at his pain. According to his father it was his fault that she had died.

He tried to remember his prayers but they tasted bitter in

his mouth now and he realized he had not prayed properly the entire term. Could God have forgotten him?

'Not out at games then, Flavelle?'

Niall lifted his head from the wall and saw the priest who taught sports descending on him. He had a large leather football tucked under his arm and, when Niall looked up, he threw it at him. Niall attempted to catch it but the pain in his hands was too great for him to get a touch and it bounced off his chest instead and went rolling off down the corridor.

The priest studied his hands and shook his head slowly. 'They're not so bad,' he said, 'but you'd better get off to sick-bay for some ointment if you want to be in the game tomorrow. Be out there in five minutes or you'll be staying back for detention, too. Do you hear?' he shouted.

'Yes, sir,' Niall said, running off down the corridor, his pulse beating hard in his ears.

There were shouts and whoops from the open window as he passed and he paused to look out on the field at his classmates playing there. They fought and rolled on the turf, struggling and panting like young puppies, enjoying some noisy fun while the master was still absent. They were a group, a solid mass and Niall knew that he did not belong and probably never would. He had none of their confidence or sheer joy in being alive. He felt only a burden of guilt for he knew not what.

A small ball of pity rose in his throat and expanded there until he could not breathe, then he had to let the tears out or he would have choked, though he hated himself all the more for being soft enough to cry.

CHAPTER TWENTY-FIVE

Cora's face was a picture. Twenty-six years old but looking forty, she stood on the station platform nervously clutching her purse, as she waited for Alexander's train to arrive.

The sisters had undergone a transformation during the time he had been away. Cora wore a dress of rose-pink damask, topped by a brass-buttoned cashmere half-coat dyed an alarming shade of fuchsia. Christina stood beside her dressed in apple-green crêpe-de-chine; a fabric so unsuited to the unseasonal weather that her skin had taken on a faint blueish hue.

On their heads they wore extravagant hats; full-brimmed creations that mercifully all but obscured their faces from view. Cora's was trimmed with dyed osprey feathers and a large swooping bird with black beaded eyes while Christina's had a cluster of hard high-glossed cherries that clicked together like a metronome as she walked.

Cora's dull features had been enhanced with a white matte powder and her cheeks had been rouged to match her dress. Christina had lost no time in telling her she looked like a streetwalker but Cora had argued that Christina's own complexion had received a pat of papier-poudre before they had left the house.

'Cora has been wearing cosmetics on her face,' Christina had reported to her papa the minute he had returned from his visit to Dublin. William, to her surprise, had seemed too distracted by other matters to take much interest in her accusations. Instead he had waved her off like a wasp, his eyes never leaving some papers he had on his desk.

'But I saw it quite clearly, Papa!' Christina had protested. 'She had powder and rouge on her face!' She moved closer to his desk as she spoke. 'And Alexander must have noticed;

196

what will he tell his mama? Now the whole family in London will know!'

'Alexander was here?' William asked. He seemed confused.

'Yes, Papa!' Christina told him. 'He left here only yesterday. He stayed during his holidays from the college, Papa. You invited him at the party!'

William rubbed his hands across his face, looking suddenly tired. 'How old is that boy?' he asked.

'Nearly twenty, Papa. He finishes college this term.'

William nodded, but his interest was back to the papers. Christina's mouth was dry with fear. She had an important question to ask her father. She licked her lips, praying she had picked the right time.

'May Alexander stay here again when he finishes college, Papa?' she asked quietly.

She waited for what seemed an eternity until he replied with a nod issued without any sign of interest in what she had asked. She felt her heart skip in her chest.

It was only as she tried to leave the room on tiptoe before he could change his mind that William looked up, seeming to see his daughter for the first time.

'Christina?' he said, and her body went rigid with fear that he might have had second thoughts.

'Yes, Papa?'

'Cora has always been wilful but she is a woman now, like yourself, and I have ceased trying to restrain her. You are both adults and must do as you please. I believe I have instilled the right virtues in both of you, despite your sister's minor indiscretions. She will come to no harm, Christina. Please do not bother me again with such trivialities. I have other, greater matters on my mind.'

Christina could barely believe what she heard.

'You are both nearly thirty years old now, am I right, Christina?' William asked.

'That's right, Papa,' his daughter told him, tears welling into her eyes.

William nodded. He had no fears for his two daughters now. They would never marry and would live with him until he died. Their plainness was a protection. It was his youngest that he feared for. It was Constance who had the gift of beauty denied the other two and beauty, however chaste and pure, would always attract corruption and vice. His duty was to protect his youngest and it was a responsibility he was to take extremely seriously.

'Christina!' he called as his daughter was leaving the room. 'Send Constance to me, will you? I believe she is out in the grounds somewhere.'

Christina nodded, too shocked to speak. Her initial pleasure at gaining her father's agreement to Alexander's second visit had evaporated completely at William's last words.

'You must do as you please,' he had told her, and the words had filled her instantly with a terrifying insecurity. She had lived her life in the shadow of her father's will. Now that protection had been stripped away in an instant and she was left feeling physically sick with fear. Christina had never done as she had pleased and the notion appalled her. Her face twitched and her heart palpitated wildly in its narrow ribcage.

'He is tired by his trip,' she told herself in an effort to keep calm. 'When he sees Cora in her make-up he will realize his mistake.'

Yet William was true to his word. Cora was the first to take advantage of their new-found freedom, paying frequent visits to town and returning with new clothes in all of the colours that she had ever heard Alexander profess a liking for.

Christina had been shocked but then had found herself feeling jealous. Perhaps Alexander would like her sister in the new colours. Perhaps he would pay her more attention, she thought, and the thought was anathema to Christina. Desperately afraid of rejection, Christina found herself accompanying her sister to town after all and returning with equally gaudy attire. Unlike Cora, though, she hated to wear the garments and was pleased that the broad-brimmed hats afforded her some security as they all but covered her small sallow face.

Alexander's reaction to their new appearance was barely discernible for his smile hardly faltered as he hung smiling from the carriage window. As soon as the brakes were applied he had flung the train door open and was bounding down the steps to reward them with a kiss on either cheek.

'Darling!' he cried, kissing Cora and then 'Darling!' too, for Christina, as he bent beneath her hat to kiss her as well. As a porter unloaded his copious luggage he bent his elbows and tucked his thumbs inside his waistcoat pockets, giving each sister her cue to take an arm.

He was dressed in tweed but his tweeds were not the hairy shapeless garments that the working men of Connemara wore. Alexander's suit was tailored to fit close to his body and his waistcoat was of a fine mustard felt with bright ochre stitching on the pockets. In his buttonhole he wore a deep red carnation and both sisters spotted it at once and wished he would give it to them as a keepsake.

'So how was Trinity?' Cora asked and Alexander laughed and shook his head.

'Oh, terrible, terrible, you'd never believe how awful!' he said, breathing a fat lungful of air as though fresh out of prison.

'It can't have been that bad,' Christina said. 'You had no time to write!'

'Oh, I'm well shot of that place, believe me!' Alexander laughed. He tipped his hat onto the front of his head. 'Now I can begin to live again,' he said. 'Where can we go for you two girls to buy me a drink, I wonder?

'Did you miss me?' he asked as they walked to the town, and neither sister could answer but just blushed and looked away instead.

'Well, there's a thing,' he commented. 'Nobody missed me.'

They sat on a bench near the docks to look at the sea and Alexander tossed some stones at seagulls that looped overhead. There was a sailor leaning on the rail nearby, a short, stocky man with Mediterranean features. He had pitted dark skin and an oily black cap that was pushed far back on his head.

'You're a bad shot, son!' he called as Alexander aimed at the birds which were all at great pains to ignore him, and the girls fussed about their things, eager to leave. Alexander stood to throw a few more stones but his attempts were half-hearted and the gulls made laughing sounds at him.

'You need to be fast for those bastards, look!' the sailor said, and he flicked a stone so quickly from his hand that it shot to the sky like a bullet. A gull crumpled in mid-flight and let out a sharp shriek of pain, its wing broken and dangling uselessly at its side.

The sisters watched it circle and fall as the sailor walked over to join them.

'They come to eat the rubbish,' he said, smiling and squinting into the sun.

The girls stood to leave but Alexander seemed impressed now by the sailor and went off to sit by the rail with him. The sisters watched the man offer him a cigarette and then sat back onto their bench as the two men stood smoking and talking. Finally Alexander came across. 'He has offered to buy us all a drink,' he said. He was smiling with excitement and his teeth were white in the dying light of dusk.

'In a bar?' Cora asked. She had never stepped inside one in her life and was shocked at the suggestion.

'We can't drink with a sailor!' Christina said.

Alexander laughed. 'He's OK,' he told them. 'He's just lonely, that's all. Come on!' he urged. 'He's a nice enough chap and I'm dying for a drink! It'll be fun, you'll see.'

The sailor tossed his cigarette into the water and they saw its red light arc through the air.

'Come on,' Alexander wheedled, 'I told him we could!'

'Suppose someone sees us?' Cora asked, secretly thrilled by the suggestion.

'Would you possibly know anyone who would be having a drink in a place like that?' Alexander retorted.

Neither sister replied.

'Then you're not likely to be seen, are you?'

The sailor made impatient noises behind them, stamping his feet and coughing loudly.

'Look,' Alexander went on. 'If you don't want to go in then you can wait here and we'll come out and join you when we have the drinks. How does that sound?'

Christina looked frightened. 'We can't sit alone outside a bar!'

'So come on then! The sailor told me there is a place in there where women can sit so you won't feel too strange, I promise!'

Cora allowed herself to be pulled from her seat but Christina would not move.

'We'll go without you, then!' Alexander warned, and she rose to join them for in fact she would have followed Alexander anywhere.

The bar was half-empty but well-lit and cheerful enough and Alexander found them a place to sit where they could see the room without been seen too much themselves. He and the sailor arrived a few minutes later with their hands full of foaming pints of beer and they set these down in front of the girls just as though it was their usual tipple.

Cora sipped at hers and then shuddered. This amused Alexander enormously and he told her she had a fine line of froth left upon her lip. A couple more sailors came to join them and the sisters became nervous but Alexander explained they were friends of the first man and that they were not to worry, just to have a good time.

It was late when they finally left the bar and Alexander appeared very drunk; so much so that he began to sing aloud on the ride to the station. The sailors left them at the quay, just before the tram arrived, and they took it in turns to embrace Alexander and to clap him on the back, telling him in broken English that he was a jolly good fellow.

They got into the house unnoticed though Maidie got out of bed to see who might be singing 'Men of Harlech' outside her door at such an hour.

The following morning Alexander arrived late for breakfast, a habit that William deplored, although he said nothing on this occasion. The sisters watched their cousin as he sat stirring a cup of cold tea without once lifting a drop to his mouth. They prayed that he would not pass out or be sick, for his face looked so green they were surprised he could sit upright in his seat.

'We'll go for a walk along the beach,' Cora whispered as she spooned egg onto his plate. 'That will clear the cobwebs from your brain all right.'

Alexander groaned and smiled thinly. 'And Christina too?' he asked, closing his eyes to the food she was serving him.

'Christina has to help in the church,' Cora said. 'It's her day for the flowers. She loves the job you know, for she has a terrible crush on the priest. Only you're not to tell, Alexander! You're not to tell I told you!'

Alexander looked concerned. 'But we cannot break up the threesome!' he said quietly. 'Perhaps we should wait until Christina has finished. I don't mind if we go later . . .'

'And spoil her precious time spent gazing at Father Devereux? No fear! She'll sulk for a month if she is forced to hurry on our account. Go get your coat now, Alexander dear, for there is a cool wind for this time of the year and we don't want you catching a chill your first day with us now, do we?'

'The sand will ruin my shoes!' Alexander grumbled as they walked along the wet beach. He was in a black mood and had complained every step of their walk. Cora stopped and they stood side by side, watching the grey heaving sea. Alexander clutched his arms about his thin body, as though shivering with the cold.

Cora looked at him and noticed that he had not dressed with his usual flair. The woollen scarf he had chosen looked old and covered with dog hairs and the jacket he had thrown quickly over his suit before they left was too big and the sleeves hung forlornly over his fingers.

'You should have taken Thomas's wellingtons,' Cora said. 'He always has plenty of pairs left in the kitchen hallway.'

'Wellingtons!' Alexander scoffed, as though he found the word distasteful. He looked across at some rocks that were sheltered from the winds and walked off by himself to sit on them.

'Tell me,' he said, once Cora had joined him, 'did Christina speak to you of anything in particular this morning?'

Cora looked puzzled. 'Nothing I can think of,' she said. 'We hardly spoke. She was too busy helping Maidie with the breakfast. Why?'

'There's something I have to tell you,' Alexander began.

She looked at his drawn face and realized he had not bothered to shave that morning. She had never seen him like that before and thought there was more to blame than just the drink. A sudden, terrible thought occurred to her that he was about to tell her that he loved Christina. She hugged her knees to her chest and wished she could stuff her gloved hands against her ears to block out his next words. She knew she could not bear it if that was what he had to say.

He looked uncomfortable. 'Did Christina seem to be unwell this morning?' he asked, looking out at the sea.

'What do you mean?' Cora asked him, her voice sounding high, like a child's.

Alexander shrugged. 'Oh, I don't know,' he said. 'I just wondered whether she seemed strange to you, that's all; whether she was acting normally or not.' He sounded as though he were about to cry.

'Christina is always strange,' Cora commented without humour.

Alexander turned to her then, with the first light of what looked like either relief or desperation in his eyes.

'Oh would you say so, Cora?' he asked, touching her arm. 'Does she often behave in a strange manner? Would there be nothing unusual in that, then?'

'Unusual in what?' Cora wondered what Christina could have done to have upset him in such a way.

Alexander looked down at his hands and Cora saw that they were shaking.

'It was the damnedest thing,' he began. 'She . . . she came into my room last night . . . you know, after . . . after I had gone to bed.'

Cora's face turned pale and her lips pursed.

Alexander smiled sheepishly. 'You know that I had one over the eight last night,' he said.

Cora nodded, desperate for him to continue but already wishing her sister were dead.

'But I remember what happened quite clearly,' Alexander went on, 'I am never so drunk that I forget what has happened . . . at least I think I remember . . . I mean, I would love it to have been a dream, you know, I really would. How grand it would be to wake up yawning in one's own bed and not be sitting here on this godforsaken beach, worrying about . . .' He paused as his voice broke and he covered his eyes with his hand. 'Cora, I wish to God that I had been dreaming,' he said, shuddering.

'What happened?' Cora asked, shaking his arm.

'I heard her knock,' Alexander continued, running his tongue across his lips. 'And for a moment I was confused. I'd been asleep, you know, and I thought it was Mama come to wish me goodnight and that I was back home in London, but then I saw that it wasn't, it was Christina and she came into my room without even waiting for me to tell her she could . . .' He paused again, wiping his face with his hands.

'I don't remember all she said,' he went on, 'but I do know that I had never heard her talk so much before. It was shocking, really. She sat there for hours, just going on about herself and her life and everything and she had so much to say but none of it made much sense to me, given the state that I was in. I believe I fell asleep at one point for I remember she became quite annoyed and I remember her shaking me quite violently to wake me. Then I did hear what she said, Cora, though I wish right now that I had not.' He shuddered again.

'What was it?' Cora urged. She felt she would die if he did not come to the point soon.

Alexander turned to look at her. 'She told me she loved me, Cora!' He broke down altogether, clutching at her arm and sobbing noisily into his hand.

Cora watched her cousin's heaving back and thought of her sister's ugly face; she wanted to laugh until her voice echoed around the wet rocks.

So Christina loved him and had been foolish enough to tell him. Poor, poor Christina, she thought; so desperate to have him that she had had to wait until he was rolling drunk before she had built up the courage to speak. Had she thought that he would be pleased, or what?

'So she said that, did she?' she asked, smiling now. 'You should take no notice, Alexander, she could have had no idea what she was saying to have come out with that. Treat it as a joke; something to tell your lads when you get back to London.'

But Alexander's eyes were wild with fear. 'Oh, she did, Cora!' he said. 'She did know what she said! She did, too! You didn't see her! I've never known her look like that! She became hysterical when I laughed and I was frightened someone might hear us and get quite the wrong idea! God, it was terrible!'

Cora hushed him, stroking his back as though he were a frightened child. 'Ignore her.'

'I can't!' he argued, becoming hysterical now himself. 'I haven't told all of it yet. She . . . she asked me to marry her, Cora, and when I laughed at her again she . . . oh, she said that she would kill herself if I refused!' He buried his head in his hands and sat, rocking back and forth, upon his rock.

Cora's hand fell away from his back and in that instant she hated her sister more than anyone on earth.

'I can't bear it!' came Alexander's muffled voice. 'I just know that she meant it! She looked so terrible!'

'What did you tell her?' Cora insisted, her voice rising. She was angry with Christina and with Alexander too, now. 'What did you say?' she shouted.

'What could I say?' Alexander asked helplessly. 'I had no choice. I know she would do it, Cora, I'm sure of that. She even told me I had no choice, unless I wanted to see her dead.'

'Then you didn't agree?' Cora was desperate.

He shook his head. 'Not in so many words,' he said, 'but then I didn't have to. She knew I couldn't say no! I couldn't let her kill herself, Cora; I couldn't live with myself if I did!'

'Do you love her?' Cora asked quietly.

Alexander looked horrified. 'Love her? Christina? How could I ... I mean, we were all great friends but ... well, surely that's all, Cora ... I never once thought of her in ... in that way ... It never occurred to me that she might ... I mean, she is so ... so ...' Words failed him again and he let out a long hopeless sigh instead.

'Leave it with me,' Cora said, firmly. 'I'll sort the problem out for you. Stop worrying now, Alexander, I'll see it all to rights.'

His face lit up at her words. 'Oh, would you, darling Cora?' he breathed, his eyes already shining with pleasure. 'I would be so grateful! Does this mean that I do not have to marry her after all?'

Cora nodded.

'Oh thank you, thank you, Cora!'

He was like a child, she thought, and it was then that the wonderful idea first came to her. 'There is only one way I can do it, though,' she said and his smile died a little.

'You will have to tell Christina that you had already proposed to me, Alexander, and that I had accepted you.'

Her cousin's eyes were empty for a moment and then the light of gratitude returned. 'I see!' he said, laughing. 'We shall pretend to be engaged! What a great joke, Cora! Do you think she will believe us?'

'Don't worry,' Cora told him, 'I shall convince her. She'll just be angry after she's heard, too angry to think about killing herself. It's me she'll be wanting to kill, not herself. It'll call her bluff all right, you see if it doesn't.'

Alexander's whole body relaxed. 'You're so clever, Cora,' he said, wiping his eyes on her hankie and blowing his nose loudly. 'I would have been in all sorts of trouble without you to help me.' He stood up and looked at her.

His clothes were crumpled and he looked a sorry sight but Cora thought she loved him all the more for that. He was her boy now, all hers and she loved him deeply, she could feel it all through her. She rose to her feet and leant to kiss him on the mouth but he turned his head with a little embarrassed laugh so her lips met his cheek instead and she had to content herself with that. His long dark lashes were wet still with tears. Cora was thrilled; she could barely believe her luck.

CHAPTER TWENTY-SIX

Dinner that night was a solemn affair. Niall had written Cora a letter saying that he was to finish at his school that term and that he would run away forever if he were made to stay any longer. William had spotted the letter in the post and had it read aloud while he sat in silence at the head of the table, considering his subsequent actions.

Cora marvelled at her brother's spirit for defying their father so openly but she was afraid for him too when she saw William's face. The thoughts were soon gone from her mind, though, when she remembered the scene that was still to come with her sister.

Christina was jumping with nerves. She watched Alexander's face like a hawk, gawping with such open adoration that Cora was surprised he could swallow his food. She would start in her seat each time he spoke or moved and was obviously awaiting his decision with wary impatience.

Alexander still looked pale and tired but he had shaved now and put on his best suit. He had smiled once at Cora when she had managed to catch his eye across the table. That small smile had earned Cora a look of pure loathing from her sister and she had felt herself glow inwardly for the vengeance that was to come.

Only Thomas and Constance seemed oblivious to all the tension. Thomas was busy poring over the plans for some new machinery he aimed to install in the farm and Constance sat calmly beside her papa, passing him the condiments and fresh napkins as required, even before he could make a move to search for them.

She had been down to dine with the others since recovering from her birthday accident and was well-mannered and silent for what she saw as a great privilege. She had dressed herself like an adult rather than a child and sat straight in her chair, her long light auburn hair coiled high on top of her head to make her appear taller.

Even Alexander was forced to smile at her solemn manners as she dabbed at her lips with the napkin before placing it carefully beside her empty plate. She ate very little but always finished what she was given, however long it took her.

'Did you hear that, Constance?' Thomas asked, knowing full well that she had. 'Niall is coming home again!'

She nodded, being careful to finish her mouthful of dessert before she spoke. 'Oh yes!' she said, smiling and looking excited. 'Cora told me! It will be good to have him home again, I've missed him so much and I know he must have missed us all, too!'

William frowned as he looked at his son.

'May I go and meet him from the station this time, Papa?' Constance asked. 'I have made him a present and I would so love to see his face when he opens it!'

Constance had been longing to see her brother since the night of the party. He was strange and quiet and so romantic, with his long absences from the house. She wanted to talk to him again, to discover how he lived and what he did at the school and their long separation had only served to increase her curiosity.

William turned to his daughter, near-speechless with anger at her affectionate words. It was Niall to whom his rage was directed, though, for he could never have felt such animosity for his daughter. His breath caught as he looked at her. In her adult dress, with her hair up in a knot, she looked so like her mother in the flickering golden candlelight that the words he had wanted to use caught in his throat.

'He may not come home . . .' he managed to say, and the look of pain and disappointment in her eyes caused him untold anguish.

'But he must want to see us!' Constance cried. 'He must

209

be so lonely, Papa, I know that he must! Make him come home, won't you, Papa?' she begged. 'I know he thinks you don't want him here but I know that can't be true for he has done nothing wrong! Tell him, Papa, it makes me miserable to think of his being away from us so long!'

Cora turned with interest to hear her father's reply.

William sat rigid in his chair and closed his eyes slowly. 'I do not want to hear your brother's name mentioned at table again,' he whispered in a voice that chilled her.

Constance opened her mouth to defy him but Cora could not bear to watch any more.

'Finish your food,' she told her sister quickly.

Constance stared at her with an anguished expression in her eyes and then she looked at her father and at the small mound of fruit mousse on her plate. Much to Cora's relief she picked up her spoon and continued to eat in silence.

Alexander caught Christina alone in the west room after the dinner was cleared.

'I must talk to you,' he said, 'there is something I have to say.'

She looked up at him with such short-sighted adoration in her eyes that he felt his dinner rise to the back of his throat and had to swallow hard to keep it down.

'Yes, Alexander?' she said, quietly.

How could she possibly have imagined that he would marry her? He thought that perhaps she was mad.

She closed her eyes, waiting for him to tell her that he loved her. She knew that he would never have been cruel enough to allow her to kill herself. Perhaps she would never have been strong enough to have attempted it, but she had known by the fear she had seen in her cousin's eyes that she had convinced him she would.

He led her to a chair and she could hardly walk, her legs were so weak.

'There . . . there is something you did not know last night, Christina,' Alexander began. 'Something that I did not tell you.' He felt her eyes upon his face but was not up to meeting their gaze.

'Tell me what it is, Alexander,' she whispered. 'There is nothing you could tell me that will make me love you less. Tell me, tell me anything.'

The clock behind him chimed the hour and he felt himself jump in alarm. He found himself looking after all into her dull, adoring eyes and discovered so much hope beaming out from behind her wire-rimmed spectacles that he was immediately filled with repulsion. How could she ever have thought that he might love her? He was to tell her he was engaged to her sister but that idea too seemed so utterly laughable that he was afraid she might not believe him. But then if she believed that he could love her anything might be feasible.

'You see . . .' he began, more sure of himself now. 'I'm afraid that, whatever my feelings for you, I would not be free to marry.'

He saw the alarm build in her eyes.

'I am already promised to another woman, Christina,' he said, 'and I must keep my word to her, whatever else I might truly want.'

He felt a sudden desire to laugh. Cora was right, this would be a great tale to tell once he got back to London. He watched his image in the mirror above the mantel. He was playing his part well, he thought, and for a moment the idea occurred to him that he might like a career on the stage.

'Who?' Christina asked. 'Who is it you are engaged to?'

He cleared his throat, relishing his role now. 'I had rather hoped you wouldn't ask,' he said. 'Though you would of course have found out in time.'

He assumed a grave expression. 'As a matter of fact it's your sister Cora,' he went on. 'She proposed to me just a few hours before you did and I'm afraid I accepted her. I'm sorry, Christina, truly I am. You were just a few hours late, that's all.'

He had to turn his back now, before he choked on his own laughter. Could she really believe he could marry her plain lump of a sister? But it was obvious that she could, for he heard her walk quickly and silently from the room, slamming the door in her wake.

Cora was waiting outside and smiled at her as she passed. Christina paused long enough only to throw her sister a look of hatred before she ran off in the direction of their father's study.

Cora leant back into the shadows, clutching herself with glee. Christina had done exactly what she had expected. Now she had only to wait until William heard of the news.

Alexander collapsed into a chair with a sigh of relief. So that was it, then, his problem was over. He had expected tears and tantrums and was delighted Christina had taken the news as she had. He fluffed up the flower in his buttonhole and looked at himself once again in the mirror before rising from the chair to stride about the room, humming quietly.

What a ridiculous scene! He could hardly believe he had been part of it. What a laugh the boys back in London would have when he told them what had occurred. He stopped by the window, experiencing a sudden urgent desire to be gone from the house. He was bored with the country-side and he was bored with the two sisters. He had enjoyed their attentions at first and all the fuss they had made of him, like two mother hens, but now he knew they would no longer spoil him and the thought made him impatient to be gone.

As he gazed from the window he saw Christina racing across the lawn, her ugly skirts billowing behind her like the sails of a ship. He chuckled a little to himself but then he stopped. Where was she heading? The barn? For one terrible moment a vision of her hanging from the rafters flashed through his mind and he wondered whether she intended carrying out her threat after all.

Then, to his relief, he saw William come into view, leading

Constance on her grey pony, and he realized it was them she was running towards after all. He hummed again to himself, watching the tableau that was being acted out before him on the grass.

Christina was shouting, though he could not hear her words, and he saw her waving her arms about like a fishwife. The reins fell from William's hands as he listened, and when she was finished the pair of them appeared to stand regarding one other in total silence. Then William looked up at Constance and said a few words. The young girl nodded and turned her pony around to ride it back in the direction of the stables.

Christina started shouting again and William placed a hand upon her arm to silence her. Then they both suddenly turned together to face the room that Alexander stood in and the moment he saw their faces the blood seemed to freeze in his veins.

William started walking towards the house with Christina running along in his wake.

'Cora!' Alexander heard the man's voice in the passageway now and then there was a sound of scuffling outside the door before William burst in, dragging Cora by the arm.

Christina stood behind them, her face a mask of vindictiveness.

'Christina tells me you have proposed marriage to her sister,' William shouted and Alexander felt his knee joints give way.

'Is this true?' William asked him.

Alexander looked from William's face to Christina's and then to Cora for help.

'Not exactly . . .' he began, unsure of himself.

Cora's face was a blank and she made no move to speak up on his behalf. What was he to say? It had never occurred to him that Christina would run and tell her father the news. Cora had not mentioned that possibility, nor what they should do if she did. He had thought that Christina would merely suffer her loss in her usual martyred silence and that he could be safely on the next train to Dublin within a few hours.

William turned to his younger daughter. 'Is this true, Cora?' he demanded.

Alexander relaxed a little, knowing that Cora would get him out of the spot.

'Yes, Papa,' he heard her say and felt his eyes start from his head.

William dropped his daughter's arm and walked across the room to Alexander. 'Did you not think it polite to ask my permission first, sir?' he asked.

Alexander looked across at Cora. 'I . . . I . . . it was only . . .' he began.

'And perhaps you can tell me why I should ever give my consent to such a union?' William shouted.

Alexander thought he saw a faint light of hope, after all. William would never allow them to marry. He could have kissed the man for all his stubborn pigheadedness. 'I'm sorry, sir,' he said, trying to look contrite, 'but I see I could not blame you if you did not. Perhaps . . .'

But then Cora spoke. 'You have no choice, Papa,' he heard her say. 'You will have to give your permission.'

Alexander turned to her in disbelief.

'What are you saying, Cora?' William whispered.

'I mean that Alexander has already had his way with me, Papa,' she said. 'We are husband and wife already in all but name. We will have to be married now, whether you agree or not.'

Alexander let out a strangled laugh and stepped back from the scene, his legs hitting the chair behind him as he did so. William's face, when he turned, was too terrible to behold and he felt he would turn to stone if he did.

'Please!' Alexander said, making one last appeal to Cora. Perhaps she was playing some strange joke on him, but one look at her face told him she was not.

The two sisters stared at one another; Christina with pure hatred in her eyes and Cora with an expression of triumph.

It was only then that he realized how expertly he had been trapped. A massive sob built up inside his body and he fought to keep it down.

Christina was not so strong. She let out a cry of grief and ran from the room, her sobs echoing as she ran down the passage.

'I shall write to your parents, Alexander,' William said, his bearded jowls shaking with rage. 'And I shall tell them of the terrible thing you have done. Were you not taught your Bible? I shiver to think of the shame you have brought on two respectable households!'

Alexander could not speak, he had become deaf and dumb with shock.

William looked across at Cora. 'There is little more to be said. "Cursed is the ground for thy sake",' he quoted. ' "In sorrow thou shall eat of it all the days of thy life." '

Even Alexander knew the passage. He and Cora were Adam and Eve being banished forever from the Garden of Eden.

'You will marry and then you will leave my house,' William announced. 'I never want to set eyes upon the pair of you again.'

Father Devereux stood before the altar of his church and gazed at the assembled congregation. He had never seen such a dismal assembly before in his life. Anyone being told that the paltry, long-faced group before him had been gathered to witness the marriage of one of the daughters of the grandest house for miles would have shaken his head in disbelief.

It was as well the organ was in full fettle, he thought, for there were no other voices joined with it as the hymns sounded out. Cora was a square figure shrouded in so many sheaths of heavy lace that her round face was all but invisible. She had arrived before her groom and stood waiting for some moments before he turned up, so unsteady on his feet that he had to be supported by a friend. He had twice burst out laughing during the service and Father Devereux strongly suspected that the boy was drunk.

The priest looked at William Flavelle in the front pew, grim-faced and straight-backed, and he found himself wondering why so few members of the Flavelle family had turned up to see Cora wed. Christina, he had been told, was unwell, though he wondered how unwell she could be, when he had seen her only that morning, angrily re-stacking the rocks around her grotto, her face red with exertion and the rain running in drips off the end of her nose.

Once the service was ended Cora threw back a layer of veil and Alexander staggered suddenly. This time it was Thomas who leapt to his aid and escorted him from the church. Father Devereux heard him being noisily sick among the tombstones and it was apparent that the other guests had heard the sound as well.

Cora stood alone, then, and it was Niall who was the first to step forward to shake her solemnly by the hand.

'Niall!' Cora exclaimed, delighted to see him. 'You should have written to tell us! When did you get here?'

'Just now. Just this morning.'

'Has Papa seen you yet?' she asked, looking behind her.

Niall shook his head. 'He knows I'm back, though,' he told her. 'He sent the trap to the station to meet me.'

'Then I'd stay out of his way, if I were you!' she laughed. 'He's in a terrible state about all this! If you're lucky, though, he may have forgotten you've finished at the school, with all the blathering he has been doing about my wedding!'

She looked happy, even with Alexander now swaying back at her side.

'He got himself drunk, the idiot!' she said, patting his arm. 'It must have been the nerves, you know, or the sight of Christina's face. She's been praying at the grotto all morning but Papa insisted she came along to the church just the same. She wasn't there for the service but I believe I see her now – look, she has grass-stains on the knees of her best

216

dress. Just wait till Papa sees her, Niall! Are you happy for
me, though?'

Niall looked at Alexander's grey face. 'Yes, of course I
am,' he said, and Cora kissed him, making him blush.

'Are you going back home after this?'

Niall pulled a face.

'You'd do better leaving here when you're old enough,'
she told him. 'Though you're quite the man now. I won't
be there to look out for you, you know. Papa won't have
me in the house after this.'

'There's Constance,' Niall said. 'I can look out for her
now.'

Cora laughed. 'Now that's a fine thought!' she said. 'You
look after Constance! Now why on earth would you want
to do that when she's looked after like a little princess
already?'

She placed a hand on Niall's cheek. 'I feel guilty to be
leaving you,' she said. 'But Alexander has his heart set on
travel. Don't cross Papa, will you, Niall? And get away as
soon as you're able. Escape, or you'll live in hell every day
of your life. Promise me, Niall?' she begged. 'Promise me
you'll go?'

Niall nodded. 'Thomas survives well enough, though,' he
said, looking at his brother, who had just emerged from the
church.

'But you're not Thomas,' Cora told him. 'You know how
Papa seems to treat you. He and Thomas have their
differences, but I think Papa loves him, for all that.'

'He hates me, though, doesn't he?' Niall whispered, and
Cora was unable to answer him.

William stared down at his daughter as she stood before
him in his study in her wedding-dress. Her round face
looked more plain than usual as it peeped out from its nest
of cream organdie and lace.

'Where will you go to, Cora?' he asked.

'To France,' Cora said, defiantly. 'To Paris first.

217

Alexander has friends there and they have offered us a home for the first few months. After that we will continue travelling.'

William walked around his desk. 'Why were you so set to marry that drunken young fool?' he asked. 'You know I will never forgive you for this shame, Cora! You know that I never can.'

Cora smiled at him and fingered her wedding ring. 'I don't ask your forgiveness, Papa,' she said. 'And I never shall. I am a married woman now, and may do exactly as I please. I married Alexander both because I love him and because marrying him was the only way to be free of this house. If I hadn't done so then I would have lived here until I died an old maid and that is a fate I find too terrible to consider.'

William stared across at his daughter. 'Go then, in sin,' he said, finally.

'I shall,' she told him, her head held high. She moved to join her husband but William stopped her at the door.

'You will return, Cora,' he said. 'You will return one day, just as Francis will return, too. You will both crawl on your knees, begging my forgiveness, and I will see you grovel at my feet before I will grant it.'

Cora smiled. 'I have told you, Papa,' she said, 'I will never be back. You may be sure of that. I would rather die than return here.'

CHAPTER TWENTY-SEVEN

On the anniversary of Sophia's death Father Devereux returned once again to the hill in the demesne where they had once met and where she had flown her precious kite. He was suffering with a cold and had told himself a thousand times to turn back as he made his pilgrimage but still he was there, his book of poetry in one hand and a large handkerchief liberally doused with lavender and ammonia water in the other.

Once on the brow of the hill, though, he found himself becoming bored. No tears had sprung up in his eyes, though the fluid from his nose should have been more than adequate compensation, and he discovered that emotions like grief were not things to be produced at will. If he had hoped to exorcize any remaining remnants of such feeling in one go then he was sadly disappointed. It would leak out slowly then, he decided, and he banged his book against his leg in irritation.

He had turned to walk back when he first saw Constance, a dot in the distance but a readily-recognizable dot nevertheless, setting out from the great house on her pony as though the hounds of hell were chasing at her tail.

Looking further, he saw that it was not hounds that followed her but William's stable-lad, running around the side of the house, his arms waving wildly as the gap between them grew greater. There was no chase, though. The boy was on foot and Constance's pony was off at a frantic pace. Father Devereux watched as the lad obviously realized she would not be stopped and set off again slowly for the stables.

She took a path that led to the west of the hill and away to the cliffs. The priest saw her more clearly now, as she neared his vantage-point. She was dressed in red velvet and the hat had been blown from her head, so that her auburn hair streamed out behind her. There was no rain that day and the pony's skin, he saw, was soon in a lather of sweat.

The pony slowed as it picked its way over the rocks on the cliff and it was only then that Father Devereux spotted Niall, standing hidden by some bushes.

Their meeting had obviously been planned. Constance leapt from her pony to greet him, flinging herself at her brother, though the boy seemed too embarrassed to respond. They stood a while talking. The boy looked tall beside his sister, more like a man than a boy. The priest wondered what it was that they spoke about. He was almost close enough to hear them but the wind blew their words away.

It was only once Constance was back in the saddle and Niall was urging her to go that he heard with any clarity.

'I will look after you, Constance!' he heard the boy cry as she flew off across the demesne. 'I will look after you forever, you know that!'

And then he heard Constance's laughter, as shrill in its echo as the cry of the gulls that circled the cliffs above them.

CHAPTER TWENTY-EIGHT

Cora lay on her back in the bed, her eyes wide open as she stared up at the painted ceiling. There was a large black fly just above her and she watched it circle the gas-lamp, wondering why it did so. She was unable to sleep and so lay instead listening to the deep but irregular breathing of her young newly-wed husband.

The room was so hot that she felt stuck to the sheets like glue. There were cakes on a plate beside the bed; left-overs from a tea they had never eaten. She pushed a finger into the cream and stuck it into her mouth. The fly left the ceiling and settled onto the plate to help her consume the rest of the pastry.

Her eyes ached from staring into the darkness and she wondered how long she could stare without blinking. There were four large pillows and a bolster on the bed and her neck ached too, from lying on them.

Alexander made a new noise beside her, a sort of snuffling, animal sound, and she turned her head to look at him. His face was grey like mud in the darkness. She saw his closed eyes slide back and forth in their sockets and realized he was dreaming. She wondered what it was he dreamed of. Then he let out a sigh of childish contentment and, without waking, thrust his thumb into his mouth. Cora turned back to look at the ceiling again.

'Alexander?' she whispered after a while, when she could stand it no more, but she did not feel him stir. It would be unfair to wake him. Alexander was sick, he had been taken ill on the crossing to France and now he still claimed to be suffering the ill-effects of the journey; a whole week later.

The previous night had been their first night alone since

their marriage and Cora had lain in her bed, much as she lay there now, waiting for him to come and claim his marital rights. She had heard him changing in the next room and then waited while he washed; while he donned his nightshirt, and even while he had sat smoking a cigarette and sipping at a brandy. Then, finally, she had heard him staggering as he entered the bedroom.

'Alexander?' she had asked as he pulled the covers back and tried to slip into the bed. He had given a small start of fright and she had realized he must have thought she was asleep. It was quiet in the room; she even heard him swallow.

'Oh no, Cora!' he had said in a whisper. 'Not that, too!'

The look of distaste on his face was obvious, even to her. 'What did you expect, Alexander?' she had asked.

'I thought . . .' he began, 'I thought perhaps . . . I mean, good God, Cora, you tricked me into marrying you, surely you can't expect . . .'

'We are husband and wife now,' she had told him, and his eyes had grown wider.

'But I thought . . .' he repeated.

'You thought what?' she asked.

'Well, I thought perhaps you had only married me to get away from your Papa! I mean we don't have to carry on with this charade, surely! I won't tell anyone, Cora!'

Cora had laughed at that and longed to take him into her arms. He was so silly, more like a child than a man!

'I married you because I love you, Alexander!' she said, to reassure him. 'Did you ever doubt that? Oh, you dear sweet child, to think you could have been so blind! I love you, you great sausage! I would never have married you for any other reason.'

Alexander's face had seemed to pucker. 'But you tricked me, Cora!' he said. 'You told your father lies about us!'

Cora had smiled at him then. 'Well he would never have given his permission if I hadn't now, would he?' she said. 'You saw the expression on his face when my dear sister

222

ran and told him! What else was I to do? He was furious! You surely don't blame me for that now, do you?'

'But could we not just be friends, Cora?' Alexander had asked. 'We had such fun back in Ireland, before . . . well, you know.'

Cora had reached out her arms to him then. 'You are my husband, Alexander,' she had told him. 'And I have my duties as a wife. I can refuse you nothing, it would be wicked in the eyes of God if I did.'

And it was then that Alexander had first become unwell and it was an illness that was to recur with alarming frequency throughout his married life.

CHAPTER TWENTY-NINE

Doctor O'Sullivan sat in the deepest chair in William Flavelle's study, his feet raised off the floor to avoid the murderously cutting draughts that blew about there. He had been summoned to the great house to see to the youngest child's health and it was a journey that he had been called upon frequently to make since the night of the party.

William Flavelle seemed to have it into his head that his daughter was frail and prone to suffer illnesses. The truth could not have been further removed but the doctor had long since given up trying to persuade him to the contrary. Constance was a strong, healthy girl, despite her doll-like appearance but William had obviously lost too many that were dear to him to believe otherwise.

And so the doctor indulged him and made the trek across the demesne as frequently as he was summoned and each time he would take pains to reassure William that all was well, but each time he felt his advice went unheeded.

They sat in silence now, in the study, the doctor sipping at a glass of Madeira before taking his leave, while William sat slicing open envelopes and quietly studying their contents. Suddenly the silence was broken as William slammed his fist down hard onto the polished surface of his desk.

The doctor found himself jolted up out of his seat by the sudden noise and when he turned he saw that William had risen to his feet and was pacing about the room.

'Is all well, William?' he asked, but received no answer. From his seat he was able to make out the heading on the notepaper that William had thrown down. It was from a company in America and, judging by the file that lay beside it, William had received much more correspondence from the same source in the past.

William Flavelle stopped at the window for a moment and then turned to make for the door.

'You must excuse me, Doctor,' he muttered. 'I have to leave you.'

Doctor O'Sullivan began to rise from his chair but William raised a hand to stop him.

'Stay and finish your drink, Doctor,' he said, 'please do not feel obliged to rush off on my account. The maid will show you out when you are finished.' And Doctor O'Sullivan was left alone in the room.

He studied the dying embers of the fire for a few moments as he sipped the last of his drink and then, finding no poker in the hearth, kicked at the feeble mound of smoking peat with the toe of his shoe, in an attempt to strike up some flames. He succeeded only in scorching his shoe-leather, though, and so he rose painfully from his chair as a prelude to braving the colder air outside.

Then curiosity somehow got the better of him, as he knew that it must. Circling the desk he glanced down at the letter that had caused William so much distress. His first assumption had been right, it was from an American company, though the letter-head was different from the papers in the file.

The letter on the desk was from a newspaper firm in New York, though it was written and signed by hand.

'Dear Mr Flavelle,' he read. 'This is a difficult letter for me to write and my difficulties are added to by the fact that we have never met and you will have no idea who I am. It is desperation that forces me to write, though, as, if I were to describe the matter involved as one of life and death, I do not feel that I could be accused of exaggeration.

'A few days ago I met with your son, Francis Flavelle. I need not describe the circumstances of our meeting but suffice it to say that I felt obliged to offer him the loan of a few dollars. Being a proud man, though obviously needy, he insisted on refusing the money unless I promised to write to his family for repayment. I made that promise, Mr

Flavelle, though I must state quite clearly that I have no need of the money myself. My father owns the company that you see on this letter-head and my situation in life is more than comfortable.

'It is your son that needs the money, Mr Flavelle. I only met with him for a short while but could see that his situation was such that he may not last long without aid. He would not accept more from me but I feel you would want to be informed of his plight.

'He told me that he was looking for his grandfather's company. Perhaps you could find him at that address. I pray for him and wish you luck in your search.'

The letter was signed by a woman: Nancy Deloitte.

The doctor whistled through his teeth and ran a hand over his hair. So Francis had somehow made his way to America! He would not have thought that the boy had it in him. He glanced across at the open doorway. William must have rushed off to the town to cable some money across. Then he looked at the letters that lay open on the file.

There were over a hundred sheets there, and all from what the doctor supposed to be Theo's company in Boston. He fanned them out slightly with his finger. Most were just accounts; lists of credits and debits and then totals, showing the dividends that William's shares had earned. Some of those sheets were yellow with age and the totals upon them were large enough to make the doctor's eyebrows raise in surprise and respect.

'William Flavelle, you old fool,' he whispered, 'you've been sitting on a fortune, you tight bastard!'

He glanced quickly at the door, impressed at his own daring and not at all ashamed of his own curiosity. There were two fresher sheets on top of the pile and he lifted the first one, to study it more closely.

'Dear Sir,' it began. 'We acknowledge the receipt of your letter of the 23rd and understand that the young man mentioned in previous correspondence is not a relation of yours and not known by you. We appreciate your speedy reply and assure you we will no longer bother about this unfortunate business.'

Doctor O'Sullivan looked up slowly, his eyes barely focused. The letter made no sense to him at first, but then he thought of the previous letter, in the woman's hand. He lifted the sheet below it. Another letter from the same company, and obviously posted before the first. A young man, ostensibly a hobo, had arrived at Theo's company, claiming to be his grandson from Ireland and demanding a job. They had no doubt that he could not be William Flavelle's son but he had seemed so insistent that they felt it better to check. Could William kindly reply by return for the winter was bitter and the young man had already spent several nights sleeping on their doorstep ... The doctor could read no more. William must have written back and denied knowledge of his own eldest son. He must have known Francis could perish out there. Even the woman – the doctor hunted for her name – Nancy Deloitte, an apparent stranger, had shown more mercy and given him money and help.

Doctor O'Sullivan pulled his jacket about him as though he were cold. He did not wish to stay in the house a moment longer. Throwing the final letter down onto the desk he made his way quickly towards the door.

CHAPTER THIRTY

Constance sat alone in her room, her small face peering anxiously between the long fat snakes of rain that slithered down her window. There had been storms for a fortnight and slates had been blown from the roof and all but the largest barn on the estate had been flattened. William had made no move to have the buildings repaired, though, and for days great planks of wood had been blowing about the yards, frightening the occupants of the house by rattling over the cobbles and slamming across windows when the winds reached their peak.

Constance had not been so much frightened by the noise as by the thought that her darling pony might come to grief overnight. So great was her fear for her pet that she had even slipped out of the house in her nightgown on the night that the storms blew their worst and had lain beside the animal all night, to give it comfort.

Her nanny had found her after hours of wild-eyed searching, during which time the woman had persuaded herself that Constance was dead.

'Oh, Miss Constance!' she had said when she found her asleep in the stables. 'I thought you were gone forever! How could you have disappeared like that? Didn't you know what I would think? I thought maybe you'd been out sleepwalking and that the Shee had got you at last! Or that you could have been thrown from the cliffs by the winds! Whatever would I have told your papa? How could you, Constance? I thought I might die of fright!' She looked down at the girl and saw she was crying.

'I can't leave him!' Constance said. 'He'll be so frightened! Please, let me stay with him!' But the nanny pulled her up by the arm.

'You're to come to the house!' she ordered, but Constance pulled away. 'I shall tell your papa if you stay,' the woman said. 'And then he will let the pony free and we'll be rid of the thing forever. Is that what you want?'

Constance shook her head, truly frightened now. 'You wouldn't tell him,' she said, though she sounded less sure of herself now.

'I shall if you stay here,' the nanny told her. She did not mean to be cruel but was genuinely frightened that the girl could die out there and that it would be seen as her fault. 'I'll tell him that you have been running off to meet your brother, too, if you're not careful! Now you didn't know I knew about that, did you?'

Constance's mouth opened in surprise. 'He's my brother,' she said. 'There's no harm in our meeting. I'm never allowed to see him in the house. I've every right to see him when I please.'

'I know you have,' the woman said. 'And that's why I've not said anything before. But I doubt your papa would agree with us and, if you want my mouth kept shut, you'll come back to your own bed right now.'

Constance got up reluctantly and, turning to give her pony one last hug, followed the nanny to the house.

'There's a good girl,' the woman soothed. 'I'm sure your pet will come to no harm out there. He's in a warm dry stable and, anyway, just what did you think you could do if he did come to grief? You're best off in your nice warm bed. Do you promise not to come back here tonight?'

Constance would have promised but she was an honest girl and she could not bear the thought that her pony might be harmed.

'Then I will have to lock your door until you do,' the nanny told her.

Constance found herself locked in her room at the top of the house. She had never been locked in before. She tried the handle quietly several times but it would not turn and so she had wandered to the window, where she sat now, staring down at the yard and the stables.

Each night was the same. The storms raged another week, wrecking ships along the coastline and providing a nightly display of heavenly pyrotechnics. At the end of the week, as they reached their furious peak, Constance watched as her worst fears became a reality. She had fallen asleep at the window, exhausted by worry, her face pressed to the glass as her head rested on the window-ledge. There had been an explosion that seemed to shake the whole house and she had jumped from her seat in time to see the next bolt of lightning split the large oak in the yard in two.

One half fell harmlessly across the kitchen garden but the other stood rigid for a moment, as though deciding where to land. It went in slow motion, in a shower of bright red sparks, and as it fell Constance screamed, for she saw it was set to fall across the roof of the stables.

She beat her white fists against the glass until they were sore and then she rushed to the door of her room but found it locked, as usual. She flew about like a moth in a bell-jar, finally collapsing onto the floor beside the door, where she was discovered, pale and exhausted, by Maidie the following morning.

The doctor was immediately sent for, for it was feared she had suffered a fit. Some sal volatile was quickly produced from the doctor's bag, though, to effect an immediate recovery. It was left to William to tell her of her pony's death. Its neck had been broken and he told her it had died before it could feel pain, which was a lie, for the poor thing had lain for an hour twitching in agony before the stable-lad could bring himself to put a bullet through its head.

Constance blamed her father for her pony's death. She refused to be comforted by him, asking instead for Niall, which broke William's heart, though he did not allow his emotions to show. He would not allow her brother into her room, no matter how hard she cried for him, and tried all ways to placate her himself, even spending several weeks and a great deal of money on finding her a similar-looking pony as a replacement. Constance would have none of it, though, and would not even look at the new horse, while all the staff were upset to hear her poor cries at night as she lay, sobbing, in her bed.

The whole affair affected William deeply. The nanny was called to his study a few days after the pony's death and was left to stand in silence while her employer finished his prayers.

'Do you pray often?' he asked the young woman once he was finished.

'Yes, sir,' she told him, lifting her chin to show she was not afraid.

'How often?' William asked.

'As often as I was brought up to pray,' she said. 'And any other time I feel the need.'

William nodded. 'And you read your Bible?'

'Yes, sir.'

'Then you understand the importance of honesty,' he said.

The woman felt a blush begin on her cheeks and she clasped her hands in front of her apron. 'Of course, sir,' she said.

'Then when I ask you to tell what it is that is bothering my daughter and making her keep away from me I can expect a full and honest answer?'

The woman swallowed. 'As honest an answer as I can possibly give,' she said.

William nodded and raised an eyebrow to tell her she was to commence.

'I believe, of course, that she is upset at the death of her pony,' the nanny said, but William waved her words away.

'There is more to it than that,' he told her. 'She must have realized as soon as she came to her senses that it was not my fault. There is something else troubling her; something else behind it, I am sure.'

The nanny paused. There was an injustice but she did not

231

know whether she should speak up. But then William had told her to be honest and she could see no harm in obeying his words.

'I believe she wishes to see more of her brother, sir,' she said.

'Thomas? Why, she can see him any time she chooses.'

'No, sir,' the woman said, 'I meant the younger brother, Master Niall. She is very fond of the boy and yet they are kept apart. I believe it upsets her to be separated from him. After all, they are closer in age than the others. She has no friends and I believe she likes the company. I believe she blames you for keeping them separated. I believe . . .'

'She can hardly know the boy,' William said, turning his back.

The woman bit her lip. 'They . . .' she began.

William turned on her in an instant. 'They what?' he demanded. 'Remember your promise to be honest,' he added.

She looked away from his gaze.

'Do they meet?' he asked.

She nodded. 'I believe they do, yes,' she said. 'Though it's harmless enough, sir, they just take walks and look at the sea . . .'

'Thank you,' William said. 'Thank you for your honesty.'

The woman smiled. William said no more and she took the interview to be at an end. She had worried needlessly about telling him, she thought. He had barely shown any emotion at the news. She pulled the door open and William's voice stopped her.

'You will leave at the end of the week,' he said, so quietly that she thought at first she had misheard.

But she found that she had not.

'Close the door behind you,' William added and she could do nothing more than obey him.

It was the following evening that the nanny was raised from her bed by the sound of Constance's crying. Barely awake, she lit a candle and made her way down the passage to the child's room. As she came nearer, though, she was suddenly aware that there was already someone standing there, staring through the open door.

With a small start of fright the woman extinguished her own candle with her fingers. It was William who stood there, she saw, and the sight of her employer made her think at once of fleeing back to the safety of her own room. She had no wish to talk to him again after their discussion in his study. He made no sign of having seen her, though, and so she kept her place, terrified he might notice her if she moved and think she was prying.

She spent a few moments there in the shadows of the passage, listening to the ticking of the great clock in the hall and waiting for William to make a move, which he did not. She felt herself shudder. Constance was quiet now and there was something strange about the way that he stared through her open door. When he finally did move it was all she could do to stop herself screaming aloud with fright. His face, as he turned, was streaked with silver tears in the moonlight. He walked past her down the passage, so close she could almost have touched him, and yet he did not see her hiding there, as though he walked in his sleep.

She ran forward as soon as he was gone and she took his place to see what it was he had stared at, but the only sight in the room was his daughter, asleep now on her bed, with the golden rosary that had belonged to her mother hanging above her head. The moonlight caught it and it glowed brilliantly in the darkness. Suddenly afraid for the child, and afraid that she would soon be leaving her altogether, the nanny slowly closed the door and made her way back to her bed.

CHAPTER THIRTY-ONE

It was the same fear that drove Constance's nanny from her bed the following night for, frightened as she was by William Flavelle, it was concern for his daughter that affected her more keenly.

She waited, shivering, in the passage outside Sophia's old room, and had just begun to tell herself that all was well and that she should return to her bed, when she heard footsteps approaching and made herself scarce in the shadows.

It was William Flavelle again, and she heard him moaning and whispering his dead wife's name. It was all the girl could do to stop from screaming aloud at the sound, for she had a morbid imagination and expected at any moment to see the ghost of Sophia Flavelle.

William emerged from the gloom, his face and nightshirt both drenched in sweat, his hands held high and feeling before him, as though he were blind. He stopped outside his wife's door, as he had on the previous night, and the nanny crossed herself in the darkness, praying that would be an end to it, and he would return to his room. As she prayed beneath her breath, though, there was a noise from the room; the sound of Constance sobbing in her sleep. William was alert to the sound in an instant, cocking his head for a moment before rushing in to be at his daughter's side.

The door was left open. Sick with fear that she might be discovered, but unable to turn back, the nanny stepped forward to peer through the crack by the hinges.

'Sophia?' William Flavelle stood at his daughter's bedside, and the way that he whispered his dead wife's name made the nanny's flesh begin to creep.

'Sophia?' The moon moved from behind a cloud and she saw his face in its light. His head was angled downward, gazing at his small daughter's face, and he was smiling.

He bent to touch her hair but Constance did not move – she was sound asleep again. He bent further to kiss her. 'Sophia!' He was sobbing, she could hear the muffled sounds as he pressed his wet face into his daughter's hair as though it were a bunch of the most beautiful roses, whose perfumes he was desperate to inhale.

The bedsprings screeched as he lay down beside her, caressing her softly as she rocked back and forth in his arms. Constance moved dreamily but her father shushed her gently and held her tighter.

'Sophia,' he crooned. 'Sophia, my darling, you have returned to me at last. Say you have forgiven me, Sophia, end my torment, I beg you.'

His whole body began to shake then; the nanny saw the trembling that gripped him from top to toe. She could no longer speak or move; what she saw affected her so profoundly that she was unable to act or do more than recite her prayers over and over again in her head.

She heard Constance's screams. 'Papa?' she cried, her eyes wide in terror as she was crushed in her father's embrace. He tried to raise her nightgown. She screamed again and his body twisted then in a spasm of uncontrollable agony and relief.

It was then that the nanny found her voice at last and her screams echoed down the corridors left untouched by Constance's feebler cries.

What had he done? She was an unworldly girl but not too innocent to know the vilest evil when she saw it. His grip relaxed as he fell back, exhausted, and Constance scuttled away from him like a small crab on the beach. She wished to go to the child, to help her, but was still too repulsed by the terrible things she had seen.

William Flavelle had sinned with his own daughter! She stared at him, stretched out and panting with the exertions

235

of his despicable passion, his great body still oozing vile excretions.

Suddenly he began to sit up, but still the girl could not move. His eyes rolled towards his daughter, huddled and sobbing beside him, and they became filled with such terror and horror that the nanny crossed herself once more.

'Constance?' he murmured. 'It was the Devil,' she heard him say. 'It was the Devil that tricked me!'

He threw his legs to the side of the bed and tried to stand but they would not take his weight, so he sat there helplessly instead, his head buried between his great hands.

He had been deaf to his daughter's cries and the nanny's screams, but now intuition told him he was not alone. He looked up in time to see the nanny running from the doorway, then another figure approached to take her place.

William Flavelle stared into the face of his youngest son.

Constance started to scream again and William suddenly found the strength to combat all his pain. He had his enemy now; God had shown him the way to his salvation. He had played host to the Devil for too long and was suffering at his cost for this generosity. The Devil had sat at his table and seduced his own wife. He had murdered two of his children and now ruined the life of a third and most precious child. William had delayed too long but now his path was clear. With tears streaming down his face he squared up to his son.

'What did you do?' Niall asked, but William barely heard him. He grabbed his son by the arm and marched him from the room, pulling him down the servants' stairs until they could no longer hear Constance's screams behind them.

Niall tried to resist but William was still the stronger. As they walked along a maze of passages William endlessly recited prayers beneath his breath.

They stopped at the door of William's study. William turned once to look at his son before opening the door and pushing the boy inside. There was a large polished wooden case inside the room that had always remained locked.

William unlocked the case and pulled out a long gleaming shotgun.

The gun was the thing, the very thing needed. He had played around too long and had hesitated time and time again. Let God now be merciful in His infinite wisdom; William Flavelle could no longer strive to be in his God's image. With the gun would come his final revenge. He would rid his house of the Devil forever; whatever form it cared to take.

CHAPTER THIRTY-TWO

The stable-lad woke quickly, his whole body tensed with fear, long before the sound that had woken him could be identified. He cried out, for the figure that stood before his small bed in the darkness was more terrible than the stuff of nightmares: William Flavelle in ghastly silhouette, his black hair wild and dishevelled, his eyes staring madly from his head.

The boy clutched at the sheets, his bony knees folded to his chin in a reflex of panic. He thought he was about to be beaten but then he saw the glint of the gun in his employer's hands and it was then that the taste of real terror flooded his mouth for the first time.

'Are you listening to me?' he heard William say. 'Are you awake?'

'Yes, sir,' the lad managed, though it took all his courage to answer. William looked like the Devil incarnate and the boy crossed himself beneath the thin sheet that covered him.

'Do you have a lantern?'

'Yes, sir,' the boy said again. He was unable to move.

William stepped towards him. 'Light it and give it to my son,' he said, and the stable-lad saw Niall standing behind his father.

'Do you understand?' William asked, his voice louder now.

The boy jumped from his bed and did as he was bid.

Niall took the lantern from him once he had it lit and the pair walked from the small room at once, leaving the boy shivering in the darkness.

William dragged his son across the yard towards the barn, which loomed like the hull of a large black ship in the empty darkness. When he pulled the great door back its hinges let out a rusty scream and Niall took his first breath of the warm stench of the rotted apples inside. Their choking smell made him sad, for it reminded him of the days before his mother had died and before Francis had left, when the apples had been fresh and the barn had simply smelt of their soft musty sweetness. He stepped slowly inside, waiting for his eyes to adjust to the meagre light once the door was closed behind them.

William found two wooden crates and kicked them until they were side by side. He raised his head and ran a hand across his hair so that it lay plastered once more to his scalp. Niall noticed that his father's long black coat was buttoned wrongly.

'Sit,' William demanded, pointing to the smaller of the crates.

Niall sat down slowly. The wood felt rough against the backs of his legs. He couldn't recall his father putting on his coat. All he could remember was Constance screaming and how he had run from his own room to help her. His father had been dressed in his nightshirt then. When Niall had seen him fetch the gun out of its box, why had he thought they were going to shoot animals? He had never hunted with his father in his life but Thomas had and for a moment he had hoped . . . but now he knew otherwise. You did not hunt small animals in a barn, unless you were looking for rats.

William stood before his son like a statue, the lantern in his hand. Niall looked about for rats. The apples lay in a decomposing pile. There had to be rats in amongst them. He stared at the mound for a long while until it seemed to move in the darkness; undulating and changing shape before his eyes.

William snuffed the flame of the lantern and Niall almost screamed. It was a moment before his eyes found any light at all. At first he was blinded by the darkness and then he slowly saw the thin beams of pale blue moonlight that shone like a network of silver swords between the wooden slats of the barn walls. His father was smiling at him and when he spoke his voice was gentle; the voice of a loving father addressing his son. It was how Niall had always longed for his father to speak to him but at this moment the sound made the hair rise on the back of his neck.

William placed the shotgun against the wall and clasped his hands before him in prayer.

'Confess now, Niall,' he said. 'I want to hear your confession.' He dipped his head, waiting.

Niall looked at his father. He had never been so close to him before in his life; never been able to smell him as he smelt him now, or studied his wet-black hair and beard in such detail. He had never heard the sounds of his father's body before; the roughness of his breathing and the deep buzzing as he cleared his throat. His brows were knitted in an agony of concentration as he waited for his son to speak. His father was waiting, waiting to hear him confess.

Niall went to rise from his crate but a strong hand pulled him back. He half-fell onto the box and a plank of wood cracked under his weight.

'You must confess,' William said again, patiently. 'You must tell me of your sins. It is the only way that I can save you.'

'Father?' Niall whispered. William's head lifted and his smile returned. Niall could see all his teeth now, save the ones right at the back. They were like white tablets of salt among the thick bushy nest of his beard.

'That is your first sin, Niall,' he said. 'For I am not your father and to call me such is a sin. Your father is the Devil, Niall. You must understand that and you must understand the repercussions.

'How did you suppose that I would have sired one like you? You should have known that, Niall, once you were old enough to understand all the wickedness you have brought with you. You have contaminated us all by your very presence in this house; your siblings first when you killed them with your germs, then your own mother, God bless her, who nursed you and was weakened by doing so, so that she could not survive the birth of her daughter. You drove Francis from the house and then, when you saw the love that I had for Constance, you were set to weave your evil corruption about her, too.

'I saw your desire for her, Niall, and it was then that I was weak and the Devil took his chance to manifest those desires in me. Your contamination has spread throughout the house now, Niall, and through it I have had taken from me all that I hold most dear.

'I believed I was strong enough to withstand all temptation but the Devil knew my weaknesses and has tortured me accordingly. I allowed the Devil into my house, Niall. I had him as a guest at my own table. I thought I was strong but I was not strong enough and I now reap the reward.

'My daughter, my darling daughter, that pure child, that innocent . . .' William broke off his ranting and sobbed, his head buried in his chest, then he breathed a huge sigh and wiped his eyes on the back of his sleeve.

'Do you see what you have done, Niall?' he asked softly. 'Do you see and understand all of the wickedness and the suffering you have brought into this family? Do you see how I suffer, Niall?'

Niall did not move or speak. He wished to become one with the darkness, to blend into the shadows until he was rendered invisible.

What was it he had done? It was the same question that had plagued him all his life. Why was he guilty? His father knew it and the priests at his school had obviously known it too, but how could he have caused his father so much suffering when he had barely known him? Surely the suffering had to be down to Francis, who had run away, or Cora, who had married? Had he really been sired by the Devil? That would have meant that his mother . . . Niall's whole body began to shake at the enormity of the thought.

'Will you tell me your sins?' his father repeated, his voice becoming louder.

Niall looked for the door in the darkness, wishing now to run away, however great the cost of his actions. He heard a quiet rustling on the floor near his feet and wondered if it was the rats. Would they eat live flesh? He longed to lift his feet from the floor but he was afraid any movement would make his father angrier.

'Will you?' William repeated.

'I can't,' Niall said, his voice sounding lonely and miserable in that huge empty space.

His father sighed and lowered himself onto the crate beside the boy. When he sat the shotgun was revealed, leaning on the wall at his side. Niall looked at its metal barrels and the shining wood of its handle.

William sat unmoving. Niall became uncomfortable. His muscles ached from being tensed and his body ached from the effort of keeping still. The pain became acute but still he dared not move. He turned his head slowly, hoping that even that small movement would not make a noise and alert his father. William appeared to be asleep. His head was tilted onto his chest again and Niall could not see if his eyes were opened or closed. Then his father blinked and he realized they were open.

Niall wanted to scratch or cough. Fear took control of his bladder and he began to panic as the desire to relieve himself became overwhelming. The only sound in the barn came when the rats scratched at the piles of sacking and woodshavings and when an owl hooted way off in the demesne. He heard wings beating as birds flew through the night skies and he longed to fly too, to be up there with them.

He knew that they were waiting, but for what? Suddenly the sound of the birds' wings took on a more sinister aspect. Was the Devil to come and reclaim him? The thought made him shudder and, having begun to shiver, he found that he could not stop. He was going to die, it was no use denying it. His eyes ached with the effort of keeping them open so he allowed the lids to drop and with them closed he found he felt better, for he could have been alone in his own bed, instead of in that barn with his father and the gun.

Hours passed as they sat still, then like a lick of flame, the sun appeared above the horizon, flooding the barn with a deep, bruised purple haze. William's head lifted at the moment the light fell across them and he turned to stare at his son, his eyes red and bloodshot, his face drawn and white.

'The time has come, Niall,' he said. He rose from the crate and lifted the gun. It looked smaller in his hands, somehow.

Niall stared as the silver barrels rose until they became two round black holes, pointed in his direction.

'The wicked must be punished, Niall,' William intoned. 'And you must be made to understand what it is you have done.'

Niall could not move. His body was numb from sitting still for so long, though he felt the shivering again and his teeth chattering together.

'You must see the fruits of your labour,' William said. 'You must see how the evil are punished.'

He stepped forward to place a hand upon his son's head. 'I am your salvation, Niall, do you understand that? You see why I must do this thing? I am your only hope, your only truth and your only light. Without me you would be damned to all eternity. Do you understand that, Niall? Through me and through me alone shalt thou find thy path. Does that make you happy? Will you rejoice with me?'

'Papa!' Niall cried, terrified now. He shook uncontrollably beneath his father's hand and a stream of hot wetness seeped slowly down his legs.

'Will you pray thanks to God with me, Niall?'

Niall bent his head and prayed until he thought his brain would burst. 'Save me, Father,' he beseeched silently. 'Save me-save me-save me!'

The weight of his father's hand lifted at last but when he opened his eyes he found that he looked up into the barrels of the gun. Tears squeezed from the corners of his eyes. He thought of his mother. Would she be waiting for him when

243

he died? Or would he go to hell, as his father had said? He began to close his eyes again but his father's words stopped him.

'Open your eyes, Niall,' he heard William say. 'You must watch to see how evil is punished and how sinners must pay for their transgressions before the eyes of the Lord.'

He tried to look but he could not. There was silence, then the scrape and click of the hammer being drawn back. Then silence again. He could hear his father breathing above him while he continued his own desperate, silent prayers to God.

'Open your eyes, Niall,' William repeated softly, and Niall did so, expecting to die with each fraction that his lids lifted.

His father stood but a few paces away, the shotgun no longer pointed in his direction; it was held instead against William's body, the butt resting on the ground, the barrels beneath his own chin.

William smiled at his son. 'Watch,' he commanded gently. 'Watch what it is that you have done.'

'Papa, no!'

Niall's scream went unheard for it was drowned by the blast as William kicked his foot against the trigger and the gun went off.

It was as though the whole world had exploded. Niall found that he had jumped up from his seat, engulfed by the noise. There was a sound of wild flapping in his ears, as though a thousand birds had taken off in fright. His mouth opened in a scream of horror. He watched his father's head jerk back, saw a misting spray of bright red veil him until he could see him no longer. The smell of dank blood choked in his throat and his legs felt too weak to hold his body which had become suddenly heavy. He sank to the floor, his limbs rotted through like the apples, and, as they turned to pulp beneath him, the darkness came at last and mercifully he remembered no more.

CHAPTER THIRTY-THREE

Cora climbed down from the carriage and stopped a moment to steady herself as she looked up at the house. She had been away for only one year and yet already it looked smaller to her, as though she were used to grander living.

'It's gone to ruin all right,' she whispered beneath her breath as she studied the crumbling brickwork and the holes in the roof where slates had been knocked down by the storms. The place was worn like a rock the sea had been battering for an eternity. It was the salt air that did it. It affected all the stonework in the district, sooner or later. The statues in Christina's grotto lost their features before a month was out and even the face of the angel in the graveyard had looked less distinct as she'd passed it, as though both grief and time had been working together to wear it away.

Cora caught the driver watching her from the corner of his eye and she rubbed her gloved hands together quickly as though ridding them of the dust of the journey. The gloves were kid, the finest she had ever possessed. She picked a few imaginary specks from the collar of her velvet jacket and generally fussed about until the driver walked round for his money. He would not help her with her cases; that much was clear to her. She had become used to good service in the time she had been away.

The Irish coins looked strange in her palm. A sea wind blew up from nowhere and she clamped her hand onto her bonnet as the driver counted her change. When the wind had dropped she ran her tongue across her lips tasting the salt there and knew that she was home again. A shudder ran the length of her body.

The door was wide open and the hallway empty. No one

came to greet her, save an inquisitive hound, as she made her way to her old room on the first floor. Her boots clicked on the wooden boards and once or twice her toe caught in the worn carpets.

Once inside her room she bolted the door and removed her hat before laying flat on her back on the bed. The mattress was bare and smelt musty but she was too tired to care. The ceiling had the same stains and a few new spots of green mould. Nothing in her room had been moved or dusted and for a moment she thought perhaps she had never been away at all. It was not a problem though, she would clean it herself. She would scrub the floors on her hands and knees if she had to, in fact the idea positively appealed to her and she would have started straight away if she had not known that she should see the others first.

She rose wearily from the bed and opened the case she had carried up with her. She pulled back a layer of soft violet-coloured tissue and ran her hand over the fur-trimmed crêpe dress that lay beneath. The velvet roses on the bodice had become crushed during the journey and, as she fluffed up their petals, she remembered the nights she had worn it.

With a sigh she stood to open the doors of her wardrobe, being careful not to look at her reflection as she did so. Her old, dull-coloured dresses hung in a line before her, their hangers rattling like the bones of disturbed corpses. Moving slowly she pulled each new dress from her case, fingering the fine fabrics, tweaking the lace and chiffon into life before placing them on hangers next to her old clothes. Alexander had been generous and they made a gaudy display.

Then she looked at herself in the mottled mirror. 'Old maid,' she whispered. 'Fat old maid.' She had become fatter in France. How could she not have done when the food was so exquisite and she had a husband who seemed to love eating and drinking above anything else? Her reflection smiled at her.

In a quick movement Cora pushed her new dresses to one side on the rail and unbuttoned the velvet she was wearing so that it slipped to the floor at her feet. Quickly pulling out one of her old brown outfits she threw it over her head and smoothed its full skirt down over her hips. Then she inspected herself again in the mirror. A fat brown sparrow, that's how she looked.

There was a knock on her door and she opened it to find Christina standing there.

'You've let yourself get fat,' was her only welcome.

She was dressed all in black, like a Victorian mourner. 'Papa is waiting,' she told her sister. 'You must come down.'

William Flavelle sat by the fireside, his expression terrible in the flickering light of the flames. Christina had written to her sister, but she had not mentioned the scarring of his face, the right-hand side of which seemed to have melted, so that his mouth was stretched constantly back in a hideous grimace, above which his dark eyes burned with bitterness and frustration. His whole body seemed shrunken, his white collar hanging wide about the livid red scars on his neck. He made no sign of having seen her as she approached and she wondered at first whether he could have been blinded as well.

'Papa?' she said, walking slowly towards him. The red fire reflected in his hair and she saw it was almost pure white now.

Christina had told her it was an accident, that he had fallen on his gun while searching for rats in the barn. The shot had taken an ear and part of his face with it and the explosion had half-paralysed him, robbing him, too, of most of his powers of speech. She had said that his mind was almost gone with the shock, and that it was a miracle he was alive at all. The doctor had all but given up on him and the priest had been called in four times for the last rites. He had survived the crises, though, and Christina had prayed for him through all the nights he had been near death and when Doctor O'Sullivan had guessed that he may have had a stroke too, to add to all his problems.

Christina had written to Cora of all these things but in

so offhand a manner that she had never guessed to see her father in such a bad way. Now she realized that her sister's tone had been tempered by her hatred for her, for tricking Alexander into marriage. She had probably not even wanted her home for a visit.

Falling to her knees in front of her father, Cora leant to take one of his hands in her own as tears of pity sprang up in her eyes.

'Papa!' she cried, turning her face towards him, but the bitterness in his eyes made her cry out in surprise.

His mouth started to move; a curious, sideways movement as though he were chewing at something large, and then his voice came; deeper and softer than before, a barely-audible whistle that issued through his misshapen lips. 'So . . . you are returned . . .' His head nodded slightly.

'Yes, Papa.' She looked across at her sister but Christina's face was an expressionless mask.

His head nodded harder. 'Beg . . .' he said.

Cora studied his terrible face, wondering what it was that he meant.

'Beg . . .' he repeated, becoming more agitated. 'Beg . . . my forgiveness . . .' And she caught the look of triumph that burned in his rolling eyes.

' "I will arise and go to my father . . ." ' Christina quoted, behind her, ' "and I will say unto him, Father, I have sinned against heaven and before thee, and am no more worthy to be called thy son; make me as one of thy hired servants." '

Saliva spilled over his lips onto a bib that was tied beneath his chin. 'So the sinner has thrown you out of his house,' he said, his head shaking with the effort of speech.

Cora's own head began to shake from side to side. 'No, Papa,' she said, unable to look her father in the face. 'I came back because of your accident . . . Christina wrote to me . . .'

'Then you will return to him after?' William asked.

Cora put her head in her hands so that he could not see her expression.

248

'Well?' William demanded when she did not reply.

'No, Papa,' Cora told him, and Christina smiled.

'You sickened him!'

'No, Papa!' Cora cried, her head shaking harder. She thought of Alexander, of the way he had treated her; how he had looked at her. Had he even noticed she was gone? She had been so stupid to believe she could make him love her, that the act of love would bind them together forever. She had thought her virginity a great prize that any man would treasure but her husband had refused the gift, and with so much distaste too, eventually begging her not to insist that he took it. He had not wanted her and later she had realized that he had not wanted any woman. She had been an idiot not to have understood before. How many times had she seen her young husband happier in the company of his own sex; even flirting with all the young Frenchmen, before the truth had finally crept into her stupid thick head?

She closed her eyes at the thought and her lips twisted behind her hands.

Innocence was no virtue, she realized now; not in a married woman of her age. On her it had lain like a crime or a sin. It was stupidity that she had suffered from, not pure and blameless innocence.

'He threw you out,' her father said. 'And you come crawling to me for forgiveness.'

Cora laughed aloud and fresh tears welled up in her eyes.

William glanced at Christina. 'Has Francis returned with her?' he asked.

'No, Papa,' Christina told him, 'not yet.'

William looked back at Cora. 'He will return before long. On his belly, like you; crawling and begging my forgiveness. "Return ye to the house of the Lord." You will all return with time and God's forgiveness shall be magnanimous.'

Far across the large room a door opened slowly and Cora looked up to see Constance appear from the shadows, her little face pale and as grave as her father's. Cora was shocked to see how ill the young girl looked.

'Constance?' she whispered, rising to her feet.

A great shudder shook her father's body as he heard his youngest daughter's name.

Constance advanced a few steps into the room and attempted a smile as Cora held her arms out to embrace her. It was Cora who was forced to take the last few steps across the room, though, for Constance stopped a long way behind her father's chair and would not be tempted any further.

'I fear that it is Papa's face that frightens her,' Christina told Cora once they had left the room and Constance had run off to play. 'She can hardly bear to have him in her sight since the accident and I know this distresses him. I never knew her to be so stubborn; she refuses to show him affection despite the fact that I have told her many times how close to death he has been.'

'She looks so unwell,' Cora said, watching Christina prepare a tray of her father's medicines.

'Constance is quite well,' Christina said, coldly. 'I had the doctor check her out but he announced her fit enough and so do I. We don't want you back here fussing, thank you, Cora. She was hysterical for three days after Papa's accident but then so were we all. It was Niall who raised the alarm, you know, though what he was doing about at that time Lord alone knows.'

She wetted a rag at the sink and set about wiping the row of sticky glass bottles. 'Constance now says she remembers nothing of that night,' she went on, 'which Doctor O'Sullivan says is quite usual with hysterics. He thinks she may remember in time but that perhaps it is as well she stays the way she is right now.

'I wish my own memory was as selective, Cora. I can never forget how Papa looked as he lay there, his head all . . .' She shuddered. 'If Niall had not found him when he did and called Thomas direct from his bed then I know we would not have had him with us today.' She crossed herself as she spoke.

Cora fetched a clean traycloth from the linen press and smoothed it over the damp wooden tray. 'Is Niall here now?' she asked.

'No. Papa will not have him in the house. The sight of the boy distresses him too much.'

'Where is he then?' Cora asked, full of concern.

Christina shrugged. 'He stays with Papa's family,' she said. 'The ones he stayed with while he was convalescing. They let him help around the farm.'

'They have him for slave labour, you mean!' Cora retorted.

Christina rounded on her angrily. 'Why did you leave him?' she demanded, her face red and her voice growing higher.

Cora looked confused. 'Leave him?' she asked, her mind full of her younger brother.

'Alexander.' Christina's mouth formed the word with obvious unwillingness.

'Oh,' Cora said, 'my husband.'

Christina looked away. 'Yes,' she said, slowly, 'your husband, Cora.'

Cora paced about the kitchen to annoy her sister, picking up empty bowls and cups and finally changing the subject altogether. 'Did Papa dismiss all the servants?' she asked, running her finger along the top of the stove and studying the dirt and grease on her fingertip.

'You stole him from me,' Christina said.

'You could have had him for all I cared,' Cora lied, continuing her tour of the kitchen.

'You stole him and now you have left him. You never wanted him, did you, Cora? You just tricked him to spite me! He must have hated you for what you did; for splitting us up like that! Is that when you left him? When you realized at last exactly what Alexander thought of you?'

Cora smiled. 'Oh, I don't think dear precious Alexander

251

ever wanted either of us, Christina,' she said, quietly. She walked over to the kitchen door and inhaled the scented air from the gardens. 'Did you stop to wonder what a butterfly like Alexander would possibly see in two old moths like us?' she asked. 'A couple of old maids who have been cloistered away in this old pile for so long that they've gone yellow with age and lack of real fresh air? What did we really have to offer a boy like that, now? True romance and beauty? I don't think so, do you, Christina?'

She leant her head against the doorpost. 'We were like two ugly great things growing beside him,' she said. 'We would have smothered him in time, clumsy old things that we are. Oh yes, he liked our attentions and our fussing over him but we weren't what he wanted, Christina, no woman ever could be.'

Christina sobbed. 'You're cruel! Cruel and wicked!'

Cora folded her arms and smiled. 'Oh, Christina,' she said. 'You could never understand.'

A chicken ran across the yard in front of her and she watched its golden feathers puff out in the sun. Alexander's distaste for her body had been like a knife through her soul. Then she had seen him with the boy; seen their long, slim naked bodies side by side in her bed, fitting together like a pair of gloves, pressed side-by-side as though they'd been ironed. She had watched them, unseen and in silence, and then she had quietly left forever and returned to her home, the place that she hated.

How could she ever have hoped to please Alexander as that boy had? She had been beyond jealousy in her grief, had felt her heart dry up in an instant. Her father could not hurt her and neither could Christina, for there was nothing left to hurt; nothing that she could feel.

The hen made its way across the yard, picking at the dust with its beak, and she found that she was almost peaceful in her misery. So her father wanted her to be a slave in the house? The thought did not worry her, it would give her something to do while the rest of her life dragged by.

Coming home and climbing into her dull old clothes made the perfect ending to her story. She had sinned in her father's eyes and now she had an eternity of punishment to look forward to.

She was home and she never should have left. Francis would return soon, too, unless he were dead.

'You know, I almost envy you, Christina,' she said, finally. 'You have never left this house and you have never seen the outside world. Do you wonder what you are missing? Did you know there's great cities out there and restaurants that stay open at night? Can you imagine women dancing on a stage and showing their pantaloons to all of the men?'

Her sister threw some cutlery noisily onto the table. 'We have to get tea,' she said, but Cora stopped her.

'*I* have to get tea,' she corrected her sister. 'I'm the new servant around here, remember? Where's Thomas, by the way?' she asked as she went about her duties.

'Oh, he's around when it suits him,' Christina said. 'Which is not very often since the accident. I believe he takes advantage of Papa's state to do as he pleases.'

'Thomas has always been pretty much his own man.'

'He drinks too much now,' Christina told her.

'A little drink now and again does a man no harm at all. You should try some yourself, Christina, it might bring the roses back into your old cheeks!'

The tray full now, she folded her arms across her chest and walked out towards the old barn where her father had met with his accident. The door was difficult to open as dirt had built up underneath and its wooden planks caught as she pushed. As it finally fell back, heat came at her in a rush, bringing with it a buzzing cloud of large black flies and the smell of rotten apples.

Cora entered a few paces, shivering, and looked about. The place was heavy with the warmth of the sun and dust hung in the long arcs of pale light that seeped through the broken slats. In the far corner of the barn stood two wooden crates, pushed side-by-side, though one had been overturned. Cora walked over and looked at them and at the stains of black blood that were on the floor beside them.

Two boxes. She felt her mouth go dry. They had been used as seats, she could tell that much. But why two of them?

'Niall!' she whispered suddenly, the realization making her hand shoot up to cover her mouth.

'You were here, Niall!' she thought. 'You were here all along!' Had her brother finally done it? Had he tried to murder his own father at last?

'Oh, holy mother of God, Niall!' Cora whispered to herself. 'What is it that you have done?'

BOOK II

CHAPTER THIRTY-FOUR

And so the months passed in Connemara and as they passed they held the occupants of the great house in their thrall, like small flies glued into the web of a large spider. Each waited with lazy indifference for fate to intervene, to change their lives in some way, or for their lives to come to an end altogether.

Cora and Christina took on the upkeep of the house as best they could but the place was rotting and whole floors had to be closed as they fell into the hands of neglect and age. The sisters had been used to servants all their lives and the job was patently too much for them. As a compromise they tackled only the jobs that were considered urgent and vital, which included caring for their papa and seeing that the family were served with meals more or less on time. No suggestion was made that Constance should be asked to help with the chores and so instead she was allowed to roam virtually unchecked.

'She is running wild,' Christina would tell Cora as they watched her riding off across the demesne, her hair streaming behind her and her clothes an obvious disgrace.

Cora would nod in agreement but they were both too busy ever to take any action.

The war came but it did not touch that remote part of Ireland. It was a war fought by other countries but then Thomas got drunk and signed up. Within the week Niall had heard of it and had rushed to join with his beloved brother. William was furious when Thomas told him what he had done.

'You are an Irishman, not an Englishman!' he raged. 'Why fight a war that does not concern you?'

'To get away from you,' Thomas could easily have

answered but instead he kept silent though astonishingly firm on the subject. 'I have English blood in my veins, from Mama's side,' he said to his father. 'And it will be an adventure, of sorts.'

He did not tell his father the truth, which was that he was bored to very death and could think of nothing worse than seeing his life out in the place where he had been born.

He was a lazy man, though, and when the recruiting officers had done their tour of the bars he had instantly seen a way out of his situation that required the least initial effort on his part. Besides, the risks as presented by the officers had seemed minimal and the sense of adventure so great that he had jumped straight from his seat and offered his name, much to the amusement of his friends and to cries of 'Traitor!' from some of his enemies. They had all laughed afterwards, though, and he had felt like a hero already, even before he had set one foot on foreign soil.

He had never intended his younger brother to sign up as well but once he had he was proud of him and glad of the companionship. Besides, he could keep an eye on the boy and ensure he came to no harm. They would probably not even fight, he thought, for all the accounts that he read said the whole thing would be over in a matter of months. Then they might just get to travel for free and see a bit of the world at last, or maybe even find their fortunes abroad.

Father Devereux was called to the house but he could not dissuade Thomas from going and nor did he want to. He would have gone himself, had he not been a man of the cloth. Thomas was a grown and healthy man and Father Devereux knew as well as any how stifling life must be for him in his father's house. The place now appalled even the priest and he paid it as few visits as possible. He would feel his soul die the minute he stepped over the threshold. The whole atmosphere seemed to suffocate the spirit and he felt most of its inhabitants well beyond redemption, especially William himself. There was quiet there but no peace. What little life there had been disappeared years before and while the priest tried to sit solemnly with Thomas, to talk him out of going, his heart at the same time urged him to get away and never to return.

'Better to die quickly on some far foreign field than to suffocate slowly in that tedious place you call home,' he found himself thinking. It was a few days before he discovered Niall had signed up too and then he became more worried, for the boy was young and less able to look after himself.

Niall was eighteen years old and, despite his height, looked younger. Father Devereux rode up to him as he dug turf for drying on his uncle's turbary. The boy had not seen him arrive and he reined in to watch him a while as he dug a trench with his spade before cutting the sods and throwing them into the air with a practised twist, so that they landed in a heap on the surface of the bog.

The difference between the two brothers was startling. Whereas Thomas had the well-fed confident air of the country squire, Niall had taken on the look of a farmhand on his uncle's farm. It was the same look the priest had seen a hundred times a day as he went about his parish; head down and shoulders hunched with shyness, eyes averted in the presence of a man of God, and little to say or too few words with which to communicate.

Niall stood before him, bareheaded in the warm sunlight, his long black hair plastered to the back of his neck, his dark brows knitted as he concentrated on his work. His skin was darker now, but he had not grown sufficiently to fill out to his height. He was still lean and gangly and had yet to build muscle on his undernourished-looking frame.

He stopped work for a moment as the priest approached.

'Niall,' Father Devereux said, dropping from his saddle and extending a hand to the boy.

'Father,' Niall acknowledged, nodding. He wiped his hands on his trousers but did not take up the offer to shake.

His awkwardness was contagious. Father Devereux

smiled and looked about, inhaling deeply as though it were his first breath of the day.

'I love the smell of the peat, don't you, Niall?' he asked, and the boy shrugged indifferently. The priest looked down into the trench, at the dark brown fibrous turf that lay there and he rubbed his hands together.

'I see you have stopped wearing your glasses,' he said, for want of better conversation.

'I had no use for them,' Niall told him, and resumed his digging. 'The others had them so I had them,' he said. 'I didn't need them.'

'Good, good!' Father Devereux cleared his throat. 'You're to be a farmer then, like Francis, are you?' he asked.

Niall stopped and looked directly at him. 'No, Father,' he said, 'I am not.'

Father Devereux patted his horse as it munched quietly at the dry patchy grass. He felt idiotic now, standing in the middle of a bog in his long black robes on a warm summer day, watching the boy work and feeling less than a man for doing so.

Niall was stripped to the waist. His brown moleskin trousers were tied with a thick leather belt and his shirt and waistcoat lay in a heap on the ground.

The priest pulled a large white handkerchief from his pocket and used it to mop the sweat from his brow. He felt sorry for the boy always but did not know how to offer him comfort or even friendship.

'I hear you've enlisted, then,' he said at last.

Niall did not stop his digging.

'Thomas told me,' Father Devereux said.

The boy looked at him then and he felt himself shiver, even in the heat of the sun. Niall had his mother's eyes; not their colour or their size, but the same dreamy way of looking, and it had shocked the priest and caught him off-balance.

'Did you come to talk me out of it, then?' Niall asked, tilting his head and squinting into the sun.

'If I thought I could,' Father Devereux said, smiling again but looking even less confident now than he felt.

'Did you talk Thomas out of going?'

'I'm afraid not.'

'Then you won't talk me out of it either.' Niall spat into the earth.

The priest walked to stand closer to him. 'You admire your brother, don't you, Niall?' he asked. The boy shrugged again.

'And are you doing this just to copy him?' Father Devereux asked. 'Do you really understand the dangers? You could be killed, you know, or badly wounded. Why not let the British fight their own battles? There's no need for you to go risking your neck.'

'Did Papa send you?'

The priest shook his head.

'Or Thomas? Or any of the others?' Father Devereux studied his shoes.

'I thought not. So why come here? No one cares if I am killed. It's Thomas you should worry about, Father, he's the one they'll be weeping over if anything happens.'

He looked up again.

'Why did you come?' he asked. He appeared to think for a while. 'Are you my real father?'

Father Devereux looked shocked. Fear hit him like pain, travelling the length of his body and making him sweat.

'Whatever are you asking?' he whispered, trying to sound indignant. The heat-haze made the boy waver in front of him, like a fading image seen in a dream. 'Of course I am not!' he said when the boy had said nothing.

Niall's face registered no emotion at the news. Perhaps he shrugged a little, but that could have been the priest's imagination. Father Devereux felt the sweat rolling down his spine and soaking his clothes. Niall turned and went on with his digging.

* * *

261

The brothers both said their farewells at the great house when it came time for them to take their leave, for Niall was allowed there for just the one occasion.

Constance cried as though her heart was fit to break at the sight of the two brothers she loved so much leaving her and even Cora shed a few tears, which was a quaint thing for them to see her do.

There was no formal farewell, for the people of the clachan had little sympathy for their cause, though there were many damp eyes watching from behind the shutters as they made their way through the main street. William had his chair rolled to the brow of the hill so that he could keep them in sight until they were little more than two specks in the distance.

On the day they were leaving he suddenly became coherent, sitting rigid in his chair, his dark eyes watching everything that happened around him. He saw Constance in her grief and his eyes filled with tears.

The two brothers stood before him at last in his study, one nearly old enough to be the other's father but so flushed with excitement that they could both have been boys. The bond between them was so strong as to be almost visible and though they looked unalike it would be obvious to anyone that they were brothers. The way that they held themselves made them seem as though they were already in uniform; both with their legs straight, a stride apart, and their hands clasped firmly behind their backs. It was all that Thomas could do to stop himself from grinning for he was to be away from there at last, which more than compensated for any risks he might face.

Niall looked less sure of himself. True, he felt proud for the first time in his life, to be standing alongside his brother and about to have some adventure at last, but he had seen Constance waiting quietly in the hall and her sobs as he had passed made him regret being part of the cause of so much grief. Now they had just their papa to say their farewells to and for Niall it was a duty that he would just have soon forgone. He did not understand why he had been summoned along with Thomas; he had been to the house so little in the past few years that he no longer thought of it as his home.

Despite the warm day there was a fire in the study, and both brother's faces were glazed with sweat.

'*Ad majorem Dei gloriam*,' William said to them, his Bible splayed out on his lap.

Niall stared at his father. He knew the madness of the man now; remembered even the smell of his blood as it had sprayed from his head and filled the air as he sat in the barn. He would never forget the horror of that night although he had tried to drive it from his brain. He saw again his father lying on the floor beside him, thinking he was dead, then seeing what remained of his face and hearing him whisper in agony that Niall should have allowed him to die. Instead he had seen his father, his face already bloody pulp, reaching out to the gun to finish the job, and he had knocked the gun from his reach and thereby saved his father's life. He thought William would hate him for that each and every day he spent dribbling in his wheelchair.

'For the greater glory of God.' It was the Jesuit motto; Niall had heard and read it so often before that it meant little to him now.

'You are in God's hands,' William told them. 'Pray that He will be merciful.'

'Yes, Papa,' Thomas said. They bowed their heads as William recited his prayers.

When he was finished he motioned Thomas towards him with his eyes.

'Think of your mother,' William told him. 'Keep yourself safe for her dear sake if not for mine. She loved you terribly, you know that.'

'Yes, Papa,' Thomas told him, straightening again.

The brothers stared down at their father a while before turning together and walking towards the door.

'Niall,' William called.

263

Niall looked at Thomas but saw a helpless look in his brother's eyes, so turned slowly and walked back towards his father's chair.

William shook as his youngest son stood before him. 'Did you confess your sins to Father Devereux?' he asked. Niall nodded, but it was a lie. He had not seen the priest since the day in the bog.

'Did you say your farewells to him?' Niall nodded again and his father seemed satisfied. 'Good.' Niall had to bend to hear his next words.

'Why did you do it?' William whispered. 'Why did you knock the gun from my reach? Why did you not allow me to die?'

Niall looked at him. 'Because I loved you,' he said. 'Because you are my father.' There was a pause and then William's cold hand came out to grasp Niall's for a second before letting it go.

'Pray to God,' William said, the tears running down his cheeks now. 'Pray to God to save your soul and your flesh, Niall.' And he turned his eyes back to watch the fire.

CHAPTER THIRTY-FIVE

Thomas wrote to his father every month for a year and then the letters became less frequent and more reflective. The brief, spirited notes and postcards were now long foolscap pages of introspective scrawl and, eventually, William could hardly bear to bring himself to read them as they seemed to be written by Thomas for himself, not for other eyes to see.

Then suddenly, towards the end of the war, a shorter note arrived that was a great deal lighter in tone, telling them that he would be home for a break and that he very much looked forward to seeing Ireland and his family again.

He was home for some weeks while a minor wound on his foot healed and the rest seemed to suit him for he became more his old self with each day that passed. That he and Niall were both still alive, he told Cora, had to be down to a bloody miracle, for most of their comrades were long dead. The pair of them, he said, had somehow got the reputation among the battalion of having 'the luck of the Irish' for having survived so long, and other soldiers lined up to serve alongside them, hoping that some of their luck would rub off.

'Touch me once for luck,' they would say to Niall or Thomas, extending their grimy hands before they went over the top and, so far, they had led charmed lives, for, apart from Thomas's foot, the pair of them were in relatively good health and high spirits.

William was pathetically happy at his son's return and distraught when the wound had healed and he had to return to active service. Thomas was less upset to go, though, for he had left Niall out there alone and was keen to be back at his side, to 'keep an eye out for him', as he described it. He had come to believe in the stories of their luck and was frightened that it might be less potent if they were apart for any length of time.

It seemed as though Thomas had only just set out on his journey from Connemara when the bicycle came up the drive and the telegram was handed to Christina as she opened the door.

'It's addressed to Papa,' she said to Cora, her face ashen and twitching.

Cora took the envelope and turned it over in her hands. 'We know what this is,' she said, her face screwing up with anguish. 'It is Niall. He must have been killed.' Her voice broke on the last word.

'I'm afraid, Cora,' Christina wailed, clutching at her sister, 'afraid to give it to him. I don't know how he will take the news.'

They stared at the envelope and then Cora ripped it open, her hands shaking as she tried to pull out the message folded inside.

She scanned the few lines of the telegram and then looked up at her sister. 'It's Niall,' she said, flatly. 'It's his initials; look, "Killed in action," it says here.'

Cora sank down onto the stairs and watched her sister standing like a statue in the empty hallway. She felt her body begin to shake, then, with an agonized sob, tears began to fall. Christina sat beside her and the two women wailed out their grief together.

William Flavelle heard their commotion from his seat near the fire in his study. They were the sounds that he had dreaded from the moment his son had left for the war. He had heard the bicycle arrive in the drive and the knock on the door that had sent his daughters scurrying from the kitchen. Now he was impatient to hear the news.

'Christina!' he screamed. 'Who is it? Which one of them has been killed?'

The yelling exhausted him and he collapsed, panting in his chair. The whole house seemed to fall silent as the women heard his shouts. William was reminded of the silence that had become a vacuum after the gun had gone off in the barn and he had shot away part of his own face. That silence had been a terrible thing; more terrible even than the pain that had followed. He had heard the sound of his own deafness and at the time it had seemed as though the world were holding its breath in horror at what he had done that day.

For a moment he had thought that he heard death approaching and that death was nothing more than silence. The notion had frightened him so much that he had been almost glad to find himself alive after all. He now feared his own death more than anything.

He breathed in again, summoning all his strength.

'Who is it?' he cried.

The door opened and he saw Cora standing there looking frightened, the telegram still in her hand. Her face was in shadows. If he could see the expression on her face then he would know, he would know at once.

'It is Niall, Papa,' she said. 'It is Niall who has been killed.'

Niall! William's entire body slumped with relief. Not Thomas, then, not his own son. Niall. The Devil's son. William felt a sense of triumph at last. His torment was at an end. They had been saved. He felt his spine sag and tried in vain to stay upright in his chair. His head sank to his chest and he felt Cora and Christina begin to fuss about him, somewhere far above.

A cup of water was pressed against his lips but he refused it angrily. 'Let me alone,' he said.

He felt them back away at last and knew he was alone with his thoughts.

How had the boy died? This concern would not go from his head, nor would the vision of Christ on the cross, though instead of Christ's face, he saw Niall's.

'Was I wrong?' William whispered, not to himself but to God. There was no answer for him this time.

'Have I been wrong?' he asked, needing reassurance. He

267

tried to pray but the words stuck. How was he to pray for a soul already lost at birth? The son of a priest. Niall had been damned his entire life and there could have been no other way. Then a new thought occurred to William and it was one that gave him the comfort he desired. Thomas was alive. The son that he loved had survived and would return.

There was a scream from the passage outside his study and he winced with pain, knowing that Constance had been told of Niall's death. She was young. She would recover. With time and prayer she would forget; they would all forget.

A letter from Thomas arrived the next day, though he made no mention of his brother's death. He wrote merely of his last week at home and of how little Ireland had changed in all the time he had been away.

'The war will be over soon, Papa, I can feel it now,' he wrote. 'All the fellows here think as much and morale is high again. Soon to be home.' It was signed with a flourish, and the last they were to receive. William placed it on his Bible and read it twenty or more times a day.

And Thomas was right; the war was soon finished and William was impatient as he waited for the return of his precious son.

They placed William's chair at the end of the drive where he could look past the huge whitewashed gateposts and wait for the first sight of Thomas. Cora had told him that he would probably not be home for weeks but her father insisted and as the weather was fine enough to allow it she would push him there each afternoon and collect him later for his tea.

Some days Constance would wait with him, praying that the telegram had been a mistake and that she would find both brothers marching proudly in step as they made their way to the house. She would lean against the gatepost, sucking on boiled·sweets that she took there in a bag, her two russet plaits crossed and tied above her head as she frowned against the sun and studied the road ahead with unswerving patience. If she saw a cart or horse arriving she would run a little way down the track but it would be only the doctor or the priest about his business, and often there were mists that obscured her view altogether and then she would feel like crying with frustration.

Constance was fourteen, nearly a woman, and very beautiful. Her body was slimmer, more like a boy's, and her pale skin shone like the moon. Her eyes could break the heart of any man. She took less care about her clothes now that her nanny was gone and on most days wore a creased linen skirt which hung in loose folds about her slender waist, with a wool jacket for the cold. Her feet tapped in impatient agitation in her brown high-buttoned boots. The boots were worn at Christina's insistence for she was convinced that a young girl's ankles were too weak to go unsupported. Constance hated them but Christina had tales of Cora's many accidents as a child to back up her theories and so they stayed.

Constance scuffed the boots against the stone of the gatepost and looked down with satisfaction at the white streaks that came off on the leather. Cora had hung some ancient faded bunting in the hallway of the house, to welcome Thomas home, and Constance was reminded of her birthday party, when she had been given her pony in the garden.

She had bought a flag of her own to wave; a small Union Jack that she thought might be appropriate, though she worried about her father's reaction when she pulled it out of her pocket.

'Papa?' she said quietly, shielding her eyes from the sun. Her father looked up from his chair.

'Papa!' she said, more excited now and scrambling at the gatepost, trying to find a foothold so that she could climb it. Using her father's chair as a lever and paying no heed to his warnings to be careful, Constance hoisted her way to the top of the wide post, where she stood on tiptoe, gazing at the horizon. She had seen a figure there; no more than a dull brown smudge, but the smudge was growing closer every second and soon she could make out arms, then legs cased in polished brown boots.

'Only one,' Constance whispered, looking in vain for a second figure. 'There's only one of them come back.' She squatted atop the post on all fours like an animal, rocking backwards and forwards on her haunches as she realized that Niall might, after all, be dead. He could not be gone, though. She refused still to believe it. Perhaps Thomas would have news of him and be able to tell them he was alive. So many men died in the war, after all. Surely the army could not account correctly for each and every one.

She pulled her small flag sadly from her pocket and waved it with all of her strength so that Thomas might see her and wave in return. Tears welled in her eyes and she found herself laughing and crying at once as her brother made his way up the track.

'Thomas!' William shouted suddenly, seeing his daughter's excitement.

Cora must have seen them for she came running from the kitchen, wiping her hands on her apron and crying out with joy. Christina saw Constance dancing on top of the gatepost and went to warn her in case she should fall but then she saw the brown figure in the distance too, pushed her hair from her face and joined in the shouting as though her very life depended upon it. To their delight the figure saw them and began to wave back and they all stood, waving and laughing at once.

It was Cora who stopped first. Her arm seemed to freeze in the air and her smile died as her eyes peered furiously into the distance. She turned first to her father and then her sisters but they continued to wave happily and so she looked back once again.

'Oh, holy mother of God!' she whispered. 'We've turned out to welcome a ghost!'

Constance heard her and stopped jumping. When finally she saw what Cora meant she let out a small scream and almost fell from the gatepost. She steadied herself, though, and clutched her flag to her chest.

'Papa,' Cora said to her father, trying to quiet him. 'Papa!' He did not hear her and so she clutched his arm instead. He looked up at her. 'Wait, Papa.'

It was Constance who said it first. 'It's Niall, Papa,' she said, pulling her hat off with delight and waving it with all her might. 'It is, Papa!' she screamed. 'It *is* Niall! It's a miracle! He was saved after all!'

She did not see the expression on her father's face but Cora felt the change with the fingers that lay on his arm. She knew at once what Constance did not; that if Niall were alive then Thomas must be dead. An initial had been wrong on the telegram, that was all. It was a simple enough mistake; just an 'N' instead of a 'T'. But then there had been Thomas's last letter . . .

Her fingers slid from her father's arm as she could not bear to touch him any more. He frightened her. His muscles had begun to tense. His head had turned away from her and his neck had become rigid, locked with grief and anger.

She should have turned his chair and pushed him back up the path but she was unable to move and so watched the tableau before her as though she were no longer a part of it.

Niall stopped waving once he had rounded the bend, his face still alight with joy and disbelief at the welcome he was getting. Even his father had shouted at him and there was his darling Constance, jumping atop the gate. He had thought to face accusations once they heard of Thomas's death, but his father had seemed pleased to see him and his heart swelled with pleasure at the thought that he was forgiven at last.

Cora would barely have recognized him as he had changed so much in the years they had been separated. He was even taller, his shoulders broader now, and his face had filled out to become almost handsome. She watched as Constance slid down from the gatepost and ran towards

271

him, flinging her arms about his neck and covering him with kisses. A smile crossed Niall's face as she did so, though his eyes had become grave and did not leave his father for an instant.

They took him back to the house and William did not speak the entire journey. No one told him they had thought him dead as Constance was too excited; clutching his arm in fear that he might disappear if she once lost her grip upon him, and Cora and Christina were too fearful of their father to discuss it. Somehow they clung to the hope that Thomas might still be alive. Constance thought that, if one miracle could happen, then two should not be impossible. Surely Thomas could rise up from the dead, too, and come marching up the path as Niall had done?

Niall shattered all their hopes when he told them the truth; or at least as much as he could bear to bring himself to admit. Thomas was dead. He had been killed on his return to the front. Their eyes asked how their brother had died but he said he did not know, although he did.

'We had a letter from him!' Christina said, still hoping that there had somehow been a mistake.

'He must have posted it before he was killed, then,' Niall told her.

He entered the dining-room and saw the cake that was lying on the table on a silver tray and all at once he realized that their welcome had not been for him. The cake was a large square fruit slab that Cora had soaked in rum and then iced with the words 'Welcome home, Thomas' in blue icing. A bone-handled knife lay beside it, waiting for his brother.

Niall read the inscription and turned to face his family. 'You thought it was me . . .' he began. 'You thought that it was me who had died . . . You were expecting Thomas . . . you thought I was him when you saw me coming up the path.'

No one spoke.

Niall stood there in front of them, tall and uncomfortable

in his uniform, wishing that he was dead, too. Cora poured him a brandy and pressed it into his hands. He swallowed it in one, staring at the bunting draped above his head. He barely tasted the drink. The cake was his brother's, as were the flags and their smiles of delight at his return. He could not bear to look at his father's face but knew exactly how it would be. He still felt his brother's death keenly but what pained him more at that moment was that he had thought the welcome had been arranged for him.

'The telegram had your initials on it . . .' Christina began. 'We thought . . .'

Only Constance had looked pleased once she had seen that it was him, but now she knew Thomas was dead she was crying quietly into her handkerchief as well.

Suddenly he hated them all. If he could have ripped his heart out there and then before them he would have done so, for it agonized him. He had thought himself a grown man now and immune from the pain his father had caused him as a child.

William stirred at last in his chair, like a great clock preparing to chime in an empty room.

Cora's hands tensed around the handles of his chair. He was at her mercy now, she thought; hers to control, for he had no real control of his own. She could have prevented what she knew was to come. She could have grabbed those handles and pushed him quickly from the room; flung him from the house before he spoke the terrible words she knew to be upon his lips. No one would have stopped her and no one would have blamed her but even so she knew that she could not do it. And so they all turned to listen, though none of them wanted to hear.

'The wrong one died,' William pronounced, his head shaking with grief. 'The wrong one died,' he repeated, looking about at their faces, ensuring each one of them understood the full meaning of his words.

'Papa!' Cora cried but it was too late, the words hung there in the empty air.

Niall looked again at Constance and at the painful smile that she tried, for his benefit, to hold on her face. He hated her too, now. He hated them all. It was not enough just to hate his father, he had to hate them all if he were to survive this agony. If he felt love for any of them he would be tied to his father's house forever and that he could not bear.

'I couldn't save him,' he said at last. 'I wasn't there when he died. It was a fluke, a stray shot.' Other men that had been with Thomas had told Niall in callous detail how he had died and the terrible vision their words had produced came into his mind now.

His father said nothing, only leant further forward in his chair.

'I saved you, Papa!' Niall thought. 'I saved your life!' but he could not bring himself to say the words aloud.

A sudden idea came to him, so simple that he almost laughed. 'I'll go,' he said, wondering why he had not thought to do so before.

'Niall?' he heard Constance cry behind him but he paid no attention to her now.

He hauled his arms into the sleeves of his greatcoat and, pulling up his collar, made his way towards the door.

'I couldn't save Thomas for you, Papa,' he said, as he passed his father's chair. 'But I can still save Francis, God willing. Did any of you get word from him while I was away?' he asked, looking about at his sisters' shocked faces.

William looked up with a sneer on his twisted face. 'Francis is in America,' he said. 'He went to look for his grandfather's firm.'

The sisters looked up in surprise as William had never given them any indication that he knew of Francis's whereabouts.

'You could never find him,' William's eyes told Niall.

Niall hitched his pack onto his shoulders. 'If he's still alive I'll find him,' he said, bending down to stare directly into his father's grotesque face. 'Would that please you, Papa?

One son lost but another saved? That sounds a fair enough deal to me. How does it sound to you?'

'You'll never trace him, Niall!' Cora exclaimed. 'There's so many damned people out there you'll die before you find him.'

'If he's alive I'll find him,' he repeated. 'It's God who decides the fate of us humans, isn't that right, Papa? I'll just be acting as God's helper, that's all. Or the Devil's; it all depends which way you look at it, doesn't it, Papa? You want a son and I shall go and find one for you. Then you can get out your damned bunting and your flags again and perhaps you can ice another cake, too, to show how pleased you are that he's returned. I upset your little party and I'm sorry for that.

'Keep your cake on the plate there, though, and I'll have a cause for your cutting it before it's grown too stale, I promise.' He looked down at the cake again, at his brother's name spelt out in the icing.

'I should have died,' he said, quietly. 'I should have died instead of him. I would have done you all a favour.'

He looked around at their faces then, at his father, slumped in his chair, at Christina and Cora, their faces wet with silent tears, and at his beloved Constance, who now seemed to him to be regarding him with an expression of horror.

'You wanted me dead, all of you,' Niall whispered. 'Damn you, damn you all to hell!' he shouted, in a burst of bitter anger. And then he was gone from the room, slamming the door behind him.

William's eyes closed slowly and his great head slumped onto his chest.

Cora stood red-faced and she watched the closed door as though Niall might change his mind any moment and return. When she finally turned to her father her eyes were wild with fury. Christina merely stared down at her hands and Constance sat sobbing quietly on the window-ledge.

'You cannot allow him to go, Papa!' Cora said. 'Stop him,' she ordered. 'Beg him to stay.'

There was no reply and Constance slipped from her seat.

'Niall!' she shouted from the window. And her cry was like the cry of a bird. Cora rushed to her side and grabbed her by the arms.

'Stop him!' Constance screamed, hysterical now, the two words echoing around the huge empty room.

But for Cora's strong hands she would have crawled to her father and begged him to return her darling brother to her.

'What has he ever done?' she asked instead. 'How can you always be so cruel?'

'The boy is evil, Constance!' William shouted. 'He was damned from birth! Now I damn him too for what he has brought to this house and for the look in your eyes when you gaze at me now!'

Constance's face drained with the shock of being shouted at by her father but she would not stop. 'He cannot be evil!' she argued. 'God saved him and brought him back from the war!'

'It was the Devil that saved him, Constance!' William raved, his eyes bulging with rage. 'Not God! The Devil! Remember that if you remember nothing else! It is the Devil's work that he does and I have watched him destroy my entire family as he does it! He is evil, Constance, and will corrupt you as well if I let him!'

He pulled his chair forward in one divine effort of will and, grabbing his daughter by the wrist before she could turn away, flung her to the floor, pulling her head up quickly until it was crushed against his chest.

'I have to protect you, Constance,' he said, sobbing, 'with any strength I have left in my body. You are my own darling daughter and I cannot allow him to take you as well.'

He rocked back and forth in his chair, clutching her to him. 'My darling,' he crooned. 'My dear darling daughter.'

Christina sobbed from self-pity and envy as she watched

her sister receive all the affection she had craved and the sound of her cries seemed to rouse Constance from her shocked state. Leaning in terror against her father's chest and feeling his tears upon her face, a memory long-hidden inside Constance's mind seemed slowly to surface at last. She became a small child again, clinging to her father's chest in fear as he suffered a fit from which she feared he would never recover. She saw the moonlight about her bed and heard her father call her by her mother's name. She heard her own child's voice begging him to stop, to release her before she suffocated against him and she remembered how he would not stop, how his hands shook as he held her.

He had been like a drowning man in her bed, pulling her down with him. He had even been wet – his nightshirt and his body. What was it that he had needed from her, to have clung to her so fiercely?

And then Constance remembered and her mouth opened wide with horror at the memory.

She had pleaded with him then as she pleaded with him now: crying for him to stop. She remembered his face, large and distorted above her own, and the pain that had made her scream until she had heard her own cries no more and the memory had been mercifully washed from her mind.

She was older now, though, and she understood. The scream rose inside her again but she kept it down through the strongest effort of will. She tore herself from her father's arms in a movement so sharp that it sent his chair spinning away from her. Cora rushed to steady it but Constance would have seen it spin forever until it was dashed upon the rocks that littered the beach beneath the cliffs. She would have seen him shatter like the wood of the chair that he sat upon and she would not have shed one solitary tear for him; not one single drop.

Her father became a blur before her eyes; a pallid shape with round black eyes and a wide black cavern for a mouth. What sins had they been guilty of that night? Incest. She knew the word from the Bible readings though she had not known that she knew it. They were damned together, then; father and child, each as guilty before the eyes of God as the other. She saw the blood that had been upon her sheets and felt herself damned for eternity by William's crime.

She looked at her sisters but knew that only Niall could help her, for her father had said that he was damned and so only he could ever understand her plight. She rushed from the room and out of the house to follow him, the mist over the ground freezing her feet inside their boots.

'Niall?' she shouted as loud as she could for she did not know which path he had taken. Birds flew, startled, from their nests, but there was no sound from her brother.

She heard the sea in the distance, breaking on the cliffs and she prayed he had not thrown himself onto the rocks in a final fit of despair.

Barely able to breathe through her tears, Constance ran around the house to the stables, pulling open the wooden door and startling the lad who was slowly raking at mounds of stale straw. Thomas's horse stood in its stall, its massive head bowed as it pulled whips of hay from the bundle the lad had just thrown down.

'Saddle him,' Constance said.

The boy looked concerned. Constance had never ridden the horse before and looked hardly suitably dressed for a journey. He opened his mouth to speak but she cut him off quickly, urging him to hurry.

She took off at a fearful pace and the stable-lad crossed himself twice for fear the horse would return riderless and he should get the blame for her accident.

Constance took the path that led to the cliffs and it was there that she had to allow her horse to slow a little as it picked its way through the rocks and loose rubble. The land about her looked bleak and grey, the clouds above golden in the mellow light of dusk. She smelt the mustiness of seaweed and thought of it lying on the shore below like mounds of slippery black eels.

278

'Niall!' she called in despair when she had reached level ground and the sea lay below her in a froth of deepest green. She stood up in the stirrups to lean over the edge of the cliff and peered down onto the wet rocks, fully expecting to see her brother's form stretched out and broken upon them.

The horse snorted and rolled its eyes, terrified by the sheer drop, and so Constance dismounted and flung herself onto the wet grass, her head hanging over the edge, to get a better view. There was no body there, she saw to her relief, and none that she could make out floating upon the crest of the foaming tide.

CHAPTER THIRTY-SIX

It was Father Devereux who found Constance at the cliff-edge. Lured to the path for reasons far removed from her own, he had come not to look for bodies but to escape them for he had spent the previous night and most of the day sitting uncomfortably at the bedside of one of his dying parishioners and craved fresh air.

His first reaction on seeing Constance lying prostrate on the grass had been to turn his mare and charge away before she saw him. The idea had occurred to him that she might be dead, which notion held little charm for him, and then the thought came unbidden into his mind that she was after all his own daughter as well as a member of his flock, and with that came the palpitations of a fear that he thought was all behind him.

His daughter. The flesh of his loins. Would this haunt him forever when for years he had tried to convince himself that she was William Flavelle's child? He was fearful of her, there was no other way that he could, if asked, have described his emotions as he gazed down at her. It was as though he were confronted by his own lusts and carnal desires, that she had been laid in his path to lure him towards further mortal sin.

Father Devereux felt as strong a desire to be gone from the cliffs as he had earlier felt to be gone from the sick-room and the guilt that arrived in the wake of that desire was every bit as potent. It was the sort of remorse that could take your breath away like the wind; an innocent girl in distress and a poor dying man ... but the distaste was a physical thing that would not be gone from him however hard he bade it.

The wind blew her hair like fine red sea-fern and her thin

hands grasped the rock like the small white paws of an animal. The cliff must feel chalky to her fingers and when she finally stood she would wipe those fingers onto her skirt, leaving white smears across her apron.

The priest thought that he should speak but his tongue felt like a round hard pebble in his mouth, making the basic action of speech impossible. He watched as one white hand released its grip of the rocks and pushed strands of hair from her eyes. If he spoke now he might startle her and perhaps she might slip, but then that looked unlikely, for he saw that her toes were dug firmly into the earth and he knew that her boots, when she rose, would also be stained, by the grass. Her ankles above the boots were thin white and straight, like brittle driftwood. His daughter . . . the idea seemed impossible to him.

When she turned to face him her expression was one of fierce anger, though it did not seem directed at the priest for her eyes had not focused upon him yet. He thought that her face was one that a man might adore from afar and then, in old age, draw deep sighs of regret for never having had the daring, as a youth, to attempt to procure for himself. There were no flaws in Constance's beauty, as there had been in her mother's, and therefore nothing to make a man confident that it might possibly be obtainable.

'Father!' she breathed, surprised to see him there, watching her so intently.

The word had a painful double meaning, he realized. She pulled her skirts down over her legs in a gesture of modesty, as though he might be shocked by those pale thin sticks. He would have offered his hand as she scrambled to her feet but it seemed inappropriate, and he was dearly afraid of her touch.

'Oh, Father, did you see Niall at all?' she asked. Her voice was breathless and soft. She appeared impatient, fairly hopping on the spot as she waited for his answer.

'Niall?' He had, and he told her as much. He had passed the boy on the edge of the demesne and had wondered why he had been ignored when he had stopped to pass the time of day. A look of relief crossed the girl's face as he spoke.

'He's well away then,' she said, suddenly looking sad. She had no need to search for his body on the rocks below, then.

A tear in her dress flapped in the wind. She studied him for a while, as though searching for something in his face. 'Thank you, Father,' she said at last and, with a miracle leap, she was back up in the saddle again and he found himself watching her back as she rode off down the winding curves that led towards the house.

It was some weeks before Father Devereux saw Constance again and then it was in his church, where he came upon her lighting a candle and saying her prayers on her knees. She was dressed in what he took to be some drab garment of Cora's; a great dark sombre dress that hung in empty folds about her slim frame.

He watched her shaking hands as she lit one little yellow candle from the flame of another and wax dripped onto her sleeve, though she made no move to wipe it off.

'Do you have time to hear me, please, Father?' she asked timidly. Her cheeks burned bright red and her eyes looked feverish. The priest sat in a pew beside her but his proximity seemed to make her more agitated.

'No, Father,' she told him gravely, 'I need to confess. I need you to hear my confession.'

There was nothing strange in a young girl's wish for confession, he knew, but he wondered why she approached him now, and with such a look in her eyes?

'Bless me, Father, for I have sinned,' she whispered once they were alone in the darkness. Her voice sounded high in the claustrophobic stillness of the box. Her urgency alarmed him; he had barely found his seat before she had begun to talk.

'Father . . .' There was a pause and then the words came tumbling out. 'I have wished to take my own life, Father, and I know that is a sin and I wished to confess before my

282

soul was damned to purgatory . . . though it probably is anyway because . . .' Her voice broke and the priest waited for her to go on.

So, she had been about to throw herself from the cliffs when he had found her. He thought of the black wet rocks below and felt his heart give a small lurch inside its ribcage.

'You wished to take your own life?' he asked. He had not wanted to repeat it but she now seemed unwilling to go on.

'Yes, Father,' she whispered.

There was a pause and he found himself listening to her breathing.

'Why did you wish to do that?' he asked. 'It is no solution to anything.'

Her foot banged listlessly against the leg of her chair.

'Why did you wish to die?' The banging became harder.

'Because I have sinned, Father,' she said in a whisper so low he had to bend his head to hear her words, 'and because my sin is so great that there could be no forgiveness for me, ever,' she finished.

Father Devereux smiled a little at her obvious exaggeration and leant back more comfortably in his chair. Constance was no longer a child, he knew, but her conception of sin was, obviously, still childlike. Her life had been sheltered and, to his knowledge, quite blameless and he sat back to wait for the sort of little confession a child would normally make: 'I teased my mamma's cat,' they would say; 'I spoke angrily to my brother'; 'I was late saying my prayers this morning'; 'I forgot to pray for my papa and I'm afraid that he will die'; 'I tore my stockings getting dressed'; 'I have sinned with my papa'.

The priest gave a start. The last voice had not been inside his own head. The last words had belonged to Constance. 'I have sinned with my papa.' The priest felt his palms become damp. He sat erect in his seat again, straining to catch the inflection of her tone.

'With your father?' he asked.

'Yes, Father.' Her voice sounded stronger, as though the confession had given relief already.

'Do you know what you are saying, my child?' Of course she did not. She had merely confused her vocabulary, that was all. He would laugh later in private over the mistake.

'Yes, Father,' she replied and her voice sounded alarmingly adult.

What should he say to her? The holy script evaded him suddenly; all of the platitudes and reassurance that one should give under such circumstances flew from his mind at the sound of her words and the horror of the vision that those words had implanted in his imagination.

William and Constance. The purest child and the most righteous man, welded together by lust; squirming in their juices like snails in their own slime. It was not possible. There had to be a mistake. Father Devereux shut his eyes quickly but the image became stronger. There was William, naked and covered with black hair, panting over his daughter's spreadeagled white body. He opened his eyes again quickly and gazed instead at the glowing red windows of the nave.

Constance was waiting. He had to find the words for her, repulsed though he was. He cleared his throat noisily. Why didn't she cry? She sounded so assured now. He wanted her tears and her cries for forgiveness while instead he saw her only as her mother's daughter; positive and confident in her sexuality and filling the box with the perfume of her body.

'You are telling me that you have had ... relations ... with your own father?' he asked.

She nodded now and the movement stirred a thousand new aromas from her; of fresh-smelling hair and the sea-spray that had whipped through each strand.

Father Devereux became afraid, as at the first trembling of a devastating earthquake. William's sin repulsed and horrified him and yet he was as involved in the man's rutting as if he had lain there in the bed beside him. He would have pulled a cover over the story there and then, sealed it with

284

wax and a holy seal if he could. But he knew that he could not if he were ever to live with his conscience again. He took a breath; deep but not comforting.

'How . . . often has this . . . this sin been repeated?' he asked, the distaste in his voice more obvious than he would have wanted.

Constance's head swung round and he could feel her eyes blaze in the darkness. 'Repeated?' she whispered, and it was she who sounded shocked now. She seemed to hold her breath until he wondered whether she would die from suffocation and he found himself holding his own breath too, in sympathy.

'It . . . was . . . just the once . . .' she began. 'I had forgotten . . . it had gone from my memory completely . . . it must have been the shock . . . I didn't even realize at the time . . . I thought that he was dying . . .' She broke off and the priest waited for the sound of her sobs. 'I thought that I had killed him . . .' she continued instead. 'I didn't know, I didn't know until now! Can an innocent be guilty, Father? Can I ever be forgiven my sins?'

'You were taken against your will, then?' Father Devereux asked, relieved.

He heard her sharp intake of breath at the idea that he could have thought otherwise. Her pale hands flew to her face and fluttered there, like startled moths.

'Oh, could you think that I would agree?' she asked. 'But then maybe there was something in my behaviour . . . perhaps it was not all his fault . . . I was a child, though, Father! Can a child be guilty of such a thing? But if you think I could have agreed then I must be damned . . .' she sobbed, 'for God will also suspect that I was to blame. What was I to do, Father? He came to me in the night . . . I was asleep . . . I had no way of knowing . . . it is only now that I realize the sin . . .'

'It was only the once then?' the priest asked.

'Yes, oh, yes!' Constance cried. 'It was the night that Papa had his terrible accident! My father . . .' she sobbed, 'my

285

own father . . . I shall kill myself from the shame of it!'

Father Devereux moved uneasily in his chair. He felt pity for the girl and knew that he had the power to relieve some aspects of her suffering.

'Constance . . .' he began, not knowing where that word would lead him, 'whatever else happens you must not consider taking your own life.'

The girl's head rose and he could smell the salt of her tears. He had sinned and badly but he had somehow managed to bury that beneath the rubble of his work as a priest. Now the result was there beside him and the power to save an innocent young girl was in his hands. And yet he balked at doing so, for it meant ruining his own reputation and livelihood. Should he confess to her and ease her burden of guilt? He could not. He knew that fact as much as he knew anything.

In the end then, a compromise.

'Constance . . .' he began, 'I have some words for you that may, in a way, provide comfort.'

Her sobbing ceased immediately and he heard her waiting in desperate anticipation.

'I will not speak to you as your priest to tell you this, my dear,' he said, 'for what I have to say was told to me in confidence and I felt that I never would tell it, only then I could never have imagined such circumstances as these. What you have told me is terrible, Constance, but I feel your guilt and your shame are augmented by the fact that it was your father who defiled you in such a way, and that it is the sin of incest that you fear above all others, am I right?'

Constance paused before nodding. 'It is the greatest of sins . . .' she began. 'Papa would have it read to us at table . . . I heard the punishments and tortures . . .'

Father Devereux held up his hand.

'What possible relief could you offer me?' she asked. 'I have committed a despicable sin. What possible hope could there be for me now?'

'God may grant forgiveness for the gravest of sin, my

286

child,' Father Devereux told her, 'and remember that in your case you were given no choice. The sin was forced upon you.'

Her head shook violently back and forth. 'God may forgive me,' she said. 'But I can never live with what I have done . . . what I was forced to do. My father, my very own father. I cannot live with that thought.'

The priest could listen no more. 'William Flavelle . . .' he began, painfully. 'He is not your natural father. The sin you have described to me was not one of incest.'

Constance sat in silence, listening.

'You must worry no more about that aspect of your misfortune,' he went on. 'What happened to you was certainly a crime and a sin but it was not incest. Do you understand?'

He thought he heard her laugh but she may have been choking on her tears. She said nothing, though, and he found her silence annoyed him, for he had expected more at his great revelation. 'The secret is a grave one,' he said, almost in rebuke. 'I hope that its telling was worth breaking the confidence. I hope it has given some relief from your suffering.' He stared at the girl's head through the grille.

'Not my father?' she whispered finally.

'No,' Father Devereux said, folding his arms. He knew he should say more but felt no compunction to do so at that moment. What if she were to guess the rest? The blood drained from his face. The idea had not occurred to him before that moment. But how could she guess, he thought, who would imagine that a priest like himself . . . ?

'I don't understand,' Constance was saying. 'What can you mean? How can he not be my father?'

The priest sighed. 'Your mama,' he began, 'she confessed to me upon her deathbed. She confided in me that William Flavelle was not the father of the child she had just given birth to. That child was, of course, you, Constance. Do you understand? I cannot go into further details. I have said as much as is necessary.'

'But how could . . .' Constance began, and then stopped. 'Who is my father, then?' she asked. 'Do you know? Did Mama tell you?'

Father Devereux felt the slimy trickle of sweat running in fat beads down his spine. 'I cannot tell you,' he said and then, in desperation, came the greatest lie: 'She did not tell me. I do not know his name.' He let out a sigh of relief at the disclosure. He had told the girl enough to help her. Surely she would not be forward enough to ask more. Now it was up to her to reach her own conclusions and she could never guess the truth. Perhaps she did not even have the knowledge of conception. Perhaps she did not connect what she had done with the creation of life. He shuddered to think of the day that she did.

'Does that knowledge lighten your burden, my child?' he asked, very much the priest again now.

'Yes, Father.' A child's voice, tiny and shocked.

'Good.' He had done his duty as he saw it. 'And you will have no more thoughts of suicide?' he asked.

'No, Father,' came the reply.

He sensed another question coming and his smile died.

'Is Niall not Papa's child, too, then?' she asked.

'Niall?' Father Devereux said. 'Why of course he is! It is only yourself, Constance. Niall is William's son, I am sure of it.'

In the silence that followed he thought of a penance for her, but dismissed the idea as inappropriate. She had suffered enough already. Perhaps a prayer, though, to restore the link with the great God Almighty. Father Devereux prayed and barely heard the girl's whispered replies as he did so. Having finished his prayer he crossed himself quickly and, quitting his seat in one grateful movement, left Constance and the wretched wooden box that she sat in for the relative peace and quiet companionship of the surrounding churchyard.

CHAPTER THIRTY-SEVEN

So now Constance had nothing more to do than merely wait. The waiting was simple but not easy, although her life demanded little more of her than that she sit at table at meal times and spend her other waking hours in a kind of listless agitation. She became like a ghost in the ruined great house and her first thought upon waking each day was of her brother Niall, whose loss she felt strongly. He would return to protect her though, she knew it and that was why she waited; for her brother's return and for her moment of revenge.

In the end she did not have long to wait. In the fine summer of 1920, some six years after his attempted suicide, William Flavelle was taken to his bed with a second stroke and, according to the doctor, was not expected to last the night. Constance heard the news with only the vaguest of reactions so that Doctor O'Sullivan suspected he would be called next to tend to her once the shock had set in.

While Cora and Christina stood white-faced in the hall, gazing up the stairway and listening for any sound that might indicate they were needed, Constance stood at the open window of her own room, high up in the large empty house, breathing the sweet night air and watching the horizon as usual for any sign of Niall's return.

With her father's illness she had felt the first shifting of the burden that she had carried for years and she thought that Niall had to feel it as well; wherever he was.

There was a gentle knocking on her door and the doctor's head appeared, looking kind and concerned. 'He is asking for you, Constance,' he said, walking over and taking one of her hands in his own.

Constance did not move and her eyes did not leave the window.

'You know you were always his favourite,' the doctor encouraged her. 'I suppose that he loved you all in his way but God knows you were the only one he felt he could show his affection for. You were a miracle in his life, Constance, I hope you realize that.'

He felt a shudder pass through the girl's hand.

'I know his death will affect you badly, my dear,' he said, and she pulled her hand away, 'but I want you to know that you provided one of the only happinesses of his life, and for that much you should feel proud. He is a difficult man, I know, but, when you were around, his whole nature and character would soften.

'Please think of your sisters, too, my dear,' he went on, 'they sought their father's love but never, I'm afraid, found it as you did. You may have been closer to him, Constance, but you should remember that his death will be every bit as hard for them as it is for you.'

Constance turned to the doctor then, and he saw that her eyes were peculiarly bright.

'Does he have his Bible with him, Doctor?' she asked.

The doctor nodded. 'He had the Father place it by his bedside this very hour.'

'Can he hear and understand all that is said to him?'

'I believe so,' Doctor O'Sullivan told her, 'though his speech is worse affected and you may find him difficult to understand. He cannot move his face enough to talk properly, no more than a few noises, and his limbs are like a dead man's, but his mind is untouched by the stroke and his hearing, if anything, seems improved. He will both hear and understand anything that you say, my dear, and I'm sure he will find comfort in your words.'

Constance closed her eyes and seemed to be holding her breath. 'Is he in any pain?' she asked.

'I believe not.'

Constance smiled. 'Good,' she said. 'Thank you, Doctor.'

The doctor had the uncomfortable feeling that he had somehow been dismissed.

William looked peaceful enough as he lay in the darkness. Only one small candle lit the room and it bathed his great face in a benign golden wash.

Father Devereux sat with him but he rose to leave the room when Constance arrived.

'Papa?' She spoke the word gently yet his eyes flickered open in an instant.

Constance took her father's hand in her own and sat down beside his bed. His hand lay inert and huge between her own two thin white ones. She watched his eyes roll in their sockets like the eyes of a cow, following her every move as she leant close towards him.

'Would you like me to read to you from the Bible, Papa?' she whispered.

His eyelids closed once: 'Yes.'

She pulled the heavy book across the bed and the ageing leather of its cover left an oxblood-red stain across the counterpane. There was a sheet of paper keeping one page and that was where Constance opened it. The paper slipped from the pages and fell onto the bed.

'A letter, Papa?' Constance asked at once. 'For me?' It was a sealed envelope and it had her name scrawled across it. William blinked once again. 'Yes.'

She turned the envelope, holding it up to the light. Across the back of it were written the words: 'To be opened only after my death.'

Constance nodded. 'I see,' she said, and placed the letter on the bedside table, propped against her father's glass. She read to him from the Bible until the candle-flame guttered and his eyes closed in sleep. It was then that she lifted the envelope again, turning it thoughtfully in her hands.

'I should open this now,' she said, and his eyes were open and pleading in an instant. 'No!' He could not say the word but his head rolled slowly on the pillow.

'I should,' she whispered, smiling. She ripped it open quickly and studied the contents while William watched horrified.

'My own darling daughter,' she read aloud. 'I pray that you continue to grow in God's grace and that you remember me after my death with at least a fraction of the love that I felt for you in life. I have loved you as purely as I have loved no other being. Pray for me if you will and rest in comfort at the thought that I shall watch over you and keep you for the rest of your natural life. I shall be with you always, Constance . . .' More words followed but Constance had read enough. Folding the page neatly she returned it to its envelope and placed it back between the Bible's pages.

William's eyes did not leave his daughter's face for an instant. Knowing how she was watched, Constance sat in silence, studying her hands carefully for a moment before she spoke.

'You never loved Niall as much as me, did you, Papa?' she asked.

His eyes did not waver.

'I wonder why?' she said, yawning and stretching. She fiddled with the gold-edged pages of the Bible, her father's most treasured possession; fluttering them upwards and downwards with her fingers so that they fanned a little draught onto his face. The movement annoyed him; she could tell by the way that his eyes blinked quickly.

'Do you know, I would say that you even loved this old book more than you loved your son,' she said. 'I wonder why? After all, it is only a book; just some papers with writing upon them, not real flesh and blood, like your own child.'

She was lifting the pages higher now and letting them drop back, one at a time, onto the cover.

William's eyes rolled from her face to the book and then back to Constance again. She smiled at him slowly and then he heard the ripping noise as she tore the first page away from its spine.

'Look, Papa!' she said, holding the torn page before him and then crumpling it into a ball.

William's mouth dropped open to speak but the muscles of his lips were dead and no coherent sound emerged.

Constance leant forward until her mouth was next to his face. 'You called him the Devil's child,' she whispered. 'Does that mean he could not be your own son?'

William's face was crooked now, his lips fell limply to one side and his eyes followed them helplessly.

Constance tore off another page and lay it on his chest, fixing his hands above it as though locked in prayer.

'Can you still hear me, Papa?' she asked. 'You were wrong, you see,' she told him, ripping more pages as she spoke, 'can you believe that? Wrong all those years and busy punishing the wrong child. Can you imagine how terrible that is?' Her tearing became fierce, and soon William's whole body was covered with their confetti.

'You see Niall was your true, legitimate child all along, Papa!' she said. 'Not the son of the Devil, or whoever else you cared to believe, but yours, all yours, and now look how you have treated him.'

William tried to move and to speak but succeeded only in producing a thin line of dribble that oozed from his mouth and slid slowly onto the pillow beside his face.

Full of concern, Constance blotted it away with a page torn from Genesis.

'Now, I hope you are listening, William,' she said, 'for I have something even more tremendous to tell you. Did you hear how I called you William just then and not "Papa"? Well, that is my news. You are not my papa at all, now isn't that surprising?'

She paused to see the effect her words had had upon him. He was making a terrible effort to talk, she could see. Even his hands trembled on his chest and managed to rise a fraction from the sheet.

Constance smiled. 'You chose the wrong child, Papa,' she said. 'It was me, not Niall. *I* am the Devil's child,

Papa, I know because the priest told me so.'

At the mention of Father Devereux, William's eyes slowly closed and he let out an animal groan.

Constance tore another page from the Bible and stuffed it into William's open mouth. 'Don't make such noises, Papa,' she whispered, 'it scares me.' The noise continued and so she stuffed more sheets inside his mouth until he was silent at last. Then she sat back in her seat and waited.

She heard William fighting for breath and saw the pupils of his eyes rolling helplessly behind his closed lids.

'He is dreaming,' she told herself. 'Dreaming of all the terrible things that he has done to his son and of all the love that he has wasted on me.'

She watched for several minutes and then his arm rolled slowly from his chest and a deep choking rattle issued from the back of his throat.

William Flavelle was dead.

Constance felt his presence lift from her shoulders like a physical weight. Crossing herself slowly she rose from her chair and picked up each torn sheet of paper, smoothing them out one at a time on the bedspread and then replacing them in their correct place in the Bible.

Gazing down at the corpse, she took his letter out of the envelope once more and read it again carefully.

'I shall watch over you and keep you for the rest of your natural life,' she read.

'Good,' she said, smiling. She lit the corner of the letter from the sunken flame of the candle at William's bedside, watching the paper burn until all the words were gone and all that remained was a small pile of ash that she trod into the floor.

'Watch me then if you must, Papa,' she said, and left the room to go in search of the doctor.

CHAPTER THIRTY-EIGHT

A heavy sea-mist covered the small graveyard on the day that William Flavelle was buried. It arrived from the shore in great grey rolling clouds, blown by the wind so that at times each mourner stood obscured from his neighbour with only the deep groan of the foghorn way out at sea and the quiet drone of the priest's voice to assure him he was not totally alone.

Father Devereux was ill, so he said, and another priest had been called in to conduct the lengthy service. The man did not take his commission lightly, either, speaking the entire service in a Gaelic so broad as to be near-incomprehensible to even the oldest parishioner. In between pious references to the mercy of God, he complained bitterly at being called out in the first place.

Watching the other mourners, Constance felt herself looking through thick frosted glass. They seemed unreal in that mist and there were times, when the wind blew without warning, that the only sight clearly enough defined was the dark slippery grass that lay beneath her own feet.

She wore a pair of light kid shoes and no overcoat atop her black dress. Cora had warned her several times that she would without doubt catch a chill, but Constance felt nothing as she stood there; not the wet from the ground as it seeped through her soles or the unseasonably cold wisps of fog as they played around her bare arms.

Her sisters flanked her and Constance found that she could smell them well enough even when she could no longer see them, for their fur collars smelt of camphor and their coats of stale damp worsted. Christina sucked at a cough lozenge throughout the service too, to ward off further germs, and each time she let out a sigh a cloud of aniseed and menthol rushed to join the other smells in the air.

Constance heard Cora rustling the pages of her prayerbook as the priest invited the mourners to join him in prayer. She heard the priest's voice and the muted responses from the crowd and she gazed long and hard at the hole that had been prepared for her father beside her mother's grave.

The mists cleared a little and she saw the fresh white roots that extended like arms from the soil at either side of the coffin's sheer descent. She looked quickly away, to a small gap between the graves. There was a low ash tree there and beside the tree she saw two tall figures; one stooped and swaying slightly, the other bolt straight, hands clasped, joining in the prayers. The two stood separate from the main group of mourners and Constance watched as the stooped figure started to move, pulling at the taller man's arm as though trying to urge him away from the graveside. The taller man shook his head quickly though and kept his place. She had thought she did not know them but as the taller man turned back towards the grave she noticed something familiar in his face.

'Niall?' Constance whispered, but then the mists reclaimed them and he was lost to her again. She felt Christina turn towards her and smelt the lozenge on her breath.

'Are you ill, Constance?' she asked and then Cora turned too and she felt her sister close beside her, offering her support. Cora's hands grasped her own, chafing them quickly.

'See?' Cora asked. 'You are frozen! What were you doing, coming out here without a coat?'

Suddenly Constance felt the cold at last and began to shiver as the chill of the mists reached her for the first time. Her head began to ache and her teeth chattered violently. She felt kind hands leading her up the sloping path to the house and the only word she could force from her lips before she was laid in her bed to fall into a deep sleep was the name of her brother, Niall.

They made her sip sherry when she awoke and took her downstairs to sit in front of the fire once she was recovered. Most of the mourners took her state as an excuse for leaving early and they stopped quickly before her chair to offer condolences before slipping away to the warmth of their own peat fires.

'I saw Niall,' Constance told Cora once the last of the mourners had taken their leave and only the doctor and the priest remained, chatting quietly at the table as they finished off a bottle of William's best malt.

Cora wrapped her sister's shawl a little tighter about her shoulders. 'Hush now,' she told her, 'I believe you're feverish. I'll have word with the doctor when he has finished setting the world to rights and see if he hasn't got some tonic about him somewhere that will set you back onto your feet again.'

But Constance grabbed her hand. 'He was at the grave-side,' she insisted. 'I saw him there with another man. I'm sure it was him, though he looked so much older. Do you think he's come back for Papa's funeral, Cora? Please, where is he? See if he is outside! He may not want to come in!'

'You must have been mistaken, Constance. The mists were too thick to see anyone properly. If Niall came back to visit he'd be standing in this house, wouldn't he? It belongs to him now, after all. There's no one here to stop him coming in when he likes now that Papa's dead.' Her voice trailed off and she crossed herself at the mention of her father.

Looking about for a diversion she smiled across at the priest and he lifted his glass to her in a toast.

'The Father seems in fine spirits again!' She laughed. 'Shall I ask him and the doctor to come over for a minute or two? I'm sure they'd like to say a piece before they leave and they might cheer you up in the process.'

Before Constance could stop her she had gone across the room, returning shortly with the two elderly men in tow.

Constance slipped the shawl from her shoulders as they arrived and extended a hand to the priest.

'Miss Flavelle,' the old man said, clasping his hands across his belly in a gesture of appropriate concern, 'I knew of your father, my dear; a great man, by all accounts, whatever his religious inclinations. I only wish I had the good fortune to have met him in the flesh. The doctor here has been telling me what a spiritual man he was.'

'My father lived by the Bible,' Constance said quietly.

'And something of an expert in that area, too, I hear,' the priest went on, taking a seat beside her. 'Doctor O'Sullivan here was telling me there was no one could touch him when it came to theology. Quite had our priest in knots over dinner on several occasions, I hear!'

The word 'dinner' seemed to inspire him for he looked about the room and sniffed the air, as though seeking signs that a meal was to be served.

'Will you stay for dinner, Father?' Constance asked.

'Oh, no, no, no!' he answered, watching as his glass was filled. 'I could not bear to put you to the trouble! You've your hands full enough with everything as it is without an extra mouth at table!' He paused, waiting for the protestations that would have talked him into staying and then looking aggrieved when none were forthcoming.

He emptied his glass and rose from his chair and the doctor moved quickly to fill his empty seat.

'So how will you ladies manage?' he asked Constance once the priest was being presented with his coat. 'You are all alone out here now, you know. I realize that William was no protection for you in his final years, but all the same . . .'

Constance smiled. 'Don't underestimate us, Doctor,' she said. 'Cora and Christina have run the house alone for long enough and I doubt we'll fall into pieces just because Papa has been taken from us at last.'

'You should take on staff,' the doctor said, 'the house is too big for just the three of you. It'll fall apart about your very heads if you don't have a mind. I doubt that roof will last another winter. And you should be getting a little more company now, too, my dear,' he added, patting her arm, 'you're a beautiful young woman and you should be out with friends of your own age. And not all of your own sex, either, if you take my meaning! I'd like to see you married to some fine young man one day!'

Constance smiled and looked away modestly.

'I mean it,' the doctor insisted. 'It's not healthy for a young girl like yourself to live up here with only your two older sisters for company. I know it will take you a while to recover from your father's death but once you do I want to see you away from this place as soon as you can. Find some relatives to stay with or something. There's still plenty of ways for a young girl like you to launch herself in society. Your father must have left a small fortune tied up somewhere so I shouldn't expect you'll want for anything.'

'I thought about Dublin or England,' Constance said quietly.

The doctor looked up in surprise at the apparent ease with which he had convinced her. 'Dublin would be tremendous for a girl like you,' he said, clapping his hands together. 'I have family there myself, if you have no one you can visit.'

Constance smiled. 'I believe we still have cousins there. Though they may be surprised to hear from us after so long. But it is too soon now. I will wait a while, until I am more recovered from Papa's death.'

The doctor nodded agreement. Poor young thing, he thought to himself; the death of her father has hit her very hard.

It was midnight when the knocking began at the front door and the sound echoed about the empty house, waking the three sisters and dragging them, white-faced and shaking, from their beds.

They congregated in the hallway, each afraid that the terrible banging would take the ancient door clean from its hinges, but each too terrified to open it to find out who was causing the noise.

'Oh, holy mother of God!' Christina cried, searching in vain for her glasses. 'It must be Papa come back from the grave to haunt us!'

Cora grabbed her to stop her shouting but the thumping began again and Cora had to shake her sister hard to prevent her from becoming hysterical.

While Christina fled to the safety of the kitchens Cora summoned up what little courage she had left and pulled the door open an inch before it sustained further damage.

Two shapes stood before her; one tall and dark with his face in shadow, the other bent over, leaning heavily against the first.

Cora's hands flew to her face in fear.

'Don't you recognize me?' a voice asked and she felt Constance pushing past her and throwing the door back wide.

'Niall!' Constance cried, her face alight with excitement.

Niall shoved her aside without a word, helping his companion into the hall where he collapsed into an armchair.

Niall pulled off his coat and they saw his face properly for the first time in the flickering light of the candles they carried. No longer the nervous pale boy that had been their brother, he was a man now and a massive presence in that dark windswept hall. He was as broad as his father, but much taller and more upright than he had been as a boy. His face was brown, as though he had come from abroad, and his features, quite handsome still, had a brooding, sullen look. His dark eyes stared with the gravest of expressions.

He was dressed in black, from the funeral, and would have reminded them more of his father had he not been clean-shaven and his dark hair unruly, curling long about his collar.

'I have brought back the master of the house,' he said, pointing to the sleeping form in the armchair. 'Take a look,' he told the women, 'master of all he surveys; William Flavelle's true son and heir, home again to the house that he loved. What a cruel twist of fate that his father should not have been here to greet him. Still,' he added, shaking the rain from his coat, 'I'm sure he will still claim his inheritance; if he can stay sober for long enough, that is.'

Cora moved slowly to the armchair and bent to peer over the slumbering form. 'Francis!' she whispered. 'You brought Francis back to us!'

'I said I would,' Niall told her. 'I kept my promise to Papa.'

'Niall!' It was Constance who called out this time. She had closed the door against the cold and rushed across to clasp her brother to her in delight at seeing him again.

Niall turned from her before she could reach him, though, and paced the hall instead, oblivious to her excitement.

Cora stood, speechless, at the rebuff. She watched poor Constance suffer in an agony of indecision, her arms still held out in welcome and the smile on her face being slowly exchanged for an expression of sad disbelief.

'We should get him to his bed while he can still walk,' Niall said, nodding towards his brother, who had all but slid from his chair.

Both men appeared expensively dressed and when Niall moved about the hall there was the faint smell of cologne and tobacco. His face looked grim as he lifted his brother from the chair, throwing Francis's arm about his broad shoulders and helping him up the flight of stairs that led to the bedrooms.

'There's no bed made up,' Cora said, but Niall just smiled sarcastically.

'I don't suppose he'll notice, will you, Francis?' he said. 'He's been sleeping rough on pavements for the past few years so I should think any bed would be a luxury to him whether it's covered in fine linen or not.'

Francis's head had lolled onto his shoulder as Niall talked and Cora followed as he took him into the bedroom and threw him onto the bed. His eyes opened hazily and he attempted to look about.

'Cora?' he asked, seeing his sister for the first time.

'Yes, it's your sister, Francis,' Niall told him. 'Now there's a touching reunion for you! Did you save the cake, Cora, like I said?'

'Did you get him into this state?' Cora asked, smelling the beer on her brother's breath.

'I bought him the drink, yes,' Niall told her. 'Though I'd say the general state of decay about him was caused more by our father than by myself. Anyway,' he added, smiling at his sister, 'it was the only way we could get ourselves to his funeral, if we were rolling drunk and stupid with it. I'd still swear he was crying when the coffin went down, though, poor bastard!'

'Watch your language!' Cora said quickly, looking to see if Constance had heard him.

'You know you're sounding very like our Christina these days!' Niall remarked. 'Where's she gone off to, by the way?'

'She fled to the kitchens at your banging. You put the fear of God into her. We thought you might raise the dead with your noise.'

'Raise the dead?' Niall asked. 'Now there's a happy thought.'

'Niall!' Cora said, crossing herself.

'Oh, I'm sorry, Cora,' Niall said. 'I'd forgotten you were all so set to play the grieving daughter today. I saw you there, with your furs and your prayer-books. You looked upset as he went down. Or were you just worried like the rest of us that the weight of the earth might not have been enough to keep him there? Now wouldn't that have been a fine sight, eh, Cora? Him clawing his way up out of his grave and the rest of us setting about him with shovels to make sure he stays put?' He laughed briefly. 'Oh, don't look at me like that, Cora!' he said. 'You're hypocrites, the lot of you, you know you are.'

He looked down at his brother and his expression softened for a second. 'Do you have a blanket or something you can throw over him?' he asked. 'I shouldn't want him freezing up overnight, poor sod.'

He picked up his coat and made to leave the room but Constance had followed them and stood before him in the doorway.

'You're not leaving again?' she said.

He stared at her with an expression that she could never have fathomed and when he answered he spoke over his shoulder to Cora, as though it were she who had asked him the question.

'Of course,' he said. 'What else?'

'Stay here,' Constance whispered. 'It's your home now.'

Niall laughed and inspected the fingers of his glove. 'This house has never been my home,' he said, 'and I will never be welcome inside it.'

'But Papa's dead now!' Constance cried, pleading with him.

'You can stay here, Niall,' Cora added. 'You can stay here as long as you like.'

'He may be dead,' Niall said, angry now, 'but you can feel him here in every brick of the place! Don't tell me that he's gone, Cora! He's here and he's watching us, or do you not feel him too?

'Did you think I'd come snuffling back cap in hand just as soon as he was put into the ground? His eyes will be upon me every minute that I spend here. You can live with his ghost if you want but don't ask me to rot here along with you!'

'Please stay!' Constance begged. 'The house is yours now! Papa is gone! You can forget him! Please, Niall, I need you here!'

But Niall pushed past her and made his way to the staircase. 'Francis owns the house, not me,' he said. 'Though what good the inheritance will do him heaven knows. Ask him what our father did for him when he wakes in the morning. If he's capable he may tell you how I found him sleeping rough on the streets of New York. Our blessed father had disowned him, that's what. He would not even send him the money to get home again and so instead he lay there, starving and rotted by drink and he most likely would have died there too, if our father had had his way. I was lucky to find him when I did.'

'But Papa wanted him home,' Cora said. 'I know he did! He looked for him every day.'

Niall stopped beside the main door. 'Did he?' he asked. 'Then why did he write to our grandfather's company denying all knowledge of him when they asked? They would have helped him if they'd known; I talked to them myself, but instead they threw him out when our father called him an imposter!'

Constance started weeping then and Niall looked at her with contempt.

'Francis will be a handful,' he whispered quickly to Cora. 'Will you care for him all right? He deserves it for all he's been through.'

Cora nodded and opened the door for Niall to leave. Constance ran quickly towards him but Cora grabbed her arms and held her inside.

'Go quickly,' she said to Niall as Constance started screaming. 'Let him go, Constance,' she told her sister, once the door was closed behind him. 'He doesn't want to be here, can't you see that? He's changed, he's not the boy we knew before.'

'But he can't have changed!' Constance cried. 'He promised to be here! He said he would always look after me!'

'Niall is a man now,' Cora said, 'and you can't go holding him to promises he made as a boy. He makes his own decisions and if he is bitter about life then I can't say I can blame him. I wish him well away from here, Constance, and so should you. Did you see that look in his eyes? I should say he came back for revenge on our father but, robbed of that chance, he could have brought it on the lot of us instead. We couldn't have him here like that, Constance, he may hate us all.'

But Constance merely shook her head and went on with her crying. Her brother loved her, she said, he had to. He had to come back, as well. Finally exhausted, she allowed herself to be led to her bed and spent a difficult night there, dreaming and crying and praying for Niall.

Francis was too weak to move from his bed for several days after his return but Christina and Cora fussed about him so much that he was eventually forced from his room to spend most of his time mooching about the yards, picking over the decaying remains of what had once been his farm.

When he became stronger he made some half-hearted attempts at a little farm work but he had none of his vigour of the old days and so would quit his labour in the early afternoon to disappear for hours before returning, quite drunk, for his dinner.

The meal itself became a miserable ritual for the surviving members of the Flavelle household. They sat in the long draughty room; a sparse gathering around the great wooden table that was still dominated by William's empty chair at its head. Christina had placed William's Bible open on the dresser but had never once asked about its torn pages, though the question tormented her from the moment she had spotted them. Instead of asking the others she had ironed them and glued them carefully back into place.

On their brother's return they had hired a woman from the clachan to cook for them and serve food. They would sit in silence while the woman made her slow and laborious way about the table, distributing food onto each of their plates. The food that she cooked was ghastly but they had not been able to pay her after the first few weeks and so dared not criticize for fear that she might leave.

Francis would be quietly drunk each evening, talking and muttering to himself as he spooned the food into his mouth. He would eat anything that was given to him and, if he was given nothing, he would never complain. Sometimes he began to curse to himself and it was then that the conversation around the table began in earnest, to drown the noise of his swearing.

One night Cora found him more sober than usual and, finding a moment alone with him, began to question him about America. He sat silently as she asked him of his circumstances out there, but finally he did speak.

'It was not just Niall who saved my life out there, Cora,' he said, and his sister looked at him with surprise.

'There was a girl . . .' he began, 'a beautiful girl. She gave me money when I was desperate. She gave money to a stranger, Cora. I had no way of repaying her. She was beautiful, Cora, and so kind. She even wrote to Grandfather's company. They told Niall, I believe. I asked him to pay her back the money. I hope that he did . . .'

Cora waited, but that was all he had to say.

Once Francis vanished for weeks and the three sisters became frantic with worry, thinking that he had to be dead. He returned later, though, and refused to say where he had been, and the same ritual was repeated after that as often as three times a year. In the end Cora, in desperation, had a tag with his name and address embroidered on it stitched to the lapel of his coat, and he found his way back much sooner like that, for people would help him or give him lifts home in their carts.

There were greater worries to occupy Cora's thoughts, though, when she discovered they were running out of money. Their solicitor was called in and the news that he brought with him was grave. Their father's financial affairs had been complicated to the point of paradox. He compared their construction to that of a giant ball of knotted twine that he himself had spent the past year slowly unravelling to find nothing lay at its core.

'Nothing?' Cora asked him.

'Almost nothing,' the solicitor corrected himself. 'But what there was only barely covered my fee. I was amazed at the man himself,' the solicitor told them, 'and I marvelled at the complexities of his business affairs. It was an intriguing problem and I found myself to be up against far more multifarious financial skills than my own. Your father took me down more blind alleys than they have in the whole of Dublin! Each time had me thinking that there was your inheritance, just out of reach of my fingers, then I'd discover the bond to be a stinker or the documents signed but invalid!'

'So are you saying there is no money?' Cora asked.

'Not quite,' the solicitor said, clearing his throat. 'There was some money there, as I told you. There is a little held in trust that may last you a few more months, and then there may be a little from America, although one can never be too sure of that source of income these days.'

'Is there some problem with the money from my grand-father's firm?' Cora asked. 'Mama led us to believe that it was quite prosperous.'

The solicitor shook his head and took a sip of tea, blowing on its surface as though it were still too hot, despite the fact that it had chilled and taken on a skin many minutes before.

'There are two problems there,' he said. 'The company stock has changed many times since your grandfather's day and, as your father showed so little interest in it, much of it was sold.

'Then there is the market to consider. Due to take a dive any day, I have heard. No idea how that may affect things, no idea at all.' He shook his head reflectively. 'I just wish I had been around to meet your father when he was alive,' he said. 'What a marvellous mind! What attention to detail! What paperwork!' His eyes suddenly lit up. 'Is his study still untouched?' he asked. 'I still find it hard to believe that he has beaten me in my search. Perhaps if I could have another look through his things? I would not charge you, of course, but would consider it a privilege . . .'

But Cora cut the man short. 'The study has been cleared,' she said. 'The only other papers there were either personal or religious. There were no more financial papers there.'

The solicitor looked crestfallen. 'No hidden drawers?' he asked. 'No locked chests?'

Cora shook her head and he sighed.

'A pity,' he told her. 'Do you know people say that the job of a solicitor is a boring one but if they could only see the fun to be had out of searching through . . .'

'How are we to live?' Cora interrupted.

'Live?' he echoed, raising his eyebrows. 'Well.' He spread his plump hands out upon his knees. 'As I see it you have only two options, my dear; either sell up and get what you can now, though that may not be much, given the state of the place, or live off the land that you own, like other people in the area. Take up a spot of farming, or something. I hear that Francis used to be able to turn his hand to farming in the old days. Perhaps if I were to broach the subject with him, though you say that he is still indisposed?'

'There's little living to be had off the land in Connemara,' Cora said. 'Or could you see us cutting the peat with our bare hands? Or maybe down at the coast, carrying seaweed?'

The solicitor held his hands out to her, palm-up to show how he sympathized. 'A tragedy then,' he said. 'Unless, as I said, you sell up and throw yourselves upon the mercy of relatives. You have another brother, I believe? Could he be enlisted to help?'

Cora stood from her seat with an abruptness that startled him. 'Niall has left,' she said. 'We have no idea where he has gone.'

The solicitor pursed his lips, tapping his index finger thoughtfully across his chin. 'A family disagreement?' he asked.

'Not exactly.'

'And if I were to find him for you, would he be able to help you, do you think? Is he a man of means?'

Cora remembered Niall's expensive clothes. 'He may be,' she said. 'But I do not want his charity. We have had no word of him since our father died. I believe he should be left alone.'

'Very well. But that still leaves us with no solution to your problem.'

It was a month before Cora returned to his offices and this time she was accompanied by her sister. Christina was in a panic. There had been fighting locally and fourteen houses had been burnt down in Clifden. The Black and Tans had been running armed raids on large houses in the district, she had heard, and they wanted Niall back now, not just for the money, but to take care of their house or they could all be killed in their beds.

The solicitor smiled with relief. 'I will trace your brother for you if it is at all possible,' he said, and the two frightened women in front of him had smiled for the first time during the interview.

CHAPTER THIRTY-NINE

The summer was so brief that year as to be barely noticed, for it rained non-stop, until the inhabitants of Connemara began to believe they lived underwater, like the fish. The whole of the great house was damp; it ran into the highest rooms and created thick rot and mildew that grew to claim much of the old timber and a lot of the furniture.

They threw the bad stuff onto the fire. Christina suffered with bronchitis, which left her with a cough that echoed around the place and which led to her grotto becoming wild and overgrown, for she could not stand the rain with her bad chest.

Constance's seventeenth birthday passed almost unmarked, and she was looking at her eighteenth when Niall finally returned to put the place into uproar again.

They were at their dinner when he arrived; sitting in their evening best, spooning caramel dessert into their silent mouths and looking for all the world as though the house were not falling to the ground about them. They paid the usual attention to their rituals; Christina read from the Bible in between bouts of coughing and they all took great care not to allow their silver spoons to scrape against their china plates, for fear the atmosphere of quiet concentration might be ruined.

The mantel-clock provided the only other noise in the room once the plates had been cleared and, when Niall slammed the door, the others nearly jumped right out of their seats.

All heads turned towards him and he found himself stared at by the ghosts of what had once been his family. Francis had never taken his father's seat at the head of the table. Instead he sat to the right of it, quietly sipping William's brandy, his head hung over his empty plate, fingering the rim of his glass as though searching for lost conversation. He looked neat enough – his sisters had seen to that – but the skin of his face was prematurely aged and his cheeks were sunken, despite the fact that he had put more flesh onto his bones.

Christina peered at Niall from behind her gold-rimmed glasses. Her illness had taken what little colour she had from her face and when she coughed she held her hand to her chest, as though the effort of coughing exhausted her. Her hair was already streaked with grey and she wore it tied in a loose plait that hung almost to her waist, making her look like a wizened little child. She was dressed in a loose-fitting grey lace tea-gown with sleeves so long that her hands were all but lost in their trim.

Cora, on the other hand, had the look of a well-stuffed sofa. Dressed in violet plush velvet she had got herself trussed into one of the S-shaped corsets that she had seen in a Macey's catalogue and which she hoped did a lot to stem the flow of her fast-expanding curves. Her hair had been cropped above her ears and her face looked rounder because of it.

Constance sat alone at the far end of the long table, facing the seat that her father had once used. Her back was straight and her face a little fuller than it had been when Niall had last visited the house. Her long auburn hair had been pinned up under a large pale green bow and she wore a simple tunic of eau-de-nil silk. Her arms were bare and she had a thin golden bracelet of her mother's twined about her slim wrist. Her hand flew to her throat when Niall walked into the room and no one spoke as he made his way across to his father's chair and threw himself down onto it.

Only Francis managed to smile at his brother; the others were all too shocked to move. They watched him pull off his gloves and lay them down on the table and the old dog came padding into the room from the hallway to nuzzle against his hand.

'You look as though you didn't expect me,' he said softly. The dog placed its huge paws upon his lap and stretched to lick at Niall's face.

'And yet you sent for me, didn't you, Cora?' he asked, looking at his sister. 'You paid that fat bastard of a solicitor to hunt me down, didn't you?'

Constance turned to look at Cora too now, the surprise obvious on her face, for her sisters had never told her of their meeting with the solicitor.

'So here I am,' Niall finished. 'And where's my dinner? It's a long cold ride from Dublin and I swear I'll starve if I don't eat soon.'

Constance made as though to rise from her place and her chair fell back with a clatter onto the floor.

'While you are up, Constance,' Cora said calmly, looking down at her hands, 'you might be good enough to ask in the kitchens if there's any hot food for our brother here.'

'Ask in the kitchens?' Niall asked. 'So you've a full complement of staff again, have you? Funny,' he added, looking around the room, 'I'd have thought the place was going to ruin, and all. That fat old bastard told me you weren't doing so well. Don't tell me the sob story he sold me was full of lies, now!'

Francis laughed loudly for no particular reason

Niall poured himself a glass of claret and raised it in a toast to his brother. 'Here's to you, Francis!' he called. 'At least you never lost the ability to laugh at your misfortunes, unlike some miserable old sods I could name!'

Francis roared with laughter at this and Christina rose quickly to join Constance in the kitchens.

'You're not going, are you?' Niall asked her. 'Not when I've only just arrived? Or did you mean to do the right thing and leave us gentlemen of the house to our smokes and our brandy? Eh? In that case you'd better go too, Cora. You won't want to stay around here and listen to men talking, now will you?'

312

Francis banged his palm on the table in approval and Cora sat straighter in her chair.

'I've no intention of moving,' she said as Christina walked out.

'My God, Cora,' Niall laughed. 'I just wish you could see your own face now! You could use it to curdle milk, I swear you could, couldn't she, Francis?'

'Stop it, Niall!' Cora whispered and Niall was upon her in an instant.

'What?' he asked, pretending not to have heard her. 'What was it that you said then, Cora?'

'I asked you to stop it,' Cora said, louder this time. 'You've changed so much and I can't bear to listen to you . . .' Her voice trailed off.

Niall laughed. 'Oh I've changed all right!' he said. 'Seeing our Francis laid out nearly dead on the street was enough to do that. He had sores on his face, Cora, and he was riddled with lice. I believe he had fleas as well, didn't you, Francis?' he asked.

Cora shuddered.

'Fleas! Can you imagine?' Niall pointed with his knife and Francis shook his head slowly and smiled.

'And all our dear departed father's fault, too,' Niall said quietly. He turned to look at Cora. 'There was something in that sight, you know,' he said, 'something to change me even more than hearing our Thomas had been blown to pieces. I wished then that I'd never stopped our precious father from shooting his head off properly like I did. I wish I'd let him do the job properly like he wanted. God knows why I did what I did.'

Cora looked shocked. 'You saved him?' she asked. 'I thought . . . I thought you'd tried to . . .'

Niall smiled. 'You thought I'd tried to kill him, is that what you're saying, Cora?'

Cora dropped her head.

'Don't worry,' he told her. 'That's what I should have done but I never had the guts.'

Cora let out a gasp at that.

'Look at yourself!' Niall said. 'Can't you see what he did with your life? With all of our lives?'

'So he tried to kill himself then,' Cora said, flatly. 'Why should he have wanted to do that?'

Her question was not asked of anyone in particular and Constance, the only one who could have supplied her with an answer, was still busy in the kitchens.

'I wondered why I'd bothered,' Niall went on, 'when I should have just sat there beside him and watched his face explode for good, but I couldn't because I still loved him then, you see, even after all he'd done. Amazing, isn't it, how tolerant a young boy can be? I loved him after all that he'd done to me; after all the million ways that he used to show how much he hated me. I couldn't believe it, you see; no one can believe that they are hated that much.'

'You're drunk,' Cora said, but Niall only laughed.

'Not me, Cora,' he said, emptying his glass, 'though I dearly wish that I were.'

Francis pushed the bottle towards him and it tipped over onto the table, spilling red wine across the white linen cloth. A few drops splashed onto the pale velvet of Cora's dress but she made no move to dab them off and so they dried there, instead, like blood.

Constance came back into the room, clutching a tray full of food, which she laid out in front of Niall. She stared at the round stain that was spreading across the cloth but she said nothing, quietly returning to her seat at the end of the table. She was afraid that they had all been arguing while she was out of the room. For a moment she had thought that the wine was blood and that Francis and Niall had been fighting. She was desperate to make a good welcome for her brother so that he would stay this time, instead of leaving as he had done before. She needed him there; she needed his presence in the house. With him there she would feel secure at last. He would understand all that had happened to her and he would care for her as he had promised so many years before.

She watched his face as he began to eat. He had shared with her the torment of abuse. He had suffered as she had at the hands of their father. She wanted the others to be gone, so that she could talk to him alone. Then she knew he would not be so cold towards her. Then he would stop ignoring her at last.

When Niall had finished eating he wiped his mouth and then sat back in William's chair.

'Now,' he said, placing his hands on the table. 'How do you suppose I can help you?'

Constance looked at the black stubble of a beard on his face and the dark rings beneath his eyes. How had he grown so tall? Her father had seemed to fill only half as much space in the chair. She could find no trace of her young brother in the strong, powerful man that sat before her. The knuckles of his hands whitened as he spoke. She looked down at her own small pink hands. She dreaded finding too much of William in his appearance. Did he know he was growing more like his father? A brief shudder ran through her at the thought.

'You're here to help us, then?' Francis asked and they all turned to him in surprise for he so rarely spoke at table.

'You are desperate,' Niall told him. 'Or that's how the solicitor you sent after me would have it, anyway. How could I turn a deaf ear to my own flesh and blood? I believe he thought I could come back and help you with the farming, Francis, though I fail to see how a few miserable cows and a pound or two of potatoes will help keep this place standing.' He threw down his napkin.

'Anyway,' he continued, 'I can tell you I've no intention of getting my hands dirty again in such a way, so farming's out of the question. You can't make a living out of these bogs, anyway; I learnt that much as a lad. And I've no desire to go cutting peat again for a living!'

'Don't you have a trade?' Cora asked Niall, the desperation obvious in her voice.

She knew the house was rotting about them but she could no longer bear the thought that they might have to leave. She had seen enough of the outside world to know that there was no place in it for her. She had no more dreams of love and passion, only a quiet desire to maintain their existence in the house. Her life now was as simple and as orderly as that of a nun. The world outside the house scared her and she saw Niall as their only salvation.

'A trade?' Niall asked her, smiling. 'How quaint that word sounds on your lips, Cora! You believe I should work to keep your house in order, do you?'

Constance was the only one able to meet his eye at the question.

'We're desperate, Niall, or we would never have asked you. You might stop mocking us, for God's sake.'

'So desperate that you'd invite the Devil to join you at table?' Niall said. 'Did you not remember that I bring only death and destruction to this house? I remember, Cora! I remember the last time that I was here and the time before that! I remember all your faces when it was I who came back from France instead of poor Thomas! I remember how you all stood sobbing around our father's grave and I see how well-kept it is with flowers and all, while our mother's lies under three feet of ivy!' He leant forward in his chair and stared at them all. 'I have no more desire to be here than you have to see me here, but I was told that you were desperate and that's why I have to stay.

'I'll sit up at night with my shotgun and I'll scare off your Black and Tans and, seeing as how you're all too polite to ask; yes, I have access to money, and can put the place to rights for you, too.'

A sigh of relief came from Cora at his words.

'Though I've spoken at length with your solicitor and he says there may be more debts than we know of, for our father's estate was in such a God-awful mess when he died.

316

Jesus Christ, the arrogance of the man!' he said, leaning back and closing his eyes. 'Did he suppose that the Lord would provide for you all once he'd drifted off the mortal coil? Did you know he's cheated you out of your inheritance all these years? There could have been a fortune from old Theo's business but our father has just let it all slip away, taking any money that was offered and then signing his rights away when he needed some more? Did you know that? Or did you think he was busy providing for you all? What were you supposed to live on, eh? Just a room stuffed with worthless bonds and papers? Some charity hand-outs from a business run from abroad that he only once condescended to correspond with and then only to deny the existence of his oldest son and heir? Jesus Christ!'

Christina had entered the room as he spoke and she crossed herself quickly at his blasphemy. She longed to press her hands over her ears so that she could no longer hear the assault he was making on her dear papa.

'Don't talk about him like that!' she whispered and, to her horror, Niall heard her.

He rose from his chair but Constance was quicker, rushing to his side and placing a hand upon his arm. Niall pulled away as though scalded and Constance all but cried out at his unkindness.

'I'll need some rooms prepared,' he said, coldly, looking at Cora. 'Just one for tonight and then I'll be needing another later. Does the lad still sleep over the stables?' he asked. 'Or do I have to see to my own horse?'

Cora made no answer for she was too busy looking at Constance, at the expression of despair on her beautiful young face.

CHAPTER FORTY

Niall had been in the house for barely two weeks before Francis saw the vision in the driveway.

He was standing near the main door, arms crossed, quietly surveying without comment or plan of action the passage of the weeds as they forced their way up through the gravel and cement to fan outward towards the lawn as though reclaiming land that had been lost to them many years before.

His mind had played idly with the idea of using weedkiller but that particular idea had quickly been dismissed as consisting of too much hard work for too little reward. Besides, Francis thought as he stood in the pale morning sunlight, he much preferred the green weeds to the grey gravel that lay beneath. He had a horror of anything urban now and, for his money, the weeds could have taken the lot of it and be damned.

Standing there, with the cool sun soothing the skin of his face while the mists still played about his ankles, Francis found himself cherishing the solitude and decrepit tranquillity of his home. It was the first time that he had been aware of any specific feelings since his return from America. He inhaled a great lungful of air which set him off coughing and when the spasm had ceased he straightened and began to whistle between his front teeth.

He was not happy but he was not exactly unhappy, either. He felt safer now that Niall was back and had taken control of the house. He was no longer referred to as master of the place and found he could drink as he liked and no one would criticize him for it. The women had their hands full with Niall and so they fussed less about Francis. Niall was busy with their finances. Francis was even given a cash allowance which more than covered his bill for drinks, and no sermonizing with it, either. The old dog emerged from nowhere and snuffled about Francis's feet. He went to kick it away but the mood of the day got the better of him and he found himself bending to pat it, instead. The dog looked up at Francis with such mindless gratitude in its great eyes that he began to laugh and to scratch its belly, causing it to roll onto its back in ecstasy.

'Stupid bugger!' Francis laughed as its thick tail banged against the gravel, its pink tongue lolling helplessly from its mouth. It was only then that Francis heard the heavy purr of the motor for the first time and he had straightened at once, alarmed by such a strange noise.

The car was making its way at great speed along the treacherous snaking path that led to the house. It stopped only once en route and Francis thought he heard the engine cough. He saw the driver slap the side of the bodywork as though it were a horse that had faltered and then, by some miracle, it had leapt into life again and it was only a matter of some minutes before it was pulling into the drive.

The driver was alone and Francis realized to his surprise that it was a woman. He had not been aware of that before, for her hair was cropped short and she wore a tailored suit made of dark navy worsted, but now he saw the short skirt that revealed her legs and he ducked back into the doorway as the dog dived for cover behind his feet.

Francis's first impulse was to vanish altogether. He had no desire for the company of strangers and his mood of well-being had evaporated the moment the car engine had stopped. He had no thought as to who the woman might be and no desire to find out. The sight of her and the sound and smells of her car engine had put his world entirely out of kilter. He wiped his palms on the sides of his trousers and then worried that it might look like a prelude to shaking hands.

The top of the woman's face was covered with a half-veil of navy netting. Her clothing was quite shocking to

Francis's eyes and he felt that he should look away, but he didn't.

'Hi there!' She lifted her veil and rolled it back onto her head. It was then that Francis realized, with a start, that he was asleep and dreaming, after all. None of what had happened that morning was real. He had to be lying drunk somewhere, for what he saw before him could not be true.

It was the girl from the newspaper office in America; the young woman who had helped him. She did not live in Ireland. He shook his head quickly, expecting her to vanish. She was still there when he looked back, though, and she was smiling at him.

'Do I unpack my own car?' she asked. She looked shy and happy and beautiful and he found himself, smiling delightedly, walking towards the car and pulling some large cases from the boot.

She touched his arm. She was real!

'Oh, I didn't mean you, Francis!' she said. 'I thought you must have staff to take care of all that . . . I mean . . . well, I don't really know what I did mean, actually, but it's awfully good to see you again. Can you manage? You still look weak.'

Francis nodded, feeling awkward and tongue-tied. He should have asked her what she was doing there but he was too pleased to see her to wonder.

'My brother is bringing more staff,' he told her, 'when things get straight. They haven't arrived yet. We used to have some . . .'

'Are you well now, Francis?' she asked. She looked so well herself. Her skin was brown and glowing from the drive and her eyes bright with the excitement of being there. He could smell her perfume and feel the weight of her hand as it rested upon his arm. There were grass seeds in her hair that must have been blown there on the ride. The handles of her cases were made of solid leather for he could feel them in his hands, and there were travel stickers on her

320

luggage that confirmed her trip from New York to Galway. How had she found him? But he didn't really care; all that Francis cared about was that she had. He remembered her kindness in America and how he must have looked to her then. She had helped out a hobo and then followed him around the world because she loved him every bit as much as he loved her.

Francis was speechless at his own luck. He had thought of her every day since he had met her but he had never supposed he would see her again. He looked down at himself, suddenly ashamed of his appearance. He had climbed from his bed and had emerged from the house that morning without shaving or dressing properly. He must look barely better to her than he had in New York. And yet she was still smiling at him. It was a miracle, nothing less.

'Niall said you would be here,' she told him. 'I was delighted when I heard.'

Niall? Francis's mind raced about, piecing the puzzle together. He would give up drink for her, he would smarten up. He would have died to see her smile at him as she was doing. He would become a man of stature that they could all look up to. It was what he wanted, he realized that then. With this girl at his side he could take up his position at the head of the house. He felt unsteady and he felt her grip on his arm become firmer as he rocked on his feet.

'I knew you weren't strong enough for those bags,' she said, looking worried. 'Is Niall about?' she asked. 'Perhaps he could help.'

It was then that the pieces of the puzzle slotted into place. It was Niall who had saved his life in America and it was in America that he must have met Nancy, during his search. Niall had recognized the value of this woman in his life and he had brought her over from America, just to help him. His brother worked miracles, he realized that now.

Niall had saved his life once and now he was doing it again. All that Niall had been able to rescue from America was the bones and the flesh of him, while this woman was here to restore his soul. How could Niall have persuaded her to pursue a hobo halfway across the world? But Francis did not know and he found that he did not care. She was there and Niall had brought her and that was all that mattered to him.

The dog rose to greet them as they crossed the dusty hall and Nancy patted its head, laughing as it licked her hand. 'I see what Niall meant when he said about all the work that had to be done here!' she said, looking about, and Francis noticed the decayed state of the house that he lived in for the very first time.

'Niall is out on his horse,' he told her and she smiled and said it was a pity but not to worry, for she had her unpacking to do.

'You're staying, then?' Francis asked, still barely able to believe his own luck and Nancy laughed and said of course, did he want her going straight back to Dublin?

'It's been a long journey all right,' she said, stretching and yawning, and it was only then that Francis remembered his manners and asked if she would like to wash and change. He ran his fingers over his chin. While she changed he would have time to get himself in order.

He called for Christina or Cora but it was Constance who arrived instead. Francis made the introductions as best he could but Nancy took over, thankfully, smiling at his sister and taking her hand in her own.

'You are so beautiful you have to be Constance,' she said.

Constance blushed a little at that and smiled shyly and Francis happily left the two women together while he retired to his room to wash and shave.

The hot water and soap lather felt good on his face and as he scraped at his skin with the cut-throat he whistled a little as he had used to when he was shaving in the old days. His hair needed cutting, he saw in the mirror, but he slicked it back instead and it didn't look half-bad. His best suit was still hanging in his wardrobe, though he had not worn it once since his return. He sniffed at it and winced, for it smelt

322

of camphor. He took it to the open window to air before he put it on.

He had lost some weight on his travels but he pulled the belt tight and slipped his hands into his trouser pockets – he thought he would pass muster for the time being. He would get off to the town in the morning and see about a haircut and some new clothes. He wiped a hand across his mouth. He was badly in need of a drink, to give him courage, but then he thought of Nancy and her beautiful, kindly smile, and he knew he had had his last taste of alcohol forever.

He heard Nancy's laughter as he came down the stairs. She had brought life into the house and Constance was laughing too; not just polite laughter but the sort of delighted giggles that they used to hear from her as a child. She had taken to Nancy straight away and was asking about her clothes, which she adored, her luggage, and even the way that she wore her hair.

'Francis!' Nancy laughed as he entered the room. 'Your young sister is so kind to us colonials! She's managed to compliment every feature of my appearance and she's not given me time to draw breath to ask about her fine Irish skin and her wonderful auburn hair!'

Constance studied her brother's new appearance with a smile of delight, though she made no comment and for that he was eternally grateful. She did not understand exactly who her brother's American visitor was, but one look at Francis's expression as he watched her made her terribly pleased that she had arrived. He could not remove his eyes from her face. When Nancy laughed he laughed and when she smiled he smiled, too. Constance had never before seen her brother so animated or so cheerful.

She fetched them some tea and when she returned Nancy was seated at their mother's piano, Francis standing behind her, turning the pages of the music as she played. She sung the last chorus and her voice was as sweet as her playing. Once the notes had faded like dust into the air, Constance clapped loudly and begged her to play more.

'Oh, it was hardly that good!' Nancy said, smiling, but Constance disagreed noisily.

'I thought that piano was to be kept closed after Mother died,' a voice said behind her and they turned to see Niall in the doorway, his face still wet from the ride and his hair plastered against his neck.

Constance rose quickly from her seat. 'You shouldn't be so rude, Niall! This is Francis's visitor. She's come from America.'

'Oh, she's Francis's visitor, is she?' Niall said softly. 'In that case I must apologize, madam, I mistook you for someone I knew.'

Nancy rose from the piano stool, looking flustered. 'The house is quite beautiful!' she said, holding out her hands.

Niall smiled. 'It's a ruin,' he replied, but she shook her head and laughed.

'You two have met, then?' Constance asked, looking confused.

Nancy's arms fell to her sides and she stared at Niall. 'You didn't tell them,' she said.

Francis leapt to his brother's side. 'It was a surprise, wasn't it, Niall?' he said, grabbing his brother's arm. 'You met Nancy in America. How on earth did you talk her into coming back here? I don't know how to thank you, Niall. You saved my life once and now I believe you have saved it again!'

'You didn't tell them,' Nancy repeated. She had not moved from the centre of the room.

'Francis!' Niall said, looking surprised. 'You're suddenly wonderfully smart! I can see my wife's had a civilizing influence on you already! How did you manage it, Nancy? You've only been in the house five minutes and you've got him spruced up and shaved. Let's introduce you to Christina and Cora and see if you can't work some miracles there and get them both smiling.'

Nancy turned quickly to Francis with an expression of

anguish on her face. 'You shouldn't tease, Niall,' she said. 'You can be so hurtful at times.'

Constance swayed slightly and grabbed at the tea-table for support.

'Your wife?' Francis said faintly, his face every bit as drained of colour as his sister's.

'Did you not introduce yourself properly?' Niall asked, turning to Nancy. 'Did you just barge your way in here without so much as a nod in the direction of good manners?'

'I thought you knew,' Nancy said, looking at Francis and Constance. 'I thought he would have told you all. I'm sorry . . .' she whispered to Francis, 'I'm so sorry . . .'

'It was through you that we met, Francis,' Niall said, pouring himself some tea. 'I placed an advertisement in the newspaper in America, asking if anyone knew of your whereabouts. Nancy here saw it before it was even in print and she contacted me at my hotel. She helped me find you, Francis, you owe her more gratitude than you do me, really. She was so relieved when I told her I had found you, weren't you, darling?'

'Yes, yes, I was . . .' Nancy began.

'You took her from me!' Francis whispered, moving backwards towards the door, his hands searching blindly behind him for the handle.

'Don't be ridiculous, Francis!' Niall said. 'You're embarrassing my wife! She was kind to you, that was all. She told me how you had met just the once and how she had bought you a coffee. Surely you didn't imagine there could be anything in that? Now you might pull yourself together enough to congratulate us, for we are not long married after all and I don't want my new bride to think I have brought her to a land of heathens and hooligans! Go and fetch some champagne up from the cellars, so that we can toast the whole thing in style.'

Francis looked from Niall to Nancy and then left the room without saying a word.

Niall tutted quietly, then turned to his sister. 'What about you then, Constance?' he asked quietly. 'Don't you have a nice word of greeting for your new sister-in-law?'

Nancy saw Constance's face and pulled at his arm to stop him but he shook her off.

'It's a shock for everyone now,' she said. 'You should have warned them . . .'

Constance moved forward quickly and kissed Nancy on the side of the cheek. 'Congratulations,' she whispered.

Nancy smiled gratefully and attempted to hug her in return but Constance froze like ice beneath her fingers. 'I hope we can carry on being friends,' Nancy said, but Constance was not listening, she was looking at her brother.

'Would you like to find Cora and Christina?' he asked. 'I'm sure they'd like to be introduced as well.'

'Shall I play the piano some more?' Nancy was desperate to bring the smile back to Constance's face.

'I'd rather you did not touch the instrument again,' Niall told her quickly. 'As I said, it belonged to my mother and I would rather it were kept locked. Perhaps Constance would like to show you the stables or take you about the house instead. She has so little company these days and I know she would be pleased for the chance to talk.'

'Well, we'll have to change all that then, won't we?' Nancy said, smiling at Constance. 'Perhaps we can have a big party so I can meet everyone some time soon.'

She looked at her husband and found him staring hard at his sister. There was a look that passed between them that Nancy did not recognize, then tears appeared in Constance's eyes. Niall's face looked set. Only the farthest corners of his mouth managed to twist upward in the semblance of a smile.

CHAPTER FORTY-ONE

Francis spent one more week in the house, then he could stand it no more and left for the relative peace of the run-down farm cottage that stood on the outskirts of the grounds, near to the gateposts. The place was barely habitable and Cora made many visits during the first few weeks of his occupancy, trying to persuade him to return home and, when that failed, to allow her to make the place more comfortable. Niall stopped her on her second visit and handed her some money.

'Here,' he said. 'You might give him this.'

Cora stared down at the folded notes. 'Why not take it to him yourself?' she asked.

Niall shrugged. 'He'd hardly accept it from me now, would he? Not while he's under the illusion that I stole his bride out from under his nose. He's a great streak of pride in him, despite everything that's happened, or hadn't you noticed?'

'He won't take it from me either, then,' Cora said.

'He'll have to. Or what else will he be buying his precious liquor with?'

Cora looked shocked. 'I can't see him drink himself to death on money I have given him!'

Niall laughed. 'So what would you have me do? Let him starve down there? At least with the money he has a choice. If he decides to use it to kill himself with booze rather than eat then that's his business.'

'I'll feed him, then,' Cora said, pushing the notes back in his hands. 'I shan't take the money but I'll take him food.'

'And that way you'll strip the poor sod of every ounce of dignity he has left.'

'It's your fault, Niall,' she retorted, anger burning in her

327

eyes. 'Bringing that woman back here without so much as warning us you were married. You could have broken it to him before she arrived! How did you think he'd feel, her just waltzing in and taking over the entire house? Letting poor Francis think it was him she had come for? There was no need for such mischief, you know!'

'Francis is crazed by the drink, Cora. Nancy and he barely met in America! How was I supposed to imagine he'd have such a fixation on her? You're talking nonsense, Cora. I thought you had more sense, you always used to.'

'And you always used to be kinder,' Cora retaliated. 'You were cruel to Francis and you are just as cruel to Constance.'

'Constance? How do you figure that? I hardly talk to her, how can I be cruel if I keep away?'

'You ignore her,' Cora said. 'She's fond of you, Niall, and you used to be close. Now you act as though she's barely there.'

'Then I am acting exactly how our father would have wanted! Constance was his child, his favourite, and he wanted me nowhere near her. He was frightened I might corrupt her, did you know that? It's best I keep my distance. This is still William Flavelle's house I'm living in and it's only right I should pay heed to his wishes.'

'It's Francis's house now, Niall,' Constance reminded him.

'Then thank heaven he is generous or foolish enough to allow you all to go on living there,' Niall said. 'Besides,' he added, quietly, 'it may not be his for too much longer.'

Cora looked up sharply. 'Who will own it then?'

Niall sighed. 'Francis has no money and it's obvious he no longer wants to live here. He needs money, Cora, the house is of no use to him. How did you imagine he would ever maintain it?'

'We thought you were going to help,' Cora said. 'You told us you had money. You said you would get everything into good repair.'

'And so I will. But you didn't think I would be foolish

enough just to pile in money without my name even being mentioned on the deeds, did you? I have offered to buy the estate from Francis – at a good price – and he's really in no position to refuse.

'If I am to pay for this place then I want it for my children, not his. Did you never wonder what might happen if he sobered himself up one day and started his own family? Did you think he would want his three spinster sisters and his younger brother and his family all waiting to receive his new bride? No, Cora, I couldn't have that. Francis can live where he pleases and this is your home for the rest of your life but don't expect me to pay for it and then find myself thrown out yet again. I'm too sharp for that, Cora, believe me!'

'But you can't take it from him! It belongs to him, it's his birthright! Papa left it to his eldest son!'

'So what would you have him do, then?' Niall asked. 'Sit and watch the whole place crumble about your ears, because that's what will happen if I don't invest in it. It's your choice, Cora; yours and Francis's and Christina's. Either you take me up on my offer and have a good home for life, or you get Francis to turn me down; in which case you had better look about for somewhere safer to live. Now what's it to be?'

Cora paused. 'Where the hell did you get so much money from?'

Niall laughed. 'Does it matter? Or did you suddenly obtain some scruples? It's all legal, Cora,' he said. 'It's the money of my darling wife, of course. Her father's as rich as Croesus and Nancy is his only child. Why else do you think I determined to marry her so quickly? Oh, you don't need to look at me like that, Cora!' He laughed at her expression. 'It's a love-match, all right. As perfect and sincere a marriage as your own, anyway!

'It's my wife, or "that woman" as you so affectionately referred to her just now, who will be paying for the renovations to your home. Now do you still feel the same about her, Cora? Or could you try a little harder to be the perfect loving sister to her I know you're really just dying to be?'

'Niall!' Cora tried to stop him but he continued regardless. He could not see what Cora had seen in the mirror over the marble mantelpiece. Nancy had entered the room quietly and was standing behind them, listening to his every word.

'Niall!' Cora spoke louder this time and he heard her at last, looking up into his wife's white, shocked face.

'Nancy!' he said, without pause. 'Come and join us! You were the subject of our conversation anyway so there is no need to eavesdrop. I was just telling Cora that I had married you for your money and she looks a little shocked to hear it, don't you think?'

Nancy attempted to smile as she approached. Niall extended an arm and she allowed herself to be pulled into an embrace.

'Niall has a dry sense of humour, don't you think?' she asked. 'It would be easy to become upset by him if you took everything he said too seriously.'

'Do I?' Niall asked, kissing the top of her head. 'I thought I was always perfectly serious.'

Nancy let out a little laugh. 'My father warned me about men like you.'

'Then your father is a very shrewd man. I should have thought you would have heeded his warnings. Or did you suppose that he was only joking, too?'

'I should be helping Christina.' Cora was anxious to get away.

Nancy smiled at her. 'I just offered to help her myself,' she said. 'But she said she was better off alone.'

'I'll bet she won't turn Cora down, though,' Niall remarked. 'I'll bet it's just you she doesn't want in the kitchen. Shall we tell her who that kitchen will belong to soon?'

Nancy smiled. 'If we're to own the house I should at least have some working knowledge of the place,' she said.

'Though we'll have staff to work down there and then Cora and Christina will have less to do. You'll be waited on hand and foot!' she told Cora, who pulled a face at the notion.

'Why don't you just go and tell Christina that, then?' Niall suggested to his wife. 'I should think the news will please her enormously. She may even share the recipe for those horrendous little rock cakes she is always serving up, you never know.'

'I don't mean to be tactless . . .' Nancy said.

'Then leave her alone. You'll only get your head bitten off if you go around where you're not wanted. Why don't you just spend your days looking beautiful instead? There's enough old rooms in this place for you to waft about like Lady Macbeth.'

'Is that how you see me?'

'Why not?' Niall asked. 'It was all our mother ever did.'

Cora had heard enough. She left the room quickly, before they could stop her, and she felt herself growing annoyed at the sound of Nancy's footsteps following quickly behind.

'Look, can we talk for a while?' Nancy asked when she caught up with her.

Cora slowed a little but would not stop.

'Do you think I should speak to Francis?'

'Why should you want to do that?' Cora asked, turning at last.

'I just feel I may have upset him,' Nancy said, running her hand through her hair. 'I don't want him out of the house on my account. I thought I might be able to make things all right with him again.'

'Why not ask Niall?'

'I did. He told me to leave well enough alone.'

Cora looked at her tilted cat's eyes and her wide, thin-lipped mouth. Her nose was a little too large for fashion but it added a certain wit and obstinacy to what would have otherwise been an ordinary, pretty face. 'Then that's it,' Cora said. 'That's what you should do.'

'You were married once, weren't you?' Nancy asked.

Cora nodded.

'Did you obey your husband in everything?'

Cora watched her silently.

'There was nothing between Francis and me in America, honestly.'

'Then I can see no use in your talking to him,' Cora retorted coldly.

'Why do you three dislike me so much?' Nancy asked quietly. 'I can understand Francis but I don't know what I have done to hurt you. I love your brother and I'm sure I can make him happy. I'll be proud to save this house for you and then you can live here for the rest of your lives . . .'

'Aren't we grateful enough, then?' Cora asked.

'No, no!' Nancy said. 'That's not what I meant!'

'The problem is,' Cora thought, though she did not speak out loud, 'that you look happy while we three do not. We cannot bear to see such happiness in this house when it is a gift that has been robbed from us, each one in turn.'

'Then perhaps you will ask me again when you are clear what you do mean,' was what she actually said, then swept off down the corridor like a ship at sail, leaving Nancy standing miserably in her wake.

CHAPTER FORTY-TWO

'Niall, is there anything I could do that might please your sisters?' Nancy asked her husband as they dressed for dinner that evening.

'Yes,' he told her, straightening his bow tie, 'you can go away.'

She turned from her mirror to look at him. 'Is that really what they want?' she asked. 'Christina barely speaks to me and Cora seems so angry somehow, and Constance . . .'

'What about Constance?' Niall asked, his voice changing.

'I don't know . . .' Nancy began, 'she was so friendly when I arrived and then when she found out I was your wife . . . I think she's jealous, Niall. She's very fond of you herself and can't stand to see you married. Perhaps she feels I've stolen her favourite brother from her.'

'Don't be stupid,' Niall said, bending to look in the mirror behind her. 'They just want us away from here, that's all. They resent having to live on your money, and it galls them that they have to. They'd probably like to see us both dead right now, so they can live in peace again.'

'That's a wicked thing to say,' Nancy said. 'Even as a joke.'

She absent-mindedly fingered the brushes and cosmetics that lay on the dressing-table before her. Niall moved behind her and she watched in the mirror as he pressed his lips against the nape of her bare neck.

'For God's sake put some lipstick on,' he whispered, 'you look like a boy with that crop you have.'

'I love you,' she told him. 'I want us happy, that's all.'

She saw his face beside hers and saw the same dark look in his eyes that she would see after they made love at night, when she would lie beside him in their bed, gorged and sated by his passion and then turn to see him lying staring at the ceiling as though his heart had been saddened by what they had just done.

She rose from her stool and crossed to the bed, where she stepped into her dinner-dress and pulled it up to her shoulders while Niall stood watching. It was the latest style; a slim-fitting sheath of bright peacock-blue shantung that had thin pencil-straps at her shoulders and a line of pearl-button fastenings at the back.

'You know you will scandalize everyone here with your clothes, don't you?' Niall was smiling and Nancy looked pleased.

'How come?' she said.

'Your skirts are too short and you show too much breast and leg. Did you not notice how Cora dresses herself up?'

'Swathed in brown serge or yards of violet velvet.' Nancy laughed.

Niall settled himself upon the bed, leaning back onto the pillows and lighting a cigarette.

'Would you rather have me covered up like that? Besides,' she added, admiring herself in the mirror, 'these styles are all the fashion in Paris and New York.'

'But this is Ireland,' Niall told her. 'Or hadn't you noticed?'

'So what will they do when they see me?' Nancy asked. 'Have me put into the stocks or burnt at the stake? Perhaps it's about time a little piece of the twentieth century visited Connemara. Look at little Constance! She gets herself dressed up each night like a quaint old-fashioned doll! Perhaps I could let her borrow from my wardrobe now and again. Maybe that would please her, d'you think?'

Nancy turned towards her husband and was shocked at the anger in his eyes.

'Leave Constance alone,' he said. 'She looks fine as she is.'

'I'm sorry . . .' Nancy began, 'I didn't mean to be unkind . . .'

Niall jumped from the bed and stubbed his cigarette out into an ashtray on the nightstand.

'You'll no doubt hear the local priest's opinion of your ensemble tonight,' he said, quickly. 'I have invited him and a few of his cronies to dinner.'

'You might have warned me!' Nancy said, turning back to the mirror.

'Why? So that you could have had time to get yourself suitably attired? You are the vainest person I know, Nancy. I shouldn't think Father Devereux would worry how you turned yourself out. He's an eye for beauty as well as the next man. I'm sure he'll appreciate your charms in the way you have chosen to display them.'

Nancy pulled a pair of long satin gloves over her arms. 'Do these match?' she asked.

'Did some precious little designer get paid a fortune by your mother to ensure that they do?'

Nancy laughed. 'Yes,' she told him, 'most likely he did.'

'Then they match.' Niall pulled the door open. 'Now come along or we'll turn up after our guests.'

Niall made a surprisingly good host that evening, but then so had his father, in the old days. Father Devereux had not been to the house for many months and he was as enchanted by the changes that had been made to the place as he was by his new hostess.

The room in which they ate was made warm and glowing from the fire and the score of yellow candles that were lit along the table, although the winds were fierce that night and the smoke kept blowing back into the room from the vast chimney, causing the guests' eyes to smart.

There were twenty places laid and nineteen turned up to eat, for the doctor had a case of pleurisy in the O'Leary household and sent word that he would be arriving later.

Father Devereux found himself seated between Nancy and Constance; while Niall took William's chair at the head of the table, though his gaze would shift uncomfortably to his wife and his sister at the opposite end.

They made a handsome pair of dinner companions, the priest thought, turning from Nancy to Constance as he spoke. There was no comparing their beauty, though. Nancy had the face of a pretty cat. Her eyes were slanted and vivacious and she had a small neat chin below a wide, ever-smiling mouth. Her smile was infectious, showing perfect white teeth between lips that had been stained with bright carmine lipstick. She was intelligent and confident and as out of place at that table as a peacock in a sparrow's nest.

It was Constance who had the real beauty, though. Her pale, radiant face and large, watchful eyes glowed with the same luminous beauty that her mother had possessed. She had come to the table like a moth drawn to a flame; quiet, reluctant but needy of the company, and she had sat staring at the diners and especially at her brother Niall. Her movements were slow and light, in direct contrast to her sister-in-law's rapid and unself-conscious gestures.

'This is a fine feast, Niall!' Father Devereux called as the dinner was served.

Niall nodded and rose to his feet. 'And we have my wife there to thank for it, Father,' he said, raising his glass. 'It is her father who provides the meal for our mouths and the roof over our heads. It is thanks to his coffers that we eat so well tonight. A toast, I think, to the new Missus Flavelle!'

The men rose hastily to their feet as the toast was called. Father Devereux turned to his hostess and saw that her face had turned scarlet with embarrassment.

When Nancy leant back in her chair Father Devereux found himself wishing that she would bend forward again, for her dress fell tight against her ample bosom and he was forced to smile as each man in the room fell silent, even the oldest.

Nancy seemed not to notice the effect she was having, though. She was busy now telling the priest about her family in New York and about the food that was currently being served at table, which was based on traditional American recipes. Only then did she lean forward to spoon some chowder into her mouth and the conversation about the table resumed, preceded by something that sounded like a collective sigh from the male guests.

'My family are second-generation Irish Catholics,' she told the priest between mouthfuls of food, 'though my father lapsed so badly when he started his business that I believe my mother still thinks he's damned to purgatory. I told her he's used to working to schedule and that he'll be sure to repent just before he goes, for he knows his deadlines better than any newspaper man in the business. He's never brought a story in late yet, Father!' she said, smiling. 'Oh! I'm sorry, Father, am I being blasphemous?' She laughed nervously but Father Devereux was charmed and dismissed her apologies as unnecessary.

He turned smiling then to Constance. Constance had not been listening, though, as she was too intent on hearing the conversation at the other end of the table.

'Oh, we'll be starting a family soon enough,' Niall was telling one of his guests. 'I need an heir to inherit all of this, you know. I have bought the place from my brother so that I have a legacy for my own children. Who knows?' he added, laughing and waving his dinner-fork in the direction of his wife, 'perhaps we already have an heir on the way!'

Constance rose abruptly from her seat at this and those around fell silent when they saw the anguished expression on her face. Her napkin slithered slowly down her skirt to the floor, from where Father Devereux made an attempt to retrieve it.

'No!' she whispered, so quietly that only Father Devereux heard.

Niall looked up, an expression of quiet amusement on his face.

A sob came from Constance's mouth and her hand shot up to cover it, to prevent any more from escaping.

Nancy rose quickly from her chair in sympathy and would have walked around to comfort her but Constance

337

fled from the room before she could reach her. Nancy followed but Niall grabbed her wrist as she ran past his chair.

'Leave her,' he said, quietly.

'But she looks so ill!'

'Then send one of your precious servants to her,' Niall said. 'I'm sure we have the staff to cover all emergencies these days. You have guests to see to, Nancy. This dinner party is in your honour and they have come to meet their new hostess.'

Nancy looked down at him for a moment in silence, then he released her wrist and she walked slowly back to her seat at the opposite end of the table.

'I believe Constance is what they call highly-strung,' she said to Father Devereux. 'She barely talks to me now, though she seemed so friendly when I arrived. Has she always been this way, Father? You must have known her all her life. I don't know what the matter is but my husband just says not to worry.'

'Then I'm sure that is the best advice, Missus Flavelle,' Father Devereux said. It was the first time he had used that name since Sophia had died and it gave him quite a jolt. He looked down the table to where Niall sat and found himself worrying, despite his reassurances to his hostess.

Perhaps he should have a word with William's youngest in private. Was the son beginning to resemble the father? Yet he could not believe it would happen. Perhaps Francis, yes, but Niall? How could he ever follow in his father's footsteps when he had been so ostracized? Father Devereux felt the need to discuss the puzzle with Doctor O'Sullivan and was considerably cheered when he saw the man arrive. Perhaps he could offer up some theories to explain Niall's manner. He wished that he had arrived earlier and seen Constance's flight from the room. Perhaps it was a medical problem after all – there were all sorts of women's ailments that could have explained the scene, he knew. But it was the look that had passed between brother and sister that so

concerned him: mute appeal from Constance, and either fear
or hatred from Niall, the priest could not be sure which.
Father Devereux gave himself a little cerebral shake and
turned back to his hostess with the most charming of smiles.
'Constance and her sisters must be secretly delighted,' he
said, 'to find their nest invaded by such a good companion
as yourself.'

Niall was on his way to bed, tired by the late evening and
the generous amount of brandy he had consumed, his head
ringing from the endless conversation, when Constance
stopped him in the passage, running up from behind and
grabbing him roughly by the arm.

Surprised by the sudden assault, he turned to look at her.

She was dressed in an old-fashioned broderie anglaise
nightgown that reached to her ankles, a stark contrast to
the sensual satin gowns that his wife wore. Constance
looked very much like a pretty child in it, with her long hair
lying loose about her shoulders. Her pale eyes were
red-rimmed, as though she had been crying. She was so
small beside him as he towered above her but the grip that
she had on his arm was a strong one and only became
stronger when he tried to shake it off.

'Did you come to apologize for your behaviour, then?'
Niall asked her quickly. 'Because if you did then it's my wife
you should be apologizing to for the scene you made earlier,
not me. It was her you embarrassed with your histrionics.'
He yawned. 'Have a word with her tomorrow,' he said.
'She'll no doubt be delighted you took the bother. She wants
you as a friend, you know.'

'Niall!' Constance cried. 'You have to stop this, I can't
bear it any more! For pity's sake don't take it any further!'

'Take what further?' Niall whispered, glancing quickly
down the corridor to make sure they were not overheard.
'Are you mad, Constance? I don't know what you are
talking about.'

'You do know, Niall!' Constance insisted. 'You know

exactly what I mean! It can't continue! I will die if you go on treating me like this! What have I done? You are wicked, Niall, you must stop it, you must!'

'Wicked?' Niall repeated. 'Do you know that's just what our father used to say? I know he thought sometimes that I was the very Devil himself. And as with him, Constance, I have no idea what it is you are talking about.'

'You don't love her, Niall!' Constance said, her eyes feverish. 'You know you don't! How can you be so wicked? You brought her here just to make me jealous and now you plan to have children with her. It isn't right, Niall! You must stop this game now, before it goes too far!'

Niall glanced down the passage again and, seeing it was still clear, pulled his sister into the nearest empty room. They stood there in the sudden darkness, staring at each other.

'I don't know what you mean,' he said, quietly. 'But I think you may be mad, Constance. Do you think I don't love my wife, is that what you are saying? You think that I brought her here just to play some crazy game with you, do you?' He shook his head slowly and sadly. 'Why should I ever do that, Constance?' he asked. 'You're my *sister*, for Christ's sake! Whatever has possessed you? I think you should have a word with Father Devereux, perhaps he can put you to rights.'

'You love me, Niall!' Constance persisted, louder now. 'I know you do!'

'Jesus Christ!' A nightmare had suddenly revealed itself to Niall. He remembered the scenes in the confession as a boy, with the Jesuits asking him: 'Do you have impure thoughts of your sister?' He had been innocent then and now he did all he could to keep her at arm's length, as his father had wanted.

'We have always loved each other!' she claimed. 'You said you would care for me! I need you, Niall! Can't you see how things are for me? You can't have changed that much, I know you can't. Look at me! We were so close as children! Show me you haven't changed! I don't believe you when you try to be cold towards me!'

Niall pushed her away and she hit the wall behind with a thump.

'Holy mother of God!' he whispered. 'How can you think such things, Constance, let alone say them? Of course I loved you, I loved you as a brother should, but that was years ago and a lot has happened since then. We can't be children all our lives! Your mind is as bad as our father's. He died in holy terror that I might be guilty of lusting after his precious young daughter! For God's sake keep quiet, Constance, you're raving!'

She closed her eyes. 'I love you, Niall,' she said. 'You are all I have to live for. I can't bear to see the two of you together.'

Niall sighed. 'She's my wife, Constance. A man has needs. He has to have a wife. Anything else would be unnatural.'

'I could have been a wife to you, Niall,' Constance whispered.

Niall grabbed her, driven half-mad at her words. 'You are my *sister*, Constance,' he repeated with more patience than he felt. 'What you are implying is evil, you must know that.'

'You pretend to hate me,' Constance said, 'but I know you don't. I know you love me. That's why you keep away from me.'

Niall groaned. 'You don't know what you are saying.'

'I know more than you think,' Constance sobbed. 'I was wife enough for William Flavelle after our mother died. Don't talk to me as though I am a child, Niall! I understand what I am offering you, truly I do!'

She had made her confession at last, then; told him what his father had done to her as a child. Now she waited for his comfort and his sympathy and for all the things that she had hoped for during those lost years since William Flavelle had abused her. The circumstances were not as she would have wanted, but what did that matter now that he would understand and would compensate for all the suffering she had endured in silence? He had thought her spoilt by their father but now he would hate her no longer, now that he knew she had suffered just as he had.

Niall's hands fell from her shoulders and she looked up into his face.

'Liar!' he whispered, and she shrank away at the sound of the word.

'You saw us!' she cried. 'You were there after it happened!'

Niall saw the scene in a terrible flash before his eyes; his father, half-naked and furiously angry; Constance, curled small and screaming in her bed. He had not understood, he would never have imagined . . . his father loved his sister above anything else in his life. But he saw the scene now through the eyes of an adult, and knew Constance was telling the truth.

'Liar!' he said again, though, for he did not want to believe. 'What is it you are trying to tell me?'

It was then that Constance became truly frightened, for instead of love and compassion in her brother's eyes she saw only shock and repulsion. She became desperate, saw her life falling from her grasp and knew the utter helplessness she would suffer if Niall were to abandon her now.

'He came into my room . . .' she said softly. 'You saw him yourself . . . you came to protect me . . . He climbed into my bed . . . I didn't know what it was that he wanted . . . I thought he was ill . . . he called me by our mother's name . . . He forced me . . . I couldn't breathe . . .' She did not hear the words as they rushed from her mouth; she watched her brother's face and saw it fill with intolerable emotion, his hands covering his ears when he could bear to hear no more.

Constance tried to pull his hands away, for he had to hear; there was no one else to understand and to help her. It was not her fault, so why did he hate her? Then the realization came to her that he might think as the priest.

Perhaps he saw her as guilty, too, thought she had been willing, an eager replacement for their mother! Could he possibly imagine . . . the idea made her feel physically sick and a bitter taste filled her mouth. Her dear father's favourite. He would see her as a collaborator; sharing the love from which he and the others were excluded. She could not bear the thought and a first flavour of madness came into her head.

She thought to tell him the rest; that William Flavelle was not her true father, but it seemed pointless for he had ceased listening.

'Niall!' she whispered as she watched him back away, no longer able to fathom the expression in his eyes.

The door opened behind them. It was Nancy, her shocked expression at the scene made ridiculous by the layer of vivid make-up still on her face.

'What is it?' she asked. 'What's going on?' Niall pushed roughly past her and ran down the corridor. Constance attempted to follow but Nancy grabbed at her nightgown, almost tearing it in her determination to find out what was wrong.

Constance struggled but Nancy was stronger and held her fast.

'Calm down,' she ordered. 'You're quite hysterical, Constance. Tell me what has happened. What has my husband done to upset you like this? Tell me!'

At the words 'my husband' Constance tore herself fiercely from Nancy's grasp and raced after Niall. She could hear Nancy following and calling after her but she was too fast now and didn't care to listen.

The front door was hanging wide open. The rain had wet the floor and made puddles of the rugs. Constance ran outside and the rain stung her face like needles, soaking her in an instant.

'Niall!' Her voice was like the shrill cry of a bird and carried no further than a few feet.

Walking was impossible. Her bare feet stuck in the mud

343

and her nightdress became heavy with water. She reluctantly took the path back to the house, her feet ripping on the sharp gravel. Once inside she ran to the large hall cupboard and pulled on a pair of ancient wellingtons, then wrapped a stiff and aged cape about her shoulders.

Outside again, she thought she saw something in the darkness of the demesne. It was a lamp, an oil-lamp, threading its way through the trees and rocks, swinging gently to and fro as Niall hurried away from the house.

Constance stumbled over the lawns, losing her footing several times in the giant boots and twice nearly falling altogether. Niall was moving quickly and for a few terrible minutes she thought that he was on horseback, but she paced out the light of the swaying lantern and to her relief saw that it swung only to footsteps, not a horse's canter.

When it seemed as though she had walked for hours she saw the light stop and she almost cried out with relief. Her legs were stiff with the effort and the boots had rubbed her feet raw. It could have been a mile away, she was not able to judge its distance, but it had stopped at last and that was all that mattered to her at that moment. She sank down onto the sodden ground and watched the small glow-worm of light ahead until some of her strength had returned.

It was an hour before she managed to walk far enough to make out the shapes before her in the darkness. The light stood upon a wall and she realized with a start of apprehension that she was in front of her family burial-ground.

Running as quickly as she could around the low wall, Constance made her way to the entrance archway and leant against the rusty gate, peering vainly into the darkness. She thought she heard noises from inside and saw a tall dark shadow move before the glow of the lantern. She knew then that it was Niall and that gave her the courage to enter.

'Niall?' she whispered. He was standing over a grave. His shoulders were hunched and she saw his head go down and then his arms come up . . .

'Niall!' she screamed. 'Stop! Oh my God!'

Niall was digging at his father's grave. She heard his breath as it rasped from his lungs and smelt the fresh-dug earth that reminded her of William's funeral.

Constance threw herself against her brother, pulling at his arms to stop him, but he barely seemed to notice and merely shrugged her off.

'He cannot lie here . . .' he was saying. 'I won't have him next to her . . . he pollutes the ground he lies in . . . she should be left in peace.'

Constance watched each heavy lift of the spade. Her brother's face in the dull lantern light looked grim and exhausted, yet he was set on his task. She looked over at the huge marble angel with their mother's face watching over them and imagined the eternal pity of its gaze as it looked down upon its two beloved children.

It was another hour before Niall's spade struck the wood of his father's coffin and the noise seemed to give him renewed strength for he set about working with such a frenzy that Constance feared that he would drop from exhaustion. He began to slide on the mud at each fresh pull of the spade and she saw him wedge himself into the sides of the hole so that he was held securely enough to remain upright as he worked.

At last he threw the spade away and began to work with his bare hands. Constance watched in silence, mesmerized by the horror of the scene. Niall paused only once, when he was no longer able to breathe, and then he leant against a wall of the hole, his head bent back so that it was stippled by the lamplight. He was panting hard and there was mud on his face. Then he looked across at Constance as though noticing her for the first time.

'Go back to the house, Constance!' he shouted. 'I don't want you out here and you'll drown in this rain!' His head collapsed backwards without waiting for her reply.

'Oh Christ,' she heard him mutter to himself. 'What other wicked things has he done?'

His tone of utter despair made Constance begin weeping

again for she was afraid her brother had gone insane and that it was her fault, for telling him of his father's sins.

'Please stop now, Niall!' she begged, though she knew he did not hear her. 'You scare me.'

With one marvellous effort Niall pulled himself from the grave and Constance heard the heavy rain drumming onto the lid of the coffin. He was walking towards her, she realized, and with a cry, she dragged herself up to run away. His face looked white and terrible.

'You are no help here, Constance,' he said, grabbing her by the arm. 'You have to get back to the house. I cannot do what I have to do with you here watching. I don't want you standing there crying, don't you see?'

He paused and looked back towards the house. 'I have to get the horse and some rope now. I can't manage without it. I'll take you back with me.'

'I'll get your horse,' Constance offered.

'Don't be stupid,' Niall snapped, but she could see he was too exhausted to argue. She pulled away from him and stumbled off across the demesne before he could stop her or call her back. He couldn't follow her in the state he was in. The walk would take her an hour at the least and she was not sure she had the energy, but she needed to help her brother and knew she would manage it somehow.

She had walked half the way when she saw lights ahead in the distance and she stopped, shielding her eyes from the rain, half-wondering whether to throw herself into the ditch for fear it was some wandering spirit come to wreak retribution upon the both of them for the job they were about. Then she heard the motor for the first time and realized it was Nancy's car, its tyres spinning in the mud as she took each narrow bend at too fast a speed.

The car pulled up some distance away from Constance and she found herself pinned in the twin arcs of its spotlights. She stood, blinded and unable to move, as the car door was opened and Nancy jumped out, still in her evening dress and with her short hair plastered to her face with the rain.

'What the hell is going on?' she demanded, walking down the path until the two women stood level. 'Where is Niall?' She looked at Constance's flailing great cape and studied her mud-caked boots. 'What's happened?' she asked quite calmly. 'Has there been an accident?'

Constance shook her head. 'No.'

'You know where he is, then?'

'He's just down the way there,' Constance said, not bothering to point. 'You're not to go, though,' she added quickly, 'he won't be wanting you there. He sent me away.'

'I see.' Nancy stood still a moment, thinking. Then she suddenly turned. 'Get into the car,' she told Constance. 'We'll drive down to wherever he is and see if he's all right.'

But Constance stood her ground. 'You're not to go, Nancy,' she said. 'He won't want you there, I told you.'

The two women stared at each other as the rain streamed down their faces and the wind howled in their ears.

'Niall is my husband, Constance,' Nancy said quietly, but loud enough for Constance to hear. 'It is not your place to tell me what he will or won't want. You don't have the right any more, do you understand? I need to see for myself, whatever you say. I know you love him but you are only his sister. We are husband and wife and that is a much closer relationship. I'm sorry, Constance, but you have to understand that.'

She motioned towards the car again and this time Constance complied. Nancy stared as she pulled the wet nightdress around her legs and clambered into the leather-lined seat, shivering a little as Nancy slammed the door shut and walked around to jump in beside her. The car smelt of petrol and the seats squeaked as the two women settled into them in their wet clothes. There was a terrible intimacy in that confined space.

347

'Now,' Nancy said, clutching the steering wheel, 'where is he?'

Constance looked straight ahead, at the rain that formed a sheet before her and at the twin spheres of country that lay frozen in the yellow arcs of the lamps.

'You'll have to take me back to the house first,' she said. 'I need to fetch something for him. That's where I was going. It's urgent, you see. We have to go there first.'

'Like hell,' Nancy said.

'It's *urgent*,' Constance said again.

'It would have to be, wouldn't it,' Nancy whispered to herself. She closed her eyes and sighed She seemed indecisive.

Constance turned to her. 'You think I'm lying,' she said.

Nancy shrugged.

'Why would I be in this state if it weren't?' Constance asked, lifting her sodden nightgown for inspection.

'You had an argument with Niall,' Nancy said.

Constance shook her head. 'No, no. We didn't argue. Niall just has something that he must do . . . something that doesn't involve you, believe me, Nancy. I have to help him, it's important. *Please*. You have to take me back. Niall will be terribly angry if you don't!'

Nancy almost laughed. 'So he'll be mad, will he?' she asked.

'And I might die of the cold!' Constance added, sounding suddenly childish. 'And besides,' she said, looking at Nancy, 'you'd never stand a hope of finding him out there in the dark unless I decided to show you the way.'

'OK,' she sighed. 'We'll do as you say, Constance, but you might just tell me what it is that you have to fetch for him.'

They drove in silence, the car jumping uncomfortably over the pitted road.

'Well?' Nancy asked as they neared the house.

'I need to get his horse.' She said nothing about the rope.

Nancy looked truly alarmed for the first time. 'Is he going away?' she asked quietly.

'No. He just needs it, that's all.'

Nancy shook her head as she steered around the driveway. 'I can see I am going to have to wait until I ask Niall,' she said, but Constance was gone as soon as the car had slowed and Nancy sat watching as she made her way around the house towards the stables.

Niall stopped work when he heard the horse's hooves drumming on the track that led towards the graveyard and he leant back, exhausted, as Constance leapt from the saddle and ran across to him.

'Did you bring some rope?' he asked. The effort of keeping the mud out of the hole that he had spent hours digging had left him drained.

She threw the rope onto the ground beside him.

'Good. Now get back to the house.'

'I can't go back,' Constance argued. 'I'm too tired to walk and anyway, Nancy's up there and she keeps asking me questions. What are you going to do, Niall?' she asked as she saw her father's coffin sticking halfway out of its grave. 'Are you mad? What are you going to do with him? He's dead, Niall! He can do us no more harm!'

'He can't lie in consecrated ground,' Niall said quietly. 'He shouldn't lie next to our mother. He polluted the very air that he breathed while he was alive and he contaminates the ground now that he's dead.

'I thought it was me, do you see? I thought I was the evil one! He told me I was the son of the Devil and that it was I who was the danger to the whole family, but it was him all the while! There I was, scared to even touch my own sister and all the time he knew that he had . . . and I wondered why he had tried to kill himself that night! I should have let him die! If I'd known then what I know now I would have done, I swear it!

'Don't you see, Constance? Do you think I could let him lie here, smug in his grave, after all that he's done to us? Do you think I could live in his house, knowing he's out

349

here in his state of grace, tormenting my soul? Look at his tombstone, Constance, have you read it? "Lying safe in the arms of the Lord". Now who the hell had that put there, I wonder? Is that how you wish to think of him, lying in the arms of the Lord while the rest of us scratch about in the hell that he has created for us upon earth? Is that what you want, Constance?' Niall's voice rose to an angry shout and Constance backed away slowly, frightened by his madness.

She watched from a quiet distance as her brother finished his task, tying the rope from the coffin to his horse and then urging the animal on until the box was pulled clear from the open grave.

At the sight of the rotted coffin, Constance began to tremble. She covered her eyes with her shivering hands and wept. She was terribly afraid; afraid that the lid might fall back from the coffin and that William Flavelle might come screaming from inside to bring vengeance upon them both.

She lowered her hands and peered over at her brother and found that he had paused in his work and was staring at the coffin as though he, too, were fearful of ghosts, but then, with a shake of his head, he resumed his grim task and, leaping into the horse's saddle, would have set off across the demesne, leaving Constance alone in the dark.

'Don't leave me, Niall!' she called out at once.

'You can't come, Constance!' he shouted. 'I have this to finish and you cannot come with me! Go home! I have to see an end to him.'

'Don't leave me!' Constance screamed, hysterical now. The open grave loomed before her and her boots were so heavy with mud she could barely move her feet to run.

She staggered over to Niall's horse and looked up at him, dark and terrible in the saddle. 'Please!' she insisted.

He held his hand down to her and she almost wept with relief as he pulled her up into the saddle behind him. She wrapped her arms about his waist as he kicked his heels into the horse's soft belly and it set off across the demesne like a horse out of hell, the coffin bouncing in its wake. Constance could hear the wood dragging in the mud and cracking on the stones but she would not look back for fear of what she might see. She felt the rope pull taut with the effort of holding it and she was sure the coffin would split open before they reached their destination.

She sobbed and prayed for her brother's soul. Surely they were both damned for what they had done that night? If Niall were mad, though, she was mad as well, she decided, for, even as she had sat terrified by William's open grave, she had found herself excited by the scene and by Niall's terrible revenge.

The horse made its way more slowly up the path that led to the cliffs. Niall urged it on, pushing his heels into its ribs and cursing when it lost its footing. In the end it had pulled the coffin up to the peak that looked down onto the sea and it was there that he reined in and stopped to untie the rope.

Constance stayed in the saddle as Niall walked towards the cliff-edge.

'Should I say a few words for you, Papa?' he asked as he pulled at the rope and the coffin slid nearer. 'How about: "Father, forgive them; for they know not what they do"?' He laughed, and Constance shuddered. 'Hardly suitable though,' he said, 'for I'm sure that you knew exactly what you were doing.'

He pulled the coffin closer to the edge and fell onto the wet grass beside it. A picture came into his mind of William with Constance beneath him, lying spread on white and swelling sheets, like the sail of a ship. He saw blood leaking from between his sister's pale legs and soon the sheet was pure crimson. The blood became a flowing pool that in turn became as great as the black heaving ocean below him.

'I had the chance to let you die,' he whispered to the coffin, 'but I could not find the courage, and for that much I am guilty. I pray to heaven to forgive me for that one sin.

'I must surely be the greatest fool that ever walked God's earth. After all that you had done to me I still could not let you die. You had come straight from her bed when you took me to that barn. Was her blood still wet upon your body? You knew she was all I had left to love after our mother died and you tried to convince me that the love I felt for her was impure, yet all the while you were planning to have her yourself, you bastard!

'Did you think that if you killed yourself then all your sins would be absolved? How did it feel when that gun exploded in your face yet you discovered you had lived and that you were not on the other side? How did it feel to sit there, dribbling in that chair each day, watching her walk about you and knowing what it was you had done to her?

'Did you still lust after her? Was that your torment, to be impotent and paralysed while all that you longed for was so nearly within your reach? Perhaps God has a sense of humour after all, to punish you in such a way. My God, you bastard, you great, hypocritical bastard!'

With a loud cry of despair that was echoed by Constance's high-pitched scream, Niall rose from the grass and pushed the coffin with all his might until it toppled over the clifftop and flew out into the dark air.

He threw himself onto the ground, lying close to the edge as he watched it soar into the blackness and then fall heavily to earth to be dashed to splinters on the rocks below.

He saw the white shape of his father's corpse, bound in its winding-sheet, rise up and lie for a moment, suspended on the foaming stones until the sea came to claim it and it was dragged out with the roaring tide, bobbing on the surface like a buoy until it was taken from sight and the waves returned, angry and empty-handed.

Niall made the sign of the cross. 'May the fishermen find you, Papa,' he said, 'rotting in their nets along with all the fish.'

The job was over. He jumped to his feet and threw the length of rope over the cliff before returning to his horse. His body shook with exhaustion but he felt reborn, his soul pure once more.

He barely noticed his sister, who sat trembling in the saddle, as he turned his horse slowly onto the path back to the graveyard. He could have slept for a decade but first he had more work to do that night. He had to fill in his father's grave before anyone else discovered the terrible thing that he had done.

CHAPTER FORTY-THREE

Constance took to her bed after that terrible night and would not be coaxed from it, despite all Cora's attempts at persuasion.

'Are you ill?' Cora asked, but she would not answer, could not reveal the awful secret, and so the doctor was eventually called and he came away saying that he could see little wrong with her apart from a slight fever, caused, no doubt, by the wetting she had had.

'You say she was running about in the storm?' he asked Nancy. 'What on earth for?'

Nancy lifted her hands in a gesture of desperation. 'Lord knows! All my husband will say is that he had to see to a fence that had been battered down by the winds but why Constance found that an occasion for such high drama I couldn't tell you. She was like a headless chicken, Doctor, saying she had to help him urgently or something. Is she all right, do you think? Is there any more that we can do to help her?'

The doctor smiled. 'Don't worry yourself, Missus Flavelle,' he said. 'Make sure she gets enough red meat to eat and maybe an odd glass of wine or two with her supper. She's of sound enough strength, despite her fragile looks.' He studied Nancy as he spoke. 'Are you well enough yourself, Missus Flavelle?' he asked, noting the paleness of her cheeks.

'I'm quite well, thank you,' Nancy said, but the doctor noted the hesitation in her voice. She folded her arms quickly about her waist.

'That is . . .' she began.

'A child is it, then?' the doctor asked her and she looked startled.

'I should know the signs by now.' The doctor laughed. 'I've delivered so many in my years in Connemara that I've lost count.' He patted her arm reassuringly. 'I'm sure we all seem like heathens and wild natives out here to you,' he said, smiling, 'but I can assure you there's not much new in modern science that can better the old methods when it comes to bringing a child into the world safely.

'I'd be proud to attend you, if you wish. It's a few years since there's been a birth of a Flavelle child in this house and I'm sure it will be one of the grandest occasions ever.' He rubbed his hands with delight at the thought. Sophia's births had always been occasions for worry and concern but this young woman looked as though she were made of stronger stuff.

'I haven't exactly thought that far ahead yet,' Nancy said, swallowing hard. 'I haven't even told my husband, I haven't found the right moment. I meant to tell him last night, after dinner, but things got a little out of hand, as you know. We were so busy fussing about Constance . . .'

'Well you can stop worrying about that young lady and start thinking of yourself now,' the doctor said, lifting his bag from the hall table. 'Mister Flavelle will be delighted when he hears the news, I'm sure of it. Tell him as soon as you can and let him fuss about you for a change!'

But the doctor felt less confident than he sounded as he tried to reassure the distressed-looking woman. Niall was an odd fish all right; much his father's son in many ways. There was no telling how Nancy's pregnancy would affect him. He had been a quiet child but he had grown into a volatile adult. He had been hospitable enough at dinner the night before, but there was something in his dark eyes that the doctor had found disturbing.

Everyone pitied Niall for the way that he had been treated by his father but then no one had gone out of their way to befriend him since his return to the house. He was like a stranger in the village now and he appeared to prefer things to stay that way.

That night Constance prayed alone in her room.

'Let him see what he is doing to me,' she prayed, 'make him see that he loves me and that I love him. What he is doing to us is wrong, I know it. I can't live with him like this, it will kill the both of us!'

Tears ran down her clenched hands and she saw her own reflection in the mirror opposite the bed. It was a child's face, ghastly white in the moonlight.

'I shall die,' she whispered to the reflection, 'I shall die without him.'

She heard voices in the hall outside her room; Nancy whispering and then Niall talking louder. She heard Nancy trying to hush him, as though they were arguing in the darkness. Constance climbed onto her bed and pulled her knees up under her chest and listened, her head cocked like a small bird. The words they spoke were muffled by the distance but she managed to hear a few.

'I thought you would be pleased,' she heard Nancy say.

Niall laughed. 'I am pleased,' he said. Nancy started to cry.

'Come on, now,' Niall said softly and then she heard Nancy laugh.

Constance's mouth opened. She knew what those words meant. Nancy was carrying her brother's child. Constance felt sick at the thought and she held her hands over her mouth while the nausea passed. She closed her eyes and rocked herself gently on the bed, listening to the sounds of her own body; waiting until her heartbeat regained its normal pace. Then she walked unsteadily across to her bureau and pulled out the stool that stood in front of it.

Her hands trembling, she lit a lamp and took some notepaper out of the drawer, dipped the pen into the ink to begin her letter. She wrote to her mother's family in Dublin, begging them to allow her to stay with them.

'I cannot stay here,' she whispered to herself, 'I shall go mad if I have to live here with them. I cannot share him with her. I have to go now.'

Composing the letter calmed her a little. Dublin was a grand place, after all; the doctor had told her as much. Niall would miss her, whatever he said. Perhaps he would even come after her. She smiled and the baby was already forgotten. She ended the letter with a flourish and signed: 'Your loving niece, Constance.'

Perhaps she would never return.

Constance took great delight in her packing, and in Niall's expression when she told him she was to go. He feigned disinterest but she could see behind his lies, just as she could see the relief in Nancy's eyes when she tried to offer her concern.

'You'll be back before the baby is born?' she asked and Constance had found it easy to smile.

'Most likely,' she said.

'You'll be its auntie, after all,' Nancy told her and Constance had been disgusted at the thought.

'Of course, I may decide to stay there,' she had said, watching Niall's face.

'Perhaps you should,' Niall remarked, quietly.

'Oh, I should think you'll miss the beautiful countryside too much to stay,' Nancy had corrected him.

'Don't you miss your home?' Constance asked her.

'This is my home,' Nancy replied.

There was an envelope waiting in her room, lying across her largest case. It was filled with money, folded inside a note from her sister-in-law.

'I know that Niall will not think to give you any,' she read, 'but you will find you will need new fashions when you arrive in Dublin. You will feel strange in the clothes that you wear now and I want you to know you can indulge yourself at your pleasure.'

Constance stood in silence, staring down at the note.

'I hope it doesn't embarrass you,' Nancy said, walking into the room. She laughed. 'Call it baby's first gift if you like,' she said. 'You don't have to spend it on clothes,' she added. 'You can spend it on whatever you like. Have some fun if you want; there's little enough of it around here.'

'And I can have more, if I want?' Constance asked. 'You'll send me more when I need it?'

'Whatever you need,' Nancy said, quietly.

'Just to have fun?'

Nancy nodded.

'And to stay away from this house,' Constance said.

Nancy said nothing.

'Thank you,' Constance told her, and stuffed the notes quickly into her purse.

CHAPTER FORTY-FOUR

Constance found that Dublin did not suit her at all at first. She missed Connemara but most of all she missed her brother. Their separation had been all her own doing and that made the suffering even harder to bear. At any moment, on any day, she would be acutely aware of the fact that she could step onto a train and be back with him in a few hours and then she would have to force herself to think of her sister-in-law, with her great swollen belly; and then all thoughts of a reconciliation would be swept instantly from her mind.

She wrote to Niall often but it was always Nancy who replied. Niall might as well have been dead to her, apart from the mention that he got in the letters from his wife, and then Nancy would only describe a man that Constance did not know.

'Niall has taken his horse across the estates,' Nancy would write; 'Niall took your sisters and myself into Clifden for the day . . .' 'Niall told an amusing tale about the priest at supper this evening . . .' 'Niall is so caring now that the baby is on the way that I feel I must be made of crystal-glass . . .'

Nancy had created a whole new character for Constance's brother and Niall became gregarious and sociable in her letters, which Constance knew he was not. She had to be lying, unless approaching fatherhood had changed him completely. Constance had considered this for a moment or two before deciding that she could not entertain such an idea and then she had screwed Nancy's letter into a ball and tossed it into the fire.

Yet when she eventually saw Niall again, when the baby was born and some six months old, she had thought at first that she had been wrong and that her brother was a changed man, after all.

It was Father Devereux who spotted her first. Walking across the demesne on his way to the great house and wishing that his old horse was not lame, for it was a rare hot day and the dust of the road coated his skirts, he turned suddenly at the sound of a motor-car behind him and there she was, raised up in her seat, her face small and excited beneath a ridiculously large-brimmed hat.

'Father!'

The sound seemed to choke him and so did the sight of her. How he had missed her presence in Connemara! Deny her as much as he could, yet still he was proud of her beauty.

Constance pushed open the car door behind her. 'Are you off to the house, Father?' she asked. 'Can we take you the rest of the way? You look awfully warm and dusty!'

Father Devereux looked down at his robes, embarrassed to be found in such a state. She was with a friend, too. The young man driving the car was fair-haired and handsome, impeccably dressed in flannels and a white shirt. He smiled at the priest as he struggled into the back seat, turning and extending his hand for a more formal introduction before they set off again.

'Hugh Chatterton,' he said.

Constance laughed. 'Hugh is my fiancé,' she informed Father Devereux. 'We're to be married, Father.'

The car engine started now and they were moving. Constance was showing Father Devereux a ring. He found himself unable to speak, though the boy looked presentable enough and he should not have been shocked. Still he felt no great pleasure at the news.

'Have you told your family yet?' he managed to ask.

Constance shook her head. 'I'm here as a surprise!' she said, and the priest felt his mood darken at her words.

Then she saw her brother and Father Devereux realized he was forgotten as she clambered up in her seat for a second time.

Niall was a mile or so along the road, casually dressed in flannels and a white shirt, like the young man who drove their car. Niall's trousers were creased, though, and his shirtsleeves rolled up in the blistering heat of the day. He wore an old straw panama pulled down over his eyes as a protection from the sun.

They heard his laugh as they drove closer and Father Devereux saw Constance smile quietly at the sound. It seemed that he had not heard them approach. He was running across the grass and suddenly he stopped, then disappeared from sight behind the ditch, reappearing just as suddenly a few seconds later with something held in his arms. Father Devereux realized with a start that Niall was playing and that what was held in his arms was a small brown and white dog.

Constance asked Hugh to stop the car again and they all watched for a few moments. Sitting on a tartan rug on the grass before her brother, solemn-faced and rocking slightly, was a tiny child; his child, and Niall had been busy amusing it with the aid of the wiry-haired dog.

Niall clapped his hands and the dog jumped into his arms and then he laughed, rolling upon the ground as though fighting with the small beast. He lay there for several minutes, pretending to have lost the battle, and then he pulled a tennis ball out from one of his pockets and threw it for the dog to retrieve. The small dog ran to fetch it, returning with it in his mouth to the child's woollen rug and it was then that the baby started to laugh, clapping its fat brown hands together for the game to continue.

Constance watched the entire game with an expression of delight on her face. Then suddenly her smile melted, to be replaced by the beginnings of a frown.

'Niall!' Father Devereux shouted and Constance looked shocked at the sound, as shocked as her brother as he spotted the car for the first time.

Niall pulled himself quickly to his feet, brushing the grass from his knees and plucking the straw hat from his head.

'Constance?' There was excitement in his voice, though his face was obscured from the priest's view by the dazzling sunshine. Constance jumped from the car in an instant and ran towards him to hug him before the advantage of surprise had worn off. Niall returned the embrace and Father Devereux relaxed slightly, thinking that all was well between them once again.

'Have you missed me?' he heard Constance ask, but she was robbed of her answer by the baby's cries, as the child suddenly realized it had been left unattended and started to complain.

Niall ran back to the child and lifted it quickly into his arms. 'This is my son,' he told her, 'Thomas Robert Liam Flavelle; heir to all the Flavelle fortunes, for what they are worth.'

His face was tanned by the sun and his eyes glowed with pride as he held up his squirming, screaming baby.

Father Devereux saw Constance's expression darken as she looked, first at her brother and then at the child. Her words became too soft to hear and he looked out across the demesne, afraid of appearing to eavesdrop.

It was some moments before he heard their footsteps approaching and Hugh jumped from his seat at the front.

'Hugh Chatterton, sir,' he said to Niall, in the same polite tone he had used for the priest.

'I can't shake,' Niall said, irritably, looking down at the offered hand, 'I've my arms full at present. And you don't need to call me sir; I'm not your father.'

The young man's smile faded slightly, and he looked over at Constance.

There was an uncomfortable silence between them all and Father Devereux felt a strange sense of pity for the young man before them, with his polite introductions and his keen young smile. There was a game afoot there, the priest decided, a game between brother and sister. He wished that he could warn the young man to go off and never return.

Niall looked at his sister, too. 'This is a friend of yours from Dublin, then?' he asked.

Constance smiled and took Hugh's arm. 'More than a friend,' she said, happily. 'Hugh has proposed marriage.'

'And you accepted him, no doubt,' Niall asked and, by way of an answer, Constance extended her left hand to show Niall her engagement ring.

The young man smiled and blushed. 'Connie said she should introduce me to her family first but I talked her into accepting me anyway. I hope you don't mind.'

'So it's Connie, is it?' Niall sneered. The child's squirms became more frantic and he started to rock it back and forth, to quiet it.

'It's a fine ring, don't you think, Niall?' Constance asked, moving her finger about in the sunlight so that the small diamond shone with tiny shards of white light.

Niall studied her face for a moment. 'You do know that you are full of ill-founded conceit, Constance?' he asked quietly, but her smile merely widened and she laughed right into his face.

At that Niall turned quickly and, pulling the rug from the ground, threw it over his shoulder like a cape and set off across the demesne, the dog chasing at his ankles.

Constance's young man looked worried. 'Did I upset your brother somehow?' he asked.

Constance laughed. 'No, don't worry. It was I who did that. I don't think he liked being caught in that way, with the child and the dog and all that. My brother is rather strange, you see, Hugh, like the rest of my family, isn't that so, Father? It's poor Father Devereux here who has the job of keeping all our souls from purgatory, you know, and I should think he has his hands full with some of us now, don't you, Father?'

She laughed even louder and Hugh joined in, bending to kiss the side of her cheek, relieved to think that she was only joking after all.

A great fuss was made of Constance's fiancé when

she introduced him at the house and he was soon put to rights again, after Niall's frosty welcome. A plate of the best country cooking was placed before him and Cora and Christina sat at his side, hanging onto his every word. He was light-hearted and witty, they soon found, and were reminded of the days when Alexander had first come to visit, before the great upset of Cora's marriage.

The two women came to life in the young man's presence; he was all that they had hoped for their beautiful sister and all that they knew they could never have themselves. They threw him hundreds of questions about Dublin and his family and even suggested a rubber of bridge at an hour when usually they would have been well tucked away in their beds.

Nancy appeared for only an hour or so that evening, as the birth had been a difficult one and she was still suffering with anaemia and her nerves and mostly confined to her bed. Father Devereux noticed how tired and uneasy she seemed and how she had soon excused herself and returned to her room. Niall appeared only once she was gone, with the story that he had some late business about the estate to see to. He was in a foul mood all evening and nothing appeared to lighten it. Hugh's determined politeness seemed only to make matters worse. He refused to join them in cards and sat apart from the others, gazing instead at the smoking fire, the muscles of his cheeks working back and forth while Constance laughed and chattered as she had used to as a child.

Soon after midnight she jumped up from her seat, nearly knocking the small card-table over in her excitement. 'Hugh has brought a gramophone!' she told the others. 'Shall we fetch it? We could have a dance! There has not been music in this house for years! Quickly, Hugh, go and get it out of the car. Would you mind, Father?' she asked, but Father Devereux waved his hand in the air, relieved to have found an excuse to leave at last.

'You might wake Nancy and the baby,' Niall protested, but Constance would hear none of it.

'We don't have to play it too loud. And, anyway, the house is so large they could never hear us from the bedrooms.'

Christina rose from her chair and tried to discourage her but Hugh was already returned, clutching a large wooden chest in his arms.

While he set the thing up Constance threw herself onto the floor to study the half-dozen or so records they had brought with them. Having finally made her selection, she pulled it from its sleeve and placed it on the felt-covered turntable. There was a loud crackling as she bent the silver arm down and the needle touched onto the surface, followed by a moment of silence before the music began. 'It's a waltz!' Cora cried, her foot tapping the floor. 'A Strauss!' she announced, delighted, when she had listened a little longer.

'They belong to Hugh's mother,' Constance remarked. 'I told Hugh how much you would enjoy them.'

Christina smiled quietly, rocking gently in her seat.

'Come on,' Constance said suddenly to Hugh. 'Help me clear back these old tables.'

She rolled the card-table back to the edge of the rug and Hugh pulled a couple of chairs away until they had room to dance.

'Would you dance with me then, Cora?' Constance asked her sister and Cora's plump face looked up at her, glowing pink in the lamplight; her eyes shining with excitement.

It was strange, so much noise and laughter in that dreary quiet house. It was as though the music had put a spell about the place and even Christina was taken in by it, for she smiled at her sisters and urged Cora from her seat.

Father Devereux had risen from his chair to take his leave quietly, but even he stood transfixed by the strange sight of such jollity in that gloomy, oppressive house.

Cora's head shook once, bashfully, and then, her face now flushed crimson, she rose like a fully-rigged ship to take her sister's outstretched hands. The pair stood awkwardly for a moment in the centre of the room and then Cora began to step out, kicking her right leg stiffly to the side and pulling her long skirts out, to help her on her way.

Constance grinned and made an effort to fall into step as they slowly began to turn on the floor, gathering speed all the while until they gained the confidence to burst out into grander steps, both their skirts flying now and their breathless laughter rising to join the notes that played about their ears.

Hugh cheered and laughed as though he had never seen a prettier sight before in his life. He looked quickly at Christina, who sat by herself, and wondered whether it was his duty to ask this much plainer sister to dance. He hoped that it was not for, kindly though he was, wild horses would not have impelled him to drag that poor twitching creature about the floor.

The music faded and stopped. Constance spun quickly away from her sister and ran to the gramophone to select another tune.

'Is there much more we can dance to here?' she asked Hugh.

'I believe there's a Charleston there somewhere,' he replied, but Constance laughed and shook her head.

'Oh that would never do, you know! My sister would think the Devil had come into the house if we played that sort of stuff, wouldn't you, Christina?'

She found another waltz instead, a slower one this time, and she pushed Hugh with her elbow until he agreed to take the floor with her. Despite the goading he turned out to be a good dancer with a more than adequate ear for the music and he turned Constance about until she cried out that she was giddy and would fall over there and then if he did not stop, and soon.

Niall had watched them both thoughtfully as they danced. Halfway through their waltz, though, he had apparently seen enough for he rose from his seat and made his way quickly and quietly to the door.

Constance saw him leaving and it was then that she had pulled away from her fiancé's arms, rushing over to stop Niall before he could leave the room altogether.

'Won't you dance with me, Niall?' she asked, blocking his way to the door.

'You know I don't dance,' he told her, the irritation clear in his tone. He reached behind her for the doorhandle but she stepped neatly in front of it.

'Dance with me,' she said again, and now her smile had vanished. 'You danced with me when we were children.'

Niall drew in a long breath. 'What is this stupid game that you are playing, Constance?'

'Game?' Constance echoed.

'That . . . that boy!' Niall said softly, and they both turned to look in the direction of the dancing. Hugh had both sisters on the floor now, and was twirling them around until the pins began to fall from their hair.

'What the hell are you about with him?' Niall asked.

Constance smiled at her brother. 'I'm to marry him,' she said. 'I told you just this morning.'

Niall looked for a moment as though he were about to strike her but she did not flinch, merely stood there smiling at him.

Turning back to the door again Niall reached behind Constance, opened it and pushed her from the room, shutting the door behind them before dragging her across the hallway by the arm and pushing her into his father's old study.

He was instantly overwhelmed by the smells in there. He smelt the books and the hair-oil and the tobacco even now, as though William were still sitting at his place behind the desk. Niall closed his eyes in the darkness and even Constance stood silently, for she also found herself overwhelmed.

The music in the distance was barely audible once the

367

door was shut behind them. Niall waited. Any moment he would hear rustling paper as his father thumbed through his Bible, looking for a place for him to read from. He felt his father's spirit in that room and the thought angered him to the point of fury. Why could Constance and he not love one another as brother and sister should? Why had this fear of corruption been planted inside his brain to destroy whatever innocent love they had felt and replace it with guilt?

He had married to protect Constance; to save her from whatever curse his father had believed their love would foster. Now he felt only resentment when he looked at her and yet he remembered how she had once been his entire life.

'This is just petty revenge,' he told her. Her face was hidden in the darkness, so that he could not see the flame of anger that burned in her eyes.

'What makes you say that?' she asked, keeping her tone level.

'You know as well as I do.' He sounded suddenly tired. 'You brought him here to spite me for my own marriage. You don't love him at all, you know you don't. Your behaviour is no better than that of a spoilt child.'

Constance's cheeks turned pink from the humiliation. 'You have no right to say such things to me!' she said.

'I have every right. You said much the same things to me, if you remember?'

'I love him every bit as much as you love that wife of yours!' Constance said. 'I thought that you'd be pleased for me! I thought it was what you would have wanted, now that you've got your own child, and all!'

She walked towards William's desk and stood with her back to him, her head bowed.

Niall sighed. 'If I thought that were true I'd be a happy man, Constance,' he said, quietly. 'And my marriage to Nancy has nothing to do with this.' The lie sounded painful, even to his own ears. He had married his wife for decency's sake, for it was the only way that he could see himself living under the same roof as his sister again.

'You can't accept that I love her, can you, Constance?' he asked.

'No,' Constance said, turning to him. 'For I cannot believe that you are capable of loving two women and I know that you love me, Niall.'

He walked towards her at that and placed his hands upon her shoulders. 'There are different types of love, Constance,' he said. 'I love Nancy as my wife. I love you as my sister. Of course a man can love two women when he loves them in those ways.'

He realized his mistake immediately. He should not have touched her. He had gone too close, like Icarus to the sun. He knew he was about to be burnt up in her flame. His body filled with anguish as her head lifted towards him. He had only to bend his head and he could have kissed her on the mouth. He had never expected such power to emanate from her; he could feel the strength of her longing the moment he touched her.

He felt the soft skin of her lips pressed against his own mouth and her breath, like the breath of a small animal, as it played against his cheek. Fear rose up in his throat, giving him the strength to push her away from him quickly, even raising his hand to strike her.

Constance saw the raised arm but did not move, just watched her brother gravely.

'You're insane,' Niall told her. He felt himself to be on the edge of the windswept cliffs, watching his father's coffin as it was swallowed up by the waves. Would his father's ghost rise up behind them at the desk, shaking its great blind head in disapproval at what they had just done? It was not what he had wanted, Niall would have sworn to his dying breath that it was not. Had William been right all along, after all?

Constance was talking, but he barely heard her words.

'Tell me now that I am wrong,' she whispered. 'Say again that you feel nothing for me, Niall.'

A terrible sadness overcame him then, an all-consuming grief for the death of the innocent love that he had once felt for her; now the pure love they had known as children would be forever tainted by the mad demands that she had made upon him.

He searched for regret in his heart, but felt only triumph flaring there.

Father Devereux stood in the dark and unlit hall, his coat clutched foolishly in his hands, his head bowed. He had meant to take his leave but instead had stood, listening in horror to the words from the study. Now his hands trembled and he felt weak and powerless as he heard how the legacy of evil had permeated down through the generations of William Flavelle's family. Pity and guilt – between them they created a burden that he was not up to shouldering – not at that hour of night, anyway. In the morning he would begin to pray for all of their souls, but right then he could pray only for the comfort of his own bed and the blissful oblivion of sleep.

There was nothing more to say then, no further arguments that Niall could put forward. He felt bone-weary, as he had done after battles in the trenches during the war.

He thought of returning to his wife, to the bed that she lay in, waiting for him. But he knew that was impossible this night. He could not lie next to her, knowing what had just happened.

Like a man in a trance he quit the room, walking through dark and silent passages until he reached the farthest point of the house, where he discovered a bedroom unused because of the damp, and it was there that he finally threw off his clothes to lie, naked and exhausted, upon the bare bed.

CHAPTER FORTY-FIVE

Niall was deeply asleep when Constance came to him. She had waited several hours, until the whole house had fallen silent save for the settling of the wooden floorboards and the soughing of the wind as it crept in under doors and between gaps in rotted window-frames.

Niall's dreams had all been of his father. He lay on the bare bed with one arm thrown up over his face, his long naked body silver-grey in the moonlight.

Constance watched him for a moment. She saw his lips move as though he talked in his sleep and when she saw the anguish on his face she guessed to whom he spoke in his dreams. The window beside his bed was pushed wide open and a cool breeze disturbed the heavy drapes about his bed. An owl cried somewhere off in the demesne and Constance stood listening like a child in her nightgown. Her long hair had been brushed and pushed back off her face and she was barely able to breathe or move for fear she might break the spell that held her brother there, forever in her power.

It was some minutes before she silently crossed the floor to his bed. The only sound came from the quiet rustle of her starched white gown. Close to she could see the life that flowed through his body; the pulses that throbbed with blood, eyes rolling slowly beneath his closed lids.

His nakedness astonished her. She had not imagined his body to be so foreign to her own. They were brother and sister; linked by the same mother and yet Niall was not her twin in any way. His body was slim and muscular, thick dark hair covering his chest and neck. She had thought that their two shapes would fall quickly into place once they were finally united but instead she found herself staring down at a stranger and she grew cold with fear at the thought of what she was about to do.

Niall felt the small hand that touched his chest and moaned at its gentleness. He felt a shape move to lie beside him but felt it only in his sleep; he had not yet woken. The hand moved about his body, touching softly, careful not to disturb him and yet arousing him nevertheless. There was a slight weight upon his chest and cool lips pressed against his neck, moving to his stomach and thighs.

A quiet rhythm built up and he was drawn into the movement until his need became so urgent, so great, that he finally awoke to find himself enveloped in softness. He groaned aloud with ecstasy and it was then that he saw his sister in his arms, her neck arched backward with pleasure. Her cries became his own cries as he held her to him forever and lost himself in the miracle of his longing.

They lay entwined until their bodies had cooled. She was little more than a child now in his arms. 'Constance,' he murmured, lifting her up to kiss her mouth. As their lips parted he heard her ask if he loved her, but he could not answer, his throat blocked with the fierceness of his emotions.

And yet she was adamant. 'Do you love me, Niall?' she asked again, her face so beautiful and her expression so intense that he could have wept with pleasure at the sight of it.

'Yes, Constance, I love you,' he managed to say at last, and realized then that he had always loved her, just as she had said, and that she was the wise one, for she had known all along what was right between them.

It was the only moment of pure joy in his life and it more than made up for all the misery he had suffered. She turned her body towards him once again and they made love for the rest of the night, sleeping only when dawn broke and they were too exhausted to move.

They clung to each other as they slept, for fear they should wake and find the other missing, and this was how

Nancy found them when she finally came to search for her husband.

She pushed the door open slowly, almost playfully, for she had turned the hunt into a game of hide-and-seek for the benefit of their child, whom she carried in her arms. She pulled an excited face as the door fell back and its hinges screamed at the intrusion. Then she saw the naked bodies on the bed and her mouth fell open with shock, her legs threatening to give way beneath her.

Her first thought was for the child. If she fainted she would drop him and he could be badly injured. She kept her emotions in check then as she gazed down on her husband and his sister, realizing suddenly that to eyes other than her own they would make a beautiful couple.

She wanted to leave but could not. Dark patches began to congeal in front of her and she let out a cry. To her horror, the baby picked up her cry, repeating it more loudly as a prelude to much stronger screams.

Nancy placed a trembling hand over the child's mouth to quiet him but that only made him more determined and it was then that Niall's eyes flickered open. She saw the look of horror that flooded them once he realized they were standing there, watching, and then she took herself quickly from the room, for she could bear to see no more.

Blinded by tears Nancy carried her screaming child back to her bedroom, where she threw open the wardrobes and started ripping clothes off hangers and throwing them into her trunk. Her strength abandoned her, though, and in the end she had to content herself with packing a few things for the baby instead.

She ran to the nursery and asked the bleary-eyed nanny to collect some of her son's most necessary requirements for a journey, having to repeat herself several times before the poor girl understood what it was that she wanted. In the end the nanny threw a selection of things into a case while Nancy stood over her, hurrying her on.

The door to the nursery was suddenly slammed back as

this hasty packing was in progress and the nanny sprang instantly to her feet, terrified by the look on her master's face as he stood angrily in the doorway. She zipped up the small bag and made to leave the room, taking the baby with her and, to her relief, Niall allowed her to pass.

It was Nancy who spoke first. 'I'm leaving you, Niall. I'm getting out of your way.'

Niall looked at the clothes that were flung about the room and then back at his wife's face. 'You're too weak,' he said. 'You should stay until you're better.'

Nancy almost laughed. 'I would not stay another night in this house if I were lying on my deathbed!'

Niall ran a hand through his hair and punched angrily at the doorframe.

Nancy flinched at the noise. 'Let me past,' she said, moving towards the door. 'I need to get my son.'

Niall stared at her in horror. 'You're not taking the boy!'

Nancy looked him full in the eyes. 'You want him raised here?' she asked. 'In this house? You really must be mad. He'll come back to America with me. With a little luck I might be able to make him forget who his father is.' She took a step further.

'Get out of my way,' she ordered, when Niall tried to stop her.

He stared at her for a moment with madness in his eyes and then his hand fell from the doorway and he allowed his wife to pass. 'I love her, Nancy,' he said quietly. 'She is the only thing I have ever truly loved in my life.'

'And she's your sister, for God's sake, Niall!' Nancy raged. 'Your *sister*!'

She stood in the passage now, challenging him to argue with her, for she still could not believe what she had just seen.

'Wherever you go, Nancy, I will come after my son and I shall get him back, whatever it takes,' Niall told her quietly. 'I want you to know that. Whatever I have done he is my child and he belongs here.'

'Do you think I would sit back and let him go mad like the rest of this household?' Nancy asked.

She turned at that and walked away from her husband and kept on walking until she had reached her car in the old stables. She took her son from his nanny and placed him in the seat beside her, then set off down the driveway without once turning to look back.

She drove until she reached the nearest town and only then did she stop. The child began to cry and she cried with him, hugging him to her chest and kissing the top of his head.

'Oh, my poor baby!' she moaned over and over again, rocking the child until her tears had cleared a little, then she placed him back onto the seat beside her and spurred the car into life again.

As she drove on she saw someone in the road. Braking sharply she pulled into a clearing and a figure ran up towards her, full of concern at their near-miss.

Wiping her eyes with the back of her hand she saw that it was Francis and she wound her window down quickly to speak to him.

'Are you all right, Nancy?' he asked, sounding sober for a change.

She shook her head. 'I'm leaving,' she told him. 'I can't live there any more. Please, Francis!' she begged, looking up at him. 'Get out of my way! I'm frightened Niall will come after me!'

Francis stepped back, shocked by her words and the expression of fear on her face. He watched while Nancy reversed her car back onto the road, then tried to approach her again to ask more, to find out exactly what his brother had done to make her leave in such a way, but she pulled away quickly and instead he was forced to watch until her car was little more than a speck upon the horizon.

CHAPTER FORTY-SIX

Niall was still in the nursery when Francis found him, sunk into an armchair, his head resting between his hands.

'What the hell did you do to her?' Francis shouted and Niall looked up in surprise. 'What did you do?' Francis repeated. 'She's left in a state. I saw her on the road, she almost knocked me down. She's sick, Niall, and she should never be out driving like that. She has the child with her, too. She could kill them both, you know!'

Niall let out a low laugh. 'You should have gone with her, Francis,' he said. 'You'd always a soft spot for Nancy, hadn't you? She's left me for good now, too, if she means what she says.'

Francis was upon him in an instant, pulling him from the chair and pummelling his fists into his brother's face and body.

'You bastard!' he cried. 'You evil fucking bastard! What have you done to her? Tell me what you've done!'

Niall tried to hold him off without hurting him but Francis was driven by rage. He grabbed his brother by the neck of his shirt and drove his fist squarely into his jaw. Niall was knocked sideways by the force of the blow, sending a table and a lamp flying to the floor as he landed.

Francis would have leapt upon him again but Niall was too strong. He knocked him away lightly, then grabbed his arms and pinned them to his sides.

Francis stared at him with hatred, his chest heaving, knowing that Niall's grip was by far the stronger and that he could not break away.

'Calm down, Francis!' Niall warned him. 'I don't want to hurt you.'

They stood for a moment in the centre of the room and then Francis seemed to let his anger out in a sigh. Niall released him and returned to his chair, rubbing his hand across his bruised jaw.

'I'm sorry,' he said, after a pause. 'I spoke out of turn. Nancy has just gone and I didn't know what it was I was saying.'

'Why has she left you?'

'Don't ask, Francis,' Niall told him. 'It isn't your business.'

There was a sound in the doorway and he looked up suddenly, his eyes starting.

Francis turned his head and saw Constance standing there dressed in her best frock, her long hair freshly-washed and carefully plaited. She looked so pretty that even Francis stared. 'Did you know his wife's left him?' he asked.

'I thought I heard fighting,' she said, quietly. 'I heard the sound of fists and then some furniture being knocked over.' She looked across at Niall but it was Francis who answered.

'He's a stupid bastard,' he said, rubbing his knuckles.

'Are you hurt?' Constance asked Niall, but he shook his head.

'She took the baby,' he said in a low voice. 'She's walked out with my child.'

'What did you expect?' She picked a baby's toy up from the floor where it had fallen and Niall leant back in the chair and closed his eyes.

'I sent Hugh off,' Constance said.

Niall opened his eyes again. 'What should I say?' he asked. 'That I am glad?'

Constance looked over at Francis, wishing he were gone from the room. She waited, watching him, but he made no move to leave. In the end it was Niall who left.

Constance grabbed his arm as he pushed past her. 'Where are you going?'

'For a ride,' he told her. 'To try and clear my head.'

She followed him into the passage. 'I could come with you.'

'No!'

'I love you,' she told him.

'She's taken my bloody child,' Niall said walking off, leaving his sister to return to the nursery to watch him from the window as he saddled up his horse and set out across the demesne.

It was dark before he returned to the house. He went straight to his room, ignoring the light under the study door where Constance sat waiting for him.

She woke to the sound of his boots on the stairs and jumped from her seat to run quickly into the hall.

'Niall?' she called but the footsteps did not stop.

She ran up the stairs after him, throwing open his bedroom door and gazing at him with fear in her eyes.

'I have to leave, Constance,' was all that he said, tossing clothes into a bag. 'I cannot allow her to go with my son. She will take him off to America and I will never see him again.'

'No!' Constance whispered quietly, as though the breath had been taken from her body. 'What about me, Niall? You cannot leave me. You can't turn your back on me twice, not now. You can't.'

He looked down at her face and the pain that he felt at hurting her ran through his entire body.

'I'm no better than he was, Constance,' he said gently, stroking her cheek. 'Look what I have done to you. At least Papa had the courage to try to take his own life after he had sinned but I don't even have the nerve for that, God help me. I spent the day on the cliffs knowing that I should throw myself over and onto the rocks but look at me, I'm still here, and now the only thing I can do is to get out of your life forever. You do understand that, don't you, Constance? We have ruined you between us, Papa and I. I can't allow it to continue, and I have to find my son before he is lost to me forever, too.'

'But you love me, Niall!' Constance whispered, her eyes glazed. 'You cannot leave me again. I couldn't live without you now. You don't understand, we belong together.'

Niall held her away from him until she could see the expression on his face.

'What did you think we would do, Constance?' he asked. 'Live together as man and wife? What we did last night was a sin and I am the guilty one, I should have known better. I should never have come back here. You are my sister, Constance, and I should not have touched you. It was wicked of me . . .'

'It wasn't wrong,' Constance cut in. 'It could never be wrong when we love one another so much. I don't care if it is a sin. I don't care if we both burn in purgatory for what we did last night.

'William was not even my father, Niall,' she said, desperately. 'The priest told me, so you are only my half-brother. Don't leave me, Niall. If you leave me here I shall die.'

Niall held her until she had quietened and then wiped the tears from her cheeks with his fingers.

'Stop it, Constance,' he said, gently. 'You are tearing me in two. I have to try and do what's right, even though it is killing me, don't you see? How easy do you think it is for me to walk out of here? I don't even know if I'll be able to stand it either, but I know I must try, for both our sakes. I've made a ruin of my own life and I can't stay to destroy yours as well.

'Perhaps Papa was right, perhaps I am the son of the Devil, or I would never have behaved as I did last night. I tried not to touch you, Constance, though God knows that was hard enough, but I thought if I told myself enough times that I hated you then I might have found myself believing it.

'You can't know how I feel after last night, Constance,' he said, the tears rolling down his own cheeks now. 'If you had any idea you would not be begging me to stay.'

He turned from her then and picked up his bag but she was onto him like a terrier, trying to wrest it from his hands. When he pushed her off she clung to his back, pummelling him with her small fists.

'No, Niall!' she shouted. 'You cannot leave me! I won't let you! You can't! I would sooner see you die here than let you go!'

But Niall shrugged her off, knowing that he had to get away. When she ran to follow him he slammed the door in her face, the sound of her tears and her fists beating against the wood following him down the stairs and, in his imagination, the entire length of the demesne.

CHAPTER FORTY-SEVEN

Niall managed to stay away for almost a year. He was lost without Constance and no longer had the strength to deny it, and the loss of his son only added to his grief.

He could not be without Constance. A life without her was, he found, no life at all and even his guilt was not enough to keep him from her for another moment. As he rode slowly up the path he believed and hoped that all his pain would be gone the minute he had her in his arms again and, as the house came into view, he spurred his exhausted horse on.

At first the place seemed deserted and a gnawing sense of fear chewed away at his heart. The door hung back on its hinges and there was no reply when he jumped from his saddle and shouted for the maid. Troubled by the silence, Niall returned to his sweating horse and led it towards the stables in search of water and feed.

He kicked open the stable doors one at a time, but every stall was empty. Tethering his horse quickly he ran around to the gardens, calling each of his sisters by name. A terrible thought occurred to him that they might be dead, but then he saw Cora, a large and ancient straw hat tied to her head, digging at some weeds in the small but desolate area of land that she liked to refer to as her kitchen garden.

'Cora!' He ran up to her, relieved

'There's no need to shout, Niall,' she told him, refusing the hand that he offered as she scrambled to her feet. She had grown even stouter.

'You are back then,' she said, peering up at his face.

Niall nodded, looking about him. 'I thought the place was deserted,' he said. 'I was worried you were all off some place or another.'

Cora looked down at the weeds that she held in her hands. 'We had to lay off most of the staff after Nancy left like that,' she said. 'We don't need many, though, not now there's just Christina and myself to care for.'

'Christina? Where is Constance, then?'

Cora pulled a face as though she had a bitter taste in her mouth. 'Constance is away,' she said.

'Where?'

'You'd better come indoors,' she said. 'I think it's about to rain.'

'Where is she, Cora?' Niall asked again once they were properly seated in the lounge.

'Did you want tea or something?' Cora asked, looking for the bell.

'I'm not a bloody guest, Cora!' Niall shouted, unable to contain his impatience any more. 'Now will you tell me where Constance has got herself off to, or do I have to ask Christina?'

But Cora was stubborn and would not be hurried. 'You were not so interested in her the last time you arrived here,' she said, discovering the bell at last beneath one of her cushions and ringing it as hard as she could. 'In fact,' she added, 'I believe the girl complained that you had quite ignored her. Why the interest now, Niall?'

Niall rose impatiently from his chair and walked across to the window. Christina was a brown speck in the distance, clambering over her precious grotto to dust all the stones and statues that were laid out there.

'She's my sister, Cora,' he said. 'I have a right to know where she is.'

Cora saw to the tea things that the maid had brought in and then, once the girl had gone, she turned to her brother, whispering as though she might be overheard. 'Constance has it into her head that she's only our half-sister,' she mouthed. 'She says she has a different father from the rest of us.' She shuddered.

'Did she tell you that, too?' Niall asked. 'I thought she

382

was hysterical when she told me. I suppose it is just wishful thinking.'

The sour look had returned to Cora's face. 'It was a wicked thing to say and I told her so,' she said. 'The thought that our mother might have . . .' but she could not go on, the idea repelled her so much. She folded her arms across her generous chest, as though fearing personal assault, and stared at her brother's face, her head tilted to one side.

'Is Constance sick, Cora? Is she all right?'

Cora inhaled deeply. 'She's well enough.'

'So where the hell is she?' Niall's temper had gone now. 'Jesus Christ, Cora, you'd test the patience of a saint!'

'She's staying with family for a few months,' Cora told him. 'She left here last summer. We felt she needed some new air in her lungs. There's no need for you to know exactly where she's gone, Niall, she'll be back soon enough. I can't see why you're in such a lather anyway,' she added, 'when you took off without so much as a by-your-leave yourself. One minute you were here with your wife and all her fine old money and the next you were gone, leaving us to fend for ourselves. Did you care how we'd manage, Niall? This is your property now, remember? You bought it off Francis and then you went and abandoned it again. Did you worry that we'd starve or did you think that God would provide?'

'Christ, Cora, will you shut up your blathering!' Niall said angrily. 'I can hardly hear myself think! Where was I to get money from after Nancy walked out on me? I sent you what I had! The rest I paid Francis for this house. What do you suppose I lived on, eh?'

Cora's mouth shut in a firm line but she had not finished with her brother yet. 'What did you want with Constance, anyway?' she asked.

Niall turned back to the window. It was raining now, but Christina still clambered over her rocks, wiping the faces of her statues with a piece of old wet rag.

'Do I have to account to *you* now?' he asked.

'And where's your wife and child? Did you manage to find her or are you back empty-handed?'

'I told you to hold your tongue, Cora!' Niall said. He walked towards the door. 'Tell me where I can find her,' he said, his hand on the doorknob.

Cora stood to face him. 'I take it you mean your sister, do you, Niall?' she asked. 'And not your wife?'

'Just tell me, Cora.' His face looked ghastly; eyes sunken and cheeks hollow.

'Leave her alone, Niall,' Cora warned.

'It is none of your business what I choose to do,' Niall retorted. 'Just tell me where my sister has gone, that's all.'

Cora's face flushed. 'So, I was right,' she whispered. She slumped into her chair and looked away. 'She was carrying a child, Niall,' she said quietly. 'We had to send her away. We could not bear the shame of having her here.'

Niall's hand dropped to his side. 'You're lying,' he said.

'Why should people always be lying, just because they say things that you don't want to hear?' Cora asked him. 'Why should I lie, Niall? It's not a thing to lie about now, is it?'

Niall walked back to his chair and dropped into it, suddenly exhausted.

Cora leant forward and busied herself with the tea things, giving him time to think.

'I did not hear you asking who the father is, Niall,' she said. 'We thought of course that it had to be young Hugh, with his charming ways and all, though he seemed a nice enough lad when he was here. Could you imagine him tiptoeing down the dark hall to our sister's bedroom after we were all asleep?' she asked. 'No, neither could we,' she finished. 'Though Constance did dismiss him from the house rather suddenly, as I remember. We wondered whether he had forced himself upon her . . . but that hardly seems possible, does it? He was so nicely brought up, good manners, and all.'

She poured brown tea into two china cups and handed one to her brother, getting up to place it on the side-table herself when he made no move to take it from her.

'Constance was quite calm, considering everything,' she said. 'In the end I wore her down, though, and she admitted poor Hugh had nothing to do with it. I'm sure she was telling the truth.'

Niall looked up at her.

'Christina now believes it was the work of the Holy Ghost and that this is the second coming,' she said. 'That's why she's out there busy polishing her statues, just in case.' She laughed. 'I have not seen her this happy for years, you know.'

'Where *is* Constance?' Niall asked.

Cora shook her head. 'This is women's business, Niall. We can take care of things better if we are left alone.'

'What do you mean "take care of things"?' Niall sat forward so suddenly that he spilled tea across the table.

'Well, she could hardly have had it now, could she?' Cora said, flatly. 'It would have been a monster, and I told her as much. It would have been deformed, Niall – could have had two heads or something! That's the way these things work. It's God's punishment, or didn't you know that? She could never have had the child and you know it!'

'Jesus Christ!' Niall said, sinking his head into his hands. 'Has she killed it, then?' His voice was muffled by his fingers.

'You should hope she has, Niall. I guessed at once, you know, but I prayed for months that it would not be true. How could you, Niall? How could you be so wicked? Your own sister! I told her how it would have turned out. I never believed you'd come here looking for her again.

'I prayed I was wrong, Niall, but one look at your face just now told me what I didn't want to know. Constance never denied it but she would not admit it, either. It didn't take a lot of guessing, though, once I thought about how your poor wife had left with your child. You had a wife, Niall! What did you want with your sister as well?'

Niall rose from his seat with a cry. 'She can't have killed it!'

'Tell me you hope it's alive and I'll call you a liar, Niall!' Cora shouted, jumping to her feet and grabbing his arm. 'You're a terrible pair of sinners, the both of you, but it's Constance who has had to suffer while you've been off to God-knows-where. And now you dare return here as though nothing has happened? Jesus, Niall, but you're an idiot!'

Niall groaned despairingly.

'What did you think you were doing?' Cora went on relentlessly. 'Do you still have no concept of sin? She's a woman, I know, but she's as innocent as a young child. How could you, Niall? How could you corrupt her in such a way? Did you think any other man would want to touch her once you've had your filthy hands over her? She could have married well and been out of this place for good, but now she'll rot here like the rest of us and God bless her damaged soul when she does go for she'll roast in hell for this one!

'I know how things were when you were a child, Niall, but why did you to go and do this, and just as you'd made something of yourself, too?'

'I loved her more than my own life, Cora,' Niall said softly. 'I always have done, and she knew it.'

'Then why did you have to go and ruin her?'

But Niall was not listening. 'She can't have killed it!' he mutterd to himself, pacing the room. 'She can't have killed our child!'

'She had no choice, Niall,' Cora said. 'Thank God no one else knows, that's all. I kept it to myself, though God knows it was hard enough. Neither Christina nor Francis know the truth and the pair of them are too stupid to have guessed.'

'Where is she, Cora?' Niall asked again, suddenly. 'Where did she go? I might be able to stop her! I could not lose another child!'

'Don't be such a great idiot!' Cora told him angrily. 'She has been gone for weeks now, I told you. You'd be too late, even if I did tell you.' She paused for breath. 'Go and find your own wife and child, Niall,' she said. 'Win them back, if they'll have you. Leave us here in peace. We don't want you.

'Papa said you were wicked and he was right, I can see that now. We needed your money, I'll admit, but if I could pay every penny back to you now I would. It was too high a price to pay for your generosity, Niall. I'd rather the place had gone to ruin.'

She pulled herself up to full height and clutched her hands about her waist.

'Get out,' she told her brother. 'Get away from this house. I know that you own it and I cannot afford to buy it back but, if you have any sense of decency left, you'll leave it and never return.'

'As you said, it's my house, Cora,' Niall said quietly. 'I mean to stay here until she comes back.'

'And then what will you do?' Cora shouted. 'Marry her? See some sense, can't you! How do you think she will feel, coming home to find you here? How long before you touch her again? How long before people start to guess? You must be mad, Niall. Let us in peace, for pity's sake!'

Niall looked at his sister with a terrible expression on his face. 'Why should I leave you in peace when I can have none?' he asked, and, before she could answer, he was gone.

CHAPTER FORTY-EIGHT

It was some months later that Father Devereux made his way across the demesne again, ostensibly on a visit to the house, though in reality he found himself walking without direction, undeniably delaying the moment when he would have to set foot inside that vast and gloomy hall.

The fact that he carried in his pocket a small book of poetry was further proof of the aimlessness of his meanderings. He had sought a dry spot near a clump of trees where he could sit and read alone but, despite the fine colour of the skies, the mists had been soon upon him like a length of damp muslin and his shoes had rapidly become wet from the grass.

He read as he walked, pausing only occasionally to check his footing in the mud or to clamber over one of the low walls that ran like tram tracks around the outskirts of the vast property.

He was reading Tennyson.

> 'Sleep, breathing love and trust against her lip:
> I go tonight: I come tomorrow morn.
> I go, but I return: I would I were
> The pilot of the darkness and the dream.'

Father Devereux felt a compression in his chest as he read the words. A strange feeling came over him; a mix of loneliness and melancholy, deep longing and regret as though he had been reminded of a scene from his youth and suddenly yearned to return there, as if his entire life since had been found wanting.

Where was his belief in God when he read words like

these? They carved cracks in his soul that his faith could no longer heal.

He did not notice where he walked.

'Sleep, breathing health and peace upon her breast,' he read. He sighed and looked about, found that he stood upon their hill – his and Sophia's – a place he had not visited for many years.

All at once the burden of his memories returned and he sank onto the wet grass, no longer mindful of the well-pressed crease in his trousers and the spotlessness of his robe. He saw how empty of true poetry his life had been, save for that time so long ago when William Flavelle's wife had loved him.

He saw her again, flying her kite, her bronze hair whipping in the wind. Her face was alive with excitement, her eyes as bright as any child's.

He became stricken with fear at the thought of his guilt. 'Forgive me, Sophia,' he whispered, knowing his apology came too late.

She turned to him, though, and the compassion and forgiveness in her eyes made him want to weep. She raised her palms towards him, letting the kite fly from her hands as she did so, and she smiled at him as it caught the currents and flew free to the clouds.

'You have lost your kite!' he called to her, the words sounding terribly sad to him, affected as he was by loneliness and self-pity. He wiped a tear away with his hand and when he looked back he saw her still, though she was pointing now to something far below in the demesne.

Her pale lips moved. 'Help her,' he heard her say.

His eyes followed the direction in which she pointed and he saw a figure, small and grey in the distance, hurrying along the path that led up to the house. It was Constance, Sophia's daughter; his daughter. She had started to run now, her long coat billowing behind her in the wind.

'Constance!' he called, cupping his hands to his mouth to

make his voice carry. But he thought that she had not heard him.

'Constance!' He had not seen her for almost a year. It was strange to see her travelling on foot, and in such an obvious hurry, but then perhaps she had been taken by the same impulse that had made him leave his horse in the barn for once and get his shoe-leather sodden.

He ran down the hill towards her, his arms held out for balance as his feet slipped in the mud. It was then that she heard him at last, turning at the sound of his voice, though she did not stop running, only slowed a little.

Father Devereux laughed with relief as he caught up with her but when he saw her face his laughter was replaced with a smile of concern. Her face was thinner and her auburn hair had frizzed out in the mist. The coat she wore was an old one and the shoes peeping out from beneath it were what Cora would have described as 'unsuited to the inclement conditions'.

He found himself extraordinarily pleased to see her, though, despite her distressed state. He was relieved to find her well and all in one piece after the message he had received from her mother.

'You've returned to us, then,' he said, shoving his book of poetry deep into his pocket. 'When did you arrive? I had not heard that you were home.'

A nervous look flickered in her eyes. 'I've not been back yet,' she said, her voice sounding faint. 'I was on my way just now . . .'

He suddenly noticed the bag that she was carrying. 'On foot?' he asked, smiling. 'That's quite a journey! They'll be glad to see you, though, it's been a while now, hasn't it? Where did you get yourself off to? Cora was extraordinarily secretive, you know, like an old mother hen! Were you partying in Dublin again?'

As soon as the question was asked he realized how stupid it had sounded. The girl looked ill and she was far from well-dressed.

'No,' she told him softly. 'I've been away in the country.'

Father Devereux laughed aloud at her unfortunate choice of words, then a silence fell between them. She could not have meant what she said. When girls of that area went 'away to the country' it usually meant they had got themselves into trouble and were off till the baby was born. Constance would have hardly known that though, he decided, living as cloistered as she did.

'Are you well?' he found himself asking.

Her right arm slid protectively about her waist. 'Well enough, thank you, Father.'

The old and battered gentleman's travelling bag that she held appeared half-empty.

'Can I carry that for you?' he asked.

Constance nodded with some relief and they fell in together, walking side-by-side along the narrow road.

'You look tired,' Father Devereux said. 'You should have taken a cart,' but Constance just shrugged. The priest managed a few hundred yards in silence before his curiosity got the better of him again.

His mind was full of the conversation he had overheard in the study on the day Constance had announced her engagement. He had prayed for her since and had long wondered at his own role in tackling the problem.

'Do you remember that little chat we had in the church some time ago?' he asked. 'I just wondered whether it had helped you or not. I wondered afterwards whether I had done the right thing in telling you about your father. In this job we learn that our judgement is not always indisputable, you know, and we priests would not be human if we did not ponder over the odd decision now and again. Did it help you, Constance? Or did it cause you further distress?

'I very much hope it did not make you think less of your mother. She was a good woman, despite that one failing. It was a terrible thing to hear, I know, but under the circumstances I hope I did the right thing.'

Constance looked at Father Devereux with a level stare.

'I should hardly think that discovering that the man who had treated you so badly as a child was not, in fact, your own father could add to your stress in such a situation, Father,' she said quietly; so quietly, in fact, that the priest was forced to bend to hear her words.

'But did it help?'

'I should say that it did. Thank you, Father.' She smiled a little. 'Did you know my real father?' she asked.

Father Devereux felt his heart lurch with fear. He had lied before. Now he remembered her mother's face.

'Was he a good man?'

'Good enough,' Father Devereux told her. His mouth had gone dry.

'Would he have come to help me had he known of my circumstances?'

'If he could have, no doubt.'

Constance smiled at him. 'I am being unfair to you,' she said, 'you have your confidences to keep and I could not ask you to break them. I understand your position, Father. I'm sorry. I just needed to know that there was someone who could help me if I was desperate, that's all.'

'God is always there to help you.'

Constance laughed. 'I believe I'm beyond the help of God now,' she said.

'No one is beyond God's help,' Father Devereux replied in some alarm.

There was a long silence between them now and it was some time before he felt able to resume the conversation.

'Is there no one else in your family that you feel you can turn to for help?' he asked. 'Surely Cora has always been more like a mother to you than a sister.'

Constance shook her head and walked on in silence.

'Niall is back at the house now too,' Father Devereux said, watching to see her reaction to the news. 'He returned several months ago, or so I heard from your sister Christina.'

Constance stopped walking so abruptly that Father

Devereux was a few paces on before he realized he walked alone. He turned to look back at her.

'Niall is there?' she asked in a whisper. 'Are you sure, Father?' Her face was so white that he thought she might faint. 'Are you sure that it was Niall, Father?' she pleaded. 'And not just Francis that Christina spoke about?'

Father Devereux took her arm to steady her. 'No, it wasn't Francis,' he said. 'I'm sure it was Niall. I'm just on my way to visit him now.'

'Is his family there?' she asked. She seemed suddenly set on turning back the way she had come.

The priest thought for a moment. 'No,' he said, finally, 'I don't believe they are. There was no mention made at all of Missus Flavelle, and I'm sure Christina would have said something.'

'No child, either?' Constance interrupted.

'Well, I should imagine not,' Father Devereux said. 'Not if his wife is not there. Perhaps he is here on some business.'

'I cannot go there,' Constance said suddenly and this time she did turn and set off in the opposite direction.

'Constance?' the priest asked, worried now. She looked too weak to walk more than a hundred yards and yet it was miles back to the village. 'You can't go back now, my dear, I don't believe you have the strength.'

As if in reply, Constance collapsed in his arms and he found himself supporting her, staring in distress down the empty path, hoping for help.

Father Devereux stumbled a half-mile or so with her and then, to his utter relief, he saw Niall approaching on his horse.

'My God, what's the matter with her?' Niall asked, throwing himself out of the saddle the minute he saw who the priest held in his arms. 'What's wrong with her, Father?'

'I believe it's a faint. If we could just get her back to the house . . .'

Niall leapt back into the saddle. 'Pass her to me,' he said, bending forward.

It was as well that Constance weighed so little. Father Devereux handed her easily up to her brother and, without another word, Niall turned his horse and set off towards the house. Once inside he carried her in his arms up the wide stairway, whispering words of reassurance all the while in her ear.

'You're home now, Constance,' he told her. 'You're safe. You can bring our child back here and I will care for you both. I will never leave you again.' He laid her gently down onto her bed, pulled a blanket over her then sat beside her, rubbing her hands to warm her.

When her eyes opened and focused she tried to smile at Niall, her thin arms coming up to cling about his neck as though she would never let him go again. She was so tired, though, that she was soon asleep and he gently lifted her arms from his neck and laid them back by her sides. He sat by her bed the entire night, watching her face as she slept, and whispering to her softly if she stirred.

She woke at dawn and saw his head on the pillow beside her. She moved only slightly but he was awake at once, taking her into his arms and making promises of love that brought the tears flooding from her eyes.

'You should have told me you carried our child, Constance,' he whispered. 'I should have been there. I was crazy when I left you. I didn't know what I was doing any more. I would have come after you, to find you, but Cora would not tell me where you had gone.'

'You weren't there, Niall,' she sobbed, 'I couldn't tell you. I thought I'd lost you forever when you walked out.'

'I made you suffer so much, Constance,' he whispered into her hair as he kissed her head. 'Where is it now, where is our baby? Cora told me you had had it killed but I knew she had to be lying. We can live here together, Constance, I won't care who knows about us, they can all go to hell! Tell me, Constance, tell me where it is. I will go and fetch it, however far the distance. I've lost one child, Constance, and that is enough. I could never lose another just because

394

of what the bastards around here might say. We'll live alone, that's all.'

Constance struggled to pull away from his arms but he gripped her more fiercely.

'Where is it?' he insisted.

Cora's voice came from behind him. 'I told you. She had it seen to.'

He leapt up in anger at the intrusion but Cora strode into the room.

'The poor deformed thing that it would have been, too,' she said. 'It has gone, hasn't it, Constance?' she asked. 'I told you, Niall, and you should have believed me. Leave the poor girl alone now, you've done enough damage already.'

Niall turned back to the bed. 'You couldn't have killed it,' he said. 'I know you, Constance, you couldn't have done. You could never have done such a thing.'

'Listen to yourself!' Cora shouted. 'What do you think you are saying? You want her to suffer the rest of her life because of some mistake she made with you? What you did was *incest*, Niall! Do you not remember our papa's warnings when we were children? Yet you expect her to keep the child of such a union? Leave her in peace, Niall, you've almost destroyed her already!'

Niall stared at Constance, barely hearing Cora's words. Her beautiful face was as blank as a mask and her eyes could no longer meet with his own. Niall's eyes filled with horror at the realization of what she had done.

'You killed it,' he said coldly. His hands released her at last and dropped back to his sides.

Constance shook her head, slowly at first but then more violently.

'You *killed* it,' Niall accused. 'You killed our child!'

Constance covered her face with her hands.

'Get out!' Cora shouted, rushing to comfort her. 'Get out of this house!'

CHAPTER FORTY-NINE

Niall ran from the house, turning only once to look back as he saddled his horse and set off on the path to the cliffs. Where was his father's God in all of this? The house looked evil to him, it seemed to bear the expression of his father's face on its grey façade, sneering and malignant, watching him as he set off on his journey.

The tragedies of Niall's life appeared in his mind as he rode through the demesne and incidents of his childhood came to mingle with the sadness of later years. He closed his eyes to block the images from his view but they merely became clearer, moving more quickly, until, spurring his horse on and screaming in anger like a banshee, he set off even faster for the sanctuary of the heaving sea.

When he reached the cliffs he slid out of the horse's saddle and clambered down the face of the rock until he had reached the small spit of land that he had visited as a child with Cora.

'The killeen,' he whispered to himself as he looked around at all the sad little graves of the unbaptized babies. A small wreath of wild flowers hung in a ragged ring about one marker. The flowers were dead and had not been replaced. Did his child, too, lie in a small unmarked grave that would never be visited?

A gull screamed overhead and he thought he heard his sister crying for him.

'Constance?' he shouted quickly, scrabbling to his feet. He pushed the hair from his eyes and searched the dark clifftop but she had not come to look for him and he knew in his heart that she would never come for him again.

Sinking to his knees once more he studied the small mounds that lay dotted about. He hated Constance for what she had done and he felt that hatred splitting their love in two.

Visions of other children went through his head. He saw his son, Thomas, the child that still lived but that was as surely dead to him. He could smell the sweet scent of his skin as he pressed him, laughing, to his face. He felt his small hands clutching, pulling his hair and ears as they played.

He saw James and Edith, his long-dead brother and sister. He could barely see their faces now, they had faded so far in his memory, but his father had blamed him when they died. They lay in graves alongside his mother.

He lifted his head and the sea-spray hit his face. His love for Constance lay solid in his heart while his hatred of her was like bile in his gut. He was lost now and he knew it. There was nothing for him, nothing left at all. What remained of his soul had perished and he could pray only for numbness to take care of all the pain, and forgiveness for all that he had done.

Mesmerized, he watched the sea throw up its white plumes of bubbling froth, and saw, in its constant ebb and flow, the unfolding of his life – childhood, schooldays, his father, Thomas who had died, his mother buried in the graveyard, the baby Constance had killed . . . The ceaseless procession continued until at last, exhausted, Niall curled up with a sigh to wait for the end of it all.

CHAPTER FIFTY

Father Devereux drove the cart himself when he collected the Flavelle family for their outing to church. They were waiting for him in the doorway, so keen were they to take advantage of his offer of a ride, and they'd brought a couple of their staff too, for good measure, which surprised the priest greatly.

All trussed up in their Sunday best they managed to look well-scrubbed and affluent and yet still as uncomfortable and shy as any others of Father Devereux's parish. The women seemed to have chosen to wear white for the occasion, while Francis stood behind them in a brown tweed suit that was dapper enough to have belonged to Thomas, which would also have accounted for the fit. He had an odd-looking bowler perched on his head and his brogues and turn-ups seemed as ill-at-ease in one another's company as his shirt-collar and his tie-knot.

Father Devereux hid a smile as he saw them gathered there, as huddled and expectant as a herd of cows for milking, in the shade of the porch, each keen to impress with their faded and ill-fitting finery.

'Father,' Cora greeted him curtly, though he guessed the outing had been her idea in the first place.

'You're looking very grand, Cora,' Father Devereux said, but she would not smile, merely raised her hand to allow herself to be assisted into the back of the cart.

'It's good to see the lot of you together like this,' the priest went on, determined to pursue the niceties of the occasion, though a glimpse of Constance's small sad face behind her sister made him less inclined towards chit-chat.

The girl's dress looked as bad a fit as her sister's, but while Cora's buttons and seams were stretched to bursting,

Constance's dress hung in folds. She held a furled parasol beneath her arm too, as though afraid of the effects of the watery sun. In the other hand she clutched her mother's gold rosary and a small, kid-bound prayer-book.

Francis placed himself next to her in the cart and Christina scrambled in last, for she would not allow the servants to lift her.

It was Christina who kept up a conversation with Father Devereux during the journey, while Cora's eyes did not move once from her younger sister's face.

'So you're not taking the service yourself this morning?' Christina asked the priest.

'No,' Father Devereux told her, smiling. 'We've a surprise for you today. A grand priest from Donegal who takes a service that is the talk of seven parishes. As I told Cora yesterday, he terrifies me, so he should knock some sense into any doubters I have in my congregation!' Father Devereux laughed aloud. 'He's a big fanatic for the perils of sin and hell,' he went on. 'I hear he can get the bravest of grown men onto their knees begging forgiveness! Perhaps he'll even have a convert if I can somehow persuade the doctor to attend!' He laughed again but his humour was not shared.

'His name's Father O'Flaherty,' he continued regardless, 'and I'll be pleased to introduce you all to him once the service is over. It's not too often that we get all the Flavelle clan in our church at one time and I'd like to make the most of the occasion, if you don't mind.'

He found that he spoke to himself now. Christina gazed absently across the demesne and the others were little more than silent ballast behind him. He felt nothing short of relief once they had reached the church and he was able to busy himself uncoupling the horse from between the shafts of the wagon and hitching its reins to the gatepost. Then the church bell began to toll loudly, further relieving him of what he felt to be an obligation to make conversation.

'We had to come here today, you know, Father,' Cora

shouted in his ear as they made their way up the nave. 'I don't care what people think, we need the blessing, God knows we do.'

Father Devereux had little understanding of exactly what it was that she meant, but did not find it difficult to hold his curiosity in check. 'Well, for whatever reasons we are all glad to see you,' he said, smiling.

They filled the small pew nearest the pulpit. There was a rustle of respect from the other worshippers as they arrived, and a few raised eyebrows at the sisters' white georgette, surely more suited to children. Cora nodded quickly at one or two familiar faces but mostly kept her head down to avoid their eager eyes. By the time the priest arrived, however, silence awaited him, and when he cleared his throat the sound echoed in the rafters like cannon-fire.

He was a big man with eyes like a cod's that rolled about the assembled congregation, holding them in thrall before he had even started to speak. They were solemn and watchful eyes, seeming intent on finding sin buried in even the most innocent. When his voice finally emerged it rolled in great waves about the pews, eliciting a small murmur of fear from the congregation.

The sinners who stood before him watched his crabbed hands as they gripped the polished wood of the pulpit like a vice, imagining those very hands diving deep inside their souls to pluck out the evil that dwelt there.

His voice quavered slightly as he spoke to them of hell and Father O'Flaherty's version was, they found, a million times worse than that promised by their own Father Devereux.

One member of the congregation in particular was transfixed by the sermon. Her hands trembling as she clutched at her prayer-book, Constance sat bolt upright in her pew as the words beat about her head with unending ferocity. She had not been ignorant of the implications of her sin: her soul was lost, her plight hopeless. But only now did the priest's fiery eloquence bring home the full force of the infinite suffering and torment to come in the afterlife, a vision far more real than any William had conjured.

The Father's eyes seemed to roll in her direction more than once and each time she would have let out a cry had Cora not placed a firm hand upon her arm. She had committed incest with her own brother and, unlike the first assault, she had been willing. She had borne his child, and would live with him even now, had he not left her. She sought no forgiveness for she could not stop loving Niall.

Choked by fear, Constance rose slowly and unsteadily from her pew. All eyes turned upon her and at that moment she would gladly have died.

'Repent all sinners!' the priest thundered, pointing a finger at her. 'For the day of judgement is nigh!'

Constance pushed past Cora and Francis and ran the length of the nave to the door of the church. Sobbing aloud, she pulled the door back and a broad arc of sunlight fell into the gloom, blinding her for the moment.

'You cannot hide from the mercy of God!' the priest called after her but she barely heard the words in her desperation.

Cora moved to follow but the priest's gaze pinned the entire family to their seats.

Father Devereux, though, could barely conceal his impatience. He waited with mounting irritation as the seemingly endless sermon continued, and then determined to slip out of the church before the service was finished. He had to see what Constance was about. He had seen her face as she had left and she had looked terrified, poor thing. He was worried that she should not be left alone. He remembered his vision of her mother on the hill and again her words came back to him: 'Help her.'

Father O'Flaherty shot him a withering glance as he stole out through the doors but it was no time for manners; he would take his rebukes later, once he knew that Constance was all right. He had expected to find her in the churchyard, crying, but she was nowhere to be seen.

'Damn you, Constance!' he whispered to himself when

he noticed one of the horses missing from the gatepost. There had been three of them there, quietly grazing, and now there were only the two. She had taken the gelding that had pulled them to the church and only Maguire's two elderly, rheumatic mares stood waiting.

How long had she been gone? Some fifteen minutes, he thought. She could be at the house by now. He walked back towards the church, thinking of hearing the last of the service, but the cliffs came unbidden to his mind and he shuddered a little while trying to tell himself he was being melodramatic.

But then she *had* looked distressed, and her whole appearance of late had given him cause for concern. Father Devereux dithered. He looked across at Maguire's horses, tethered side-by-side and he wondered if it would be considered stealing if he were to borrow one of them for a few hours. There was no other way of following Constance and yet he knew how it would seem if he stole one of his parishioner's horses, merely to chase after a hysterical girl. Perhaps he would find her sitting comfortably in her own drawing-room, sipping tea and looking alarmed at his sudden and dramatic appearance.

The old horses turned to look at Father Devereux as though sympathetic to his predicament. He stood there for a moment, staring back at the animals, and then, with a muttered 'Damn you!', he strode over to begin his pursuit.

Father Devereux cursed himself for his stupidity every stumbling step of the journey to the house. The congregation would be emerging into the sunlight now, he thought, and Maguire would be scratching his bare scalp in the empty churchyard before he stirred up a commotion over the theft of his old horse. Father Devereux wondered whether it would last the journey anyway. Its ribs were heaving hard beneath his knees and the pace that it kept up was little faster than a fit man could run. At least twice it stumbled over loose earth and he thought that in time they might both be found lying in one of the bogs; the horse dead from age and himself crushed beneath it. If Constance were in trouble, he thought, his was hardly the heroic rescue of which epic poems are made.

Finally, though, Father Devereux had the house in his sights and it was only then that he reined in his horse and allowed it to recover a bit. It was pathetically grateful for the rest, heaving as it was like a pair of old bellows.

There was a man walking towards the house, he saw, rising up in his stirrups. He appeared to have entered the place, too, for he did not emerge again from the shadows of the porch. It had looked like Niall, Father Devereux thought, but surely Cora said he had left for good. Did Constance know he was there, he wondered? Was that why she left the service so early? Father Devereux shielded his eyes with his hand but he saw nothing to give him a clue as to what was happening up there.

Niall entered the house quietly. He had seen them all leave for church and knew the place was empty. He wanted to be alone there one last time; to try to come to terms with what had happened. He needed to hear the sound of his own footsteps ringing in the hall and to breathe the scents that his sister had left behind. He wanted to play a few notes on his mother's piano and to feel the hatred inside him once again as he stood in his father's old study. That was all that he had come for; to be alone and to say a few farewells.

Before he could even reach the study, though, the anger had begun to overpower him. Once the house was empty it had become his father's again. He could feel the man's presence in every room. He expected to see him everywhere; in the hallway, waiting for guests, in the dining-room, ordering them to read from his huge Bible, and most of all in the study, where Niall found his father's spirit overpowering. He thought he had rid himself of the man but he realized he existed in the very essence of the house itself.

He buried his face in his hands and laughed aloud, pressing his fists into his eye sockets until they ached. He could even hear his father then, he found: his footsteps on the stairs and down across the hall, and at the sound he felt the old, childish fears rise anew.

His father's laughter echoed triumphantly, while his own bore the tone of approaching madness. When he looked up he gasped aloud for his father towered above him, his dark face livid and scarred from the gunshot.

Niall closed his eyes quickly but the vision would not fade. 'You were no better than I,' the voice intoned. 'Your sins were greater, you could not keep away from her. Read to me from the Bible once again, Niall. Repeat the passage that mentions your terrible sin. Read it aloud, for all the world to hear!'

Niall screamed but no sound emerged, and when he opened his eyes again the apparition had gone. He walked across to his father's study and pulled the door open, slamming it quickly behind him. The large Bible lay open on the desk, waiting for him to read from it. He lifted the page and it came away in his hand and he saw that it had been torn, as had many of the others.

'The Devil's own boy!' He heard his father's mocking voice and pulled a handful of the torn pages angrily from the book and took them to the fireplace to burn.

His hands shaking, he found a match and, scratching it down the stonework to light it, gazed a while at its small bright flame before setting it against the paper. The pages flared quickly, he had to throw them into the grate before they burned his fingers. As the dry pages disintegrated, so his father's voice suddenly ceased. Niall allowed himself a small smile at the thought that he should be silenced so easily.

He pulled some papers off the desk and threw them into the flames. There was no noise now, no sound at all, save the crackling of the flames as they hungrily consumed the papers. Niall knew then that he had found his only chance of peace. As long as the house existed they were none of them safe. His father, his mother, the memory of his dead child, all would be exorcized if the house were no longer standing.

Niall kicked some of the flaming papers out of the hearth and onto the worn rug in front of it. They smouldered there for a moment and then started to catch. Niall pulled a couple of books from the shelves and threw them onto the pyre. It was his house now, not his father's, and he could do with it as he pleased.

He turned to his father's wooden desk and pushed that closer to the flames, too. The smoke billowed into his eyes and he could smell the acridness of the charring varnished wood above the pungent smoke from the paper. He began to cough but he would not leave the room until he was sure he had seen his job done.

Niall watched the red flames lick at the dry, ancient fabric of the curtains and there was a noise like a loud intake of breath as the fire shot up them to the ceiling. Exhilarated, he threw himself quickly towards the door. He felt the scorching heat of the small explosion of flame against his back and stared in fascination as his clothes began to smoulder. There was no air in the room now, only smoke, and it filled his lungs and eyes until he was unable to breathe or to see.

Father Devereux thought he saw the sun's rays glowing scarlet and golden in the windows of the house. He still worried over what he should say when he finally burst in upon Constance, who he knew would be recovered from her upset and taking tea with her brother by now. He thought perhaps that he should not go into the house at all but then he told himself that it had been a long and perilous ride for nothing if he did not.

What would the other parishioners think of him, though? That he had become an old fussing busybody like his predecessor? Still, the horse was on the move again now, busily plodding forward, and the priest was in no mind to stop it.

Then he saw the smoke that rose in a thin spiral against the turquoise sky and heard the splintering crash as the windows, that had just that minute been so majestically lit in crimson light, split open, flying to the ground in a shower of razor-sharp shards. 'Jesus Christ!' he breathed and threw himself from the saddle to take the last few hundred yards on foot.

There was a beast-like roar from the chimneys and smoke began to seep from between the tiles of the roof. Father Devereux could not make himself believe the sight that was before him. His mouth dropped open and he stood gawping, unable to move. Then he saw a great belch of orange flame burst from a lower window, leaving blackened stains on the outside stonework as it retreated, and a terrible thought occurred to him. He ran to the back of the house and there, in the yard, was his horse. So she *had* returned; he knew for sure now.

'Constance!' he bellowed, his voice sounding hoarse. 'Jesus Christ, *Constance*!' And then he suddenly stopped, for Niall stood in front of him, his clothes blackened, his hair wild and singed, watching the flames from the pathway as though staring into a garden bonfire on an autumn evening.

'Good God, Niall!' Father Devereux shouted, grabbing him by the shoulders. 'Whatever's happened? Is Constance out of there? Is she safe, man?'

Niall looked at the priest and smiled, his teeth showing white against the darkness of his face. 'She is safe now, Father,' he said. 'I have saved her from all this.' He looked back at the flames. 'The house was empty, don't worry. I saw them all leave for church; the servants, too.'

'She came back!' Father Devereux screamed. 'She left during the sermon! Oh, Jesus Christ save her!' He saw Niall staring at the top of the house with a terrible look in his eyes. Father Devereux followed his gaze and it was then that he saw her.

Constance's face was white against the window of her bedroom, her small fists beating against the glass, her eyes dark circles of fear.

'Constance!' Father Devereux saw his own daughter there

406

and realized that he had been charged with the duty of saving her. Now he understood what Sophia's vision had meant. He muttered a prayer beneath his breath, feeling only relief that he had been given this chance to redeem himself before Sophia's spirit and before the eyes of his God. The burden of guilt that had oppressed him for years would be lifted from his shoulders at last with this one final act of salvation. He felt Sophia watching him as he ran through the open doorway, his black robes billowing in the smoke.

He had no experience of fire. He had not known how dense the smoke could be, nor how it choked the lungs and scalded the throat. The hallway was full of it and, for a moment, he found himself disorientated in the darkness. He turned around once, then spun quickly in his panic. There was crackling, like gunshot, in his ears, as ancient wood exploded in the heat.

He fell to the floor on all fours and there he found air that was clear enough to breathe. His eyes streaming, he crawled towards the stairs and made his way upward towards Sophia's old room. He came to William's room first. The flames had not touched it, so he ran inside to allow his eyes to clear. He pulled his cloak off and doused it with water from a large china jug on the washstand. William Flavelle. He had feared the man for years yet never admitted it. A huge dark face before him made him start and cry out with shock but it was his own face that he saw, not William's, blackened by the smoke and staring out at him from the washstand mirror.

'Constance!' he had to find her soon, or they were both dead. Throwing the wet cape about his head he ran to her room, but it was empty and the door hung wide open.

'Constance!' he shouted again, but the smoke muffled the sound and he heard no reply.

There was another floor. He ran to the top of the house, to the rooms the children had used as a nursery and it was there that he found her, gazing quietly from the window, her long hair dishevelled and her dress as blackened by the smoke as his face. 'Constance,' Father Devereux said with relief, but she did not turn at his words. The room was quiet and untouched by either flame or smoke.

'He is down there in the gardens,' she said softly. 'Niall is down there waiting for me.'

'Constance, my dear,' Father Devereux began, 'you must leave here at once or we will both be killed. The stairs may be impassable even now. Come with me quickly, take my hand.'

She turned then, and he saw the terror in her eyes.

'Come, my dear,' he repeated gently, stretching out his hand.

Constance shook her head slowly. 'I cannot leave,' she said, 'my papa will not allow it. He has me locked in this room. He will not let me out to see Niall.'

Father Devereux stepped towards her, hoping to catch her for he could see she was hysterical with fear, but she shrank away before he could touch her.

'Niall will come for me,' she whispered, 'he promised he would take care of me. I will wait for him.'

'I have come for you,' Father Devereux told her, his voice rising in panic. 'Trust in me, Constance, allow me to take you to safety. There is nothing to fear. Trust me.'

There was a great cracking noise from below and the priest chose the diversion to grab at the frightened girl.

Constance screamed as he caught her but he quickly wrapped his cloak about her as she fought and shivered like a trapped bird.

'Shush, shush,' he soothed. 'You are safe now. I am your father, dear, I have come to save you. You have nothing to fear. God will protect us.'

'My father?' She looked up into his grimy face.

'Your true father,' he affirmed, staggering with her towards the open door.

'I knew you would come for me,' Constance said, but her words were like a sigh, lost in the heavy fabric of the cloak. With tears streaming down his face, Father Devereux lifted his daughter into his arms and made his way towards the landing.

Niall's eyes could not leave the spot in the window where his sister's face had been. He opened his mouth to call for her, but the shock had taken his voice.

'Constance!' he found the sound again and the name lasted an eternity.

He could not believe it was her. He had seen her leave with Cora; seen her in her Sunday best. Perhaps she was a vision, like the vision of his father. Perhaps the flames would rid the house of her ghost, so that she could live in peace at last.

She moved, though, the white face at the window moved. He saw her fists again, beating hard until they bled, and he knew that she was calling for him, for she had seen him at last on the path. Then she was suddenly still, staring at him, and then, just as suddenly, she had disappeared.

He knew then that he had killed her. He ran to follow the priest but the doorway was already on fire so he ran to the servants' entrance.

The kitchen looked strangely normal inside, the flames had not yet reached it. There were things laid for dinner; cold foods put out ready for their return from church. He saw a meat pie with a muslin cover to protect it from the flies; some pickles, a loaf, ready for slicing. Then he heard a scream, a new roar of flames, and he raced through the narrow network of back corridors until he was in the main hallway.

He threw his coat over his head and plunged up the stairs, taking them two at a time. He ran down the wide passage, frantically calling for her, shouting out her name while choking on the smoke. Then he reached her room and nearly fell over them, hidden as they were by the dense smoke. They were laid out on the floor before him; Constance and the priest; their handsome features blackened by smoke, but untouched by the flames, as far as he could see. They lay coiled together like lovers. Father Devereux still held

Constance fast in the huge black cloak, just as a father would do to protect his beloved child from danger.

'Constance!'

Retching badly, trying to breathe, Niall pulled his sister from the priest's arms and lifted her gently into his own. Her head fell back and her mouth opened slightly. He paused to pull her face down onto his shoulder so that she was free from all the smoke and then arranged his coat about her to protect her from the flames.

With his remaining strength, Niall ran down the stairs with his beautiful Constance held fast in his arms, all the time whispering endearments, assuring her that she was safe at last. As he reached the main doorway the hall erupted behind them and he fell out onto the gravel path, his ears singing as he fought for each scorching breath.

He laid Constance on the grass, away from the smoke. 'Constance.' He bent to kiss her open lips, to give her life so that she would not be lost to him. He pressed her head to his chest and rocked her there, like a child.

'Constance, my darling love,' he wept. 'You are safe now. I came back for you.' He buried his face into her blackened hair and sobbed: he knew she was gone, and that never again would she hear him tell her that he loved her.

He lay there beside her lifeless body, and when he finally looked up into the sky, in the last few blood-red rays of the setting sun he saw a hot-air balloon high overhead, its green silk billowing in the wind like the sails of a ship.

It rose above the hills and he cradled his sister's head in his arms as he watched it soar above them. It floated nearer then, as the air currents took it and he could see two people in the basket that hung below, watching. He thought that they smiled and waved at him, but he had to be mistaken, for they looked like his mother and the priest. When he looked again, the balloon had gone, the skies were clear and Niall was alone.

EPILOGUE

It is now some twenty years since the great house was destroyed by the fire. It stands, a charred and blackened ruin, the long straggling ivy obliterating what is left of its walls, save for the charred bricks of the upper floors. The rafters of its roof are like the huge burnt bones of a carcass poking viciously into the turquoise sky overhead. The window of Constance's room hangs free from its frame and fronds of wild fern reach from the spot where her white arms once waved.

The small farmer's cottage in the demesne, totally untouched by any modern convenience, is the family home now, where Cora and Christina live like the two elderly spinsters they were always destined to be. By choice, they have become totally isolated from the local community, the shame of the long-ago scandal too much for them to bear.

Cora has no need of a bed, preferring to sleep upright in a chair by the fireside at night. The chair that she uses is a tapestry-covered smoking-chair, one of the only items rescued from the house after the fire. The rest of the furniture has been left to rot, along with the gutted ruins.

Niall will only enter the cottage to eat his food when the weather is at its coldest and his hands so frozen that he is unable to lift his mug of soup to his mouth. Cora knows that he prefers to rest in the shelter of the ruined house at night, though he has never told her exactly where he sleeps. He says very little these days. He works their small farm along with some help from Cora and together they manage to survive without outside assistance.

Francis is dead. At least, he left them on the day of the tragedy and has never returned. Cora believes he would not have survived twenty years by himself, and so, when

411

she visits the family graveyard, she includes him in her prayers.

Constance is buried close to her mother, though her true father was laid to rest in his own churchyard. Father Devereux was placed there a few days after the fire and a plaque was put up in the church, telling how he died bravely trying to save one of his young parishioners from the blaze. His grave is visited often and is kept neat as a mark of affection and respect, but Constance's has been claimed by the same ivy that laid siege to her mother's stone many years before.

Father Devereux's replacement in the parish, Father Murray, has taken great pride in building up the legend of his predecessor's good works. The people of the parish have needed little bidding to come forward with their tales of his goodness and it is Father Murray's greatest wish to have published a book that he is writing, chronicling Father Devereux's life and ultimate martyrdom.

If Constance had only survived he would have had dreams of seeing the man made a saint as, only a few days after his death, the people of the village were already recounting the stories of his great works.

Niall was never blamed for his sister's death by anyone other than himself. He has carried this guilt inside him through the years and it has all but eroded what sanity he had left. At first he realized that he was unaware of Constance's presence in the house when he set fire to it, but he gradually came to believe that he killed her for destroying their child.

He visits the cliffs regularly and sometimes he sees her, flying a kite beside their mother. He visits the killeen still, believing their child to be buried in one of those graves. He is able to work on the land and at night he rests beneath Constance's ruined room. When he sleeps there he feels he is close to her, and that she will be with him through the night.

The sisters managed to deter most visitors to the cottage

many years before and now any that care to make the journey will find the paths hidden by undergrowth, so that the last mile or so will have to be taken on foot. It is easy to get lost, too, without some knowledge of the route.

Father Murray still makes the trek regularly, to sing hymns with the two sisters once evensong is over, but even he is forced to make his visits less frequently as he suffers now from rheumatics and his legs ache all night after the long walk. He persuaded some of the hardier locals to cut the paths afresh a few summers ago, but by winter they were gone again through neglect.

Some local lads still find themselves forced to make the journey through the bogs to bring the charity parcels that the church will often donate but, as the house has the reputation of being haunted, the boxes are usually left with only the most perfunctory knock at the back door.

The visitor calling today, though, appears to have no such apprehensions and waits after knocking, even though the place looks apparently deserted. It is a warm day for Connemara and the young woman, who is dressed lightly enough in a pair of pale beige slacks and a white shirt, pulls a handkerchief from her shoulder-bag and blots it against her face while she waits. She has walked for two miles and has lost her way more than once but she is young and fit enough to have enjoyed the journey, even so. Her clothes look surprisingly fresh and uncreased and she has somehow managed to keep her expensive, well-polished shoes free of mud. Her bright russet hair is neatly styled, though she pushes a few stray strands back under her hairband as she waits, the hairs at the nape of her neck damp and plastered to her collar from the heat.

Her small car is parked way back on the road, at the precise spot that Father Murray warned her that she would be forced to get out and walk.

She waits longer than would normally be considered reasonable after knocking and she jangles her car keys in her hand. Then she takes a step back to look up at the windows and Christina pulls back only just in time, to duck out of sight beneath the ledge. She crouches there, trembling with unknown terrors, her grey hair covering her face. She would never have the courage to open the door and for once she wishes Cora were there to do the job for her.

There is another knock, sending Christina scurrying on her knees to the opposite wall of her small room. With her eyes wide with fear she reaches onto her nightstand for her Bible and, pulling it onto her lap, prays to God to make the stranger go away.

The young woman, meanwhile, has become tired of waiting at the front and has set off around the back of the house to search the gardens, instead.

It is there that she finds Cora, old, fat and bent in her long brown overcoat tied at the waist with a length of string. She digs at a patch of hard dark earth, her foot against the shovel and the whole weight of her body behind it. She is muttering encouragement to herself as she works and there are thick lines of exertion across her round face.

She stops suddenly when she sees the young woman approaching and the shovel falls from her hands. She makes no move to retrieve it. Her face becomes first pale, then white, and her hands rise to her throat, as if fending off an unseen strangler.

The woman appears not to have noticed the effect her appearance is having. She steps forward with a smile and extends her hand. 'Miss Flavelle?' she asks, politely.

Cora manages to shake her head at this but does not take the offered hand.

'I'm sorry,' the girl says. 'Do you know the Flavelles, though? I was told that they live here.'

Her hair looks alight in the brilliant sun. Cora studies her face for a while before answering. Her initial shock at the girl's appearance is slowly receding. She is being foolish. It is not who she thought it was, after all. And yet in the sunlight . . . 'My name was Flavelle,' she tells the woman, 'before I married.'

The girl's eyes shine with relief. 'Thank the Lord for that!' she says. 'I thought I had come all this way for nothing! When I saw the burnt-out house I wondered . . .' She looks towards the ruin, shielding her eyes from the sun, and Cora suddenly feels annoyed and embarrassed by the wreck of their old home.

She wears no wedding-band, Cora notices. Her accent is not local, either.

'Then I saw this house,' she continues, 'and I guessed that this was where the priest meant after all. I just hoped you'd be the same Flavelle family I am looking for. Would you mind if I asked you for a glass of water?' she adds, smiling politely. 'It's been a long walk and the sun is rather warm.'

Cora leads her grudgingly into the house. The woman pauses on the doorstep once she spots the state of the interior, but she is too polite to refuse to enter. The place is a ruin. Books are piled everywhere, most of them mildewed with age. They are tied into bundles with the same thick yellow string that Cora has tied about her waist. There is little furniture and what there is is rotted and covered with cats.

The cats are everywhere, she sees, as her eyes become used to the dark. Some turn their heads to stare as she enters but mostly she is regally ignored. One large cat pushes past her as she stands in the doorway and she bends quickly to brush the hairs from the leg of her slacks.

While Cora disappears to get some water the young woman tilts her head sideways to see if she can make out any of the titles of the books. The nearest pile seems to consist mostly of works of poetry. She pulls open the corner of one of them and sees a poem of Byron's that she knows by heart. Then Cora returns and she quickly lets the page fall.

Cora is carrying a chipped cup and she offers it to the young woman. The water inside it tastes stale and warm.

'It's from our well,' Cora tells her and the woman places it down on the table after just one sip.

There is a noise from upstairs; the rapping of quick running feet, but the sound stops as quickly as it began and Cora seems not to have noticed.

'I don't know of any polite way to put this . . .' the young woman begins. 'You see, I am trying to trace my parents – my real parents, that is.' She looks about for somewhere to sit but Cora occupies the only chair in the room.

'I was adopted as a child, you see,' the woman continues. 'I had no idea until a year ago, when my parents told me. I was at college at the time and so this is the first chance I have had to do anything about it. I know you should live with what you've got, but it's only natural to be curious, isn't it?'

She takes a deep breath and looks about the room.

'At first it didn't matter much,' she says. 'But then my father – my adopted father – has just died.' She pauses while Cora crosses herself.

'I didn't want to cause any more grief for my mother but then I started wondering . . .'

Cora watches her, her mind already ahead of the story, and she badly wants this young woman to be gone from her house.

'My mother told me that my real mother was called Flavelle and that she came from Connemara,' she continues. 'I asked the local priest and he said you lived up here and that you were the only ones of that name in the district.

'He told me the Flavelles used to be wealthy but that there was a fire and that their great house was burnt down. I saw the ruin from the hillside. I'm sorry,' she adds, blushing. 'It must have been a terrible shock to you, the fire and all . . . you were lucky to have this house to live in.' She tails off, painfully aware that there can have been no luck in that house for many a year.

'Do you know Constance Flavelle?' she asks suddenly. 'Is she a relation of yours at all?'

The name is like a knife through Cora's heart. She folds

416

her arms across her chest and looks away. 'Did the priest tell you any more?' she demands, angrily.

'No. He said it was before his time here.'

'Constance Flavelle died in the fire that destroyed the house,' Cora states flatly.

The woman looks shocked. 'Dead?' she says, with grief in her voice.

'It was a long time ago,' Cora tells her, hoping that she will go now. But the woman begins to cry.

'I'm sorry,' she says, drying her eyes on a handkerchief.

Cora just shrugs.

'She was my mother,' the woman says, and Cora shrugs again. 'Did you know her?'

'No,' Cora lies. 'I came here after she died. I just knew about the fire, that's all.'

The young woman straightens and tries to smile. 'Thank you for the water,' she says. She turns to leave, for Cora has made it quite obvious by now that she is not welcome. But then she turns back.

'Would you mind if I just took a look at the ruined house?' she asks. 'As my mother used to live there?'

Cora minds very much but knows there is little she can say. 'If you like.'

The young woman walks slowly towards the house but Niall has already seen her approach and is watching from the hill. He begins to run but she arrives at the house first. He believes that he has seen a ghost, just as Cora thought when she first saw her. She very much resembles her mother, though in her hair and her height she is more like Sophia, her grandmother.

'Constance!' Niall whispers, believing in the forgiveness of God, for returning his love to him at last. Then she turns and looks into the sun and he sees her modern dress and he clutches the wall for balance because he is suddenly confused.

She has not seen him. She pulls a camera from her bag and lines up a shot of what would have been her family home. Then she sees Niall in her view-finder; an old man, a farmer, staring at her with an expression of shock. She nearly drops the camera.

They stare at one another for a minute and then she seems to relax and walks towards him with a smile. He is only an old man, after all, and if he worked for the family at some time, he may know something about her mother.

'Good morning!' she says and when he does not answer she wonders whether he is simple or deaf. 'Have you worked around here many years?' she asks.

He cannot reply, though. Her face, out of the sunlight, is alarming. She is not Constance and she is not Sophia yet she has features of them both; enough to make his heart ache at the sight of her.

'You see I'm trying to trace my mother,' she says. 'She lived in this house once. I wonder if you knew her at all. I asked the lady at the cottage but she couldn't help. My mother's name was Constance Flavelle and I was told that she died in the fire here. I never knew her, you see. She had me adopted as a baby. I suppose there was some scandal or other and that she couldn't keep me.

'My father's name was never mentioned, though I'd dearly love to trace him, if he's alive. Were you here at the time? Do you remember Constance Flavelle vanishing from sight for a few months or so? It would have been nearly twenty-one years ago. Did you know my mother? I'd so like to hear about her if you did. I guess she wasn't married or I suppose she would have kept me. I don't mind if there was a scandal like that, for it all seems a little old-fashioned these days.'

She smiles encouragement but Niall turns away from his daughter to hide the tears that are, by now, running freely down his cheeks. So she was not killed and she was not buried in the killeen. His daughter is beautiful, too, not the monster that Cora had said she would be.

'No,' he says, slowly. 'I remember no one of that name here.'

The young woman waits a moment or two, looking at him strangely, and then he hears her leave and he relaxes a little, closing his eyes to imprint her face upon his memory. He wonders why Constance lied to him and then his daughter is gone and he is alone at last with his grief.

He stumbles around to the back of the ruined house and he looks up at the small window where he last saw Constance alive. Her face is no longer there, no longer watching for him.

They lied to him, Constance and Cora. The fire was for nothing, his child was always alive. His eyes strain to search for Constance. He needs to see her again, to speak to her, to explain things. The pain does not lessen for him with the years. He feels her there now, teasing him, tantalizing him. She is so close, if only he could see her.

Instead he turns to look for the girl. He should have stopped her. She is all that he has left. He stares at her back as she makes her way slowly down the hill. Then, by some miracle, she turns to look at him once again. He should call to her, but he is unable to move. God will return her to him, he thinks. He waits.

But Niall's daughter does not return. She studies the scene before her for a few moments: the strange old man with the haunted eyes standing dumb before the burnt-out building. She had almost forgotten to take a shot of it. She raises her camera to her eye to record the peculiar scene. His face is so comic that it amuses her. The shot taken, she lowers the camera again and does not see his arm rise to wave at her, for she turns to make her slow way back to her car.